LINDA HOWARD

Linda Howard says that whether she's reading them or writing them, books have long played a profound role in her life. She cut her teeth on Margaret Mitchell and from then on continued to read widely and eagerly. In recent years her interest has settled on romance fiction, because she's "easily bored by murder, mayhem and politics." After twenty-one years of penning stories for her own enjoyment, Ms. Howard finally worked up the courage to submit a novel for publication—and met with success! Happily, the Alabama author has been steadily publishing ever since.

BEVERLY BARTON

Beverly Barton has been in love with romance since her grandfather gave her an illustrated book of *Beauty and the Beast.* An avid reader since childhood, Beverly wrote her first book at the age of nine. After marriage to her own "hero" and the births of her daughter and son, Beverly chose to be a full-time homemaker, aka wife, mother, friend and volunteer. The author of over thirty-five books, Beverly is a member of Romance Writers of America and helped found the Heart of Dixie chapter in Alabama. She has won numerous awards and has made the Waldenbooks and *USA Today* bestseller lists.

MACKENZIE'S PLEASURE

LINDA HOWARD

DEFENDING HIS OWN

Beverly BARTON

Silhouette Books

Published by Silhouette Books

America's Publisher of Contemporary Romance

SILHOUETTE BOOKS

RECYCLED PAPER · RECYCLED PAPER

Copyright in the collection:
© 2001 by Harlequin Books S.A.

ISBN 0-373-48432-1

Cover illustration © Kevin Ghiglione/i2i Art

The publisher acknowledges the copyright holders
of the individual works as follows:

MACKENZIE'S PLEASURE
Copyright © 1996 by Linda Howington

DEFENDING HIS OWN
Copyright © 1995 by Beverly Beaver

This edition published by arrangement with Harlequin Books S.A.

® and TM are trademarks of Harlequin Books S.A., used under license. Trademarks indicated with ® are registered in the United States Patent and Trademark Office, the Canadian Trade Marks Office and in other countries.

Visit Silhouette at www.eHarlequin.com

Printed in U.S.A.

MACKENZIE'S PLEASURE
by Linda Howard

* * *

Mackenzie's Pleasure is dedicated
to all the wonderful fans who fell as much in love
with the Mackenzies as I did.

Dear Reader,

The whole Mackenzie brood touched a chord with me and readers alike, but Zane holds a special place in my heart. There was just something about that quiet, controlled boy that told me he was one of the few, the different, the deadly—a Navy SEAL. The men who make it through SEAL training are extremely focused and intelligent, and if I wore a hat I'd take it off to them. They have my total respect.

Because he's a Mackenzie, Zane's capacity for love is enormous. With such an example in his family life, how could he be otherwise? He's wise and wily, cautious and cunning, but when he meets Barrie he knows almost immediately that she's the one for him. Getting her, however, costs him some trouble and blood. First he has to rescue her from terrorists, then he has to fight through layers of security to get to her, then he finds that the terrorists who kidnapped her in the first place still haven't given up, and he's in a fight for their lives to protect her.

A lesser man couldn't have pulled it off, but Zane was in no way a lesser man. He was a Mackenzie.

Sincerely,

Linda Howard

Prologue

Wolf Mackenzie slipped out of bed and restlessly paced over to the window, where he stood looking out at the stark, moonlit expanse of his land. A quick glance over his bare shoulder reassured him that Mary slept on undisturbed, though he knew it wouldn't be long before she sensed his absence and stirred, reaching out for him. When her hand didn't encounter his warmth, she would wake, sitting up in bed and drowsily pushing her silky hair out of her face. When she saw him by the window she would slide out of bed and come to him, nestling against his naked body, sleepily resting her head on his chest.

A slight smile touched his hard mouth. Like as not, if he stayed out of bed long enough for her to awaken, when they returned to the bed it wouldn't be to sleep but to make love. As he remembered, Maris had been conceived on just such an occasion, when he had been restless because Joe's fighter wing had just been deployed overseas during some flare-up. It had been Joe's first action, and Wolf had been as tense as he'd been during his own days in Vietnam.

Luckily, he and Mary were past the days when spontaneous passion could result in a new baby. Nowadays they had grandkids, not kids of their own. Ten at the last count, as a matter of fact.

But he was restless tonight, and he knew why.

The wolf always slept better when all of his cubs were accounted for.

Never mind that the cubs were adults, some of them with children of their own. Never mind that they were, one and all, supremely capable of taking care of themselves. They were *his,* and he was there if they needed him. He also liked to know, within reason, where they were bedding down for the night. It wasn't necessary for him to be able to pinpoint their location—some things a parent was better off not knowing—but if he knew what *state* they were in, that was usually enough. Hell, sometimes he would have been glad just to know which *country* they were roaming.

His concern wasn't for Joe, this time. He knew where Joe was—the Pentagon. Joe wore four stars now, and sat on the Joint Chiefs of Staff.

Joe would still rather strap on a metal bird and fly at twice the speed of sound, but those days were behind him. If he had to fly a desk, then he would damn sure fly it the best it could be flown. Besides, as he'd once said, being married to Caroline was more challenging than being in a dogfight and outnumbered four to one.

Wolf grinned when he thought of his daughter-in-law. Genius IQ, doctorates in both physics and computer sciences, a bit arrogant, a bit quirky. She'd gotten her pilot's license just after the birth of their first son, on the basis that the wife of a fighter pilot should know something about flying. She had received her certification on small jet aircraft around the time the third son had made his appearance. After the birth of her fifth son, she had grumpily told Joe that she was calling it quits with that one, because she'd given him five chances and obviously he wasn't up to the job of fathering a daughter.

It had once been gently suggested to Joe that Caroline should quit her job. The company that employed her was heavily engaged in government contract work, and the appearance of any favoritism could hurt his career. Joe had turned his cool, blue laser gaze on his superiors and said, "Gentlemen, if I have to choose between my wife and my career, I'll give you my resignation immediately." That was *not* the answer that had been expected, and nothing else was said about Caroline's work in research and development.

Wolf wasn't worried about Michael, either. Mike was the most settled of all his children, though just as focused. He had decided at an early age that he wanted to be a rancher, and that's exactly what he was. He owned a sizable spread down toward Laramie, and he and his wife were happily raising cattle and two sons.

The only uproar Mike had ever caused was when he decided to marry Shea Colvin. Wolf and Mary had given him their blessing, but the problem was that Shea's mother was Pam Hearst Colvin, one of Joe's old girlfriends—and Pam's father, Ralph Hearst, was as adamantly opposed to his beloved granddaughter marrying Michael Mackenzie as he had been to his daughter dating Joe Mackenzie.

Michael, with his typical tunnel vision, had ignored the whole tempest. His only concern was marrying Shea, and to hell with the storm erupting in the Hearst family. Quiet, gentle Shea had been torn, but she wanted Michael and refused to call off the wedding as her grandfather demanded. Pam herself had finally put an end to it, standing nose to nose with her father in the middle of his store.

"Shea *will* marry Michael," she'd stormed, when Ralph had threatened to take Shea out of his will if she married one of those damn breeds. "You didn't want me to date Joe, when he was one of the most decent men I've ever met. Now Shea wants Michael, and she's going to have him. Change your will, if you like. Hug your hate real close, because you won't be hugging your granddaughter— or your great-grandchildren. Think about that!"

So Michael had married Shea, and despite his growling and grumping, old Hearst was nuts about his two great-grandsons. Shea's second pregnancy had been difficult, and both she and the baby had nearly died. The doctor had advised them not to have any more children, but they had already decided to have only two, anyway. The two boys were growing up immersed in cattle ranching and horses. Wolf was amused that Ralph Hearst's great-grandchildren bore the Mackenzie name. Who in hell ever would have thought?

Josh, his third son, lived in Seattle with his wife, Loren, and their three sons. Josh was as jet-mad as Joe, but he had opted for the Navy rather than the Air Force, perhaps because he wanted to succeed on his own, not because his older brother was a general.

Josh was cheerful and openhearted, the most outgoing of the bunch, but he, too, had that streak of iron determination. He'd barely survived the crash that left him with a stiffened right knee and ended his naval career, but in typical Josh fashion, he had put that behind him and concentrated on what was before him. At the time, that had been his doctor—Dr. Loren Page. Never one to dither around, Josh had taken one look at tall, lovely Loren and begun his courtship from his hospital bed. He'd still been on crutches when they married. Now, three sons later, he worked for an aeronautics firm, developing new fighter aircraft, and Loren practiced her orthopedic specialty at a Seattle hospital.

Wolf knew where Maris was, too. His only daughter was currently in Montana, working as a trainer for a horse rancher. She was considering taking a job in Kentucky, working with Thoroughbreds. From the time she'd been old enough to sit unaided on a horse, her ambitions had all centered around the big, elegant animals. She had his touch with horses, able to gentle even the most contrary or vicious beast. Privately Wolf thought that she probably surpassed his skill. What she could do with a horse was pure magic.

Wolf's hard mouth softened as he thought of Maris. She had wrapped his heart around her tiny finger the moment she had been placed in his arms, when she was mere minutes old, and had looked up at him with sleepy dark eyes. Of all his children, she was the only one who had his dark eyes. His sons all looked like him, except for their blue eyes, but Maris, who resembled Mary in every other way, had her father's eyes. His daughter had light, silvery brown hair, skin so fine it was almost translucent, and her mother's determination. She was all of five foot three and weighed about a hundred pounds, but Maris never paid any attention to her slightness; when she made up her mind to do something, she persisted with bulldog stubbornness until she succeeded. She could more than hold her own with her older, much larger and domineering brothers.

Her chosen career hadn't been easy for her. People tended to think two things. One was that she was merely trading on the Mackenzie name, and the other was that she was too delicate for the job. They soon found out how wrong they were on both counts, but it was a battle Maris had fought over and over. She kept at it, though, slowly winning respect for her individual talents.

The mental rundown of his kids next brought him to Chance. Hell, he even knew where Chance was, and that was saying something. Chance roamed the world, though he always came back to Wyoming, to the mountain that was his only home. He had happened to call earlier that day, from Belize. He'd told Mary that he was going to rest for a few days before moving on. When Wolf had taken his turn on the phone, he had moved out of Mary's hearing and quietly asked Chance how bad he was hurt.

"Not too bad," Chance had laconically replied. "A few stitches and a couple of cracked ribs. This last job went a little sour on me."

Wolf didn't ask what the last job had entailed. His soldier-of-fortune son occasionally did some delicate work for the government, so Chance seldom volunteered details. The two men had an unspoken agreement to keep Mary in the dark about the danger Chance faced on a regular basis. Not only did they not want her to worry, but if she knew he was wounded, she was likely to hop on a plane and fetch him home.

When Wolf hung up the phone and turned, it was to find Mary's slate blue gaze pinned on him. "How bad is he hurt?" she demanded fiercely, hands planted on her hips.

Wolf knew better than to try lying to her. Instead he crossed the room to her and pulled her into his arms, stroking her silky hair and cradling her slight body against the solid muscularity of his. Sometimes the force of his love for this woman almost drove him to his knees. He couldn't protect her from worry, though, so he gave her the respect of honesty. "Not too bad, to use his own words."

Her response was instant. "I want him here."

"I know, sweetheart. But he's okay. He doesn't lie to us. Besides, you know Chance."

She nodded, sighing, and turned her lips against his

chest. Chance was like a sleek panther, wild and intolerant of fetters. They had brought him into their home and made him one of the family, binding him to them with love when no other restraint would have held him. And like a wild creature that had been only half-tamed, he accepted the boundaries of civilization, but lightly. He roamed far and wide, and yet he always came back to them.

From the first, though, he had been helpless against Mary. She had instantly surrounded him with so much love and care that he hadn't been able to resist her, even though his light hazel eyes had reflected his consternation, even embarrassment, at her attention. If Mary went down to fetch Chance, he would come home without protest, but he would walk into the house wearing a helpless, slightly panicked "Oh, God, get me out of this" expression. And then he would meekly let her tend his wounds, pamper him and generally smother him with motherly concern.

Watching Mary fuss over Chance was one of Wolf's greatest amusements. She fussed over all of her kids, but the others had grown up with it and took it as a matter of course. Chance, though…he had been fourteen and half wild when Mary had found him. If he'd ever had a home, he didn't remember it. If he had a name, he didn't know it. He'd evaded well-meaning social authorities by staying on the move, stealing whatever he needed, food, clothes, money. He was highly intelligent and had taught himself to read from newspapers and magazines that had been thrown away. Libraries had become a favorite place for him to hang out, maybe even spend the night if he could manage it, but never two nights in a row. From what he read and what little television he saw, he understood the concept of a family, but that was all it was to him—a concept. He trusted no one but himself.

He might have grown to adulthood that way if he hadn't

contracted a monster case of influenza. While driving home from work, Mary had found him lying on the side of a road, incoherent and burning up with fever. Though he was half a foot taller than she and some fifty pounds heavier, somehow she had wrestled and bullied the boy into her truck and taken him to the local clinic, where Doc Nowacki discovered that the flu had progressed into pneumonia and quickly transferred Chance to the nearest hospital, eighty miles away.

Mary had driven home and insisted that Wolf take her to the hospital—immediately.

Chance was in intensive care when they arrived. At first the nursing staff hadn't wanted to let them see him, since they weren't family and in fact didn't know anything about him. Child services had been notified, and someone was on the way to take care of the paperwork. They had been reasonable, even kind, but they hadn't reckoned with Mary. She was relentless. She wanted to see the boy, and a bulldozer couldn't have budged her until she saw him. Eventually the nurses, overworked and outclassed by a will far stronger than their own, gave in and let Wolf and Mary into the small cubicle.

As soon as he saw the boy, Wolf knew why Mary was so taken with him. It wasn't just that he was deathly ill; he was obviously part American Indian. He would have reminded Mary so forcibly of her own children that she could no more have forgotten about him than she could one of them.

Wolf's expert eye swept over the boy as he lay there so still and silent, his eyes closed, his breathing labored. The hectic color of fever stained his high cheekbones. Four different bags dripped an IV solution into his muscular right arm, which was taped to the bed. Another bag hung at the side of the bed, measuring the output of his kidneys.

Not a half-breed, Wolf had thought. A quarter, maybe. No more than that. But still, there was no doubting his heritage. His fingernails were light against the tanned skin of his fingers, where an Anglo's nails would have been pinker. His thick, dark brown hair, so long it brushed his shoulders, was straight. There were those high cheekbones, the clear-cut lips, the high-bridged nose. He was the most handsome boy Wolf had ever seen.

Mary went up to the bed, all her attention focused on the boy who lay so ill and helpless on the snowy sheets. She laid her cool hand lightly against his forehead, then stroked it over his hair. "You'll be all right," she murmured. "I'll make sure you are."

He had lifted his heavy lids, struggling with the effort. For the first time Wolf saw the light hazel eyes, almost golden, and circled with a brown rim so dark it was almost black. Confused, the boy had focused first on Mary; then his gaze had wandered to Wolf, and belated alarm flared in his eyes. He tried to heave himself up, but he was too weak even to tug his taped arm free.

Wolf moved to the boy's other side. "Don't be afraid," he said quietly. "You have pneumonia, and you're in a hospital." Then, guessing what lay at the bottom of the boy's panic, he added, "We won't let them take you."

Those light eyes had rested on his face, and perhaps Wolf's appearance had calmed him. Like a wild animal on guard, he slowly relaxed and drifted back to sleep.

Over the next week, the boy's condition improved, and Mary swung into action. She was determined that the boy, who still had not given them a name, not be taken into state custody for even one day. She pulled strings, harangued people, even called on Joe to use his influence, and her tenacity worked. When the boy was released from the hospital, he went home with Wolf and Mary.

He had gradually become accustomed to them, though by no stretch of the imagination had he been friendly, or even trustful. He would answer their questions, in one word if possible, but he never actually *talked* with them. Mary hadn't been discouraged. From the first, she simply treated the boy as if he was hers—and soon he was.

The boy who had always been alone was suddenly plunged into the middle of a large, volatile family. For the first time he had a roof over his head every night, a room all to himself, ample food in his belly. He had clothing hanging in the closet and new boots on his feet. He was still too weak to share in the chores everyone did, but Mary immediately began tutoring him to bring him up to Zane's level academically, since the two boys were the same age, as near as they could tell. Chance took to the books like a starving pup to its mother's teat, but in every other way he determinedly remained at arm's length. Those shrewd, guarded eyes took note of every nuance of their family relationships, weighing what he saw now against what he had known before.

Finally he unbent enough to tell them that he was called Sooner. He didn't have a real name.

Maris had looked at him blankly. "Sooner?"

His mouth had twisted, and he'd looked far too old for his fourteen years. "Yeah, like a mongrel dog."

"No," Wolf had said, because the name was a clue. "You know you're part Indian. More than likely you were called Sooner because you were originally from Oklahoma—and that means you're probably Cherokee."

The boy merely looked at him, his expression guarded, but still something about him had lightened at the possibility that he hadn't been likened to a dog of unknown heritage.

His relationships with everyone in the family were complicated. With Mary, he wanted to hold himself away, but he simply couldn't. She mothered him the way she did the rest of her brood, and it terrified him even though he delighted in it, soaking up her loving concern. He was wary of Wolf, as if he expected the big man to turn on him with fists and boots. Wise in the ways of wild things, Wolf gradually gentled the boy the same way he did horses, letting him get accustomed, letting him realize he had nothing to fear, then offering respect and friendship and, finally, love.

Michael had already been away at college, but when he did come home he simply made room in his family circle for the newcomer. Sooner was relaxed with Mike from the start, sensing that quiet acceptance.

He got along with Josh, too, but Josh was so cheerful it was impossible not to get along with him. Josh took it on himself to be the one who taught Sooner how to handle the multitude of chores on a horse ranch. Josh was the one who taught him how to ride, though Josh was unarguably the worst horseman in the family. That wasn't to say he wasn't good, but the others were better, especially Maris. Josh didn't care, because his heart was wrapped up in planes just the way Joe's had been, so perhaps he had been more patient with Sooner's mistakes than anyone else would have been.

Maris was like Mary. She had taken one look at the boy and immediately taken him under her fiercely protective wing, never mind that Sooner was easily twice her size. At twelve, Maris had been not quite five feet tall and weighed all of seventy-four pounds. It didn't matter to her; Sooner became hers the same way her older brothers were hers. She chattered to him, teased him, played jokes on him—in short, drove him crazy, the way little sisters were supposed to do. Sooner hadn't had any idea how to handle the way she treated him, any more than he had with Mary. Sometimes he had watched Maris as if she was a ticking time bomb, but it was Maris who won his first smile with her teasing. It was Maris who actually got him to enter the family conversations: slowly, at first, as he learned how families worked, how the give-and-take of talking melded them together, then with more ease. Maris could still tease him into a rage, or coax a laugh out of him, faster than anyone else. For a while Wolf had wondered if the two might become romantically interested in each other as they grew older, but it hadn't happened. It was a testament to how fully Sooner had become a part of their family; to both of them, they were simply brother and sister.

Things with Zane had been complicated, though.

Zane was, in his own way, as guarded as Sooner. Wolf knew warriors, having been one himself, and what he saw in his youngest son was almost frightening. Zane was quiet, intense, watchful. He moved like a cat, gracefully, soundlessly. Wolf had trained all his children, including Maris, in self-defense, but with Zane it was something more. The boy took to it with the ease of someone putting on a well-worn shoe; it was as if it had been made for him. When it came to marksmanship, he had the eye of a sniper, and the deadly patience.

Zane had the instinct of a warrior: to protect. He was immediately on guard against this intruder into the sanctity of his family's home turf.

He hadn't been nasty to Sooner. He hadn't made fun of him or been overtly unfriendly, which wasn't in his nature. Rather, he had held himself away from the newcomer, not rejecting, but certainly not welcoming, either. But because they were the same age, Zane's acceptance was the most crucial, and Sooner had reacted to Zane's coolness by adopting the same tactics. They had ignored each other.

While the kids were working out their relationships,

Wolf and Mary had been pushing hard to legally adopt Sooner. They had asked him if that was what he wanted and, typically, he had responded with a shrug and an expressionless, "Sure." Taking that for the impassioned plea it was, Mary redoubled her efforts to get the adoption pushed through.

As things worked out, they got the word that the adoption could go forward on the same day Zane and Sooner settled things between them.

The dust was what had caught Wolf's attention.

At first he hadn't thought anything of it, because when he glanced over he saw Maris sitting on the top rail of the fence, calmly watching the commotion. Figuring one of the horses was rolling in the dirt, Wolf went back to work. Two seconds later, however, his sharp ears caught the sound of grunts and what sounded suspiciously like blows.

He walked across the yard to the other corral. Zane and Sooner had gotten into the corner, where they couldn't be seen from the house, and were ferociously battering each other. Wolf saw at once that both boys, despite the force of their blows, were restraining themselves to the more conventional fisticuffs rather than the faster, nastier ways he'd also taught them. He leaned his arms on the top rail beside Maris. "What's this about?"

"They're fighting it out," she said matter-of-factly, without taking her eyes from the action.

Josh soon joined them at the fence, and they watched the battle. Zane and Sooner were both tall, muscular boys, very strong for their ages. They stood toe to toe, taking turns driving their fists into each other's faces. When one of them got knocked down, he got to his feet and waded back into the fray. They were almost eerily silent, except for the involuntary grunts and the sounds of hard fists hitting flesh.

Mary saw them standing at the fence and came out to investigate. She stood beside Wolf and slipped her small hand into his. He felt her flinch every time a blow landed, but when he looked at her, he saw that she was wearing her prim schoolteacher's expression, and he knew that Mary Elizabeth Mackenzie was about to call the class to order.

She gave it five minutes. Evidently deciding this could go on for hours, and that both boys were too stubborn to give in, she settled the matter herself. In her crisp, clear teaching voice she called out, "All right, boys, let's get this wrapped up. Supper will be on the table in ten minutes." Then she calmly walked back to the house, fully confident that she had brought detente to the corral.

She had, too. She had reduced the fight to the level of a chore or a project, given them a time limit and a reason for ending it.

Both boys' eyes had flickered to that slight retreating figure with the ramrod spine. Then Zane had turned to Sooner, the coolness of his blue gaze somewhat marred by the swelling of his eyes. "One more," he said grimly, and slammed his fist into Sooner's face.

Sooner picked himself up off the dirt, squared up again and returned the favor.

Zane got up, slapped the dirt from his clothes and held out his hand. Sooner gripped it, though they had both winced at the pain in their knuckles. They shook hands, eyed each other as equals, then returned to the house to clean up. After all, supper was almost on the table.

At supper, Mary told Sooner that the adoption had been given the green light. His pale hazel eyes had glittered in his battered face, but he hadn't said anything.

"You're a Mackenzie now," Maris had pronounced with

great satisfaction. "You'll have to have a real name, so choose one."

It hadn't occurred to her that choosing a name might require some thought, but as it happened, Sooner had looked around the table at the family that pure blind luck had sent him, and a wry little smile twisted up one side of his bruised, swollen mouth. "Chance," he said, and the unknown, unnamed boy became Chance Mackenzie.

Zane and Chance hadn't become immediate best friends after the fight. What they had found, instead, was mutual respect, but friendship grew out of it. Over the years, they became so close that they could well have been born twins. There were other fights between them, but it was well known around Ruth, Wyoming, that if anyone decided to take on either of the boys, he would find himself facing both of them. They could batter each other into the ground, but by God, no one else was going to.

They had entered the Navy together, Zane becoming a SEAL, while Chance had gone into Naval Intelligence. Chance had since left the Navy, though, and gone out on his own, while Zane was a SEAL team leader.

And that brought Wolf to the reason for his restlessness. Zane.

There had been a lot of times in Zane's career when he had been out of touch, when they hadn't known where he was or what he was doing. Wolf hadn't slept well then, either. He knew too much about the SEALs, having seen them in action in Vietnam during his tours of duty. They were the most highly trained and skilled of the special forces, their stamina and teamwork proven by grueling tests that broke lesser men. Zane was particularly well-suited for the work, but in the final analysis, the SEALs were still human. They could be killed. And because of the nature of their work, they were often in dangerous situations.

The SEAL training had merely accentuated the already existing facets of Zane's nature. He had been honed to a perfect fighting machine, a warrior who was in top condition, but who used his brain more than his brawn. He was even more lethal and intense now, but he had learned to temper that deadliness with an easier manner, so that most people were unaware they were dealing with a man who could kill them in a dozen different ways with his bare hands. With that kind of knowledge and skill at his disposal, Zane had learned a calm control that kept him in command of himself. Of all Wolf's offspring, Zane was the most capable of taking care of himself, but he was also the one in the most danger.

Where in hell *was* he?

There was a whisper of movement from the bed, and Wolf looked around as Mary slipped from between the sheets and joined him at the window, looping her arms around his hard, trim waist and nestling her head on his bare chest.

"Zane?" she asked quietly, in the darkness.

"Yeah." No more explanation was needed.

"He's all right," she said with a mother's confidence. "I'd know if he wasn't."

Wolf tipped her head up and kissed her, lightly at first, then with growing intensity. He turned her slight body more fully into his embrace and felt her quiver as she pressed to him, pushing her hips against his, cradling the rise of his male flesh against her softness. There had been passion between them from their first meeting, all those years ago, and time hadn't taken it from them.

He lifted her in his arms and carried her back to bed, losing himself in the welcome and warmth of her soft body. Afterward, though, lying in the drowsy aftermath, he turned his face toward the window. Before sleep claimed him, the thought came again. Where was Zane?

Chapter 1

Zane Mackenzie wasn't happy.

No one aboard the aircraft carrier USS *Montgomery* was happy; well, maybe the cooks were, but even that was iffy, because the men they were serving were sullen and defensive. The seamen weren't happy, the radar men weren't happy, the gunners weren't happy, the Marines weren't happy, the wing commander wasn't happy, the pilots weren't happy, the air boss wasn't happy, the executive officer wasn't happy, and Captain Udaka sure as hell wasn't happy.

The combined unhappiness of the five thousand sailors on board the carrier didn't begin to approach Lieutenant-Commander Mackenzie's level of unhappiness.

The captain outranked him. The executive officer outranked him. Lieutenant-Commander Mackenzie addressed them with all the respect due their rank, but both men were uncomfortably aware that their asses were in a sling and their careers on the line. Actually, their careers were probably in the toilet. There wouldn't be any court-martials, but neither would be there any more promotions, and they would be given the unpopular commands from now until they either retired or resigned, their choice depending on how clearly they could read the writing on the wall.

Captain Udaka's broad, pleasant face was one that wore responsibility easily, but now his expression was set in lines of unhappy acceptance as he met the icy gaze of the lieutenant-commander. SEALs in general made the captain nervous; he didn't quite trust them or the way they operated outside normal regulations. This one in particular made him seriously want to be somewhere—anywhere—else.

He had met Mackenzie before, when both he and Boyd, the XO, had been briefed on the security exercise. The SEAL team under Mackenzie's command would try to breach the carrier's security, probing for weaknesses that could be exploited by any of the myriad terrorist groups so common these days. It was a version of the exercises once conducted by the SEAL Team Six Red Cell, which had been so notorious and so far outside the regulations that it had been disbanded after seven years of operation. The concept, however, had lived on, in a more controlled manner. SEAL Team Six was a covert, counterterrorism unit, and one of the best ways to counter terrorism was to prevent it from happening in the first place, rather than reacting to it after people were dead. To this end, the security of naval installations and carrier battle groups was tested by the SEALs, who then recommended changes to correct the weaknesses they had discovered. There were always weaknesses, soft spots—the SEALs had never yet been completely thwarted, even though the base commanders and ships' captains were always notified in advance.

At the briefing, Mackenzie had been remote but pleasant. Controlled. Most SEALs had a wild, hard edge to them, but Mackenzie had seemed more regular Navy, recruiting-poster perfect in his crisp whites and with his coolly courteous manner. Captain Udaka had felt comfortable with him, certain that Lieutenant-Commander Mackenzie was the administrational type rather than a true part of those wild-ass SEALs.

He'd been wrong.

The courtesy remained, and the control. The white uniform looked as perfect as it had before. But there was nothing at all pleasant in the deep voice, or in the cold fury that lit the pale blue gray eyes so they glittered like moonlight on a knife blade. The aura of danger surrounding him was so strong it was almost palpable, and Captain Udaka knew that he had been drastically wrong in his assessment of Mackenzie. This was no desk jockey; this was a man around whom others should walk very lightly indeed. The captain felt as if his skin was being flayed from his body, strip by strip, by that icy gaze. He had also never felt closer to death than he had the moment Mackenzie had entered his quarters after learning what had happened.

"Captain, you were briefed on the exercise," Zane said coldly. "Everyone on this ship was advised, as well as notified that my men wouldn't be carrying weapons of any sort. Explain, then, *why in hell two of my men were shot!*"

The XO, Mr. Boyd, looked at his hands. Captain Udaka's collar felt too tight, except that it was already unbuttoned, and the only thing choking him was the look in Mackenzie's eyes.

"There's no excuse," he said rawly. "Maybe the guards were startled and fired without thinking. Maybe it was a stupid, macho turf thing, wanting to show the big bad SEALs that they couldn't penetrate our security, after all. It doesn't matter. There's no excuse." Everything that happened on board his ship was, ultimately, his responsibility.

The trigger-happy guards would pay for their mistake—and so would he.

"My men had *already* penetrated your security," Zane said softly, his tone making the hairs stand up on the back of the captain's neck.

"I'm aware of that." The breach of his ship's security was salt in the captain's wounds, but nothing at all compared to the enormous mistake that had been made when men under his command had opened fire on the unarmed SEALs. His men, his responsibility. Nor did it help his feelings that, when two of their team had gone down, the remainder of the SEAL team, *unarmed*, had swiftly taken control and secured the area. Translated, that meant the guards who had done the shooting had been roughly handled and were now in sick bay with the two men they had shot. In reality, the phrase "roughly handled" was a euphemism for the fact that the SEALS had beaten the hell out of his men.

The most seriously wounded SEAL was Lieutenant Higgins, who had taken a bullet in the chest and would be evacuated by air to Germany as soon as he was stabilized. The other SEAL, Warrant Officer Odessa, had been shot in the thigh; the bullet had broken his femur. He, too, would be taken to Germany, but his condition was stable, even if his temper was not. The ship's doctor had been forced to sedate him to keep him from wreaking vengeance on the battered guards, two of whom were still unconscious.

The five remaining members of the SEAL team were in Mission Planning, prowling around like angry tigers looking for someone to maul just to make themselves feel better. They were restricted to the area by Mackenzie's order, and the ship's crew was giving them a wide berth. Captain Udaka wished he could do the same with Mackenzie. He had the impression of cold savagery lurking just beneath the surface of the man's control. There would be hell to pay for this night's fiasco.

The phone on his desk emitted a harsh *brr*. Though he was relieved by the interruption, Captain Udaka snatched up the receiver and barked, ''I gave orders I wasn't to be—'' He stopped, listening, and his expression changed. His gaze shifted to Mackenzie. ''We'll be right there,'' he said, and hung up.

''There's a scrambled transmission coming in for you,'' he said to Mackenzie, rising to his feet. ''Urgent.'' Whatever message the transmission contained, Captain Udaka looked on it as a much-welcomed reprieve.

Zane listened intently to the secure satellite transmission, his mind racing as he began planning the logistics of the mission. ''My team is two men short, sir,'' he said. ''Higgins and Odessa were injured in the security exercise.'' He didn't say *how* they'd been injured; that would be handled through other channels.

''Damn it,'' Admiral Lindley muttered. He was in an office in the U.S. Embassy in Athens. He looked up at the others in the office: Ambassador Lovejoy, tall and spare, with the smoothness bequeathed by a lifetime of privilege and wealth, though now there was a stark, panicked expression in his hazel eyes; the CIA station chief, Art Sandefer, a nondescript man with short gray hair and tired, intelligent eyes; and, finally, Mack Prewett, second only to Sandefer in the local CIA hierarchy. Mack was known in some circles as Mack the Knife; Admiral Lindley knew Mack was generally considered a man who got things done, a man whom it was dangerous to cross. For all his decisiveness, though, he wasn't a cowboy who was likely to endanger people by going off half-cocked. He was as thorough as he was decisive, and it was through his contacts that they had obtained such good, prompt information in this case.

The admiral had put Zane on the speakerphone, so the other three in the room had heard the bad news about the SEAL team on which they had all been pinning their hopes. Ambassador Lovejoy looked even more haggard.

"We'll have to use another team," Art Sandefer said.

"That'll take too much time!" the ambassador said with stifled violence. "My God, already she could be—" He stopped, anguish twisting his face. He wasn't able to complete the sentence.

"I'll take the team in," Zane said. His amplified voice was clear in the soundproofed room. "We're the closest, and we can be ready to go in an hour."

"You?" the admiral asked, startled. "Zane, you haven't seen live action since—"

"My last promotion," Zane finished dryly. He hadn't liked trading action for administration, and he was seriously considering resigning his commission. He was thirty-one, and it was beginning to look as if his success in his chosen field was going to prevent him from practicing it; the higher-ranking the officer, the less likely that officer was to be in the thick of the action. He'd been thinking about something in law enforcement, or maybe even throwing in with Chance. There was nonstop action there, for sure.

For now, though, a mission had been dumped in his lap, and he was going to take it.

"I train with my men, Admiral," he said. "I'm not rusty, or out of shape."

"I didn't think you were," Admiral Lindley replied, and sighed. He met the ambassador's anguished gaze, read the silent plea for help. "Can six men handle the mission?" he asked Zane.

"Sir, I wouldn't risk my men if I didn't think we could do the job."

This time the admiral looked at both Art Sandefer and Mack Prewett. Art's expression was noncommittal, the Company man refusing to stick his neck out, but Mack gave the admiral a tiny nod. Admiral Lindley swiftly weighed all the factors. Granted, the SEAL team would be two members short, and the leader would be an officer who hadn't been on an active mission in over a year, but that officer happened to be Zane Mackenzie. All things considered, the admiral couldn't think of any other man he would rather have on this mission. He'd known Zane for several years now, and there was no better warrior, no one he trusted more. If Zane said he was ready, then he was ready. "All right. Go in and get her out."

As the admiral hung up, Ambassador Lindley blurted, "Shouldn't you send in someone else? My daughter's life is at stake! This man hasn't been in the field, he's out of shape, out of practice—"

"Waiting until we could get another team into position would drastically lower our chances of finding her," the admiral pointed out as kindly as possible. Ambassador Lindley wasn't one of his favorite people. For the most part, he was a horse's ass and a snob, but there was no doubt he doted on his daughter. "And as far as Zane Mackenzie is concerned, there's no better man for the job."

"The admiral's right," Mack Prewett said quietly, with the authority that came so naturally to him. "Mackenzie is so good at what he does it's almost eerie. I would feel comfortable sending him in alone. If you want your daughter back, don't throw obstacles in his way."

Ambassador Lindley shoved his hand through his hair, an uncharacteristic gesture for so fastidious a man; it was a measure of his agitation. "If anything goes wrong…"

It wasn't clear whether he was about to voice a threat or was simply worrying aloud, but he couldn't complete the sentence. Mack Prewett gave a thin smile. "Something always goes wrong. If anyone can handle it, Mackenzie can."

After Zane terminated the secure transmission he made his way through the network of corridors to Mission Planning. Already he could feel the rush of adrenaline pumping through his muscles as he began preparing, mentally and physically, for the job before him. When he entered the room with its maps and charts and communication systems, and the comfortable chairs grouped around a large table, five hostile faces turned immediately toward him, and he felt the surge of renewed energy and anger from his men.

Only one of them, Santos, was seated at the table, but Santos was the team medic, and he was usually the calmest of the bunch. Ensign Peter "Rocky" Greenberg, second in command of the team and a controlled, detail-oriented kind of guy, leaned against the bulkhead with his arms crossed and murder in his narrowed brown eyes. Antonio Withrock, nicknamed Bunny because he never ran out of energy, was prowling the confines of the room like a mean, hungry cat, his dark skin pulled tight across his high cheekbones. Paul Drexler, the team sniper, sat cross-legged on top of the table while he wiped an oiled cloth lovingly over the disassembled parts of his beloved Remington bolt-action 7.62 rifle. Zane didn't even lift his eyebrows at the sight. His men were supposed to be unarmed, and they had been during the security exercise that had gone so damn sour, but *keeping* Drexler unarmed was another story.

"Planning on taking over the ship?" Zane inquired mildly of the sniper.

His blue eyes cold, Drexler cocked his head as if considering the idea. "I might."

Winstead "Spooky" Jones had been sitting on the deck, his back resting against the bulkhead, but at Zane's entrance he rose effortlessly to his feet. He didn't say anything, but his gaze fastened on Zane's face, and a spark of interest replaced some of the anger in his eyes.

Spook never missed much, and the other team members had gotten in the habit of watching him, picking up cues from his body language. No more than three seconds passed before all five men were watching Zane with complete concentration.

Greenberg was the one who finally spoke. "How's Bobcat doing, boss?"

They had read Spooky's tension, but misread the cause, Zane realized. They thought Higgins had died from his wounds. Drexler began assembling his rifle with sharp, economical motions. "He's stabilized," Zane reassured them. He knew his men, knew how tight they were. A SEAL team had to be tight. Their trust in each other had to be absolute, and if something happened to one of them, they all felt it. "They're transferring him now. It's touchy, but I'll put my money on Bobcat. Odie's gonna be okay, too." He hitched one hip on the edge of the table, his pale eyes glittering with the intensity that had caught Spooky's attention. "Listen up, children. An ambassador's daughter was snatched a few hours ago, and we're going into Libya to get her."

Six black-clad figures slipped silently along the narrow, deserted street in Benghazi, Libya. They communicated by hand signals, or by whispers into the Motorola headsets they all wore under their black knit balaclava hoods. Zane was in his battle mode; he was utterly calm as they worked their way toward the four-story stone building where Barrie Lovejoy was being held on the top floor, if their intelligence was good, and if she hadn't been moved within the past few hours.

Action always affected him this way, as if every cell in his body had settled into its true purpose of existence. He had missed this, missed it to the point that he knew he wouldn't be able to stay in the Navy without it. On a mission, all his senses became more acute, even as a deep center of calm radiated outward. The more intense the action, the calmer he became, as time stretched out into slow motion. At those times he could see and hear every detail, analyze and predict the outcome, then make his decision and act—all within a split second that felt like minutes. Adrenaline would flood his body—he would feel the blood racing through his veins—but his mind would remain detached and calm. He had been told that the look on his face during those times was frighteningly remote, jarring in its total lack of expression.

The team moved forward in well-orchestrated silence. They each knew what to do, and what the others would do. That was the purpose of the trust and teamwork that had been drilled into them through the twenty-six weeks of hell that was formally known as BUD/S training. The bond between them enabled them to do more together than could be accomplished if each worked on his own. Teamwork wasn't just a word to the SEALs, it was their center.

Spooky Jones was point man. Zane preferred using the wiry Southerner for that job because he had unfrayable nerves and could ghost around like a lynx. Bunny Withrock, who almost reverberated with nervous energy, was bringing up the rear. No one sneaked up on Bunny—except the Spook. Zane was right behind Jones, with Drexler, Greenberg and Santos ranging between him and Bunny. Greenberg was quiet, steady, totally dependable. Drexler was uncanny with that rifle, and Santos, besides being a damn good SEAL, also had the skill to patch them up and keep them going, if they were patchable. Overall, Zane had never worked with a better group of men.

Their presence in Benghazi was pure luck, and Zane knew it. Good luck for them and, he hoped, for Miss Lovejoy, but bad luck for the terrorists who had snatched her off the street in Athens fifteen hours ago. If the *Montgomery* hadn't been just south of Crete and in perfect position for launching a rescue, if the SEALs hadn't been on the carrier to practice special insertions as well as the security exercise, then there would have been a delay of precious hours, perhaps even as long as a day, while another team got supplied and into position. As it was, the special insertion into hostile territory they had just accomplished had been the real thing instead of just a practice.

Miss Lovejoy was not only the ambassador's daughter, she was an employee at the embassy, as well. The ambassador was apparently very strict and obsessive about his daughter, having lost his wife and son in a terrorist attack in Rome fifteen years before, when Miss Lovejoy had been a child of ten. After that, he had kept her secluded in private schools, and since she had finished college, she had been acting as his hostess as well as performing her "work" at the embassy. Zane suspected her job was more window dressing than anything else, something to keep her busy. She had never really worked a day in her life, never been out from under her father's protection—until today.

She and a friend had left the embassy to do some shopping. Three men had grabbed her, shoved her into a car and driven off. The friend had immediately reported the abduction. Despite efforts to secure the airport and ports— cynically, Zane suspected deliberate foot-dragging by the Greek authorities—a private plane had taken off from Athens and flown straight to Benghazi.

Thanks to the friend's prompt action, sources on the ground in Benghazi had been alerted. It had been verified that a young woman of Miss Lovejoy's description had been taken off the plane and hustled into the city, into the very building Zane and his team were about to enter.

It had to be her; there weren't that many red-haired Western women in Benghazi. In fact, he would bet there was only one—Barrie Lovejoy.

They were betting her life on it.

Chapter 2

Barrie lay in almost total darkness, heavy curtains at the single window blocking out most of whatever light would have entered. She could tell that it was night; the level of street noise outside had slowly diminished, until now there was mostly silence. The men who had kidnapped her had finally gone away, probably to sleep. They had no worries about her being able to escape; she was naked, and tied tightly to the cot on which she lay. Her wrists were bound together, her arms drawn over her head and tied to the frame of the cot. Her ankles were also tied together, then secured to the frame. She could barely move; every muscle in her body ached, but those in her shoulders burned with agony. She would have screamed, she would have begged for someone to come and release the ropes that held her arms over her head, but she knew that the only people who would come would be the very ones who had tied her in this position, and she would do anything, give anything, to keep from ever seeing them again.

She was cold. They hadn't even bothered to throw a blanket over her naked body, and long, convulsive shivers kept shaking her, though she couldn't tell if she was chilled from the night air or from shock. She didn't suppose it mattered. Cold was cold.

She tried to think, tried to ignore the pain, tried not to give in to shock and terror. She didn't know where she was, didn't know how she could escape, but if the slightest opportunity presented itself, she would have to be ready to take it. She wouldn't be able to escape tonight; her bonds were too tight, her movements too restricted. But tomorrow—oh, God, tomorrow.

Terror tightened her throat, almost choking off her breath. Tomorrow they would be back, and there would be another one with them, the one for whom they waited. A violent shiver racked her as she thought of their rough hands on her bare body, the pinches and slaps and crude probings, and her stomach heaved. She would have vomited, if there had been anything to vomit, but they hadn't bothered to feed her.

She couldn't go through that again.

Somehow, she had to get away.

Desperately she fought down her panic. Her thoughts darted around like crazed squirrels as she tried to plan, to think of something, anything, that she could do to protect herself. But what *could* she do, lying there like a turkey all trussed up for Thanksgiving dinner?

Humiliation burned through her. They hadn't raped her, but they had done other things to her, things to shame and terrorize her and break her spirit. Tomorrow, when the leader arrived, she was sure her reprieve would be over. The threat of rape, and then the act of it, would shatter her and leave her malleable in their hands, desperate to do anything to avoid being violated again. At least that was what they planned, she thought. But she would be damned if she would go along with their plan.

She had been in a fog of terror and shock since they had grabbed her and thrown her into a car, but as she lay there in the darkness, cold and miserable and achingly vulnerable in her nakedness, she felt as if the fog was lifting, or maybe it was being burned away. No one who knew Barrie would ever have described her as hot-tempered, but then, what she felt building in her now wasn't as volatile and fleeting as mere temper. It was rage, as pure and forceful as lava forcing its way upward from the bowels of the earth until it exploded outward and swept away everything in its path.

Nothing in her life had prepared her for these past hours. After her mother and brother had died, she had been pampered and protected as few children ever were. She had seen some—most, actually—of her schoolmates as they struggled with the misery of broken parental promises, of rare, stressful visits, of being ignored and shunted out of the way, but she hadn't been like them. Her father adored her, and she knew it. He was intensely interested in her safety, her friends, her schoolwork. If he said he would call, then the call came exactly when he'd said it would. Every week had brought some small gift in the mail, inexpensive but thoughtful. She'd understood why he worried so much about her safety, why he wanted her to attend the exclusive girls' school in Switzerland, with its cloistered security, rather than a public school, with its attendant hurly-burly.

She was all he had left.

He was all she had left, too. When she'd been a child, after the incident that had halved the family, she had clung fearfully to her father for months, dogging his footsteps when she could, weeping inconsolably when his work took him away from her. Eventually the dread that he, too, would disappear from her life had faded, but the pattern of overprotectiveness had been set.

She was twenty-five now, a grown woman, and though in the past few years his protectiveness had begun to chafe, she had enjoyed the even tenor of her life too much to really protest. She liked her job at the embassy, so much that she was considering a full-time career in the foreign service. She enjoyed being her father's hostess. She had the duties and protocol down cold, and there were more and more female ambassadors on the international scene. It was a moneyed and insular community, but by both temperament and pedigree she was suited to the task. She was calm, even serene, and blessed with a considerate and tactful nature.

But now, lying naked and helpless on a cot, with bruises mottling her pale skin, the rage that consumed her was so deep and primal she felt as if it had altered something basic inside her, a sea change of her very nature. She would *not* endure what they—nameless, malevolent "they"—had planned for her. If they killed her, so be it. She was prepared for death; no matter what, she would not submit.

The heavy curtains fluttered.

The movement caught her eye, and she glanced at the window, but the action was automatic, without curiosity. She was already so cold that even a wind strong enough to move those heavy curtains couldn't chill her more.

The wind was black, and had a shape.

Her breath stopped in her chest.

Mutely she watched the big black shape, as silent as a shadow, slip through the window. It couldn't be human; people made *some* sound when they moved. Surely, in the total silence of the room, she would have been able to hear the whisper of the curtains as the fabric moved, or the faint, rhythmic sigh of breathing. A shoe scraping on the floor, the rustle of clothing, anything—if it was human.

After the black shape had passed between them, the curtains didn't fall back into the perfect alignment that had blocked the light; there was a small opening in them, a slit that allowed a shaft of moonlight, starlight, street light— whatever it was—to relieve the thick darkness. Barrie strained to focus on the dark shape, her eyes burning as she watched it move silently across the floor. She didn't scream; whoever or whatever approached her, it couldn't be worse than the only men likely to come to her rescue.

Perhaps she was really asleep and this was only a dream. It certainly didn't feel real. But nothing in the long, horrible hours since she had been kidnapped had felt real, and she was too cold to be asleep. No, this was real, all right.

Noiselessly the black shape glided to a halt beside the cot. It towered over her, tall and powerful, and it seemed to be examining the naked feast she presented.

Then it moved once again, lifting its hand to its head, and it peeled off its face, pulling the dark skin up as if it was no more than the skin of a banana.

It was a mask. As exhausted as she was, it was a moment before she could find a logical explanation for the nightmarish image. She blinked up at him. A man wearing a mask. Neither an animal, nor a phantom, but a flesh-and-blood man. She could see the gleam of his eyes, make out the shape of his head and the relative paleness of his face, though there was an odd bulkiness to him that in no way affected the eerily silent grace of his movements.

Just another man.

She didn't panic. She had gone beyond fear, beyond everything but rage. She simply waited—waited to fight, waited to die. Her teeth were the only weapon she had, so she would use them, if she could. She would tear at her attacker's flesh, try to damage him as much as possible before she died. If she was lucky, she would be able to get him by the throat with her teeth and take at least one of these bastards with her into death.

He was taking his time, staring at her. Her bound hands clenched into fists. Damn him. Damn them all.

Then he squatted beside the cot and leaned forward, his head very close to hers. Startled, Barrie wondered if he meant to *kiss* her—odd that the notion struck her as so unbearable—and she braced herself, preparing to lunge upward when he got close enough that she had a good chance for his throat.

"Mackenzie, United States Navy," he said in a toneless whisper that barely reached her ear, only a few inches away.

He'd spoken in *English,* with a definitely American accent. She jerked, so stunned that it was a moment before the words made sense. *Navy. United States Navy.* She had been silent for hours, refusing to speak to her captors or respond in any way, but now a small, helpless sound spilled from her throat.

"Shh, don't make any noise," he cautioned, still in that toneless whisper. Even as he spoke he was reaching over her head, and the tension on her arms suddenly relaxed. The small movement sent agony screaming through her shoulder joints, and she sucked in her breath with a sharp, gasping cry.

She quickly choked off the sound, holding it inside as she ground her teeth against the pain. "Sorry," she whispered, when she was able to speak.

She hadn't seen the knife in his hand, but she felt the chill of the blade against her skin as he deftly inserted the blade under the cords and sliced upward, felt the slight tug that freed her hands. She tried to move her arms and found that she couldn't; they remained stretched above her head, unresponsive to her commands.

He knew, without being told. He slipped the knife into its scabbard and placed his gloved hands on her shoulders, firmly kneading for a moment before he clasped her forearms and gently drew her arms down. Fire burned in her joints; it felt as if her arms were being torn from her shoulders, even though he carefully drew them straight down, keeping them aligned with her body to lessen the pain. Barrie set her teeth again, refusing to let another sound break past the barrier. Cold sweat beaded her forehead, and nausea burned in her throat once more, but she rode the swell of pain in silence.

He dug his thumbs into the balls of her shoulders, massaging the sore, swollen ligaments and tendons, intensifying the agony. Her bare body drew into a taut, pale arch of suffering, lifting from the cot. He held her down, ruthlessly pushing her traumatized joints and muscles through the recovery process. She was so cold that the heat emanating from his hands, from the closeness of his body as he bent over her, was searingly hot on her bare skin. The pain rolled through her in great shudders, blurring her sight and thought, and through the haze she realized that now, when she definitely needed to stay conscious, she was finally going to faint.

She couldn't pass out. She refused to. Grimly she hung on, and in only a few moments, moments that felt much longer, the pain began to ebb. He continued the strong kneading, taking her through the agony and into relief. She went limp, relaxing on the cot as she breathed through her mouth in the long, deep drafts of someone who has just run a race.

"Good girl," he whispered as he released her. The brief praise felt like balm to her lacerated emotions. He straight-

ened and drew the knife again, then bent over the foot of
the cot. Again there was the chill of the blade, this time
against her ankles, and another small tug, then her feet were
free, and involuntarily she curled into a protective ball, her
body moving without direction from her brain in a belated,
useless effort at modesty and self-protection. Her thighs
squeezed tightly together, her arms crossed over and hid
her breasts, and she buried her face against the musty ticking of the bare mattress. She couldn't look up at him, she
couldn't. Tears burned her eyes, clogged her throat.

"Have you been injured?" he asked, the ghostly whisper
rasping over her bare skin like an actual touch. "Can you
walk?"

Now wasn't the time to let her raw nerves take over.
They still had to get out undetected, and a fit of hysteria
would ruin everything. She gulped twice, fighting for control of her emotions as grimly as she had fought to control
the pain. The tears spilled over, but she forced herself to
straighten from the defensive curl, to swing her legs over
the edge of the cot. Shakily she sat up and forced herself
to look at him. She hadn't done anything to be ashamed
of; she would get through this. "I'm okay," she replied,
and was grateful that the obligatory whisper disguised the
weakness of her voice.

He crouched in front of her and silently began removing
the web gear that held and secured all his equipment. The
room was too dark for her to make out exactly what each
item was, but she recognized the shape of an automatic
weapon as he placed it on the floor between them. She
watched him, uncomprehending, until he began shrugging
out of his shirt. Sick terror hit her then, slamming into her
like a sledgehammer. My God, surely *he* wasn't—

Gently he put the shirt around her, tucking her arms into
the sleeves as if she was a child, then buttoning each button,

taking care to hold the fabric away from her body so his fingers wouldn't brush against her breasts. The cloth still held his body heat; it wrapped around her like a blanket, warming her, covering her. The sudden feeling of security unnerved her almost as much as being stripped naked. Her heart lurched inside her chest, and the bottom dropped out of her stomach. Hesitantly she reached out her hand in an apology, and a plea. Tears dripped slowly down her face, leaving salty tracks in their wake. She had been the recipient of so much male brutality in the past day that his gentleness almost destroyed her control, where their blows and crudeness had only made her more determined to resist them. She had expected the same from him and instead had received a tender care that shattered her with its simplicity.

A second ticked past, two: then, with great care, he folded his gloved fingers around her hand.

His hand was much bigger than hers. She felt the size and heat of it engulf her cold fingers and sensed the control of a man who exactly knew his own strength. He squeezed gently, then released her.

She stared at him, trying to pierce the veil of darkness and see his features, but his face was barely distinguishable and blurred even more by her tears. She could make out some details, though, and discern his movements. He wore a black T-shirt, and as silently as he had removed his gear, he now put it on again. He peeled back a flap on his wrist, and she caught the faint gleam of a luminous watch. "We have exactly two and a half minutes to get out of here," he murmured. "Do *what* I say, *when* I say it."

Before, she couldn't have done it, but that brief moment of understanding, of connection, had buoyed her. Barrie nodded and got to her feet. Her knees wobbled. She stiffened them and shoved her hair out of her face. "I'm ready."

She had taken exactly two steps when, below them, a staccato burst of gunfire shattered the night.

He spun instantly, silently, slipping away from her so fast that she blinked, unable to follow him. Behind her, the door opened. A harsh, piercing flood of light blinded her, and an ominous form loomed in the doorway. The guard— of course there was a guard. Then there was a blur of movement, a grunt, and the guard sagged into supporting arms. As silently as her rescuer seemed to do everything else, he dragged the guard inside and lowered him to the floor. Her rescuer stepped over the body, snagged her wrist in an unbreakable grip and towed her from the room.

The hallway was narrow, dirty and cluttered. The light that had seemed so bright came from a single naked bulb. More gunfire was erupting downstairs and out in the street. From the left came the sound of pounding feet. To the right was a closed door, and past it she could see the first step of an unlit stairway.

He closed the door of the room they had just left and lifted her off her feet, slinging her under his left arm as if she was no more than a sack of flour. Barrie clutched dizzily at his leg as he strode swiftly to the next room and slipped into the sheltering darkness. He had barely shut the door when a barrage of shouts and curses in the hallway made her bury her face against the black material of his pants leg.

He righted her and set her on her feet, pushing her behind him as he unslung the weapon from his shoulder. They stood at the door, unmoving, listening to the commotion just on the other side of the wooden panel. She could discern three different voices and recognized them all. There were more shouts and curses, in the language she had heard off and on all day long but couldn't understand. The curses turned vicious as the guard's body, and her absence, were discovered. Something thudded against the wall as one of her kidnappers gave vent to his temper.

"This is One. Go to B."

That toneless whisper startled her. Confused, she stared at him, trying to make sense of the words. She was so tired that it took her a moment to realize he must be speaking a coded message into a radio. Of course he wasn't alone; there would be an entire team of rescuers. All they had to do was get out of the building, and there would be a helicopter waiting somewhere, or a truck, or a ship. She didn't care if they'd infiltrated on bicycles; she would gladly walk out—barefoot, if necessary.

But first they had to get out of the building. Obviously the plan had been to spirit her out the window without her kidnappers being any the wiser until morning, but something had gone wrong, and the others had been spotted. Now they were trapped in this room, with no way of rejoining the rest of his team.

Her body began to revolt against the stress it had endured for so many long hours, the terror and pain, the hunger, the effort. With a sort of distant interest she felt each muscle begin quivering, the shudders working their way up her legs, her torso, until she was shaking uncontrollably.

She wanted to lean against him but was afraid she would hinder his movements. Her life—and his—depended completely on his expertise. She couldn't help him, so the least she could do was stay out of his way. But she was desperately in need of support, so she fumbled her way a couple of steps to the wall. She was careful not to make any noise, but he sensed her movement and half turned, reaching behind himself with his left hand and catching her. Without speaking he pulled her up against his back, keeping her within reach should he have to change locations in a hurry.

His closeness was oddly, fundamentally reassuring. Her

captors had filled her with such fear and disgust that every
feminine instinct had been outraged, and after they had finally left her alone in the cold and the dark, she had wondered with a sort of grief if she would ever again be able
to trust a man. The answer, at least with *this* man, was yes.

She leaned gratefully against his back, so tired and weak
that, just for a moment, she had to rest her head on him.
The heat of his body penetrated the rough fabric of the web
vest, warming her cheek. He even smelled hot, she noticed
through a sort of haze; his scent was a mixture of clean,
fresh sweat and musky maleness, exertion and tension heating it to an aroma as heady as that of the finest whiskey.
Mackenzie. He'd said his name was Mackenzie, whispered
it to her when he crouched to identify himself.

Oh, God, he was so warm, and she was still cold. The
gritty stone floor beneath her bare feet seemed to be wafting
cold waves of air up her legs. His shirt was so big it
dwarfed her, hanging almost to her knees, but still she was
naked beneath it. Her entire body was shaking.

They stood motionless in the silent darkness of the empty
room for an eternity, listening to the gunfire as it tapered
off in the distance, listening to the shouts and curses as
they, too, diminished, listened for so long that Barrie drifted
into a light doze, leaning against him with her head resting
on his back. He was like a rock, unmoving, his patience
beyond anything she had ever imagined. There were no
nervous little adjustments of position, no hint that his muscles got tired. The slow, even rhythm of his breathing was
the only movement she could discern, and resting against
him as she was, the sensation was like being on a raft in a
pool, gently rising, falling....

She woke when he reached back and lightly shook her.
"They think we got away," he whispered. "Don't move
or make any sound while I check things out."

Obediently she straightened away from him, though she almost cried at the loss of his body heat. He switched on a flashlight that gave off only a slender beam; black tape had been placed across most of the lens. He flicked the light around the room, revealing that it was empty except for some old boxes piled along one wall. Cobwebs festooned all of the corners, and the floor was covered with a thick layer of dust. She could make out a single window in the far wall, but he was careful not to let the thin beam of light get close to it and possibly betray their presence. The room seemed to have been unused for a very long time.

He leaned close and put his mouth against her ear. His warm breath washed across her flesh with every word. "We have to get out of this building. My men have made it look as if we escaped, but we probably won't be able to hook up with them again until tomorrow night. We need someplace safe to wait. What do you know about the interior layout?"

She shook her head and followed his example, lifting herself on tiptoe to put her lips to his ear. "Nothing," she whispered. "I was blindfolded when they brought me here."

He gave a brief nod and straightened away from her. Once again Barrie felt bereft, abandoned, without his physical nearness. She knew it was just a temporary weakness, this urge to cling to him and the security he represented, but she needed him now with an urgency that was close to pain in its intensity. She wanted nothing more than to press close to him again, to feel the animal heat that told her she wasn't alone; she wanted to be in touch with the steely strength that stood between her and those bastards who had kidnapped her.

Temporary or not, Barrie hated this neediness on her part; it reminded her too sharply of the way she had clung to her father when her mother and brother had died. Granted, she had been just a child then, and the closeness that had developed between her and her father had, for the most part, been good. But she had seen how stifling it could be, too, and quietly, as was her way, she had begun placing increments of distance between them. Now this had happened, and her first instinct was to cling. Was she going to turn into a vine every time there was some trauma in her life? She didn't want to be like that, didn't want to be a weakling. This nightmare had shown her too vividly that all security, no matter how solid it seemed, had its weak points. Instead of depending on others, she would do better to develop her own strengths, strengths she knew were there but that had lain dormant for most of her life. From now on, though, things were going to change.

Perhaps they already had. The incandescent anger that had taken hold of her when she'd lain naked and trussed on that bare cot still burned within her, a small, white-hot core that even her mind-numbing fatigue couldn't extinguish. Because of it, she refused to give in to her weakness, refused to do anything that might hinder Mackenzie in any way. Instead she braced herself, forcing her knees to lock and her shoulders to square. "What are we going to do?" she whispered. "What can I do to help?"

Because there were no heavy blackout curtains on this grimy window, she was able to see part of his features as he looked at her. Half his face was in shadow, but the scant light gleamed on the slant of one high, chiseled cheekbone, revealed the strong cut of his jaw, played along a mouth that was as clearly defined as that of an ancient Greek statue.

"I'll have to leave you here alone for a little while," he said. "Will you be all right?"

Panic exploded in her stomach, her chest. She barely

choked back the scream of protest that would have betrayed them. Grinding her teeth together and electing not to speak, because the scream would escape if she did, she nodded her head.

He hesitated, and Barrie could feel his attention focusing on her, as if he sensed her distress and was trying to decide whether or not it was safe to leave her. After a few moments he gave a curt nod that acknowledged her determination, or at least gave her the benefit of the doubt. "I'll be back in half an hour," he said. "I promise."

He pulled something from a pocket on his vest. He unfolded it, revealing a thin blanket of sorts. Barrie stood still as he snugly wrapped it around her. Though it was very thin, the blanket immediately began reflecting her meager body heat. When he let go of the edges they fell open, and Barrie clutched frantically at them in an effort to retain that fragile warmth. By the time she had managed to pull the blanket around her, he was gone, opening the door a narrow crack and slipping through as silently as he had come through the window in the room where she had been held. Then the door closed, and once again she was alone in the darkness.

Her nerves shrieked in protest, but she ignored them. Instead she concentrated on being as quiet as she could, listening for any sounds in the building that could tell her what was going on. There was still some noise from the street, the result of the gunfire that had alarmed the nearby citizenry, but that, too, was fading. The thick stone walls of the building dulled any sound, anyway. From within the building, there was only silence. Had her captors abandoned the site after her supposed escape? Were they in pursuit of Mackenzie's team, thinking she was with them?

She swayed on her feet, and only then did she realize that she could sit down on the floor and wrap the blanket around her, conserving even more warmth. Her feet and legs were almost numb with cold. Carefully she eased down onto the floor, terrified she would inadvertently make some noise. She sat on the thin blanket and pulled it around herself as best she could. Whatever fabric it was made from, the blanket blocked the chill of the stone floor. Drawing up her legs, Barrie hugged her knees and rested her head on them. She was more comfortable now than she had been in many long hours of terror and, inevitably, her eyelids began to droop heavily. Sitting there alone in the dark, dirty, empty room, she went to sleep.

Chapter 3

Pistol in hand, Zane moved silently through the decrepit old building, avoiding the piles of debris and crumbled stone. They were already on the top floor, so, except for the roof, the only way he could go was down. He already knew where the exits were, but what he didn't know was the location of the bad guys. Had they chosen this building as only a temporary hiding place and abandoned it when their victim seemingly escaped? Or was this their regular meeting place? If so, how many were there, and *where* were they? He had to know all that before he risked moving Miss Lovejoy. There was only another hour or so until dawn; he had to get her to a secure location before then.

He stopped at a turn in the corridor, flattening himself against the wall and easing his head around the corner just enough that he could see. Empty. Noiselessly, he moved down the hallway, just as cautiously checking the few rooms that opened off it.

He had pulled the black balaclava into place and smeared

dust over his bare arms to dull the sheen of his skin and decrease his visibility. Giving his shirt to Miss Lovejoy and leaving his arms bare had increased his visibility somewhat, but he judged that his darkly tanned arms weren't nearly as likely to be spotted as her naked body. Even in the darkness of the room where they had been keeping her, he had been able to clearly make out the pale shimmer of her skin. Since none of her clothes had been in evidence, giving her his shirt was the only thing he could have done. She'd been shaking with cold—evidence of shock because the night was warm—and she likely would have gone into hysterics if he'd tried to take her out of there while she was stark naked. He had been prepared, if necessary, to knock her out. But she'd been a little trooper so far, not even screaming when he had suddenly loomed over her in the darkness. With his senses so acute, though, Zane could feel how fragile her control was, how tightly she was strung.

It was understandable. She had likely been raped, not once but many times, since she had been kidnapped. She might fall apart when the crisis was over and she was safe, but for now she was holding together. Her gutsiness made his heart clench with a mixture of tenderness and a lethal determination to protect her. His first priority was to get her out of Libya, not wreak vengeance on her kidnappers—but if any of the bastards happened to get in his way, so be it.

The dark maw of a stairwell yawned before him. The darkness was reassuring; it not only signaled the absence of a guard, it would shield him. Humans still clung to the primitive instincts of cave dwellers. If they were awake, they wanted the comfort of light around them, so they could see the approach of any enemies. Darkness was a weapon that torturers used to break the spirit of their captives, because it emphasized their helplessness, grated on their nerves. But he was a SEAL, and darkness was merely a circumstance he could use. He stepped carefully into the stairwell, keeping his back to the wall to avoid any crumbling edges of the stone. He was fairly certain the stairs were safe, otherwise the kidnappers wouldn't have been using them, but he didn't take chances. Like idiots, people stacked things on stair steps, blocking their own escape routes.

A faint lessening of the darkness just ahead told him that he was nearing the bottom of the steps. He paused while he was still within the protective shadow, listening for the slightest sound. There. He heard what he'd been searching for, the distant sound of voices, angry voices tripping over each other with curses and excuses. Though Zane spoke Arabic, he was too far away to make out what they were saying. It didn't matter; he'd wanted to know their location, and now he did. Grimly he stifled the urge to exact revenge on Miss Lovejoy's behalf. His mission was to rescue her, not endanger her further.

There was a stairwell at each end of the building. Knowing now that the kidnappers were on the ground floor at the east end, Zane began making his way to the west staircase. He didn't meet up with any guards; as he had hoped, they thought the rescue had been effected, so they didn't see any point now in posting guards.

In his experience, perfect missions were few and far between, so rare that he could count on one hand the number of missions he'd been on where everything had gone like clockwork. He tried to be prepared for mechanical breakdowns, accidents, forces of nature, but there was no way to plan for the human factor. He didn't know how the kidnappers had been alerted to the SEALs' presence, but he had considered that possibility from the beginning and made an alternate plan in case something went wrong.

Something had—exactly what, he would find out later: except for that brief communication with his men, telling them to withdraw and switch to the alternate plan, they had maintained radio silence.

Probably it was pure bad luck, some late-night citizen unexpectedly stumbling over one of his men. Things happened. So he had formulated Plan B, his just-in-case plan, because as they had worked their way toward the building, he'd had an uneasy feeling. When his gut told him something, Zane listened. Bunny Withrock had once given him a narrow-eyed look and said, "Boss, you're even spookier than the Spook." But they trusted his instincts, to the point that mentally they had probably switched to Plan B as soon as he'd voiced it, before he had even gone into the building.

With Miss Lovejoy to consider, he'd opted for safety. That was why he had gone in alone, through the window, after Spook's reconnaissance had reported that the kidnappers had set guards at intervals throughout the first floor. There were no lights in any of the rooms on the fourth floor, where Miss Lovejoy was reportedly being held, so it was likely there was no guard actually in the room with her; a guard wouldn't want to sit in the darkness.

The kidnappers had inadvertently pinpointed the room for him: only one window had been covered with curtains. When Zane had reached that room, he had carefully parted the heavy curtains to make certain they hadn't shielded an interior light, but the room beyond had been totally dark. And Miss Lovejoy had been there, just as he had expected.

Now, ostensibly with nothing left to guard, the kidnappers all seemed to be grouped together. Zane cat-footed through the lower rooms until he reached the other staircase, then climbed silently upward. Thanks to Spooky, he knew of a fairly secure place to take Miss Lovejoy while they waited for another opportunity for extraction; all he had to do was get her there undetected. That meant he had to do it before dawn, because a half-naked, red-haired Western woman would definitely be noticeable in this Islamic country. He wouldn't exactly blend in himself, despite his black hair and tanned skin, because of his dark cammies, web gear and weaponry. Most people noticed a man with camouflage paint on his face and an automatic rifle slung over his shoulder.

He reached the room where he'd left Miss Lovejoy and entered as quietly as he'd left. The room was empty. Alarm roared through him, every muscle tightening, and then he saw the small, dark hump on the floor and realized that she had curled up with the thin survival blanket over her. She wasn't moving. Zane listened to the light, almost inaudible evenness of her breathing and realized she had gone to sleep. Again he felt that subtle inner clenching. She had been on edge and terrified for hours, obviously worn out but unable to sleep; the slight measure of security he'd been able to give her, consisting of his shirt, a blanket and a temporary, precarious hiding place, had been enough for her to rest. He hated to disturb her, but they had to move.

Gently he put his hand on her back, lightly rubbing, not shaking her awake but easing her into consciousness so she wouldn't be alarmed. After a moment she began stirring under his touch, and he felt the moment when she woke, felt her instant of panic, then her quietly determined reach for control.

"We're moving to someplace safer," he whispered, removing his hand as soon as he saw she was alert. After what she had been through, she wouldn't want to endure a man's touch any more than necessary. The thought infuriated him, because his instinct was to comfort her; the women in his family, mother, sister and sisters-in-law, were adored and treasured by the men. He wanted to cradle Bar-

rie Lovejoy against him, whisper promises to her that he
would personally dismember every bastard who had hurt
her, but he didn't want to do anything that would under-
mine her fragile control. They didn't have time for any
comforting, anyway.

She clambered to her feet, still clutching the blanket
around her. Zane reached for it, and her fingers tightened
on the fabric, then slowly loosened. She didn't have to explain her reluctance to release the protective cloth. Zane
knew she was still both extrasensitive to cold and painfully
embarrassed by her near nudity.

"Wear it this way," he whispered, wrapping the blanket
around her waist sarong-style so that it draped to her feet.
He tied the ends securely over her left hipbone, then bent
down to check that the fabric wasn't too tight around her
feet, so she would have sufficient freedom of movement if
they had to run.

When he straightened, she touched his arm, then swiftly
lifted her hand away, as if even that brief touch had been
too much. "Thank you," she whispered.

"Watch me closely," he instructed. "Obey my hand signals." He explained the most basic signals to her, the raised
clenched fist that meant "Stop!" and the open hand that
meant merely "halt," the signal to proceed and the signal
to hide. Considering her state of mind, plus her obvious
fatigue, he doubted she would be able to absorb more than
those four simple commands. They didn't have far to go,
anyway; if he needed more commands than that, they were
in deep ca-ca.

She followed him out of the room and down the west
staircase, though he felt her reluctance to step into the Sty-
gian depths. He showed her how to keep her back to the
wall, how to feel with her foot for the edge of the step. He
felt her stumble once, heard her sharply indrawn breath. He

whirled to steady her; his pistol was in his right hand, but his left arm snaked out, wrapping around her hips to steady her as she teetered two steps above him. The action lifted her off her feet, hauling her against his left side. She felt soft in his grip, her hips narrow but nicely curved, and his nostrils flared as he scented the warm sweetness of her skin.

She was all but sitting on his encircling arm, her hands braced on his shoulders. Reluctantly he bent and set her on her feet, and she immediately straightened away from him. "Sorry," she whispered in the darkness.

Zane's admiration for her grew. She hadn't squealed in alarm, despite nearly falling, despite the way he'd grabbed her. She was holding herself together, narrowing her focus to the achievement of one goal: freedom.

She was even more cautious in her movements after that one misstep, letting more distance grow between them than he liked. On the last flight of steps he stopped, waiting for her to catch up with him. Knowing that she couldn't see him, he said, "Here," when she was near, so she wouldn't bump into him.

He eased his way down the last couple of steps into the faint light. There was no one in sight. With a brief wave of his hand he signaled her forward, and she slipped out of the darkness of the stairwell to stand beside him.

There was a set of huge wooden double doors that opened onto the street, but Zane was aware of increased noise outside as dawn neared, and it was too risky to use that exit. From their left came a raised voice, shouting in Arabic, and he felt her tense. Quickly, before the sound of one of her kidnappers unnerved her, he shepherded her into a cluttered storage room, where a small, single window shone high on the wall. "We'll go out this window," he murmured. "There'll be a drop of about four feet to the ground, nothing drastic. I'll boost you up. When you hit the ground, move away from the street but stay against the side of the building. Crouch down so you'll present the smallest possible silhouette. Okay?''

She nodded her understanding, and they picked their way over the jumbled boxes and debris until they were standing under the window. Zane stretched to reach the sill, hooked his fingers on the plaster and boosted himself up until he was balanced with one knee on the sill and one booted foot braced against a rickety stack of boxes. The window evidently hadn't been used in a long time; the glass was opaque with dust, the hinges rusty and stiff. He wrestled it open, wincing at the scraping noise, even though he knew it wouldn't carry to where the kidnappers were. Fresh air poured into the musty room. Like a cat he dropped to the floor, then turned to her.

''You can put your foot in my hand, or you can climb on my shoulders. Which do you prefer?''

With the window open, more light was coming through. He could see her doubtful expression as she stared at the window, and for the first time he appreciated the evenness of her features. He already knew how sweetly her body was shaped, but now he knew that Miss Lovejoy didn't hurt his eyes at all.

''Can you get through there?'' she whispered, ignoring his question as she eyed first the expanse of his shoulders and then the narrowness of the window.

Zane had already made those mental measurements. ''It'll be a tight fit, but I've been through tighter ones.''

She gazed at his darkened face, then gave one of her sturdy nods, the one that said she was ready to go on. Now he could see her calculating the difficulty of maneuvering through the window with the blanket tied around her waist, and he saw the exact moment when she made her decision. Her shoulders squared and her chin came up as she untied the blanket and draped it around her like a long scarf, winding it around her neck and tossing the ends over her shoulders to dangle rakishly down her back.

"I think I'd better climb on your shoulders," she said. "I'll have more leverage that way."

He knelt on the floor and held his hands up for her to catch and brace herself. She went around behind him and daintily placed her right foot on his right shoulder, then lifted herself into a half crouch. As soon as her left foot had settled into place and her hands were securely in his, he rose steadily until he was standing erect. Her weight was negligible compared to what he handled during training. He moved closer to the wall, and she released his right hand to brace her hand against the sill. "Here I go," she whispered, and boosted herself through the window.

She went through it headfirst. It was the fastest way, but not the easiest, because she had no way of breaking her fall on the other side. He looked up and saw the gleam of pale, bare legs and the naked curves of her buttocks; then she vanished from sight, and there was a thump as she hit the ground.

Quickly Zane boosted himself up again. "Are you all right?" he whispered harshly.

There was silence for a moment, then a shaky, whispered answer. "I think so."

"Take the rifle." He handed the weapon to her, then dropped to the floor while he removed his web gear. That, too, went through the window. Then he followed, feet first, twisting his shoulders at an angle to fit through the narrow opening and landing in a crouch. Obediently, she had moved to the side and was sitting against the wall with the blanket once more clutched around her and his rifle cradled in her arms.

Dawn was coming fast, the remnants of darkness no

more than a deep twilight. "Hurry," he said as he shrugged into the web vest and took the rifle from her. He slid it into position, then drew the pistol again. The heavy butt felt reassuring and infinitely familiar in his palm. With the weapon in his right hand and her hand clasped in his left, he pulled her into the nearest alley.

Benghazi was a modern city, fairly Westernized, and Libya's chief port. They were near the docks, and the smell of the sea was strong in his nostrils. Like the vast majority of waterfronts, it was one of the rougher areas of the city. From what he'd been able to tell, no authorities had shown up to investigate the gunfire, even supposing it had been reported. The Libyan government wasn't friendly—there were no diplomatic relations between the United States and Libya—but that didn't mean the government would necessarily turn a blind eye to the kidnapping of an ambassador's daughter. Of course, it was just as likely that it would, which was why diplomatic channels hadn't been considered. The best option had seemed to go in and get Miss Lovejoy out as quickly as possible.

There were plenty of ramshackle, abandoned buildings in the waterfront area. The rest of the team had withdrawn to one, drawing any pursuers away from Zane and Miss Lovejoy, while they holed up in another. They would rendezvous at oh-one-hundred hours the next morning.

Spooky had chosen the sites, so Zane trusted their relative safety. Now he and Miss Lovejoy wended their way through a rat's nest of alleyways. She made a stifled sound of disgust once, and he knew she'd stepped on something objectionable, but other than that she soldiered on in silence.

It took only a few minutes to reach the designated safe area. The building looked more down than up, but Spooky had investigated and reported an intact inner room. One outer wall was crumbled to little more than rubble. Zane straddled it, then caught Miss Lovejoy around the waist and effortlessly lifted her over the heap, twisting his torso to set her on the other side. Then he joined her, leading her under half-fallen timbers and around spiderwebs that he wanted left undisturbed. The fact that he could see those webs meant they had to get under cover, fast.

The door to the interior room hung haphazardly on one hinge, and the wood was rotting away at the top. He pulled her inside the protective walls. "Stay here while I take care of our tracks," he whispered, then dropped to a crouch and moved to where they had crossed the remnants of the outer wall. He worked backward from there, scattering dirt to hide the signs of their passage. There were dark, wet places on the broken pieces of stone that were all that remained of the floor. He frowned, knowing what those dark patches meant. Damn it, why hadn't she said something? Had she left a trail of blood straight to their hiding place?

Carefully he obliterated the marks. It wasn't completely her fault; he should have given more thought to her bare feet. The truth was, his mind had been more on her bare butt and the other details of her body that he'd already seen. He was far too aware of her sexually; the proof of it was heavy in his loins. After what she had been through that was the last thing she needed, so he would ignore his desire, but that didn't make it go away.

When he had worked his way to the room, he silently lifted the door and reset it in the frame, bracing it so it wouldn't sag again. Only then did he turn to face her. "Why didn't you tell me you'd cut your foot? When did it happen?" His voice was low and very even.

She was still standing where he'd left her, her face colorless in the half light coming through the open shutters of the window, her eyes so huge with fatigue and strain that she looked like a forlorn, bedraggled little owl. A puzzled frown knit her brows as she looked at her feet. "Oh," she said in dazed discovery as she examined the dark stains on her left foot. "I didn't realize it was cut. It must have happened when I stepped in that…whatever…in the alley. I remember that it hurt, but I thought there was just a sharp rock under the…stuff."

At least it hadn't happened any sooner than that. Their position should still be safe. He keyed the radio, giving the prearranged one click that told the team he was in the safe area and receiving two clicks in return, meaning his men were secure in their position, too. They would check in with each other at set intervals, but for the most part they would spend the day resting. Relieved, Zane turned his mind to other matters.

"Sit down and let me see your foot," he ordered. The last thing he needed was for her to be hobbled, though from what he'd seen of her so far, she wouldn't breathe a word of complaint, merely limp along as fast as she could.

There was nothing to sit on except the broken stones of the floor, so that was where she sat, carefully keeping the blanket wrapped around her waist. Her feet were filthy, caked with the same mess that caked his boots. Blood oozed sullenly from a cut on the instep of her left foot.

Zane shucked off his black hood and headset, took off his web vest and removed his gloves; then he unpacked his survival gear, which included a small and very basic first-aid kit. He sat cross-legged in front of her and lifted her foot to rest on his thigh. After tearing open a small packet containing a premoistened antiseptic pad, he thoroughly cleaned the cut and the area around it, pretending not to notice her involuntary flinches of pain, which she quickly tried to control.

The cut was deep enough that it probably needed a couple of stitches. He took out another antiseptic pad and pressed it hard over the wound until the bleeding stopped. "How long has it been since your last tetanus vaccination?" he asked.

Barrie thought that she had never heard anything as calm as his voice. She could see him clearly now; it was probably a good thing she hadn't been able to do so before, because her nerves likely couldn't have stood the pressure. She cleared her throat and managed to say, "I don't remember. Years," but her mind wasn't on what she was saying.

His thick black hair was matted with sweat, and his face was streaked with black and green paint. The black T-shirt he wore was grimy with mingled dust and sweat, not that the shirt she had on was in much better shape. The material strained over shoulders that looked a yard wide, clung to a broad chest and flat stomach, stretched over powerful biceps. His arms were corded with long, steely muscles, his wrists almost twice as thick as hers; his long-fingered hands were well-shaped, callused, harder than any human hands should be—and immensely gentle as he cleansed the wound on her foot.

His head was bent over the task. She saw the dense black eyelashes, the bold sweep of his eyebrows, the thin and arrogantly high bridge of his nose, the chiseled plane of his cheekbones. She saw his mouth, so clear-cut and stern, as if he seldom smiled. Beard stubble darkened his jaw beneath the camouflage paint. Then his gaze flicked up to her for a moment, cool and assessing, as if he was gauging her reaction to the sting of the antiseptic, and she was stunned by the clear, pale beauty of his blue gray eyes. He had silently and efficiently killed that guard, then stepped over the body as if it didn't exist. A wicked, ten-inch black blade rode in a scabbard strapped to his thigh, and he handled both pistol and rifle with an ease that bespoke a familiarity that went far beyond the normal. He was the most savage, dangerous, lethal thing, man or beast, that she had ever seen—and she felt utterly safe with him.

He had given her the shirt off his back, treating her with a courtesy and tenderness that had eased her shock, calmed her fears. He had seen her naked; she had been able to ignore that while they were still trapped in the same building with her kidnappers, but now they were relatively safe, and alone, and she was burningly aware of both his intense masculinity and of her nakedness beneath his shirt. Her skin felt unusually sensitive, as if it was too hot and tight, and the rasp of the fabric against her nipples was almost painfully acute.

Her foot looked small and fragile in his big hands. He frowned in concentration as he applied an antibiotic ointment to the cut, then fashioned a butterfly bandage to close the wound. He worked with a swift, sure dexterity, and it was only a moment before the bandaging was complete. Gently he lifted her foot off his leg. "There. You should be able to walk with no problem, but as soon as we get you to the ship, get the doc to put in a couple of stitches and give you an injection for tetanus."

"Yes, sir," she said softly.

He looked up with a swift, faint smile. "I'm Navy. That's, 'Aye, aye, sir.'"

The smile nearly took her breath. If he ever truly smiled, she thought, she might have heart failure. To hide her reaction, she held out her hand to him. "Barrie Lovejoy. I'm pleased to make your acquaintance."

He folded his fingers around hers and solemnly shook hands. "Lieutenant-Commander Zane Mackenzie, United States Navy SEALs."

A SEAL. Her heart jumped in her chest. That explained it, then. SEALs were known as the most dangerous men alive, men so skilled in the arts of warfare that they were in a class by themselves. He didn't just look lethal; he *was* lethal.

"Thank you," she whispered.

"My pleasure, ma'am."

Hot color flooded her face as she looked at her blanket-covered lap. "Please, call me Barrie. After all, your shirt is the only thing I..." Her voice trailed off, and she bit her lip. "I mean, formality at this point is—"

"I understand," he said gently, breaking into her stumbling explanation. "I don't want you to be embarrassed, so the circumstances are strictly between us, if you prefer. But I advise you to tell the ship's surgeon, or your own doctor, for the sake of your health."

Barrie blinked at him in confusion, wondering what on earth her health had to do with the fact that he'd seen her naked. Then comprehension dawned; if she hadn't been so tired, she would have realized immediately what conclusion he had drawn from the situation.

"They didn't rape me," she whispered. Her face flushed even hotter. "They—they touched me, they hurt me and did some...other things, but they didn't actually rape me. They were saving that for today. Some important guy in their organization was supposed to arrive, and I suppose they were planning a sort of p-party."

Zane's expression remained calm and grave, and she knew he didn't believe her. Why should he? He'd found her tied up and naked, and she'd already been in the kidnappers' hands for most of a day. Chivalry wasn't part of their code; they had refrained from rape only on orders from their leader, because he wanted to be there to enjoy her himself before the others had their turn on her.

He didn't say anything, and Barrie busied herself with the used antiseptic pads, which were still damp enough to clean the rest of the disgusting muck from her feet. She longed for a bath, but that was so far out of the question that she didn't even voice the wish.

While she busied herself with tidying up, he explored the small room, which didn't take long, because there was nothing in it. He closed the broken shutters over the window; the wooden slats were rotted away at the top, allowing some light through but preventing any passersby from seeing inside.

With the room mostly dark once more, it was like being in a snug, private cave. Barrie smothered a yawn, fighting the fatigue that dragged on her like lead weights. The only sleep she'd had was that brief nap while Zane had been finding a way out of the building, and she was so tired that even her hunger paled in comparison.

He noticed, of course; he didn't miss anything. "Why don't you go to sleep?" he suggested. "In a couple of hours, when more people are moving around and I won't be as noticeable, I'll go scrounge up something for us to eat and liberate some clothes for you."

Barrie eyed the paint streaking his face. "With makeup like that, I don't believe you're going to go unnoticed no matter how crowded the streets are."

That faint smile touched his lips again, then was gone. "I'll take it off first."

The smile almost kept her awake. Almost. She felt her muscles slowly loosening, as if his permission to sleep was all her body needed to hear. Her eyelids were too heavy for her to hold open anymore; it was like a veil of darkness descending. With her last fraction of consciousness, she was aware of his arms around her, gently lowering her to the floor.

Chapter 4

She had gone to sleep like a baby, Zane thought, watching her. He'd seen it often enough in his ten nephews, the way little children had of dropping off so abruptly, their bodies looking almost boneless as they toppled over into waiting arms. His gaze drifted over her face. Now that dawn was here, even with the shutters closed, he could plainly see the exhaustion etched on her face; the wonder was that she had held up so well, rather than that she'd gone to sleep now.

He could use some rest himself. He stretched out beside her, keeping a slight distance between them; not touching, but close enough that he could reach her immediately if their hiding place was discovered. He was still wired, too full of adrenaline to sleep yet, but it felt good to relax and let himself wind down while he waited for the city to come completely awake.

Now he could also see the fire in her hair, the dark auburn shade that, when she stood in the sun, would glint with gold and bronze. Her eyes were a deep, soft green, her brows and lashes like brown mink. He wouldn't have been surprised by freckles, but her skin was clear and creamy, except for the bruise that mottled one cheek. There were bruises on her arms, and though he couldn't see them, he knew the shirt covered other marks left by brutal men. She'd insisted they hadn't raped her, but probably she was ashamed for anyone else to know, as if she'd had any choice in the matter. Maybe she wanted to keep it quiet for her father's sake. Zane didn't care about her reasons; he just hoped she would get the proper medical care.

He thought dispassionately about slipping to the building where they'd held her and killing any and all of the bastards who were still there. God knew they deserved it, and he wouldn't lose a minute's worth of sleep over any of them. But his mission was to rescue Miss Lovejoy—Barrie—and he hadn't accomplished that yet. If he went back, there was the chance that he would be killed, and that would endanger her, as well as his men. He'd long ago learned how to divorce his emotions from the action so he could think clearly, and he wasn't about to compromise a mission now... But *damn,* he wanted to kill them.

He liked the way she looked. She wasn't drop-dead gorgeous or anything like that, but her features were regular, and asleep, with her woes put aside for the moment, her expression was sweetly serene. She was a pretty little thing, as finely made as an expensive porcelain figurine. Oh, he supposed she was probably of middle height for a woman, about five feet five, but he was six-three and outweighed her by at least a hundred pounds, so to him she was little. Not as little as his mother and sister, but they were truly slight, as delicate as fairies. Barrie Lovejoy, for all her aristocratic bloodlines, had the sturdiness of a pioneer. Most women, with good reason, would have broken down long before now.

He was surprised to feel himself getting a little drowsy. Despite their situation, there was something calming about lying here beside her, watching her sleep. Though he was solitary by nature and had always preferred sleeping alone after his sexual appetite had been satisfied, it felt elementally right, somehow, to guard her with his body as they slept. Had cavemen done this, putting themselves between the mouth of the cave and the sleeping forms of their women and children, drowsily watching the gentle movements of their breathing as the fires died down and night claimed the land? If it was an ancient instinct, Zane mused, he sure as hell hadn't felt it before now.

But he wanted to touch her, to feel the softness of her flesh beneath his hand. He wanted to fold her within the warm protection of his body, tuck her in close, curl around her and keep her there with an arm draped around her waist. Only the knowledge that the last thing in the world she would want now was a man's touch kept him from doing just that.

He wanted to hold her. He ached to hold her.

She was dwarfed by his shirt, but he'd seen the body hidden by the folds of cloth. His night vision was very good; he'd been able to discern her high, round breasts, not very big, but definitely mouth-watering, and tipped with small, tight nipples. She was curvy, womanly, with a small waist and rounded hips and a neat little triangle of pubic hair. He'd seen her buttocks. Just thinking about it made him feel hollowed out with desire; her butt was fine indeed. He would like to feel it snuggled up against his thighs.

He wasn't going to be able to sleep, after all. He was fully aroused, desire pulsing through his swollen and rigid flesh. Wincing, he turned onto his back and adjusted himself to a more comfortable position, but the comfort was relative. The only way he would truly find ease was within the soft, hot clasp of her body, and that wasn't likely to happen.

The small room grew brighter and warmer as dawn developed into full morning. The stone walls would protect them from most of the day's heat, but soon they would need water. Water, food, and clothes for her. A robe would be better than Western-style clothing, because the traditional Muslim attire would cover her hair, and there were enough traditionalists in Benghazi that a robe wouldn't draw a second glance.

The streets were noisy now, the waterfront humming with activity. Zane figured it was time for him to do some foraging. He wiped the camouflage paint from his skin as best he could and disguised what was left by smearing dirt on his face. He wasn't about to go unarmed, so he pulled the tail of his T-shirt free from his pants and tucked the pistol into the waistband at the small of his back, then let the shirt fall over it. Anyone who paid attention would know the bulge for what it was, but what the hell, it wasn't unusual for people to go armed in this part of the world. Thanks to his one-quarter Comanche heritage, his skin had a rich bronze hue, and in addition he was darkly tanned from countless hours of training in the sun and sea and wind. There was nothing about his appearance that would attract undue notice, not even his eyes, because there were plenty of Libyans with a European parent.

He checked Barrie, reassuring himself that she was still sleeping soundly. He'd told her that he would be slipping out for a while, so she shouldn't be alarmed if she woke while he was gone. He left their crumbling sanctuary as silently as he had entered it.

It was over two hours before he returned, almost time for the designated check-in time with his men. He had a definite talent for scavenging, he thought, though outright thievery would probably be a better term. He carried a woman's black robe and head covering, and wrapped up in it was a selection of fruit, cheese and bread, as well as a pair of slippers he hoped would fit Barrie. The water had been the hardest to come by, because he'd lacked a container. He'd solved that by stealing a stoppered gallon jug of wine, forbidden by the Koran but readily available anyway. He had poured out the cheap, sour wine and filled the jug with water. The water would have a definite wine taste to it, but it would be wet, and that was all they required.

While he had the opportunity, he disguised the entrance to their lair a bit, piling some stones in front of it, arranging a rotted timber so that it looked as if it blocked the door. The door was still visible, but looked much less accessible. He tested his handiwork to make certain they could still get out easily enough, then slipped inside and once again braced the door in its sagging frame.

He turned to check on Barrie. She was still asleep. The room was considerably warmer, and she had kicked the blanket aside. His shirt was up around her waist.

The kick of desire was like taking a blow to the chest. He almost staggered from it, his heart racing, his breath strangling in his throat. Sweat beaded on his forehead, ran down his temple. *God.*

He should turn away. He should put the blanket over her. He should put sex completely out of his mind. There were any number of things he should do, but instead he stared at her with a hunger so intense he ached with it, quivered with it. Greedily his gaze moved over every female inch of her. His sex was throbbing like a toothache. He wanted her more intensely than he'd ever wanted a woman before. His famous cool remoteness had failed him—there wasn't a cool inch on him, and his desire was so damn strong and immediate, he was shaking from the effort of resisting it.

Moving slowly, stiffly, he set his purloined goodies on the floor. His breath hissed between his clenched teeth. He hadn't known sexual frustration could be this painful. He'd never had any trouble getting a woman whenever he'd wanted one. This woman was off-limits, though, from even an attempt at seduction. She'd been through enough without having to fend off her rescuer, too.

As warm as the room was now, if he spread the blanket over her she would only kick it off again. Gingerly he went down on one knee beside her and with shaking hands pulled the shirt tail down to cover her. With slight disbelief he eyed the fine tremor of his fingers. He never trembled. He was rock steady during the most tense and dangerous situations, icily controlled in combat. He had parachuted out of a burning plane, swum with sharks and sewn up his own flesh. He had ridden unbroken horses and even bulls a time or two. He had killed. He had done all of that with perfect control, but this sleeping, red-haired woman made him shake.

Grimly he forced himself to turn aside and pick up the radio headset. Holding the earpiece in place, he clicked once and immediately heard two clicks in response. Everything was okay.

Maybe some water would cool him down. At least thinking about it was better than thinking about Barrie. He dropped a couple of purification tablets into the jug, in case the small amount of wine that had remained in it wasn't enough to kill all the invisible little critters. The tablets didn't improve the taste any—just the opposite—but they were better than a case of the runs.

He drank just enough to relieve his thirst, then settled down with his back to a wall. There was nothing to do but wait and contemplate the walls, because he sure as hell didn't trust himself to look at Barrie.

Voices woke her. They were loud, and close by. Barrie bolted upright, her eyes huge with alarm. Hard arms grabbed her, and an even harder hand clamped itself over her mouth, stifling any sound she might have made. Confused, disoriented, in sheer terror she began to fight as much as she could. Teeth. She should use her teeth. But his fingers were biting hard into her jaw, and she couldn't open her mouth. Desperately she tried to shake her head, and he merely gathered her in tighter, tucking her against him in a way that was oddly protective.

"Shh" came that toneless whisper, and the familiarity of it cut through the panic and fog of sleep. Zane.

Instantly she relaxed, weak with relief. Feeling the tension leave her muscles, he tilted her face, still keeping his hand over her mouth. Their eyes met in the shadowed light, and he gave a brief nod as he saw that she was awake now, and aware. He released her jaw, his hard fingers trailing briefly over her skin in apology for the tightness of his grip. The barely there caress went through her like lightning. She shivered as it seared a path along nerve endings throughout her body and instinctively turned her face into the warm hollow created by the curve of his shoulder.

The arm around her had loosened immediately when she shivered, but at her action she felt him hesitate a fraction of a second, then gather her snugly against him once more.

The voices were closer, and added to them were some thuds and the sound of crumbling rock. She listened to the rapid, rolling syllables of Arabic, straining to concentrate on the voices. Were they the same voices she had heard through yesterday's long nightmare? It was difficult to tell. She didn't understand the language; hers had been a finishing-school education, suited to an ambassador's daughter. She spoke French and Italian fluently, Spanish a little less so. After her father's posting in Athens she had made it a point to study Greek, too, and had learned enough that she could carry on a simple conversation, though she understood more than she spoke.

Fiercely she wished she had insisted on lessons in Arabic, too. She had hated every moment she'd spent in the kidnappers' hands, but not speaking the language had made her feel even more helpless, more isolated.

She would rather die than let them get their hands on her again.

She must have tensed, because Zane gave her a light squeeze of reassurance. Swiftly she glanced at his face. He wasn't looking at her; instead he was concentrating on the fragile, half-rotted door that protected the entrance to their sanctuary, and on the voices beyond. His expression was utterly calm and distant. Abruptly she realized that he *did* understand Arabic, and whatever was being said by the people picking through the ruins of the building, he wasn't alarmed by it. He was alert, because their hiding place could be compromised at any moment, but evidently he felt confident of being able to handle that problem.

With reason, no doubt. From what she'd seen, she thought he was capable of handling just about any situation. She would trust him with her life—and had.

The voices went on for a long time, sometimes coming so close to their hiding place that Zane palmed that big pistol and held it aimed unwaveringly at the door. Barrie stared at that hand, so lean and powerful and capable. There wasn't the slightest tremor visible; it was almost unreal, almost inhuman, for any man to be that calm and have such perfect control over his body.

They sat silently in the warm, shadowy little room, their

breathing for the most part their only movements. Barrie noticed that the blanket no longer covered her legs, but the shirt, thank God, kept her reasonably decent. It was too hot to lie under the blanket, anyway.

Time crept by at a sloth's pace. The warmth and silence were hypnotic, lulling her into a half dream state of both awareness and distance. She was ferociously hungry, but unaffected by it, as if she was merely aware of someone else's hunger. After a while her muscles began to ache from being in one position for so long, but that didn't matter, either. Thirst, though, was different. In the increasing heat, her need for water began to gnaw at her. The kidnappers had given her some water a couple of times, but she'd had nothing to drink in hours—since she had learned they expected her to relieve herself in their presence, in fact. She had chosen to do without water rather than provide them with such amusement again.

Sweat streaked down Zane's face and dampened his shirt. She was perfectly content to remain where she was, nestled against his side. The arm around her made her feel safer than if their hiding place had been constructed of steel, rather than crumbling stone and plaster, and rotting wood.

She had never been exposed to a man like him before. Her only contact with the military had been with the senior officers who attended functions at the embassy, colonels and generals, admirals, the upper brass; there were also the Marine guards at the embassy, with their perfect uniforms and perfect manners. Though she supposed the Marine guards had to be exemplary soldiers or they wouldn't have been chosen as embassy guards, still, they were nothing like the man who held her so protectively. They were soldiers; he was a warrior. He was as different from them as the lethal, ten-inch black blade strapped to his thigh was from a pocketknife. He was a finely honed weapon.

For all that, he wasn't immortal, and they weren't safe. Their hiding place could be discovered. He could be killed; she could be recaptured. The hard reality of that was something she couldn't ignore as she could hunger and cramped muscles.

After a long, long time, the voices went away. Zane released her and walked noiselessly to the door to look out. She had never before seen anyone move with such silent grace, like a big jungle cat on velvet paws instead of a battle-hardened warrior in boots.

She didn't move until he turned around, the faint relaxation of his expression telling her the danger was past. "What were they doing?" she asked, taking care to keep her voice low.

"Scavenging building materials, picking up blocks, any pieces of wood that hadn't rotted. If they'd had a sledgehammer, they probably would have dismantled these walls. They carted the stuff off in a wheelbarrow. If they need more, they'll probably be back."

"What will we do?"

"The same thing we did this time—hunker down and keep quiet."

"But if they come in here—"

"I'll handle it." He cut her worry short before she could completely voice it, but he did it with a tone of reassurance. "I brought some food and water. Interested?"

Barrie scrambled to her knees, eagerness in every line of her body. "Water! I'm so thirsty!" Then she halted, her recent experience fresh in her mind. "But if I drink anything, where will I go to…you know."

He regarded her with faint bemusement, and she blushed a little as she realized that wasn't a problem he normally encountered. When he and his men were on a mission, they would relieve themselves wherever and whenever they needed.

"I'll find a place for you to go," he finally said. "Don't let that stop you from drinking the water you need. I also found some clothes for you, but as hot as it's getting in here, you'll probably want to wait until night before you put them on."

He indicated the black bundle beside his gear, and she realized it was a robe. She thought of the modesty it would provide, and gratitude flooded her; at least she wouldn't have to face his men wearing nothing more than his shirt. But he was right; in the heat of day, and in the privacy of this small room, she would prefer wearing his shirt. They both knew she was bare beneath it; he'd already seen her stark naked, and demonstrated his decency by giving her the shirt and ignoring her nakedness, so there was no point now in swathing herself in an ankle-length robe.

He produced a big jug and unstoppered it. "It'll taste funny," he warned as he passed the jug to her. "Purification tablets."

It did taste funny—warm, with a chemical flavor. But it was wonderful. She drank a few swallows, not wanting to make her stomach cramp after being empty for so long. While she was drinking, he unwrapped the bits of food he'd procured—a loaf of hard bread, a hunk of cheese and several oranges, plums and dates. It looked like a feast.

He straightened the blanket for her to sit on, then took out his knife and cut small portions of both the loaf and cheese and gave them to her. She started to protest that she was hungry enough to eat much more than that, but realized that what he had would have to last them all day, and perhaps longer than that. She wasn't about to complain about the amount of food she *did* have.

She had never been particularly fond of cheese, and she suspected that if she hadn't been so hungry she wouldn't have been fond of this cheese, either, but at the moment it was delicious. She nibbled at both bread and cheese, finding satisfaction in the simple act of chewing. As it happened, she had overestimated her appetite. The small portion he had given her was more than enough.

He ate more heartily, and polished off one of the oranges. He insisted that she eat a couple of the juicy slices and drink a bit more water. Feeling replete, Barrie yawned and refused the offer of another orange slice.

"No, thanks, I'm full."

"Would you like to freshen up now?"

Her head whipped around, sending her red hair flying. Amusement twinkled in his pale eyes at her eager, pleading expression. "There's enough water?"

"Enough to dampen a bandana."

She didn't have a bandana, of course, but he did. Carefully he poured just enough water from the jug to wet the square cloth, then politely turned his back and busied himself with his gear.

Slowly Barrie smoothed the wet cloth over her face, sighing in pleasure at the freshness of the sensation. She hadn't realized how grimy she felt until now, when she was able to rectify the situation. She found a sore place on her cheek, where one of the men had hit her, and other tender bruises on her arms. Glancing at Zane's broad back, she quickly unbuttoned the shirt just enough that she could slide the handkerchief inside and rub it over her torso and under her arms. After she fastened the garment, her dusty legs got the same attention. The dampness was wonderfully cooling, almost voluptuous in the sensual delight it gave her.

"I'm finished," she said, and returned the dark bandana

to him when he turned around. "It felt wonderful. Thank you."

Then her heart leaped in her chest, because he evidently felt the same need to cool off as she had, but unlike her, he didn't keep his shirt on. He peeled the snug black T-shirt off over his head and dropped it on the blanket, then sat on his heels while he moistened the bandana and began scrubbing it over his face.

Oh, my. Helplessly she stared at the rippling muscles of his chest and stomach, the way they flexed and relaxed with the flow of his movements. The dim light caught the deep bronze of his skin, gleamed on the smooth, powerful curve of his shoulder. Her fascinated gaze wandered over the slant of his shoulder blades, the diamond of black hair that stretched from nipple to nipple on his chest. He twisted around to reach for something, and she found his back equally fascinating, with the deep furrow of his spine bisecting two muscular planes.

There was an inch-long scar on his left cheekbone. She hadn't noticed it before because his face had been so dirty, but now she could plainly see the silvery line of it. It wasn't a disfiguring scar at all, just a straight little slash, as precise as a surgeon's cut. The scar along his rib cage was different, easily eight or nine inches in length, jagged, the scar tissue thick and ridged. Then there were the two round, puckered scars, one just above his waist, the other just below his right shoulder blade. Bullet wounds. She'd never seen one before, but she recognized them for what they were. There was another slash running along his right bicep, and God only knew how many other scars there were on the rest of his body. The warrior hadn't led a charmed life; his body bore the signs of battle.

He squatted half-naked, unconcernedly rubbing the damp handkerchief across his sweaty chest, lifting his arms to wash under them, exposing the smooth undersides and intriguing patches of hair. He was so fundamentally, elementally male, and so purely a warrior, that her breath strangled in her lungs as she watched him.

The rush of warmth through her body told her that she was more female than she'd ever imagined.

A little dazed, she sat back, resting against the wall. Absently she made certain the shirt tail preserved her modesty, but thoughts were tumbling through her mind, dizzyingly fast yet very clear.

They weren't out of danger yet.

During the past twenty-four horrific hours, she hadn't spent a lot of time wondering about the motive behind her kidnapping. She'd had too much to deal with as it was, the sheer terror, the confusion, the pain of the blows they'd given her.

She'd been blindfolded much of the time, and disoriented. She'd been humiliated, stripped naked and roughly fondled, taunted with the prospect of rape, and yet they had stopped short of rape—for a reason. Sheer psychological torture had undoubtedly played a role, but most of all they'd had orders to save her for the man who was to arrive today.

Who was he? He was the one behind her kidnapping; he had to be. But why?

Ransom? When she thought about it now, coolly and clearly, she didn't think so. Yes, her father was rich. Many a diplomat came from a moneyed background; it wasn't unusual. But if money had been the motive, there were others who were richer, though perhaps she had been chosen specifically because it was well known that her father would beggar himself to keep her safe. Perhaps.

But why would they have taken her out of the country? Wouldn't they have wanted to keep her close by, to make the exchange for money easier? No, the very fact that they'd taken her out of the country meant they'd kidnapped her for another reason. Maybe they would have asked for money anyway; since they already had her, why not? But money wasn't the primary object. So what was?

She didn't know, and since she didn't know who the leader was, she had no way of guessing what he truly wanted.

Not herself. She dismissed that notion out of hand. She wasn't the object of obsession, because no man so obsessed with a woman that he was driven to such lengths would let his men maul her. Nor was she the type to inspire obsession, she thought wryly. Certainly none of the men she'd dated had shown any signs of obsessive behavior.

So…there was something else, some piece of puzzle she was missing. Was it someone she knew? Something she'd read or seen?

Nothing came to mind. She wasn't involved in intrigue, though of course she knew which employees at the embassy were employed by the CIA. That was standard, nothing unusual. Her father often spoke privately with Art Sandefer and, lately, Mack Prewett, too. She'd often thought that Art was more bureaucrat than spy, though the intelligence in his tired gaze said he'd done his time in the field, too. She didn't know about Mack Prewett. There was something restless and hard about him, something that made her uneasy.

Her father said Mack was a good man. She wasn't certain about that, but neither did he seem like a villain. Still, there had been that time a couple of weeks ago when she hadn't known anyone was with her father and had breezily walked in without knocking. Her father had been handing a thick manila envelope to Mack; both of them had looked startled and uncomfortable, but her father wasn't a diplomat for

nothing. He'd efficiently smoothed over the slight awk-
wardness, and Mack had left the office almost immediately,
taking the envelope with him. Barrie hadn't asked any
questions about it, because if it was CIA business, then it
wasn't her business.

Now she wondered what had been in that envelope.

That small incident was the only thing the slightest bit
untoward that she could remember. Art Sandefer had once
said that there was no such thing as coincidence, but could
that moment be linked to her kidnapping? Could it be the
cause of it? That was a reach.

She didn't know what was in the envelope, hadn't shown
any interest in it. But she had seen her father giving it to
Mack Prewett. That meant...what?

She felt as if she was feeling her way through a mental
maze, taking wrong turns, stumbling into dead ends, then
groping her way back to logic. Her father would never, in
any way, do anything that would harm her. Therefore, that
envelope had no significance—unless he was involved in
something dangerous and wanted out. Her kidnapping made
sense only if someone was using her as a weapon to make
her father do something he didn't want to do.

She couldn't accept the idea of her father doing anything
traitorous—at least, not voluntarily. She wasn't blind to his
weaknesses. He was a bit of a snob, he didn't at all like
even the idea that someday she might fall in love and get
married, he was protective to the point of smothering her.
But he was an honorable man, and a truly patriotic man. It
could be that the kidnappers were trying to force her father
to do something, give them some information, perhaps, and
he had resisted; she could be the means they were using to
force him to do what they wanted.

That felt logical. The envelope probably had nothing at

all to do with her kidnapping, and Art Sandefer was wrong about coincidence.

But what if he wasn't?

Then, despite her instincts about him, her father was involved in something he shouldn't be. The thought made her sick to her stomach, but she had to face the possibility, had to think of every angle. She had to face it, then put it aside, because there was nothing she could do about it now.

If the kidnappers had been going to use her as a weapon against her father, then they wouldn't give up. If it had just been ransom, they would have thrown up their hands at her supposed escape and said the Arabic equivalent of, "Ah, to hell with it."

The leader hadn't been here. She didn't even know where "here" was; she'd had too much on her mind to ask questions about her geographic location.

"Where are we?" she murmured, thinking she really should know.

Zane lifted his eyebrows. He was sitting down, lounging against the wall at a right angle to her, having finished cleaning up, and she wondered how long she'd been lost in thought. "The waterfront district," he said. "It's a rough section of town."

"I meant, what town?" she clarified.

Realization dawned in his crystal clear eyes. "Benghazi," he said softly. "Libya."

Libya. Stunned, she absorbed the news, then went back to the mental path she'd been following.

The leader had been flying in today. From where? Athens? If he'd been in contact with his men, he would know she'd somehow escaped. But if he had access to the embassy, and to her father, then he would also know that she hadn't been returned to the embassy. Therefore, she would logically still be in Libya. Also logically, they would be actively searching for her.

She looked at Zane again. His eyes were half-closed, he looked almost asleep. Because of the heat, he hadn't put his T-shirt back on. But despite the drowsy look on his face, she sensed that he was vitally aware of everything going on around them, that he was merely letting his body rest while his mind remained on guard.

After the humiliation and pain her guards had dealt her, Zane's concern and consideration had been like a balm, soothing her, helping to heal her bruised emotions before she even had time to know how deep the damage went. Almost before she knew it, she had been responding to him as a woman does to a man, and somehow that was all right.

He was the exact opposite of the thugs who had so delighted in humiliating her. Those thugs were probably searching all over the city for her, and until she was out of this country, the possibility existed that they would recapture her. And if they did, this time there would be no respite.

No. It was intolerable. But if the unthinkable happened, she would be damned if she would give them the satisfaction they'd been anticipating. She would be damned if she would let them take her virginity.

She had never thought of her virginity as anything other than a lack of experience and inclination. At school in Switzerland there had been precious few opportunities for meeting boys, and she hadn't been particularly interested in those she had met. After she left school, her father's protective possessiveness, as well as her duties at the embassy, had restricted any social life she might have developed. The men she met hadn't seemed any more interesting than the few boys she had met while in school. With AIDS added in as a threat, it simply hadn't seemed worth the risk to have sex simply for the experience.

But she had dreamed. She had dreamed of meeting a man, growing to love him, making love with him. Simple, universal dreams.

The kidnappers had almost taken all that from her, almost wrecked her dream of loving a man by abusing her so severely that, if she had remained in their hands much longer, she knew she would have been so severely traumatized that she might never have been able to love a man or tolerate his touch. If Zane hadn't taken her out of there, her first sexual experience would have been one of rape.

No. A thousand times no.

Even if they managed to recapture her, she wouldn't let them murder that dream.

Scrambling to her feet, Barrie took the few steps to where Zane lounged against the wall. She saw his muscled body come to alertness at her action, though he didn't move. She stood over him, staring at him with green eyes burning in the dim light. The look he gave her was hooded, unreadable.

"Make love to me," she said in a raw voice.

Chapter 5

"Barrie..." he began, his tone kind, and she knew he was going to refuse.

"No!" she said fiercely. "Don't tell me I should think about it, or that I really don't want to do it. I know what I went through with those bastards. I know you don't believe it, but they *didn't* rape me. But they looked at me, they touched, and I couldn't stop them." She stopped and drew a deep breath, steadying herself. "I'm not stupid. I know we're still in danger, that you and your men could be wounded or even killed trying to rescue me and that I could end up back in their hands anyway. I've never made love before, with anyone. I don't want my first time to be rape, do you understand? I don't want them to have that satisfaction. *I want the first time to be with you.*"

She had surprised him, she saw, and she had already noticed that Zane Mackenzie wasn't a man whose expression revealed much of what he was thinking. He sat up straight, his pale eyes narrowed as he examined her with a piercing gaze.

He was still going to refuse, and she didn't think she could bear it. "I promise," she blurted desperately. "They didn't do that to me. I can't have any disease, if that's what you're worried about."

"No," he said, his voice suddenly sounding strained. "That isn't what I'm worried about."

"Don't make me beg," she pleaded, wringing her hands together, aware that she was already doing exactly that.

Then the expression in those pale eyes softened, grew warmer. "I won't," he said softly, and rose to his feet with that powerful, feline grace of his. He towered over her, and for a moment Barrie felt the difference in their sizes so sharply that she wondered wildly what she thought she was doing. Then he moved past her to the blanket; he knelt and smoothed it, then dropped down on it, stretching out on his back, and watched her with a world of knowledge in his slightly remote, too-old eyes.

He knew. And until she read that knowledge in his eyes, she hadn't even been aware of what she really needed. But watching him lie down and put himself at her service, something inside her shattered. *He knew.* He understood the emotions roiling deep inside her, understood what had brought her to him with her fierce, startling demand. It wasn't just that she wanted her first time to be of her own volition, with the man of her choice; the kidnappers had taken something from her, and he was giving it back. They had tied her down, stripped her, humiliated her, and she had been helpless to stop them. Zane was giving control back to her, reassuring her and at the same time subtly letting her exact her vengeance against the male of the species.

She didn't want to lie helpless beneath him. She wanted

to control this giving of her body, wanted things to move at her pace instead of his, wanted to be the one who decided how much, how far, how fast.

And he was going to let her do it.

He was giving control of his body to her.

She could barely breathe as she sank to her knees beside him. The warm, bare, richly tanned flesh lured her hands closer, closer, until the urge overcame her nervousness and her fingers lightly skimmed over his stomach, his chest. Her heart hammered wildly. It was like petting a tiger, knowing how dangerous the animal was but fascinated beyond resistance by the rich pelt. She wanted to feel all of that power under her hands. Carefully she flattened her hands along his ribs, molding his flesh beneath her palms, feeling the resilience of skin over the powerful bands of muscle and, beneath that, the strong solidity of bone. She could feel the rhythmic thud of his heartbeat, the expansion of his ribs as he breathed.

Both heartbeat and breathing seemed fast. Swiftly she glanced at his face and blushed at what she saw there, the heat in his heavy-lidded eyes, the deepened color of his lips. She knew what lust looked like; she'd seen the cruel side of it on the faces of her captors, and now she saw the pleasurable side of it in Zane. It startled her, because somehow she hadn't considered lust in the proposition she'd made to him, and her hands fell away from his body.

His lips parted in a curl of amusement that revealed the gleam of white teeth, and she felt her heart almost stop. His smile was even more potent than she'd expected. "Yeah, I'm turned on," he said softly. "I have to be, or this won't work."

He was right, of course, and her blush deepened. That was the trouble with inexperience. Though she knew the mechanics of lovemaking, and once or twice her escort for the evening had kissed her with unexpected ardor and held her close enough for her to tell that he was aroused, still, she'd never had to deal directly with an erection—until now.

This particular one was there for her bidding. Furtively she glanced at the front of his pants, at the ridge pushing against the cloth.

"We don't have to do this," he offered once again, and Barrie flared from hesitance to determination.

"Yes, I do."

He moved his hands to his belt. "Then I'd better—"

Instantly she stopped him, pushing his hands up and away, forcing them down on each side of his head. "I'll do it," she said, more fiercely than she'd intended. This was her show.

"All right," he murmured, and again she knew that he understood. Her show, her control, every step of the way. He relaxed against the blanket, closing his eyes as if he was going to take a nap.

It was easier, knowing he wasn't watching her, which of course had been his intention. Barrie didn't want to fumble, didn't want to underline her inexperience any more than she already had, so before she reached for his belt she studied the release mechanism for a moment to make certain she understood it. She didn't give herself time to lose her nerve. She simply reached out, opened the belt and unfastened his pants. Under the pants were black swim trunks. Puzzled, Barrie stared at them. Swim trunks?

Then she understood. He was a SEAL; the acronym stood for SEa, Air and Land. He was at home in all three elements, capable of swimming for miles. Since Benghazi was a seaport, that was probably how his team had infiltrated, from the sea. Maybe they'd used some sort of boat to reach land, but it was possible they'd been dropped off some distance from the port and had swum the rest of the way.

He had risked his life to save her, was still doing so, and now he was giving her his body. Everything inside her squeezed tight, and she trembled from the rush of emotion. Oh, God. She had learned more about herself in the past twenty-four hours than in the entire past twenty-five years of her life. Perhaps the experience had changed her. Either way, something had happened inside her, something momentous, and she was learning how to deal with it.

She had let her father wrap her in a suffocating blanket of protection for fifteen years; she couldn't blame him for it, because she'd *needed* that blanket. But that time was past. Fate had pitched her headlong into life, ripped her out of her protective cocoon, and like a butterfly, she couldn't draw the silken threads back around her. All she could do was reach out for the unknown.

She slipped her hands under the waistband of the swim trunks and began working them, and his pants, down his hips. He levered his pelvis off the ground to aid her. "Don't take them all the way off," he murmured, still keeping his eyes closed and his hands resting beside his head. "I can handle things if I get caught with my pants down, but if they're completely off, it would slow me down some."

Despite her nervousness, Barrie smiled at that supreme self-confidence, the wry humor. If he wasn't so controlled, he could be described as cocky. He had no doubt whatsoever about his fighting ability.

Her hands stroked down his buttocks as she slipped her hands inside his garments. An unexpected frisson of pleasure rippled through her at the feel of his butt, cool and smooth, hard with muscle. Tush connoisseurs would envy her the moment, and she wished she had the nerve to linger, to fully appreciate this male perfection. Instead she tugged at his clothes, pulling them down to the middle of his thighs. He relaxed, letting his hips settle on the blanket again, and Barrie studied the startling reality of a naked man. She'd read books that described sexual arousal, but seeing it firsthand, and at close range, was far more impressive and wondrous.

Blindly she reached out, her hand drawn as if by a magnet. She touched him, stroking one fingertip down the length of his swollen sex. It pulsed and jerked upward, as if following the caress. He inhaled sharply. His reaction warmed her, and the tightness in her chest, her body, clenched once more, then began to loosen with that rush of warmth. Bolder now, she folded her fingers around him, gently sighing with pleasure as she felt the heat beneath the coolness, iron beneath silk, the urgent throbbing.

And she felt her own desire, rushing like a heated river through her flesh, turning angry determination into lovemaking. *This is how it should be,* she thought with relief; they should come together in pleasure, not in anger. And she didn't want to wait, didn't want to give herself time to reconsider, or she would lose her nerve.

Swiftly she straddled him, mounted him. No longer in anger at other men, no longer in desperation. *Pleasure,* warm and sweet. With her knees clasping his hips, acting on instinct, she held the thick shaft in position and slowly sank down on him, guiding their bodies together.

The first brush of his flesh against hers was hot, startling, and she instinctively jerked herself upright, away from the alien touch. Zane quivered, the barest ripple of reaction, then once more lay motionless between her legs, his eyes still closed, letting her proceed at her own pace.

Her chest was so constricted she could barely breathe; she sucked in air in quick little gasps. That contact, brief as it had been, had touched off an insistent throbbing between her legs, as if her body, after its initial startled rejection, had paused in instinctive recognition of female for male. Her breasts felt tight and feverish beneath the black fabric of his shirt. Alien, yes...but infinitely exciting. Desire wound through her, the river rising.

She told herself that she was prepared for the sudden acute sense of vulnerability, for her body's panic at the threat of penetration, even though desire was urging her on to that very conclusion. More gingerly, she settled onto him again, holding herself steady as she placed him against the entrance to her body and let her weight begin to impale her on the throbbing column of flesh.

The discomfort began immediately and was worse than she'd expected. She halted her movement, gulping as she tried to control her instinctive flinching away from the source of pain. He was breathing deeply, too, she noticed, though that was the only motion he made. She pushed harder, gritting her teeth against the burning sensation of being stretched, and then she couldn't bear any more and jerked herself off him. This time the discomfort between her legs didn't go away but continued to burn.

It wasn't going to get any better, she told herself. She might as well go ahead and do it. Breathing raggedly, once more she lowered herself onto him. Tears burned in her eyes as she struggled to complete the act. Why wouldn't it just go *in?* The pressure between her legs was enormous, intolerable, and a sob caught in her throat as she surged upward.

"Help me," she begged, her voice almost inaudible.

Slowly his eyes opened, and she almost flinched at the pale fire that burned there. He moved just one hand, the right one. Gently he touched her cheek, his callused fingertips rough and infinitely tender; then he trailed them down her throat and lightly over the shirt to her left breast, where they lingered for a heart-stopping moment at her nipple, then finally down to the juncture of her legs.

The caress was as light as a whisper. It lingered between her legs, teasing, brushing, stroking. She went very still, her body poised as she concentrated on this new sensation. Her eyes closed as all her senses focused on his hand and what it was doing, the way he was touching her. It was delicious, but not...quite... enough. He tantalized her with the promise of something more, something that was richer, more powerful, and yet that lightly stroking finger never quite touched her where she wanted. Barrie inhaled deeply, her nipples rising in response. Her entire body hung in suspense. She waited, waited for the gentle touch to brush her with ecstasy, waited.... Her hips moved, her body instinctively seeking, following his finger.

Ah. There. Just for a moment, *there*. A low moan bubbled up in her throat as pleasure shot through her. She waited for him to repeat the caress, but instead his fingers moved maddeningly close, teasing and retreating. Again her hips followed, and again she was rewarded by that lightning flash of pure sensation.

A subtle, sensual dance began. He led, and she followed. The just-right touches came more often, the pleasure became more shattering as the intensity built with each repetition. Between her legs, his male shaft still probed for entrance, and somehow each movement of her hips seemed to ease him a bit closer to that goal. Her body rocked, swaying in the ancient rhythm of desire, surging and retreating like the tides. She could feel him stretching her, feel the discomfort sharpened by her movements...and yet the desire lured her onward like a Lorelei, and somehow she began to need him inside her, need him to the point that the pain no longer mattered. She braced her hands on his chest, and her movements changed, lifting and falling rather than swaying side to side. His touch changed, too, suddenly pressing directly on the place where she most wanted it.

She bit her lip to keep from crying out. His thumb rubbed insistently, releasing a torrent, turning the warm river into something wild and totally beyond her control. She was so hot that she was burning up with desire, aching with emptiness. The pain no longer mattered; she had to have what his body promised, what hers needed. With a low moan she pressed downward, forcing her soft flesh to admit the intruder. She felt the resistance, the inner giving; then suddenly his hot, swollen sex pushed up inside her.

It hurt. It hurt a lot. She froze in place, and her eyes flew open, huge with distress. Their gazes locked, hers dark with pain, his burning with ruthlessly restrained desire. Suddenly she became aware of how taut the muscled body beneath her was, how much his control was costing him. But he had promised to let her set the pace, and he had kept that promise, moving only when she had asked for help.

Part of her wanted to stop, but a deeper, more powerful instinct kept her astride him. She could feel him throbbing inside her, feel the answering tightening of her body, as if the flesh knew more than the mind, and perhaps it did. He tensed even more. His skin gleamed with sweat, his heartbeat hammered beneath her palm. She felt a jolt of excitement at having this supremely male, incredibly dangerous warrior as hers to command, just for this time suspended from reality. They had met only hours ago; they had only hours left before they would likely never see each other again. But for now he was hers, embedded inside her, and she wasn't going to forgo a moment of the experience.

"What do I do now?" she whispered.

"Just keep moving," he whispered in return, and she did.

Rising. Falling. Lifting herself almost off him, then sinking down. Over and over, until she forgot about the pain and lost herself in the primeval joy. His hand remained between her legs, continuing the caress that urged her onward, even though she no longer needed to be urged. She moved on him, faster and faster, taking him deeper and deeper. His powerful body flexed between her thighs, arching, and a growl rumbled in his throat. Immediately he forced himself to lie flat again, chained by his promise.

Up. Down. Again. And again, the crescendo building inside her, the heat rising to an unbearable fever, the tension coiling tighter and tighter, until she felt as if she would shatter if she moved another muscle. She froze in place over him, whimpering, unable to push herself over the final hurdle.

The growl rumbled in his throat again. No, deeper than a growl; it was the sound of a human volcano exploding from the forces pent up inside. His control broke, and he moved, fiercely clamping both hands on her hips and pulling her down hard even as he arched once more and thrust himself in her to the hilt. He hadn't gone so deep before; she hadn't taken that much of him. The sensation was electric. She stifled a scream as he convulsed beneath her, heaving upward between her thighs, lifting her so that her knees left the ground. His head was thrown back, his neck corded with the force of his release, his teeth bared. Barrie felt the hot spurting of his release, felt him so deep inside her that he was touching the very center of her being, and it was enough to push her over the edge.

Pure lightning speared through her. She heard herself cry out, a thin cry of ecstasy that nothing could stifle. All her inner muscles contracted around him, relaxed, squeezed again, over and over, as if her body was drinking from his.

Finally the storm subsided, leaving her weak and shaking. Her bones had turned to jelly, and she could no longer sit upright. Helplessly she collapsed forward, folding on him like a house of cards caught in an earthquake. He caught her, easing her down so that she lay on his chest, and he wrapped his arms around her as she lay there gasping and sobbing. She hadn't meant to cry, didn't understand why the tears kept streaming down her face. "Zane," she whispered, and couldn't say anything more.

His big, hard hands stroked soothingly up and down her back. "Are you okay?" he murmured, and there was something infinitely male and intimate in his deep voice, an undertone of satisfaction and possessiveness.

Barrie gulped back the tears, forcing herself to coherency. "Yes," she said in a thin, waterlogged tone. "I didn't know it would hurt so much. Or feel so good," she added, because she was crying for both reasons. Odd, that she should have been as unprepared for the pleasure as she had been for the pain. She felt overwhelmed, unbalanced. Had she truly been so foolish as to think she could perform such an intimate act and remain untouched emotionally? If she had been capable of that kind of mental distance she wouldn't have remained a virgin until now. She would have found a way around her father's obsessive protectiveness if she had wanted to, if any man had ever elicited one-tenth the response in her this warrior had aroused within two minutes of their meeting. If her rescuer had been any other man, she wouldn't have asked such an intimate favor of him.

Their lovemaking had forged a link between them, a bond of the flesh that was far stronger and went far deeper than she'd imagined. Despite her chastity, had she believed the modern, permissive notion that making love could have no more lasting meaning than simple fun, like riding a roller coaster? Maybe, for some people, *sex* could be as trivial as a carnival ride, but she would never again think of lovemaking as anything that shallow. True lovemaking was deep and elemental, and she knew she would never be the same. She hadn't been from the moment he had given her his shirt and she had fallen in love with him. Without even seeing his face, she had fallen in love with the essence of the man, his strength and decency. It wouldn't have mattered if, when morning came, his features had been ugly or twisted with scars. In the darkness of that barren room, and the darkness of her heart, she had already seen beneath whatever lay on the surface, and she had loved him. It was that simple, and that difficult.

Just because she felt that way didn't mean he did. Barrie knew what a psychologist would say. It was the white-knight syndrome, the projection of larger-than-life characteristics onto a person because of the circumstances. Patients fell in love with their doctors and nurses all the time. Zane had simply been doing his job in rescuing her, while to her it had meant her life, because she hadn't for a moment supposed that her captors would let her live. She owed him her life, would have been grateful to him for the rest of that life—but she didn't think she would have loved just any man who had crawled through that window. She loved Zane.

She lay silently on him, her head nestled against his throat, their bodies still linked. She could feel the strong rhythm of his heartbeat thudding against her breasts, could feel his chest expand with each breath. His hot, musky scent excited her more than the most expensive cologne. She felt more at home here, lying with him on a blanket in the midst of a shattered building, than she ever had in the most luxurious and protected environment.

She knew none of the details of his life. She didn't know how old he was, where he was from, what he liked to eat or read or what programs he watched on television. She didn't know if he'd ever been married.

Married. My God, she hadn't even asked. She felt suddenly sick to her stomach. If he was married, then he wouldn't be the man she had thought he was, and she had just made the biggest mistake of her life.

But neither would the fault be entirely his. She had begged him, and he had given her more than one chance to change her mind. She didn't think she could bear it if he'd made love to her out of pity.

She drew a deep breath, knowing she had to ask. Ignorance might be bliss, but she couldn't allow herself that comfort. If she had done something so monumentally wrong, she wanted to know.

"Are you married?" she blurted.

He didn't even tense but lay utterly relaxed beneath her. One hand slid up her back and curled itself around her neck. "No," he said in that low voice of his. "You can take your claws out of me now." The words were lazily amused.

She realized she was digging her fingernails into his chest and hastily relaxed her fingers. Distressed, she said, "I'm sorry, I didn't mean to hurt you."

"There's pain, and there's pain," he said comfortably. "Bullets and knives hurt like hell. In comparison, a little she-cat's scratching doesn't do much damage."

"She-cat?" Barrie didn't know if she should be affronted or amused. After a brief struggle, amusement won. None of her friends or associates would ever have described her in such terms. She'd heard herself described as ladylike, calm, circumspect, conscientious, but certainly never as a she-cat.

"Mmm." The sound was almost like a purr in his throat. His hard fingers lazily massaged her neck, while his other hand slipped down her back to burrow under the shirt and curl possessively over her bottom. His palm burned her flesh like a brand. "Dainty. And you like being stroked."

She couldn't deny that, not when he was the one doing the stroking. The feel of his hand on her bottom was startlingly erotic. She couldn't help wiggling a little, and then gasped as she felt the surge of his flesh inside her. His breath caught, too, and his fingers dug into the cleft of her buttocks.

"I need to ask you a couple of questions," he said, and his voice sounded strained.

Barrie closed her eyes, once again feeling the warm loosening deep inside that signaled the return of desire. That had been a remarkable sensation, when his sex had expanded inside her, both lengthening and getting thicker. Oh, dear. She wanted to do it again, but she didn't think she had the strength. "What?" she murmured, distracted by what was happening between her legs.

"Did you get rid of the ghosts?"

Ghosts. He meant her lingering horror at the way those men had touched her. She thought about it and realized, with some surprise, that she had. She was still angry at the way she'd been treated, and she would dearly love to have Zane's pistol in her hands and those men in her sights, even though she'd never held a pistol before in her life. But the wounded, feminine part of her had triumphed by finding pleasure in making love with Zane, and in doing so she had healed herself. Pleasure… somehow the word fell far short of what she had experienced. Even ecstasy didn't quite describe the intensity, the sensation of imploding, melting, becoming utterly lost in her physical self.

"Yes," she whispered. "The ghosts are gone."

"Okay." His voice still sounded strained. "Second question. Will that damn shirt have to be surgically removed?"

She was startled into sitting upright. The action drove him deeper inside her and wrenched a sharp gasp from her, a groan from him. Panting, she stared at him. They had just made love—were, in fact, *still* making love—but the shirt she wore was what had kept her from going to pieces when he'd first found her, had given her the nerve to run barefoot down dark alleys, had become the symbol of a lot more than just modesty. Maybe she wasn't as recovered as she'd thought. The kidnappers had stripped her, forced her to be naked in front of them, and when Zane had first entered the room and seen her that way, she had been mortified. She didn't know if she could be naked with him now, if she could let him see the body that had been pinched and bruised by other men.

His crystal clear gaze was calm, patient. Again he understood. He knew what he was asking of her. He could have left things as they were, but he wanted more. He wanted her trust, her openness, with no dark secrets between them.

He wanted them to become lovers.

The realization was sharp, almost painful. They had loved each other physically, but with restraint like a wall between them. He had done what she had asked of him, had held himself back until the last moment, when his climax had shattered his control. Now he was asking something of her, asking her to give as he had given.

Almost desperately she clutched the front of the shirt. "I—they left marks on me."

"I've seen bruises before." He reached up and gently touched her cheek. "You have one right here, as a matter of fact."

Instinctively she reached up to the cheek he'd touched, feeling the tenderness. As soon as she released the front of the shirt, he moved his hands to the buttons and slowly began unfastening them, giving her time to protest. She bit her lip, fighting the urge to grab the widening edges of the cloth and hold them together.

When the garment was open all the way down, he slid his hands inside and cupped her breasts, his palms hot as they covered the cool mounds. Her nipples tingled as they hardened, reaching out for the contact. "The bruises shame *them*," he murmured. "Not you."

She closed her eyes as she sat astride him, feeling him hard and hot inside her, his hands just as hard and hot on her breasts. She didn't protest when his hands left her breasts, left them feeling oddly tight and aching, while he pushed the black shirt off her shoulders. The fabric puddled around her arms, and he lifted each in turn, slipping them free.

She was naked. The warm air brushed against her bare skin with the lightest of touches, and then she felt his fingertips doing the same, trailing so gently over each of the dark marks on her shoulders, her arms and breasts, her stomach, that she barely felt him. "Lean down," he said.

Slowly she obeyed, guided by his hands, down, down— and he lifted his head, meeting her mouth with his.

Their first kiss...and they'd already made love. Barrie was shocked at how she could have been so foolish as to forgo the pleasure of his kisses. His lips were firm, warm, hungry. She sank against him with a little sound of mingled surprise and delight humming in her throat. Her breasts flattened against him, the crisp hair on his chest rasping her ultrasensitive nipples, another joy she had unknowingly skipped.

Oh, this was delicious. His tongue probed for entrance, and she immediately gave it.

Several minutes later he let his head drop to the blanket.

He was panting slightly, his eyes heavy-lidded. "I have another question."

"What?" She didn't want to give up the delights of his mouth. She'd never enjoyed kissing so much before, but he was diabolically good at it. She followed him down, nipping at his lower lip, depositing hot little kisses.

He chuckled beneath her mouth. The deep, rusty sound charmed her. She sensed that his laughter was even rarer than his smiles, therefore doubly precious.

"Will you let me be on top this time?"

The question surprised her into laughter. She stifled it as best she could, burying her head against his neck, but her body shook with giggles. He slipped out of her, making her laugh even harder. She was still laughing when he wrapped one strong arm around her and rolled, lifting her so they didn't roll off the blanket, efficiently tucking her beneath him and settling between her legs. Her laughter caught on a gasp as he surged heavily into her.

Her senses swam as she was bombarded by new feelings, when she had already experienced so much. She'd known he was a big man, but lying beneath him sharply brought home the difference in their sizes. Though he propped his weight on his forearms to keep from crushing her, she still felt the heaviness of that iron-muscled body. His shoulders were so broad that he dwarfed her, wrapped around her, shielded her. When she had been on top, she had controlled the depth of his penetration. The control was his now, her thighs spread wide by his hips. He felt bigger, harder than he had before.

He waited a moment to see how she would accept the vulnerability of her position. But she didn't feel vulnerable, she realized. She felt utterly secure, buffered by his strength. Tremulously she smiled at him and lifted her arms to wind them around his neck.

He smiled in return. And then Zane Mackenzie made love to her.

Chapter 6

There seemed to be scarcely a moment for the rest of the day when they weren't making love, resting from making love or about to make love. The sounds of the waterfront surrounded them, the low bellow of ships, truck horns, the sounds of chains and cranes, but inside that small, dim room there seemed to be nothing else in the world but each other. Barrie lost herself in the force of his unbridled sensuality and discovered within herself a passion that matched his. The need to be quiet only added to the intensity.

He kissed the bruises on her breasts and sucked her nipples until they throbbed with pleasure. His beard-stubbled chin rasped against her breasts, her belly, but he was always careful not to cause her pain as he searched for all the other bruises on her body and paid them the same tender homage.

"Tell me how they hurt you," he murmured, "and I'll make it better."

At first Barrie shied away from divulging the details, even to him, but as the hot afternoon wore on and he pleasured her so often she was drunk with the overload on her senses, it began to seem pointless to keep anything from him. Haltingly she began to whisper things to him.

"Like this?" he asked, repeating the action that had so upset her—except it wasn't the same. What had been meant to punish at the hands of the kidnappers became purest pleasure in Zane Mackenzie's hands. He caressed her until her body forgot those other touches, until it remembered only him.

She whispered another detail, and he wiped out that memory, too, replacing the bad with caresses that lifted her to peak after sensual peak. She couldn't imagine being handled more tenderly than he handled her, or with such delight. He didn't try to hide how much he enjoyed looking at her, touching her, making love to her. He reveled in her body, in the contrast between her soft curves and his hard muscularity. It aroused her to be the focus of such intense masculine pleasure, to feel his absorption with the texture of her skin, the curve of her breast, the snug sheathing between her legs. He explored her; he petted her, he drowned her in sexuality. The area around them was still so busy they didn't dare converse much, so they communicated with their bodies.

Three times, while they were lying drowsily in the aftermath of loving, he checked his watch and reached for the headset radio. He would click it once, listen, then put it aside.

"Your men?" she asked, after the first time.

He nodded. "They're hiding out, waiting until it's safe to rendezvous."

Then the chatter of voices outside became louder as some people approached, and they fell silent.

The afternoon wore on, and the light began to dim. She wasn't particularly hungry, but Zane insisted that she eat.

He pulled up his pants; she once more donned his shirt. More formally attired now, they sat close together on the blanket and finished off the bread and fruit, but neither of them wanted any of the cheese. The water was warm and still tasted of chemicals. Barrie sat within the curve of his arm and dreaded leaving.

She wanted to be safe and comfortable again, but she hated to lose this closeness with Zane, this utter reliance and companionship and intimacy. She wouldn't push him to continue their relationship; under the circumstances, he might feel responsible and think he would have to let her down gradually, and she didn't want to put him in that position. If he indicated that he wanted to see her afterward, then…why, then her heart would fly.

But even if he did, it would be difficult for them to see each other regularly. He was more than just a military man; he was a SEAL. Much of what he did couldn't be discussed. He would have a home base, duties, missions. If they escaped safely, the danger to him didn't end there. A chill settled around her heart when she thought of the times in the future when, because it was his job, he would calmly and deliberately walk into a deadly situation. While they were hidden in this small room might be the only time she could ever be certain he was safe and unharmed.

The fear and uncertainty would almost drive her mad, but she would endure them, she would endure anything, for the opportunity to see him, to grow closer to him. Their relationship, if there was to be one, would have to grow in reverse. Usually people came to know each other, grew to trust and care, and then became lovers; they had become lovers almost immediately, and now they would have to get to know each other, find out all the quirks and personal history and tastes that made them individuals.

When she got back, she would have to deal with her

father. He must be frantic, and once she was safely home, he would be even more paranoid and obsessive. But if Zane wanted her, she would have to deliberately hurt her father's feelings for the first time in her life; he would be supplanted as number one in her life. Most parents handled the change in their offsprings' lives with happiness, assuming the chosen mate was decent, but Barrie knew it wouldn't matter who she fell in love with, her father would be opposed to him. No man, to him, was good enough for her. Even more, he would bitterly resent anything that would take her out of his protection. She was all he had left of his family, and it didn't help that she greatly resembled her mother. As ambassador, her father had a very active social life, but he'd only ever loved one woman, and that was her mother.

She would never turn her back on her father, because she loved him dearly, but if the chance for a relationship, possibly a lifetime, with Zane was in the balance, she would put as much distance between herself and her father as necessary until he accepted the situation.

She was planning her life around dreams, she thought wryly as she brushed the bread crumbs from the blanket. She would do better to let the future take care of itself and concern herself with how they were going to get out of Benghazi.

"What time do we leave?"

"After midnight. We'll give most people time to get settled down for the night." He turned to her with the heavy-lidded gaze she had already learned signaled arousal and, reaching out, he began to unbutton her shirt. "Hours," he whispered.

Afterward they lay close together, despite the heat, and dozed. She didn't know how long it was before she woke, but when she did it was to almost total darkness. Unlike the night before, though, when she had lain in cold, lonely terror, now she was pressed against Zane's side, and his arms securely held her. Her head was pillowed on his shoulder, one bare leg was hooked over his hips. She stretched a bit and yawned, and his arms tightened, letting her know that he was awake. Perhaps he had never slept at all, but had held her and safeguarded her. The noise beyond the ruined building had died down; even the sounds from the docks were muted, as if the darkness smothered them.

"How much longer?" she asked, sitting up to fumble for the jug of water. She found it and drank; the taste wasn't too bad, she decided. Maybe she was becoming used to the chemicals, whatever they were.

He peeled the cover from his watch so he could see the luminous dial. "Another few hours. I need to check in with the guys in a couple of minutes."

She passed the water jug to him, and he drank. They lay back down, and she cuddled close. She put her right hand on his chest and felt the strong, healthy thudding of his heart. Idly she twirled her fingers in the crisp hairs, delighting in the textures of his body.

"What happens then? When we leave, I mean."

"We get out of the city, make our rendezvous point just at sunrise, and we're picked up."

He made it sound so simple, so easy. She remembered the swim trunks he wore and lifted her head to frown at him, even though she knew he couldn't see her. "Is our rendezvous point on dry land?"

"Not exactly."

"I see. I hope you have a boat?" It was a question, not a statement.

"Not exactly."

She caught his chest hairs and gave them a tug. "*Exactly* what *do* you have?"

"Ouch!" Snagging her hand, he disentangled it and

lifted it to his mouth, lightly brushing his lips across her knuckles. "*Exactly,* we have a Zodiac, a seven-man, motorized inflatable craft. My team came in short two men, so there are only six of us. We'll be able to fit you in."

"I'm so glad." She yawned and snuggled her head more securely into the hollow of his shoulder. "Did you leave someone behind so there would be room for me?"

"No," he said shortly. "We're undermanned because of a problem I'll have to take care of when we get back. If there had been any other team available, we wouldn't be here, but we were the closest, and we needed to get you out in a hurry, before they moved you."

His tone dissuaded her from asking about the problem that put him in such a black mood, but she'd seen him in action; she knew she wouldn't want to be on the receiving end of his anger when he got back. She waited while he picked up the headset and checked in with his men, then returned to her questions.

"Where do we go in the Zodiac?"

"Out to sea," he said simply. "We radio ahead, and we'll be picked up by a helicopter from the *Montgomery,* an aircraft carrier. You'll be flown home from the carrier."

"What about you?" she whispered. "Where will you go?" That was as close as she would allow herself to get to asking him about his future plans.

"I don't know. My team was performing exercises on the *Montgomery,* but that's blown to hell now, with two of them injured. I'll have to clean up that mess, and I don't know how long it will take."

He didn't know where he would be, or if he did, he wasn't saying. Neither was he saying that he would call her, though he *did* know where *she* would be. Barrie closed her eyes and listened painfully to all that he wasn't saying. The hurt was worse than she'd anticipated, but she closed it off in a place deep inside. Later it would come out, but if she only had a few hours left with him, she didn't intend to waste them crying about what might have been. Few women would have a chance to even know a man like Zane Mackenzie, much less love him. She was greedy; she wanted it all, wanted everything, but even this little bit was more than a lot of people experienced, and she would have to be grateful for that.

Whatever happened, she could never return to the safe little cocoon her father had fashioned for her. She couldn't let herself forget the kidnapping and the unknown *why* of it. Of course, her father would know why; the kidnapper would already have made his demands. But Barrie wanted to know the reason, too; after all, she had been more directly affected than anyone else.

Lightly Zane touched her nipple, circling it with his callused fingertips and bringing it erect. "I know you have to be sore," he said, sliding his hand down her belly to nestle it between her legs. "But can you take me again?" With the utmost care he eased one long finger into her; Barrie winced, but didn't flinch away from him. Yes, she was sore; she had been sore since the first time. She had discovered that the discomfort was easily discounted when the rewards were so great.

"I could be persuaded," she whispered, sliding her hand down his belly to measure his immediate seriousness. She found that he was very serious. Granted, she had no experience against which to compare this, but she had read magazine articles and knew that usually only teenage boys and very young men could maintain this pace. Maybe it was because he was in such superb physical condition. Maybe she was just lucky, though twenty-four hours before she hadn't thought so. But circumstances had changed, and so had she.

Fate had given her this man for now, and for a few more hours, she thought as he leaned over her and his mouth captured hers. She would make the most of it.

Once more he led her through the maze of alleys, but this time she was clad in the enveloping black robe, and a chador covered her hair. Her feet were protected by slippers, which were a little too big and kept slipping up and down on her heels, but at least she wasn't barefoot. It felt strange to have on clothes, especially so many, even though she was bare underneath the robe.

Zane was once more rigged out with his gear and weaponry, and with the donning of those things he had become subtly more remote, almost icily controlled, the way he'd been the night before when he'd first found her. Barrie sensed his acute alertness and guessed that he was concentrating totally on the job at hand. She silently followed him, keeping her head a little bowed as a traditional Muslim woman would do.

He halted at the corner of a building and sank to his haunches, motioning for her to do the same. Barrie copied him and took the extra precaution of drawing the chador across her face.

"Two, this is One. How's it looking?" Once more he was speaking in that toneless whisper that barely carried to her, though she was right behind him. After a moment he said, "See you in ten."

He glanced around at Barrie. "It's a go. We don't have to shift to Plan C."

"What was Plan C?" she whispered.

"Run like hell for Egypt," he said calmly. "It's about two hundred miles due east."

He would do it, too, she realized. He would steal some kind of vehicle and go for it. His nerves must be made of solid iron. Hers weren't; she was shaking inside with nervousness, but she was holding up. Or maybe it wasn't nervousness; maybe it was exhilaration at the danger and excitement of action, of *escaping*. As long as they were still in Benghazi, in Libya, they hadn't really gotten free.

Ten minutes later he stopped in the shadow of a dilapidated warehouse. Perhaps he clicked his radio; in the dark, she couldn't tell. But suddenly five black shapes materialized out of the darkness, and they were surrounded before she could blink.

"Gentlemen, this is Miss Lovejoy," Zane said. "Now let's get the hell out of Dodge."

"With pleasure, boss." One of the men bowed to Barrie and held out his hand. "This way, Miss Lovejoy."

There was a certain rough élan about them that she found charming, though they didn't let it interfere with the business at hand. The six men immediately began moving out in choreographed order, and Barrie smiled at the man who'd spoken as she took the place he had indicated in line. She was behind Zane, who was second in line behind a man who moved so silently, and blended so well into the shadows, that even knowing he was there, sometimes she couldn't see him. The other four men ranged behind her at varying distances, and she realized that she couldn't hear them, either. In fact, she was the only one of the group who was making any noise, and she tried to place her slippered feet more carefully.

They wound their way through the alleys and finally stopped beside a battered minibus. Even in the darkness Barrie could see the huge dents and dark patches of rust that decorated the vehicle. They stopped beside it, and Zane opened the sliding side door for her. "Your chariot," he murmured.

Barrie almost laughed as he handed her into the little

bus: if she hadn't had experience navigating long evening gowns, she would have found the ankle-length robe awkward, but she managed it as if she was a nineteenth-century lady being handed into a carriage. The men climbed in around her. There were only two bench seats; if there had ever been a third one in the back, it had long since been removed, perhaps to make room for cargo. A wiry young black man got behind the steering wheel, and Zane took the other seat in front. The eerily silent man who had been on point squeezed in on her left side, and another SEAL sat on her right, carefully placing her in a human security box. The other two SEALs knelt on the floorboard behind them, their muscular bodies and their gear filling the limited space.

"Let's go, Bunny Rabbit," Zane said, and the young black man grinned as he started the engine. The minibus looked as though it was on its last wheels, but the motor purred.

"You shoulda been there last night," the black guy said. "It was tight for a minute, real tight." He sounded as enthusiastic as if he was describing the best party he'd ever attended.

"What happened?" Zane asked.

"Just one of those things, boss," the man on Barrie's right said with a shrug evident in his voice. "A bad guy stepped on Spook, and the situation went straight into fubar."

Barrie had been around enough military men to know what fubar meant. She sat very still and didn't comment.

"Stepped right *on* me," the SEAL on her left said in an aggrieved tone. "He started squalling like a scalded cat, shooting at everything that moved and most things that didn't. Aggravated me some." He paused. "I'm not staying for the funeral."

"When we got your signal we pulled back and ran like hell," the man on her right continued. "You must've already had her out, because they came after us like hound dogs. We laid low, but a couple of times I thought we were going to have to fight our way out. Man, they were walking all over us, and they kept hunting all night long."

"No, we were still inside," Zane said calmly. "We just stepped into the next room. They never thought to check it."

The men snorted with mirth; even the eerie guy on her left managed a chuckle, though it didn't sound as if he did it often enough to be good at it.

Zane turned around in the seat and gave Barrie that brief twitch of a smile. "Would you like some introductions, or would you rather not know these raunchy-smelling bums?"

The atmosphere in the bus *did* smell like a locker room, only worse. "The introductions, please," she said, and her smile was plain in her voice.

He indicated the driver. "Antonio Withrock, Seaman Second Class. He's driving because he grew up wrecking cars on dirt tracks down South, so we figure he can handle any situation."

"Ma'am," said Seaman Withrock politely.

"On your right is Ensign Rocky Greenberg, second in command."

"Ma'am," said Ensign Greenberg.

"On your left is Seaman Second Class Winstead Jones."

Seaman Winstead Jones growled something unintelligible. "Call him Spooky or Spook, not Winstead," Zane added.

"Ma'am," said Seaman Jones.

"Behind you are Seamen First Class Eddie Santos, our medic, and Paul Drexler, the team sniper."

"Ma'am," said two voices behind her.

"I'm glad to meet you all," Barrie said, her sincerity plain. She had trained her memory at countless official functions, so she had their names down cold. She hadn't yet put a face to Santos or Drexler, but from his name she figured Santos would be Hispanic, so that would be an easy distinction to make.

Greenberg began to tell Zane the details of everything that had happened. Barrie listened and didn't intrude. The fact was, this midnight drive through Benghazi felt a little surreal. She was surrounded by men armed to their eye-teeth, but they were traveling through an area that was still fairly active for so late at night. There were other vehicles in the streets, pedestrians on the sidewalks. They even stopped at a traffic light, with other vehicles around them. The driver, Withrock, hummed under his breath. No one else seemed concerned. The traffic light changed, the battered little minibus moved forward, and no one paid them any attention at all.

Several minutes later they left the city. Occasionally she could see the gleam of the Mediterranean on their right, which meant they were traveling west, toward the center of Libya's coast. As the lights faded behind them, she began to feel lightheaded with fatigue. The sleep she had gotten during the day, between bouts of lovemaking, hadn't been enough to offset the toll stress had taken on her. She couldn't see herself leaning on either of the men beside her, however, so she forced herself to sit upright and keep her eyes open.

She suspected that she was more than a little punch-drunk.

After a while Zane said, "Red goggles."

She was tired enough that she wondered if that was some kind of code, or if she'd misunderstood him. Neither, evidently. Each man took a pair of goggles from his pack and donned them. Zane glanced at her and said in explanation, "Red protects your night vision. We're going to let our vision adjust now, before Bunny kills the headlights."

She nodded, and closed her eyes to help her own vision adjust. She realized at once that, if she wanted to stay awake, closing her eyes for whatever reason wasn't the smartest thing to do, but her eyelids were so heavy that she couldn't manage to open them again. The next thing she knew, the minibus was lurching heavily from side to side, throwing her against first Greenberg, then Spooky. Dazed with sleep, she tried to hold herself erect, but she couldn't seem to find her balance or anything to hold on to. She was about to slide to the floorboard when Spooky's forearm shot out in front of her like an iron bar, anchoring her in the seat.

"Thank you," she said groggily.

"Anytime, ma'am."

Sometime while she had been asleep, Bunny had indeed killed the headlights, and they were plunging down an embankment in the dark. She blinked at something shiny looming in front of them; she had a split second of panic and confusion before she recognized the sea, gleaming in the starlight.

The minibus lurched to a halt. "End of the line," Bunny cheerfully announced. "We have now reached the hidey-hole for one IBS. That's military talk for inflatable boat, small," he said over his shoulder to Barrie. "These things are too fancy to be called plain old rafts."

Zane snorted. Barrie remembered that he'd described it as exactly that, a raft.

Watching them exit the minibus was like watching quicksilver slip through cracks. If there had been a working overhead light when the SEALs had commandeered the vehicle, they had taken care of that detail, because no light came on when the doors were cracked open. Spooky slipped past her, no mean feat given the equipment he was carrying, and when Greenberg slid the side door open a few inches, Spooky wiggled on his stomach through the small opening. One second he was there, the next he was gone. Barrie stared at the door with widened eyes in full appreciation of how he'd acquired his nickname. He was definitely spooky.

The others exited the minibus in the same manner; it was as if they were made of water, and when the doors opened they simply leaked out. They were that fluid, that silent. Only Bunny, the driver, remained behind with Barrie. He sat in absolute silence, pistol in hand, as he methodically surveyed the night-shrouded coast. Because he was silent, she was too. The best way not to be any trouble to them, she thought, was to follow their example.

There was one quick little tap on the window, and Bunny whispered, "It's clear. Let's go, Miss Lovejoy."

She scooted over the seat to the door while Bunny eeled out on the driver's side. Zane was there, opening the door wider, reaching in to steady her as she slid out onto the ground. "Are you holding up okay?" he asked quietly.

She nodded, not trusting herself to speak, because she was so tired her speech was bound to be slurred.

As usual, he seemed to understand without being told. "Just hold on for another hour or so, and we'll have you safe on board the carrier. You can sleep then."

Without him, though; that fact didn't need stating. Even if he intended to continue their relationship, and he hadn't given any indication of it, he wouldn't do so on board the ship. She would put off sleeping forever if it would postpone the moment when she had to admit, once and for all, that their relationship had been a temporary thing for him, prompted by both the hothouse of intimacy in which they'd spent the day, and her own demands.

She wouldn't cry; she wouldn't even protest, she told herself. She'd had him for a day, for one incredibly sensual day.

He led her down to the small, rocky strip of beach, where the dark bulk of the IBS had been positioned. The other five men were gathered around it in specific positions, each standing with his back to the raft while he held his weapon at the ready, edgily surveying the surroundings.

Zane lifted her into the IBS and showed her where to sit. The IBS bobbed in the water as the men eased it away from the shore. When the water was chest deep on Santos, the shortest one, they all swung aboard in a maneuver they had practiced so many times it looked effortless. Spooky started the almost soundless motor and aimed the IBS for the open sea.

Then a roar erupted behind them, and all hell broke loose.

She recognized the sharp *rat-tat-tat* of automatic weapons and half turned to look behind them. Zane put his hand on her head and shoved her down to the bottom of the boat, whirling, already bringing his automatic rifle around as he did so. The IBS shot forward as Spooky gave it full throttle. The SEALs returned fire, lightning flashing from the weapons, spent cartridges splattering down on her as she curled into a ball and drew the chador over her face to keep the hot brass from burning her.

"Drexler!" Zane roared. "Hit those bastards with explosives!"

"Got it, boss!"

Barrie heard a grunt, and something heavy and human fell across her. One of the men had been hit. Desperately she tried to wriggle out from under the crushing weight so she could help him, but she was effectively pinned, and he groaned every time she moved.

She knew that groan.

Terror such as she had never felt before raced through her veins. With a hoarse cry she heaved at the heavy weight, managing to roll him to the side. She fought her way free of the enveloping chador and didn't even notice the hot cartridge shell that immediately skimmed her right cheek.

An explosion shattered the night, lighting up the sea like fireworks, the percussion knocking her to the bottom of the boat again. She scrambled to her knees, reaching for Zane. "No," she said hoarsely. "No!"

The light from the explosion had sharply delineated every detail in stark white. Zane lay sprawled half on his side, writhing in pain as he pressed his hands to his abdomen. His face was a colorless blur, his eyes closed, his teeth exposed in a grimace. A huge wet patch glistened on the left side of his black shirt, and more blood was pooling beneath him.

Barrie grabbed the chador and wadded it up, pressing it hard to the wound. A low animal howl rattled in his throat, and he arched in pain. "Santos!" she screamed, trying to hold him down while still holding the chador in place. "*Santos!*"

With a muttered curse the stocky medic shouldered her aside. He lifted the chador for a second, then quickly pressed it into place and grabbed her hand, guiding it into position. "Hold it," he rapped out. "Press down—hard."

There was no more gunfire, only the hum of the motor. Salt spray lashed her face as the boat shot through the waves. The team maintained their discipline, holding their assigned positions. "How bad is it?" Greenberg yelled.

Santos was working feverishly. "I need light!"

Almost instantly Greenberg had a flashlight shining down on them. Barrie bit her lip as she saw how much blood had puddled around them. Zane's face was pasty white, his eyes half-shut as he gasped for breath.

"He's losing blood fast," Santos said. "Looks like the bullet got a kidney, or maybe his spleen. Get that damn helicopter on the way. We don't have time to get into international waters." He popped the cap off a syringe, straightened Zane's arm and deftly jabbed the needle into a vein. "Hang on, boss. We're gonna get you airlifted outta here."

Zane didn't reply. He was breathing noisily through his clenched teeth, but when Barrie glanced at him she could see the gleam of his eyes. His hand lifted briefly, touched her arm, then fell heavily to his side.

"Damn you, Zane Mackenzie," she said fiercely. "Don't you *dare*—" She broke off. She couldn't say the word, couldn't even admit to the possibility that he might die.

Santos was checking Zane's pulse. His eyes met hers, and she knew it was too fast, too weak. Zane was going into shock, despite the injection Santos had given him.

"I don't give a damn how close in we still are!" Greenberg was yelling into the radio. "We need a helo *now*. Just get the boss out of here and we'll wait for another ride!"

Despite the pitching of the boat, Santos got an IV line started and began squeezing a bag of clear plasma into Zane's veins. "Don't let up on the pressure," he muttered to Barrie.

"I won't." She didn't take her gaze off Zane's face. He was still aware, still looking at her. As long as that connection was maintained, he would be all right. He had to be.

The nightmare ride in the speeding boat seemed to take forever. Santos emptied the first bag of plasma and connected a second one to the IV. He was cursing under his breath, his invectives varied and explicit.

Zane lay quietly, though she knew he was in terrible pain. His eyes were dull with pain and shock, but she could sense his concentration, his determination. Perhaps the only way he could remain conscious was by focusing so intently on her face, but he managed it.

But if that helicopter didn't get there soon, not even his superhuman determination would be able to hold out against continued blood loss. She wanted to curse, too, wanted to glare at the night sky as if she could conjure a helicopter out of thin air, but she didn't dare look away from Zane. As long as their gazes held, he would hold on.

She heard the distinctive *whap-whap-whap* only a moment before the Sea King helicopter roared over them, blinding lights picking them out. Spooky throttled back, and the boat settled gently onto the water. The helicopter circled to them and hovered directly overhead, the powerful rotors whipping the sea into a frenzy. A basket dropped almost on their heads. Working swiftly, Santos and Greenberg lifted Zane into the basket and strapped him in, maneuvering around Barrie as she maintained pressure on the wound.

Santos hesitated, then indicated for her to let go and move back. Reluctantly she did. He lifted the chador, then immediately jammed it back into place. Without a word he straddled the basket, leaning hard on the wound. "Let's go!" he yelled. Greenberg stepped back and gave the thumbs-up to the winch operator in the helicopter. The basket rose toward the hovering monster, with Santos perched precariously on top of Zane. As the basket drew even with the open bay, several pairs of hands reached out and drew them inward. The helicopter immediately lifted away, banking hard, roaring toward the carrier.

There was an eerie silence left behind. Barrie slumped against one of the seats, her face rigid with the effort of maintaining control. No one said a word. Spooky started the motor again, and the little craft shot through the darkness, following the rapidly disappearing lights of the helicopter.

It was over an hour before the second helicopter settled onto the deck of the huge carrier. The remaining four members of the team leaped to the deck almost before the helicopter had touched down. Barrie clambered after them, ran with them. Greenberg had one hand clamped on her arm to make certain she didn't get left behind.

Someone in a uniform stepped in front of them. "Miss Lovejoy, are you all right?"

Barrie gave him a distracted glance and dodged around him. Another uniform popped up, but this one was subtly different, as if the wearer belonged on board this gigantic ship. The first man had worn a dress uniform, marking him as a non-crew member. Greenberg skidded to a halt. "Captain—"

"Lieutenant-Commander Mackenzie is in surgery," the captain said. "Doc didn't think he'd make it to a base with such a high rate of blood loss. If they can't get the bleeding stopped, they'll have to remove his spleen."

The first uniformed officer had reached them. "Miss Lovejoy," he said firmly, taking her arm. "I'm Major Hodson. I'll escort you home."

The military moved at its own pace, to its own rules. She was to be taken home immediately; the ambassador wanted his daughter back. Barrie protested. She yelled, she cried, she even swore at the harried major. None of it did any good. She was hustled aboard another aircraft, this time a cargo transport plane. Her last glimpse of the *Montgomery* was as the sun's first rays glistened on the blue waters of the Mediterranean, and the sight was blurred by her tears.

Chapter 7

By the time the transport touched down in Athens, Barrie had cried so hard and for so long that her eyes were swollen almost shut. Major Hodson had tried everything to pacify her, then to console her; he assured her that he was just following orders, and that she would be able to find out how the SEAL was doing later. It was understandable that she was upset. She'd been through a lot, but she would have the best medical care—

At that, Barrie shot out of the uncomfortable web seat, which was all the transport plane afforded. "*I'm* not the one who was shot!" she yelled furiously. "I don't need medical care, best, worst or mediocre! I want to be taken to wherever Zane Mackenzie is taken. I don't care what your orders are!"

Major Hodson looked acutely uncomfortable. He tugged at the collar of his uniform. "Miss Lovejoy, I'm sorry. I can't do anything about this situation. After we're on the ground and your father is satisfied that you're okay, then where you go is up to you."

His expression plainly said that as far as he was concerned, she could go to hell. Barrie sat down, breathing hard and wiping away tears. She'd never acted like that before in her life. She'd always been such a lady, a perfect hostess for her father.

She didn't feel at all ladylike now; she felt like a ferocious tigress, ready to shred anyone who got in her way. Zane was severely wounded, perhaps dying, and these *fools* wouldn't let her be with him. Damn military procedure, and damn her father's influence, for they had both wrenched her away from him.

As much as she loved her father, she knew she would never forgive him if Zane died and she wasn't there. It didn't matter that he didn't know about Zane; nothing mattered compared to the enormous horror that loomed before her. *God, don't let him die!* She couldn't bear it. She would rather have died herself at her kidnappers' hands than for Zane to be killed while rescuing her.

The flight took less than an hour and a half. The transport landed with a hard thump that jerked her in the web seat, then taxied for what seemed like an interminable length of time. Finally it rolled to a stop, and Major Hodson stood, plainly relieved to be free of his unpleasant burden.

A door was slid open, and a flight of steps rolled up to it. Clutching the black robe around her, Barrie stepped out into the bright Athens sunlight. It was full morning now, the heat already building. She blinked and lifted a hand to shield her eyes. It felt like forever since she'd been in the sunshine.

A gray limousine with darkly tinted windows was waiting on the tarmac. The door was shoved open, and her father bounded out, dignity forgotten as he ran forward. "Barrie!" Two days of worry and fear lined his face, but there was an almost desperate relief in his expression as he hurried up the steps to fold her in his arms.

She started crying again, or maybe she had never stopped. She buried her face against his suit, clutching him with desperate hands. "I've got to go back," she sobbed, the words barely intelligible.

He tightened his arms around her. "There, there, baby," he breathed. "You're safe now, and I won't let anything else happen to you, I swear. I'll take you home—"

Wildly she shook her head, trying to pull away from him. "No," she choked out. "I've got to get back to the *Montgomery*. Zane—he was shot. He might die. Oh, God, I've got to go back *now!*"

"Everything will be all right," he crooned, hustling her down the steps with an arm locked around her shoulders. "I have a doctor waiting—"

"I don't need a doctor!" she said fiercely, jerking away from him. She'd never done that before, and his face went blank with shock. She shoved her hair out of her face. The tangled mass hadn't been combed in two days, and it was matted with sweat and sea spray. "Listen to me! The man who rescued me was shot. *He might die.* He was still in surgery when Major Hodson forced me on board this plane. I want to go back to the ship. I want to make sure Zane is okay."

William Lovejoy firmly took hold of his daughter's shoulders again, leading her across the tarmac to the waiting limo. "You don't have to go back to the ship, sweetheart," he said soothingly. "I'll ask Admiral Lindley to find out how his man is doing. He *is* one of the SEAL team, I presume?"

Numbly she nodded.

"There wouldn't be any point in going back to the ship, I'm sure you can see that. If he survived surgery, he'll be airlifted to a military hospital."

If he survived surgery. The words were like a knife, hot and slicing, going through her. She balled her hands into fists, every cell in her body screaming for her to ignore logic, ignore the attempts to soothe her. She needed to get to Zane.

Three days later, she stood in her father's office with her chin high and her eyes colder than he'd ever seen them. "You told Admiral Lindley to block my requests," she accused.

The ambassador sighed. He removed his reading glasses and carefully placed them on the inlaid walnut desk. "Barrie, you know I've denied you very little that you've asked for, but you're being unreasonable about this man. You know that he's recovering, and that's all you need to know. What point would there be in rushing to his bedside? Some tabloid might find out about it, and then your ordeal would be plastered in sleazy newspapers all over the world. Is that what you want?"

"My ordeal?" she echoed. "*My* ordeal? What about his? He nearly died! That's assuming Admiral Lindley told me the truth, and he really is still alive!"

"Of course he is. I only asked Joshua to block any inquiries you made about his location." He unfolded his tall form from the chair and came around to lean against the desk and take her resistant hands in his. "Barrie, give yourself time to get over the trauma. I know you've invested this…this guerrilla fighter with all sorts of heroic characteristics, and that's only normal. After a while, when you've regained your perspective, you'll be glad you didn't embarrass yourself by chasing after him."

It was almost impossible to contain the volcanic fury rising in her. Nobody was listening; no one wanted to listen. They kept going on and on about her ordeal, how she would heal in time, until she wanted to pull her hair out. She had insisted over and over that she hadn't been raped, but she had fiercely refused to be examined by a doctor,

which of course had only fueled speculation that the kidnappers had indeed raped her. But she'd known her body
bore the marks of Zane's lovemaking, marks and traces that
were precious and private, for no one else's eyes. Everyone
was treating her as if she was made of crystal, carefully not
mentioning the kidnapping, until she thought she would go
mad.

She wanted to see Zane. That was all. Just see him, assure herself that he would be all right. But when she'd
asked one of the Marine officers stationed at the embassy
to make some inquiries about Zane, it was Admiral Lindley
who had gotten back to her instead of the captain.

The dignified, distinguished admiral had come to the ambassador's private quarters less than an hour before. Barrie
hadn't yet returned to her minor job in the embassy, feeling
that she couldn't keep her mind on paperwork, so she had
received the admiral in the beautifully appointed parlor.

After polite conversation about her health and the
weather, the admiral came to the point of his visit. "You've
been making some inquiries about Zane Mackenzie," he
said kindly. "I've kept abreast of his condition, and I can
tell you now with complete confidence that he'll fully recover. The ship's surgeon was able to stop the bleeding,
and it wasn't necessary to remove his spleen. His condition
was stabilized, and he was transferred to a hospital. When
he's able, he'll be sent Stateside for the remainder of his
convalescence."

"Where is he?" Barrie had demanded, her eyes burning.
She'd scarcely slept in three days. Though she was once
more impeccably clothed and coifed, the strain she'd been
under had left huge dark circles under her eyes, and she
was losing weight fast, because her nerves wouldn't let her
eat.

Admiral Lindley sighed. "William asked me to keep that
information from you, Barrie, and I have to say, I think

he's right. I've known Zane a long time. He's an extraordinary warrior. But SEALs are a breed apart, and the characteristics that make them such great warriors don't, as a whole, make them model citizens. They're trained weapons, to put it bluntly. They don't keep high profiles, and most information about them is restricted.''

''I don't want to know about his training,'' she said, her voice strained. ''I don't want to know about his missions. I just want to see him.''

The admiral shook his head. ''I'm sorry.''

Nothing she said budged him. He refused to give her even one more iota of information. Still, Zane was alive; he would be all right. Just knowing that made her feel weak inside, as the unbearable tension finally relaxed.

That didn't mean she would forgive her father for interfering.

''I love him,'' she now said deliberately. ''You have no right to keep me from seeing him.''

''Love?'' Her father gave her a pitying look. ''Barrie, what you feel isn't love, it's hero-worship. It will fade, I promise you.''

''Do you think I haven't considered that?'' she fired back. ''I'm not a teenager with a crush on a rock star. Yes, I met him under dangerous, stressful circumstances. Yes, he saved my life—and he nearly died doing it. I know what infatuation is, and I know what love is, but even if I didn't, the decision isn't yours to make.''

''You've always been reasonable,'' he argued. ''At least concede that your judgment may not be at its sharpest right now. What if you acted impulsively, married this man— I'm sure he'd jump at the chance—and then realized that you really didn't love him? Think what a mess it would be. I know it sounds snobbish, but he isn't our kind. He's a sailor, and a trained killer. You've dined with kings and danced with princes. What could the two of you have in common?''

"First, that doesn't just *sound* snobbish, it *is* snobbish. Second, you must not think much of me as a person if you consider your money my only attraction.''

"You know that isn't what I meant," he said, genuinely shocked. "You're a wonderful person. But how could someone like that appreciate the life you live? How do you know he wouldn't have his eye on the main chance?''

"Because I know him," she declared. "I know him in a way I never would have if I'd met him at an embassy party. According to you, a SEAL couldn't be kind and considerate, but he was. They all were, for that matter. Dad, I've told you over and over that I wasn't raped. I know you don't believe me, and I know you've suffered, worrying about me. But I swear to you—I *swear*—that I wasn't. They were planning to, the next day, but they were waiting for someone. So, though I was terrified and upset, I haven't been through the trauma of a gang rape the way you keep thinking. Seeing Zane lying in a pool of blood was a hell of a lot more traumatic than anything those kidnappers did!''

"Barrie!" It was the first time her father had ever heard her curse. Come to think of it, she had never cursed at all, until rough men had grabbed her off the street and subjected her to hours of terror. She had cursed them, and meant it. She had cursed Major Hodson, and meant that, too.

With an effort, she regulated her tone. "You know that the first attempt to get me out didn't quite work.''

He gave an abrupt nod. He'd suffered agonies, thinking their only hope of rescuing her had failed and imagining what she must be suffering. That was when he'd given up hope of ever seeing her alive again. Admiral Lindley hadn't been as pessimistic; the SEALs hadn't checked in, and though there were reports of gunfire in Benghazi, if a team of SEALs had been killed or captured, the Libyan government would have trumpeted it all over the world. That meant they were still there, still working to free her. Until they heard from the team that the rescue had failed, there was still hope.

"Well, it did work, in a way. Zane came in alone to get me, while the rest of the team was a diversion, I guess, in case things went wrong. He had a backup plan, what to do if they were spotted, because you can't control the human factor." She realized she was repeating things Zane had said to her during those long hours when they had lain drowsily together, and she missed him so much that pain knotted her insides. "The team was so well-hidden that one of the guards didn't see Spooky until he actually stepped on him. That's what gave the alarm and started the shooting. A guard had been posted in the corridor outside the room where they had me tied up, and he ran in. Zane killed him," she said simply. "Then, while the others were chasing the team, he got me out of the building. We were separated from the team and had to hide for a day, but I was safe."

The ambassador listened gravely, soaking up these details of how she had been returned to him. They hadn't talked before, not about the actual rescue. She had been too distraught about Zane, almost violent in her despair. Now that she knew he was alive, even though she was still so angry she could barely contain it, she was able to tell her father how she had been returned to him alive.

"While I stayed in our hiding place, Zane risked his life by going out and stealing food and water for us, as well as the robe and chador for me. He took care of the cut on my foot. When scavengers were practically dismantling the place around us, he kept himself between me and any danger. That's the man I fell in love with, that's the man you say isn't 'our kind.' He may not be yours, but he's definitely mine!''

The expression in her father's eyes was stunned, almost panicked. Too late, Barrie saw that she had chosen the wrong tack in her argument. If she had presented her concern for Zane as merely for someone who had done so much for her, if she had insisted that it was only right she thank him in person, her father could have been convinced. He was very big on preserving the niceties, on behaving properly. Instead, she had convinced him that she truly loved Zane Mackenzie, and too late she saw how much he had feared exactly that. He didn't want to lose her, and now Zane presented a far bigger threat than before.

"Barrie, I..." He fumbled to a stop, her urbane, sophisticated father who was never at a loss for words. He swallowed hard. It was true that he'd seldom denied her anything, and those times he had refused had been because he thought the activity she planned or the object she wanted—once it had been a motorcycle—wasn't safe. Keeping her safe was his obsession, that and holding tightly to his only remaining family, his beloved child, who so closely resembled the wife he'd lost.

She saw it in his eyes as his instinct to pamper her with anything she desired warred with the knowledge that this time, if he did, he would probably lose her from his life. He didn't want occasional visits from her; they had both endured that kind of separation during her school years. He wanted her *there,* in his everyday life. She knew part of his obsession was selfish, because she made domestic matters very easy for him, but she had never doubted his love for her.

Pure panic flashed in his expression. He said stiffly, ''I still think you need to give yourself time for your emotions to calm. And surely you realize that the conditions you describe are what that man is *used* to. How could he ever fit into your life?''

''That's a moot question, since marriage or even a relationship was never discussed. I want to see him. I don't want him to think that I didn't care enough even to check on his condition.''

''If any sort of relationship was never discussed, why would he expect you to visit him? It was a mission for him, nothing more.''

Barrie's shoulders were military straight, her jaw set, her green eyes dark with emotion. ''It was more,'' she said flatly, and that was as much of what had happened between her and Zane as she was willing to discuss. She took a deep breath and pulled out the heavy artillery. ''You owe it to me,'' she said, her gaze locked with his. ''I haven't asked any details about what happened here, but I'm an intelligent, logical person—''

''Of course you are,'' he interrupted, ''but I don't see—''

''Was there a ransom demanded?'' She cut across his interruption.

He was a trained diplomat; he seldom lost control of his expression. But now, startled, the look he gave her was blank with puzzlement. ''A ransom?'' he echoed.

A new despair knotted itself in her stomach, etched itself in her face. ''Yes, ransom,'' she said softly. ''There wasn't one, was there? Because money wasn't what *he* wanted. He wants something from you, doesn't he? Information. He's either trying to force you to give it to him, or you're already in it up to your eyebrows and you've had a falling out with him. Which is it?''

Again his training failed him; for a split second his face revealed panicked guilt and consternation before his expression smoothed into diplomatic blandness. ''What a ridiculous charge,'' he said calmly.

She stood there, sick with knowledge. If the kidnapper had been using her as a weapon to force her father into betraying his country, the ambassador most likely would have denied it, because he wouldn't want her to be worried, but that wasn't what she'd read in his face. It was guilt.

She didn't bother responding to his denial. "You owe me," she repeated. "You owe Zane."

He flinched at the condemnation in her eyes. "I don't see it that way at all."

"You're the reason I was kidnapped."

"You know there are things I can't tell you," he said, releasing her hands and walking around the desk to resume his seat, symbolically leaving the role of father and entering that of ambassador. "But your supposition is wrong, and, of course, an indication of how off-balance you still are."

She started to ask if Art Sandefer would think her supposition was so wrong, but she couldn't bring herself to threaten her father. Feeling sick, she wondered if that made her a traitor, too. She loved her country; living in Europe as much as she had, she had seen and appreciated the dramatic differences between the United States and every other country on earth. Though she liked Europe and had a fondness for French wine, German architecture, English orderliness, Spanish music and Italy in general, whenever she set foot in the States she was struck by the energy, the richness of life where even people who were considered poor lived well compared to everywhere else. The United States wasn't perfect, far from it, but it had something special, and she loved it.

By her silence, she could be betraying it.

By staying here, she remained in danger. Kidnapping her had failed once, but that didn't mean *he,* the unknown, faceless enemy, wouldn't try again. Her father knew who *he* was, she was certain of it. Immediately she saw how it would be. She would be confined to the embassy grounds, or allowed out only with an armed escort. She would be a prisoner of her father's fear.

There was really no place she would be entirely safe, but remaining here only made the danger more acute. And once she was away from the enclave of the embassy, she would have a better chance of locating Zane, because Admiral Lindley's influence couldn't cover every nook and cranny of the globe. The farther away from Athens she was, the thinner that influence would be.

She faced her father, knowing that she was deliberately breaking the close ties that had bound them together for the past fifteen years. "I'm going home," she said calmly. "To Virginia."

Two weeks later, Zane sat on the front porch of his parents' house, perched on top of Mackenzie's Mountain, just outside Ruth, Wyoming. The view was breathtaking, an endless vista of majestic mountains and green valleys. Everything here was as familiar to him as his own hands. Saddles, boots, some cattle but mostly horses. Books in every room of the sprawling house, cats prowling through the barns and stables, his mother's sweet, bossy coddling, his father's concern and understanding.

He'd been shot before; he'd been sliced up in a knife fight. He'd had his collarbone broken, ribs cracked, a lung punctured. He had been seriously injured before, but this was the closest he'd ever come to dying. He'd been bleeding to death, lying there in the bottom of the raft with Barrie crouched over him, pressing the chador over the wound with every ounce of her weight. Her quickness, her determination, had made the difference. Santos squeezing the plasma from the bags into his veins had made the difference. He had been so close that he could pick out a dozen details that had made the difference; if any one of them hadn't happened, he would have died.

He'd been unusually quiet since leaving the naval hospital and returning home for convalescence. It wasn't that he was in low spirits, but rather that he had a lot of thinking to do, something that hadn't been easy when practically the entire family had felt compelled to visit and reassure themselves of his relative well-being. Joe had flown in from Washington for a quick check on his baby brother; Michael and Shea had visited several times, bringing their two rapscallion sons with them; Josh and Loren and their three had descended for a weekend visit, which was all the time Loren's job at the hospital in Seattle had allowed. Maris had driven all night to be there when he was brought home. At least he'd been able to walk on his own by then, even if very slowly, or likely she would still be here. She had pulled up a chair directly in front of him and sat for hours, her black eyes locked on his face as if she was willing vitality from her body into his. Maybe she had been. His little sister was fey, magical; she operated on a different level than other people did.

Hell, even Chance had shown up. He'd done so warily, eyeing their mother and sister as if they were bombs that might go off in his face, but he was here, sitting beside Zane on the porch.

"You're thinking of resigning."

Zane didn't have to wonder how Chance had known what was on his mind. After nearly battering each other to death when they were fourteen, they had reached an unusual communion. Maybe it was because they'd shared so much, from classes to girls to military training. Even after all this time, Chance was as wary as a wounded wolf and didn't like people to get close to him, but even though he resisted, he was helpless against family. Chance had never in his life been loved until Mary had brought him home with her and the sprawling, brawling Mackenzies had knocked him flat. It was fun to watch him still struggle against the family intimacy each time he was drawn into the circle, because within an hour he always surrendered. Mary wouldn't let him do anything else; nor would Maris. After accepting him as a brother, Zane had never even acknowledged Chance's wariness. Only Wolf was willing to give his adopted son time to adjust—but there was still a limit on how much time he would allow.

"Yeah," he finally said.

"Because you nearly bought it this time?"

Zane snorted. "When has that ever made any difference to either of us?" He alone of the family knew the exact details of Chance's work. It was a toss-up which of them was in the most danger.

"Then it's this last promotion that did it."

"It took me out of the field," Zane said quietly. Carefully he leaned back in the chair and propped his booted feet on the porch railing. Though he was a fast healer, two and a half weeks wasn't quite long enough to let him ignore the wound. "If two of my men hadn't been wounded in that screwup on the *Montgomery,* I wouldn't have been able to go on this last mission."

Chance knew about the screwup. Zane had told him about it, and screwup was the most polite description he'd used. As soon as he'd regained consciousness in the naval hospital, he'd been on the phone, starting and directing the investigation. Though Odessa would fully recover, it was likely Higgins would have to retire on disability. The guards who had shot the two SEALs might escape court-martial if their counsel was really slick, but at the very least they would be cashiered out of the service. The extent of the damage to the careers of Captain Udaka and Executive Officer Boyd remained to be seen; Zane had targeted the shooters, but the ripple effect would go all the way up to the captain.

"I'm thirty-one," Zane said. "That's just about the upper limit for active missions. I'm too damn good at my job, too. The Navy keeps promoting me for it, then they say I'm too highly ranked to go on missions.''

"You want to throw in with me?" Chance asked casually.

He'd considered it. Very seriously. But something kept nagging at him, something he couldn't quite bring into focus.

"I want to. If things were different, I would, but..."

"What things?"

Zane shrugged. At least part of his uneasy feeling could be nailed down. "A woman," he said.

"Oh, hell." Chance kicked back and surveyed the world over the toes of his boots. "If it's a woman, you won't be able to concentrate on anything until you've gotten her out of your system. Damn their sweet little hides," he said fondly. Chance generally had women crawling all over him. It didn't hurt that he was drop-dead handsome, but he had a raffish, daredevil quality to him that brought them out of the woodwork.

Zane wasn't certain he could get Barrie out of his system. He wasn't certain he wanted to. He didn't wonder why she had disappeared without even saying goodbye, hope you're feeling better. Bunny and Spook had told him how she'd been dragged, kicking and yelling and swearing, aboard a plane and taken back to Athens. He figured her father, combined with the Navy's policy of secrecy concerning the SEALs, had prevented her from finding out to which hospital they'd taken him.

He missed her. He missed her courage, her sturdy willingness to do whatever needed doing. He missed the serenity of her expression, and the heat of her lovemaking.

God, yes.

The one memory, more than any of the others, that was

branded in his brain was the moment when she had reached
for his belt and said in that fierce whisper, "I'll do it!"

He'd understood. Not just why she needed to be in control, but the courage it took her to wipe out the bad memories and replace them with good ones. She'd been a virgin;
she had told the truth about that. She hadn't known what
to do, and she hadn't expected the pain. But she had taken
him anyway, sweetly, hotly, sliding her tight little body
down on him and shattering his control the way no other
woman had ever done.

She could have been a spoiled, helpless little socialite;
she *should* have been exactly that. Instead she had made
the best of a tense, dangerous situation, done what she
could to help and hadn't voiced a single complaint.

He liked being with her, liked talking to her. He was too
much of a loner to easily accept the word love in connection with anyone other than family, but with Barrie...maybe. He wanted to spend more time with her, get
to know her better, let whatever would develop get to developing.

He wanted her.

First things first, though. He had to get his strength back;
right now he could walk from room to room without aid,
but he would think twice about heading down to the stables
by himself. He had to decide whether or not he was going
to stay in the Navy; it felt like time to be moving on, since
the reason he'd joined in the first place was being taken
away from him as he moved up the ranks. If he wasn't
going to remain a SEAL, then what would he do for a
living? He had to decide, had to get his life settled.

Barrie might not be interested in any kind of relationship
with him, though from the way Spook and Bunny had described her departure, he didn't think that was the case. The
day of lovemaking they had shared had been more than
propinquity for both of them.

Getting in touch with her could take some doing, though. That morning he had placed a call to the embassy in Athens. He'd given his name and asked to speak to Barrie Lovejoy. It had been Ambassador William Lovejoy who had come on the line, however, and the conversation hadn't been cordial.

"It isn't that Barrie doesn't appreciate what you did, but I'm sure you understand that she wants to put all of that behind her. Talking with you would bring it all back and needlessly upset her," the ambassador had said in a cool, well-bred voice, his diction the best money could buy.

"Is that her opinion, or yours?" Zane had asked, his tone arctic.

"I don't see that it matters," the ambassador had replied, and hung up.

Zane decided he would let it rest for now. He wasn't in any shape to do much about it, so he would wait. When he had his mind made up about what he was going to do, there would be plenty of time to get in touch with Barrie, and now that he knew the ambassador had given orders for his calls not to be routed to her, the next time he would be prepared to do an end run around her father.

"Zane," his mother called from inside the house, pulling his thoughts to the present. "Are you getting tired?"

"I feel fine," he called back. It was an exaggeration, but he wasn't unduly tired. He glanced at Chance and saw the smirk on his brother's face.

"With all the worry about you, she forgot about my cracked ribs," Chance whispered.

"Glad to be of service," Zane drawled. "Just don't expect me to get shot every time you bang yourself up a little." The entire family thought it was hilarious the way Chance reacted to Mary's coddling and fussing, as if the attention terrified him, even though he was never able to resist her. Chance was putty in Mary's hands, but then, they all were. They'd grown up with the fine example of their father to emulate, and Wolf Mackenzie might growl and stomp, but Mary usually got her way.

"Chance?"

Zane controlled a grin as Chance stiffened, the smirk disappearing from his face as if it had never been.

"Ma'am?" he answered cautiously.

"Are you still keeping a pressure wrap on your ribs?"

That familiar panicked expression was in his eyes now. "Ah...no, ma'am." He could have lied; Mary would have believed him. But none of them ever lied to her, even when it was in their best interests. It would hurt the little tyrant's feelings too much if she ever discovered any of her kids had lied to her.

"You know you're supposed to wrap them for another week," said the voice from inside the house. It was almost like hearing God speak, except this voice was light and sweet and liquidly Southern.

"Yes, ma'am."

"Come inside and let me take care of that."

"Yes, ma'am," Chance said again, resignation in his voice. He got up from his rocking chair and went into the house. As he passed Zane, he muttered, "Getting shot didn't work. Try something else."

Chapter 8

Two months later, Sheriff Zane Mackenzie stood naked at the window of the pleasant two-bedroom Spanish-style house he had bought in southern Arizona. He was staring out over the moonlit desert, something wild and hot running through him at the sight. His SEAL training had taught him how to adapt to any environment, and the hot, dry climate didn't bother him.

Once he'd made up his mind to resign his commission, things had rapidly fallen into place. Upon hearing that he was leaving the Navy, a former SEAL team member who was now on the governor's staff in Phoenix had called and asked if he would be interested in serving the remaining two years of the term of a sheriff who had died in office.

At first Zane had been taken aback; he'd never considered going into law enforcement. Moreover, he didn't know anything about Arizona state laws.

"Don't worry about it," his friend had said breezily. "Sheriff is a political position, and most of the time it's more administrative than anything else. The situation you'd be going into is more hands-on, though. A couple of the deputies have quit, so you'd be shorthanded until some more can be hired, and the ones still there will resent the hell out of you because one of them wasn't appointed to finish out the sheriff's term.''

''Why not?'' Zane asked bluntly. ''What's wrong with the chief deputy?''

''She's one of the ones who quit. She left a couple of months before the sheriff died, took a job on the force in Prescott.''

''None of the others are qualified?''

''I wouldn't say that.''

''Then what would you say?''

''You gotta understand, there's not a lot of selection here. A couple of the young deputies are good, real good, but they're *too* young, not enough experience. The one twenty-year guy isn't interested. A fifteen-year guy is a jerk, and the rest of the deputies hate his guts.''

Sheriff. Zane thought about it, growing more intrigued with the idea. He had no illusions about it being a cakewalk. He would have difficulties with the fifteen-year veteran, at least, and likely all the other deputies would have some reservations and resistance about someone from the outside being brought in. Hell, he liked it better that way. Cakewalks didn't interest him. He'd rather have a challenging job any day. ''Okay, I'm interested. What does it involve?''

''A lot of headache, mostly. The pay's decent, the hours are lousy. A reservation sits on part of the county, so you'll have to deal with the BIA. There's a big problem with illegal immigrants, but that's for the INS to worry about. Generally, this isn't a high crime area. Not enough people.''

So here he was, his strength back, the owner of a house and a hundred acres of land, newly sworn in as sheriff. He'd brought in a few of his horses from his parents' place in Wyoming. It was a hell of a change from the Navy.

It was time to see about Barrie. He'd thought about her a lot over the past few months, but lately he couldn't think about anything else. The uneasy feeling was persisting, growing stronger. He'd put his resources to work, and to his surprise found that she'd left Athens within a week of being returned there. She was currently living at the Lovejoy private residence in Arlington, Virginia. Moreover, last month the ambassador had abruptly asked to be replaced, and he, too, had returned to Virginia. Zane wished Mr. Lovejoy had remained in Athens, but his presence was a problem that could be handled.

No matter what her father did or said, Zane was determined to see Barrie. There was unfinished business between them, a connection that had been abruptly cut when he'd been shot and she had been forced aboard a flight to Athens. He knew the hot intimacy of those long hours together could have been a product of stress and propinquity, but at this point, he didn't give a damn. There were other considerations, ones he couldn't ignore. That was why he had a flight out of Tucson to Washington in the morning. He needed to be sleeping, but one thought kept going around and around in his head. She was pregnant.

He couldn't say why he was so convinced of it. It was a gut feeling, an intuition, even a logical conclusion. There hadn't been any means of birth control available; they had made love several times. Put the two facts together, and the possibility of pregnancy existed. He didn't think it was a mere possibility, though; he thought it was a fact.

Barrie was going to have his baby.

The rush of fierce possessiveness he felt was like a tidal wave, sweeping away all his cautious plans. There wouldn't be any gradual getting-to-know-each-other stage, no easing into the idea of a serious relationship. If she was pregnant, they would get married immediately. If she didn't like the idea, he would convince her. It was as simple as that.

She was pregnant. Barrie hugged the precious knowledge to herself, not ready yet to let anyone else know, certainly not her father. The kidnapping and the aftermath had driven a wedge between them that neither of them could remove. He was desperate to restore their former relationship; nothing else could have induced him to resign from a post, an action that could have had serious repercussions for his career if it hadn't generally been thought that he had resigned because she had been so traumatized by the kidnapping that she couldn't remain in Athens and he wanted to be with her.

She tried not to think about whatever he might be involved in, because it hurt. It hurt horribly that he might be a traitor. Part of her simply couldn't believe it; he was an old-fashioned man, a man to whom honor wasn't just a word but a way of life. She had no proof, only logic and her own deductions…that, and the expression he hadn't quite been able to hide when she had asked him directly if he was involved in anything that might have resulted in her being kidnapped.

It also hurt horribly that he had kept her from Zane. She had made inquiries once she reached Virginia, but once again she had collided with a stone wall. No one would give her any information at all about him. She had even contacted SEAL headquarters and been politely stone-walled again. At least with the SEALs it was probably policy to safeguard the team members' identities and location, given the sensitive nature of the antiterrorism unit.

She was having his baby. She wanted him to know about it. She wouldn't expect anything of him that he didn't want to give, but she wanted him to know about his child. And she desperately wanted to see him again. She was adrift and lonely and frightened, her emotions in turmoil, and she needed some security in that part of her life, at least. He wasn't the kind of man who would blithely walk away from his offspring and ignore their existence. This baby would be a permanent link between them, something she could count on.

She doubted her father would relent concerning Zane even if he knew about the baby; his possessiveness would probably extend to a grandchild, even an illegitimate one. He would take steps to keep her pregnancy quiet, and even when the news got around, as it inevitably would, people would assume it was a child of rape, and they would look at her pityingly and talk about how brave she was.

She thought she would go mad. She had escaped to Virginia only to have her father follow. He panicked if she went anywhere unescorted. She had her own car, but he didn't want her driving it; he wanted his driver to take her wherever she wanted to go. She had had to sneak to a pharmacy to buy a home pregnancy test, though she had been sure fairly early on that she was pregnant. The test had merely confirmed what her body had already told her.

Barrie knew she should be worried and upset about this unplanned pregnancy, but it was the only thing in her life right now that made her happy. She was intensely lonely; the kidnapping and the long hours alone with Zane had set her apart from the other people in her life. She had memories they couldn't share, thoughts and needs no one could understand. Zane had been there with her; he would have understood her occasional pensiveness, her reticence in talking about it. It wasn't that she was secretive, for she would have liked to talk to someone who understood. But what she had shared with Zane was like a combat experience, forming a unique bond between the people who had lived it.

She wouldn't be able to keep her pregnancy secret much longer; she had to arrange prenatal care, and all telephone calls were now recorded. She supposed she could sneak out again and set up a doctor's appointment from a pay phone, but she would be damned if she would.

Enough was enough. She was an adult, and soon to be a mother. She hated the fact that her relationship with her father had deteriorated to the point where they barely spoke, but she couldn't find a way to mend it. As long as the possibility of his involvement in treasonous activities remained, she was helpless. She wanted him to explain, to give her a plausible reason why she had been kidnapped. She wanted to stop looking over her shoulder every time she went out; she didn't want to feel as if she truly *needed* to be guarded. She wanted to live a normal life. She didn't want to raise her baby in an atmosphere of fear.

But that was exactly the atmosphere that permeated the house. It was stifling her. She had to get away, had to remove herself from the haunting fear that, as long as her father was involved in whatever had given him such a guilty expression, she could be kidnapped again. The very thought made her want to vomit, and she didn't have just herself to worry about now. She had her baby to protect.

The fatigue of early pregnancy had gotten her into the habit of sleeping late, but one morning she woke early, disturbed by a pair of raucous birds fighting for territory in the tree outside her window. Once she was awake, nausea soon followed, and she made her usual morning dash to the bathroom. Also as usual, when the bout of morning sickness had passed, she felt fine. She looked out the window at the bright morning and realized she was inordinately hungry, the first time in weeks that the idea of food was appealing.

It was barely six o'clock, too early for Adele, the cook, to have arrived. Breakfast was normally at eight, and she had been sleeping past that. Her stomach growled. She couldn't wait another two hours for something to eat.

She put on her robe and slippers and quietly left her room; her father's bedroom was at the top of the stairs, and she didn't want to disturb him. Even more, she didn't want him to join her for an awkward tête-à-tête. He tried so hard to carry on as if nothing had happened, and she couldn't respond as she had before.

He should still be asleep, she thought, but when she reached the top of the stairs she heard him saying something she couldn't understand. She paused, wondering if he'd heard her after all and had been calling out to her. Then she heard him say *Mack* in a sharp tone, and she froze.

A chill roughened her entire body, and the bottom dropped out of her stomach. The only Mack she knew was Mack Prewett, but why would her father be talking to him? Mack Prewett was still stationed in Athens, as far as she knew, and since her father had resigned, he shouldn't have had any reason to be talking to him.

Then her heart leaped wildly as another possibility occurred to her. Perhaps he had been saying *Mackenzie* and she'd heard only the first syllable. Maybe he was talking about Zane. If she listened, she might find out where he was, or at least *how* he was. With no additional information about his condition, it had been hard to believe Admiral Lindley's assurance that he would fully recover. Belief required trust, and she no longer trusted the admiral, or her father.

She crept closer to his door and put her ear against it.

"—finished soon," he was saying sharply, then he was silent for a moment. "I didn't bargain on this. Barrie wasn't supposed to be involved. Get it wrapped up, Mack."

Barrie closed her eyes in despair. The chill was back, even colder than before. She shook with it, and swallowed hard against the return of nausea. So he *was* involved, he and Mack Prewett both. Mack was CIA. Was he a double agent, and if so, for whom? The world situation wasn't like it had been back in the old days of the Cold War, when the lines had been clearly drawn. Nations had died since then, and new ones taken their place. Religion or money seemed to be the driving force behind most differences these days; how would her father and Mack Prewett fit into that? What information would her father have that Mack wouldn't?

The answer eluded her. It could be anything. Her father had friends in every country in Europe, and any variety of confidential information could come his way. What didn't make sense was why he would sell that information; he was already a wealthy man. But money, to some people, was as addictive as a narcotic. No amount was ever enough; they had to have more, then still more, always looking for the next hit in the form of cash and the power that went with it.

Could she have been so wrong in her judgment of him? Had she still been looking at him with a child's eyes, seeing only her father, the man who had been the security in her life, instead of a man whose ambitions had tainted his honor?

Blindly she stumbled to her bedroom, not caring if he heard her. He must still have been engrossed in his conversation, though, or she didn't make as much noise as she thought she had, because his door remained closed.

She curled up on the bed, protectively folding herself around the tiny embryo in her womb.

What was it he hadn't bargained on? The kidnapping? That was over two months in the past. Had there been a new threat to use her as a means of ensuring he did something?

She was helplessly fumbling around in the dark with these wild conjectures, and she hated it. It was like being in alien territory, with no signs to guide her. What was she supposed to do? Take her suspicions to the FBI? She had nothing concrete to go on, and over the years her father had made a lot of contacts in the FBI; who could she trust there?

Even more important, if she stayed here, was she in danger? Maybe her wild conjectures weren't wild at all. She had seen a lot during her father's years in foreign service and noticed even more when she had started working at the embassy. Things happened, skulduggery went on, dangerous situations developed. Given the kidnapping, her father's reaction and now his unreasonable attitude about her safety, she didn't think she could afford to assume everything would be okay.

She had to leave.

Feverishly she began trying to think of someplace she could go where it wouldn't be easy to find her, and how she could get there without leaving a paper trail that would lead a halfway competent terrorist straight to her. Meanwhile, Mack Prewett wasn't a halfway competent bureaucrat, he was frighteningly efficient; he was like a spider, with webs of contacts spreading out in all directions. If she booked a flight using her real name, or paid for it with a credit card, he would know.

To truly hide, she had to have cash, a lot of it. That meant emptying her bank account, but how could she get there without her father knowing? It had reached the point where she would have to climb out the window and walk to the nearest pay phone to call a cab.

Maybe the house was already being watched.

She moaned and covered her face with her hands. Oh, God, this was making her paranoid, but did she dare *not* suspect anything? As some wit had observed, even paranoids had enemies.

She had to think of the baby. No matter how paranoid an action seemed, she had to err on the side of safety. If she had to dress in dark clothing, slither out a window in the wee hours of the morning and crawl across the ground until she was well away from this house…as ridiculous as it sounded, she would do it. Tonight? The sooner she got away, the better.

Tonight.

That decision made, she took a deep breath and tried to think of the details. She would have to carry some clothing. She would take her checkbook and bank book, so she could close out both her checking and savings accounts. She would take her credit cards and get as much cash as she could on them; everything together would give her a hefty amount, close to half a million dollars. How would she carry that much money? She would need an empty bag.

This was beginning to sound ludicrous, even to her. How was she supposed to crawl across the lawn in the darkness, dragging two suitcases behind her?

Think! she fiercely admonished herself. Okay, she wouldn't have to carry either clothes or suitcases with her. All she would need to carry was her available cash, which was several hundred dollars, her checkbook and savings account book, and her credit cards, which she would de-

stroy after they had served their purpose. She could buy
new clothes and makeup, as well as what luggage she
would immediately need, as soon as a discount store
opened. She could buy do-it-yourself hair coloring and dye
her red hair brown, though not until after she had been to
the bank. She didn't want the teller to be able to describe
her disguise.

With cash in her possession, she would have several options. She could hop on Amtrak and go in any direction,
then get off the train before her ticketed destination. Then
she could buy a cheap used car, pay cash for it, and no one
would know where she went from there. To be on the safe
side, she would drive that car for only one day, then trade
it in on a better car, again paying cash.

These were drastic measures, but doable. She still wasn't
certain she wasn't being ridiculous, but did she dare bet
that way, when her life, and that of her child, could hang
in the balance? *Desperate times call for desperate measures.* Who had said that? Perhaps an eighteenth-century
revolutionary; if so, she knew how he had felt. She had to
disappear as completely as possible. She would mail her
father a postcard before she left town, letting him know
that she was all right but that she thought it would be better
to get away for a while, otherwise he would think she had
indeed been kidnapped again, and he would go mad with
grief and terror. She couldn't do that to him. She still loved
him very much, even after all he had done. Again a wave
of disbelief and uncertainty hit her. It seemed so impossible
that he would sell information to terrorists, so opposite to
the man she had always known him to be. She was aware
that he wasn't universally well liked, but the worst accusation she had ever heard leveled against him was that he
was a snob, which even she admitted was accurate. He was
very effective as a diplomat and ambassador, working with

the CIA, which was of course set up in every embassy, using his social standing and contacts to smooth the way whenever a problem cropped up. He had personally been acquainted with the last six presidents, and prime ministers called him a friend. This man was a traitor?

It couldn't be. If she had only herself to consider, she would give him the benefit of the doubt.

But there was the baby, the tiny presence undetectable to any but herself. She could feel it in her breasts, which had become so tender she was always aware of them, and in the increased sensitivity and pressure low down in her abdomen, as her womb began to swell with amniotic fluid and increased blood flow. It was almost a hot feeling, as if the new life forming within her was generating heat with the effort of development.

Zane's baby.

She would do anything, no matter how Draconian, to keep it safe. She had to find some secure place where she could get the prenatal care she needed. She would have to change her name, get a new driver's license and a new social security card; she didn't know how these last two would be accomplished, but she would find out. There were always shady characters who could tell her. The driver's license could be forged, but the social security card would have to come through the regular administration. Even though social security was being phased out, until it was completely gone, everyone still had to have a number in order to get a legitimate job.

There was something else to consider. It would be stupid of her to live off her cash until it was all gone. She would need a job, anything that paid enough to keep a roof over their heads and food in their stomachs. She had degrees in art and history, but she wouldn't be able to use her own name, so she wouldn't be able to use those degrees to get a teaching job.

She didn't know what the job situation would be wherever she settled; she would simply have to wait and see. It didn't matter what she did, waiting tables or office work, she would take whatever was available.

She glanced at the clock: seven-thirty. Nerves notwithstanding, she was acutely hungry now, to the point of being sick with it. Her pregnant body had its own agenda, ignoring upset emotions and concentrating only on the business at hand.

The thought brought a smile to her face. It was almost as if the baby was already stomping a tiny foot and demanding what it wanted.

Tenderly she pressed her hand over her belly, feeling a slight firmness that surely hadn't been there before. "All right," she whispered to it. "I'll feed you."

She showered and dressed, mentally preparing herself to face her father without giving anything away. When she entered the breakfast room, he looked up with an expression of delight, quickly tempered by caution. "Well, it's a pleasure to have your company," he said, folding the newspaper and laying it aside.

"Some birds woke me up," she said, going to the buffet to help herself to toast and eggs. She fought a brief spell of nausea at the sight of sausage and changed her mind about the eggs, settling on toast and fruit. She hoped that would be enough to satisfy the demanding little creature.

"Coffee?" her father asked as she sat down. He already had the silver carafe in his hand, poised to pour.

"No, not today," she said hastily, as her stomach again clenched warningly. "I've been drinking too much caffeine lately, so I'm trying to cut down." That was a direct lie. She had stopped drinking anything with caffeine in it as soon as she suspected she might be pregnant, but it was as if her system was still warning her against it. "I'll drink orange juice." So far, that hadn't turned her stomach.

She applied herself to her food, replying civilly to his conversational gambits, but she couldn't bring herself to wholeheartedly enter into a discussion with him the way she once would have done. She could barely look at him, afraid her feelings would be plain on her face. She didn't want him any more alert than he already was.

"I'm having lunch with Congressman Garth," he told her. "What are your plans for the day?"

"None," she replied. Her plans were all for the night.

He looked relieved. "I'll see you this afternoon, then. I'll drive myself, so Poole will be available to drive you if you do decide to go anywhere."

"All right," she said, agreeing with him because she wasn't going anywhere.

Once he'd left the house, she spent the day reading and occasionally napping. Now that she had made up her mind to go, she felt more peaceful. Tomorrow would be an exhausting day, so she needed to rest while she could.

Her father returned in the middle of the afternoon. Barrie was sitting in the living room, curled up with a book. She looked up as he entered and immediately noticed how the drawn look of worry eased when he saw her. "Did you have a nice lunch?" she asked, because that was what she would have done before.

"You know how these political things are," he said. Once he would have sat down and told her all about it, but this time he smoothly evaded talking specifics. Senator Garth was on several important committees concerning national security and foreign affairs. Before she could ask any more questions, he went into his study, closing the door behind him. Before, he had always kept it open as an invitation to her to visit whenever she wanted. Sadly Barrie looked at the closed door, then returned to her book.

The doorbell startled her. She put the book aside and went to answer it, cautiously looking through the peephole before opening the door. A tall, black-haired man was standing there.

Her heart jumped wildly, and a wave of dizziness swept over her. Behind her, she heard her father coming out of his study. "Who is it?" he asked sharply. "Let me get it."

Barrie didn't reply. She jerked the door open and stared up into Zane's cool, blue gray eyes. Her heart was pounding so hard she could barely breathe.

That sharp gaze swept down her body, then came up to her face. "Are you pregnant?" he asked quietly, his voice pitched low so her father couldn't hear, even though he was rapidly approaching.

"Yes," she whispered.

He nodded, a terse movement of his head as if that settled that. "Then we'll get married."

Chapter 9

Her father reached them then, and shouldered Barrie aside. "Who are you?" he demanded, still in that sharp tone.

Zane coolly surveyed the man who would be his father-in-law. "Zane Mackenzie," he finally replied, when he had finished his appraisal. His darkly tanned face was impassive, but there was a piercing quality to his pale eyes that made Barrie suddenly aware of how dangerous this man could be. It didn't frighten her; under the circumstances, this quality was exactly what she needed.

William Lovejoy had been alarmed, but now his complexion turned pasty, and his expression froze. He said stiffly, "I'm sure you realize it isn't good for Barrie to see you again. She's trying to put that episode behind her—"

Zane looked past Lovejoy to where Barrie stood, visibly trembling as she stared at him with pleading green eyes. He hadn't realized how green her eyes were, a deep forest green, or how expressive. He got the impression that she wasn't pleading for him to be nice to her father, but rather that she was asking for help in some way, with some thing. His battle instincts stirred, his senses lifting to the next level of acuity. He didn't know exactly what she was asking of him, but he would find out, as soon as he dealt with the present situation. It was time to let the former ambassador know exactly where he stood.

"We're getting married," he said, still looking at Barrie, as he cut through the ambassador's continuing explanation on why it would be best if he left immediately. His steely voice, which had instantly commanded the attention of the deadliest guerrilla fighters in the world, cut through Lovejoy's stuffy, patronizing explanation.

The ambassador broke off, and a look of panic flashed across his face. Then he said, "Don't be ridiculous," in a strained tone. "Barrie isn't going to marry a sailor who thinks he's something special because he's a trained assassin."

Zane's cool gaze switched from Barrie to her father and went arctic cold, the blue fading to a gray that glinted like shards of ice. Lovejoy took an involuntary step back, his complexion going from pasty to white.

"Barrie, will you marry me?" Zane asked deliberately, keeping his gaze focused on Lovejoy.

She glanced from him to her father, who tensed as he waited for her answer.

"Yes," she said, her mind racing. Zane. She wouldn't question the miracle that had brought him here, but she was so desperate that she would have married him even if she hadn't loved him. Zane was a SEAL; if anyone could keep her safe from the unknown enemy who had her father so on edge, he could. She was carrying his child, and evidently that possibility was what had brought him to Virginia in search of her. He was a man who took his responsibilities seriously. She would have preferred that he cared for her as deeply as she did for him, but she would take what she could get. She knew he was attracted to her; if he wasn't, she wouldn't be pregnant.

She would marry him, and perhaps with time he would come to love her.

Her father flinched at her answer. Half turning to her, he said imploringly, "Baby, you don't want to marry someone like him. You've always had the best, and he can't give it to you."

Squaring her shoulders, she said, "I'm going to marry him—as soon as possible."

Seeing the intractability in her expression, her father looked at Zane. "You won't get a penny of her inheritance," he said with real venom.

"Dad!" she cried, shocked. She had her own money, inheritances from her mother and grandparents, so she wasn't worried about being destitute even if he carried through on his threat; it was the fact that he'd made the threat at all, that he would try to sabotage her future with Zane in such a blatant, hurtful manner, that hurt.

Zane shrugged. "Fine," he said with deceptive mildness. Barrie heard the pure iron underlying the calm, even tone. "Do what you want with your money, I don't give a damn. But you're a fool if you thought you could keep her with you for the rest of your life. You can act like an ass and cheat yourself out of your grandchildren if you want, but nothing you say is going to change a damn thing."

Lovejoy hung there, his face drawn with pain. Anguish darkened his eyes as he looked at his daughter. "Don't do it," he pleaded, his voice shaking.

Now it was her turn to wince, because in spite of everything, she hated to hurt him. "I'm pregnant," she whispered, straightening her shoulders against any other hurtful thing he might say. "And we're getting married."

He swayed on his feet, stunned by her announcement. She hadn't thought it possible he could turn any whiter, but he did. "What?" he croaked. "But—but you said you weren't raped!"

"She wasn't," Zane said. There was a soft, drawling, very masculine undertone in his voice.

Their eyes met. Barrie gave him a soft, wry smile. "I wasn't," she verified, and despite everything, a sudden, subtle glow lit her face.

Her father couldn't think of anything else to say. He gaped at them for a moment, unable to handle this turn of events. Then a red tide of anger ran up his face, chasing away the pallor. "You bastard!" he choked out. "You took advantage of her when she was vulnerable—"

Barrie grabbed his arm and jerked him around. "Stop it!" she yelled, her slender body tense with fury. Her nerves had been shredded since that morning, and this confrontation was only making them worse. Zane's sudden appearance, though it made her almost giddy with happiness, was another shock to her system, and she'd had enough. "If anyone took advantage, *I* did. If you want the details I'll give them to you, but I don't think you really want to know!"

It was on the tip of her tongue to ask him if he'd thought he could keep her a virgin forever, but she bit the bitter words off unspoken. That would be too hurtful, and once said, she would never be able to take the words back. He loved her, perhaps too much; his fear of losing her was why he was lashing out. And, despite everything, she loved him, too. Pain congealed inside her as she stared starkly at him, all pretense gone. "I know," she whispered. "Do you understand? I *know*. I know why you've been so paranoid every time I've left the house. *I have to leave.*"

He inhaled sharply, shock ripping away his last vestige of control. He couldn't sustain her burning gaze, and he looked away. "Keep her safe," he said to Zane in a stifled voice, then walked stiffly toward his study.

"I intend to." That difficulty solved, he spared no more than a glance for his departing foe. His gaze switched to Barrie, and a slow, heart-stopping smile touched his lips. "Go get packed," he said.

They were on their way within the hour.

She hurried up to her bedroom and filled her suitcases, bypassing the evening gowns and designer suits in favor of more practical clothing. The ankle-length cotton skirt she was already wearing was comfortable enough for travel; she pulled on a silk shirt over the sleeveless blouse she wore and let it go at that. Every instinct she had was screaming at her to hurry.

She dragged the bags to the top of the stairs. It didn't require a lot of effort, they all had wheeled bottoms, but when Zane saw her, he left his post by the door and took the stairs two at a time. "Don't lift those," he ordered, taking the bags from her hands. "You should have called me."

His tone was the same one he had used in commanding his men, but Barrie was too nervous to fight that battle with him right now. He lifted all three cases with an ease that made her blink and started down the stairs with them. She rushed after him. "Where are we going? Are we flying or driving?"

"Las Vegas. Flying."

"You already have the tickets?" she asked in surprise.

He paused and glanced over his shoulder at her, the dark

wings of his eyebrows lifting fractionally. "Of course," he said, and resumed his trip down the stairs.

Such certainty and self-assurance were daunting. Briefly she wondered what on earth she was getting herself into. More and more she was becoming aware of just how much in control Zane Mackenzie was, of himself and everything around him. She might never be able to break through that barrier. *Except in bed.* The memory zinged through her, bringing a flush to her cheeks that wasn't caused by rushing around. He had lost control there, and it had been... breathtaking.

"What time is the flight?" Once more she hurried to catch up to him. "Will we have time to go to my bank? I need to close out my accounts—"

"You can transfer them to a local bank when we get home."

While he carried her bags out to the rental car he was driving, Barrie went to the study and knocked softly on the door. There was no answer; after a moment she opened the door anyway. Her father was sitting at the desk, his elbows propped on top of it and his face buried in his hands.

"Bye, Dad," she said softly.

He didn't answer, but she saw his Adam's apple bob as he swallowed.

"I'll let you know where I am."

"No," he said, his voice strangled. "Don't." He lifted his head. His eyes were anguished. "Not yet. Wait...wait a while."

"All right," she whispered, understanding slicing through her. It was safer for her that way. He must suspect the phone line was tapped.

"Baby, I—" He broke off and swallowed hard again. "I only want you to be happy—and safe."

"I know." She felt dampness on her cheeks and wiped away the tears that were wetting them.

"He isn't the kind of man I wanted for you. The SEALs are—well, never mind." He sighed. "Maybe he *can* keep you safe. I hope so. I love you, baby. You've been the center of my life. You know I never meant—" He halted, unable to go on.

"I know," she said again. "I love you, too."

She quietly closed the door and stood with her head bowed. She didn't hear him approach, but suddenly Zane was there, his arm hard around her waist as he drew her with him out to the car. He didn't ask any questions, just opened the door for her and helped her inside, then closed the door with a finality that was unmistakable.

She sat tensely during the drive to the airport, watching the traffic buzz around them.

"This is the most privacy we'll have for a while," Zane said as he competently threaded the car through the insanity of rush hour. "Why don't you tell me what's going on?" He had slipped on a pair of sunglasses, and his eyes were hidden from her view, but she didn't have to see them to know how cool and remote the expression in them was.

She lifted her chin and stared straight ahead, considering the way his suggestions sounded like orders. This wasn't going to be easy, but he had to know everything. She needed his protection, at least while she still carried his child. He wouldn't be on guard unless he knew there was a threat. She had to be honest with him. "I want you to know—one of the reasons I agreed to marry you is that I need protection, and you're a SEAL. If any-thing...dangerous...happens, you'll know how to handle it."

"Dangerous, how?" He sounded very matter-of-fact, al-most disinterested. She supposed that, given his job, danger was so common to him that it was more the rule than the exception.

"I think the kidnappers may try again. And now I have more than just myself to worry about." Briefly, unconsciously, her hand moved to her lower belly in the instinctive way a pregnant woman touched the growing child within, as if reassuring it of its safety.

He glanced in the rearview mirror, calmly studying the traffic behind and around them. After a moment of consideration, he went straight to the heart of the matter. "Have you notified the FBI? The police?"

"No."

"Why not?"

"Because I think Dad may be involved," she said, almost strangling on the words.

Once again he checked the rearview mirror. "In what way?"

He sounded so damn remote. She clenched her hands into fists, determined to hold on to her control. If he could be self-contained, then so could she. She forced her voice to evenness. "The reason for the kidnapping wasn't ransom, so they must want information from him. I can't think of anything else it *could* be."

He was silent for a moment, deftly weaving in and out of the tangle of vehicles. She could almost hear that cool, logical brain sorting through the ramifications. Finally he said, "Your father must be in it up to his neck, or he'd have gone to the FBI himself. You would have been taken to a safe place and surrounded by a wall of agents."

He'd reached exactly the same conclusion she had. That didn't make her feel any better. "Since we've been back in Virginia, he's been impossible. He doesn't want me to leave the house by myself, and he's monitoring all telephone calls. He was always protective, but not like this. At first I thought he was overreacting because of what happened in Athens, but when I thought it through, I realized the threat still existed.'' She swallowed. ''I'd made up my mind to sneak out tonight and disappear for a while.''

If Zane had waited another day, she would have been gone. He wouldn't have had any idea where to find her, and she had no way of contacting him. Tears burned her eyes at the thought. Dear God, it had been so close.

''Hold on,'' he said, then jerked the steering wheel to the right, cutting across a lane of traffic and throwing the car into a sharp turn into another street. The tires squealed, and horns blared. Even with his warning, she barely had time to brace herself, and the seat belt tightened with a jerk.

''What's wrong?'' she cried, struggling to right herself and ease the strangling grip of the seat belt.

''There's a possibility we had company. I didn't want to take any chances.''

Alarmed, Barrie twisted around in the seat, staring at the cars passing through the intersection behind them, vainly trying to see anyone who looked familiar or any vehicle making an obvious effort to cut across traffic and follow them. The traffic pattern looked normal.

''Two Caucasian men, in their thirties or forties, both wearing sunglasses,'' Zane said with no more emphasis than if he'd been observing the clouds in the sky. She remembered this almost supernatural calmness from before. In Benghazi, the more tense the situation, the cooler he had become, totally devoid of emotion. For him to take the action he had, he'd been certain they were being followed. The bottom dropped out of her stomach, and she fought a sudden rise of nausea. To suspect she was in danger was one thing, having it confirmed was something else entirely.

Then what he'd said registered in her brain. ''Caucasian?'' she echoed. ''But—'' She stopped, because of course it made sense. While she had subconsciously been looking for Libyans, she had to remember that this Gordian knot of intrigue involved both Libyans and Mack Prewett's cohorts; given his resources, she had to be suspicious of everyone, not just Middle Easterners. Black, white or Oriental, she couldn't trust anyone—except Zane.

''Since they know what I'm driving, we're going to ditch the car.'' Zane took another turn, this time without the dramatics, but also without signaling or slowing down more than was necessary. ''I'll make a phone call and have the car taken care of. We'll get a ride to the airport.''

She didn't ask who he would call; the area was crawling with military personnel from all the branches of service. Someone in dress whites would collect the car and return it to the rental company, and that would be that. By then, she and Zane would be on their way to Las Vegas.

''They'll be able to find me anyway,'' she said suddenly, thinking of the airline ticket in her name.

''Eventually. It'll take a while, though. We have a substantial grace period.''

''Maybe not.'' She bit her lip. ''I overheard Dad talking to Mack Prewett this morning. Mack's CIA, deputy station chief in Athens. Dad told him that he wanted this finished, that he never meant for me to be involved.''

Zane lifted his eyebrows. ''I see.''

She supposed he did. If her father was working with the CIA in anything legitimate, he would have been able to protect her through legal channels. Mack Prewett's involvement changed the rules. He would have access to records that ordinary people wouldn't have. Even though the CIA didn't operate within the United States, the tentacles of influence were far-reaching. If Mack wanted to know if she'd taken a flight out of either of the major area airports, he would have that information within minutes.

"If they were sharp enough to get the license plate number on the car, they'll have my name very shortly," he said. "If they didn't get the number, then they won't have a clue about my identity. Either way, it's too late to worry about it now. They either have it or they don't, and there's no need to change our immediate plans. We'll take the flight to Las Vegas and lose them there, at least for a while."

"How will we lose them? If Mack can get access to your records…"

"I resigned my commission. I'm not a SEAL anymore."

"Oh," she said blankly. She struggled to adjust to yet another change. She had already been imagining and mentally preparing for life as the wife of a military officer, with the frequent moves, the politics of rank. It wouldn't have been much different from life in the embassy, just on a different level. Now she realized she had no idea what kind of life they would have.

"What will we do, then?" she asked.

"I've taken the job of sheriff in a county in southern Arizona. The sheriff died in office, so the governor appointed me to complete his term. There are two years left until new elections, so we'll be in Arizona for at least two years, maybe more."

A sheriff! That was a definite surprise, and the offhand manner with which he had announced it only deepened her sense of unreality. She struggled to focus on the important things. "What your job is doesn't matter," she said as evenly as possible. "It's your training that counts."

He shrugged and wheeled the car into the entrance of a parking garage. "I understand." His voice was flat, emotionless. "You agreed to marry me because you think I'll be able to protect you." He let down the window and leaned out to get the ticket from the automatic dispenser. The red barrier lifted, and he drove through.

Barrie wound her fingers together. Her initial flush of happiness had given way to worry. Zane had come after her, yes, and asked her to marry him, but perhaps she'd been wrong about the attraction between them. She felt uprooted and off-balance. Zane didn't seem particularly happy to see her, but then, she had certainly tossed a huge problem into his lap. He would become a husband and a father in very short order, and on top of that, he had to protect them from an unknown enemy. He hadn't even kissed her, she thought, feeling close to tears, and she was a little surprised at herself for even thinking of such a thing right now. If he was right and someone had been following them, then the danger had been more immediate than she had feared. How could she worry about his reasons for marrying her? After all, the baby's safety was one of the reasons she was marrying *him*. "I want you to protect our baby," she said quietly. "There are other reasons, but that's the main one." Her feelings for him were something she could have handled on her own; she wouldn't take that chance with her baby's safety.

"A damn important one. You're right, too." He gave her a brief glance as he pulled the car into a parking slot on the third level. "I won't let anything hurt you or the baby."

He pulled off his sunglasses and got out of the car with a brief "Wait here," and strode off toward a pay phone. When he reached it, he punched in a series of numbers, then turned so he could watch her and the car while he talked.

Barrie felt her nerves jolt and her stomach muscles tighten as she stared across the parking deck at him. She was actually marrying this man. He looked taller than she remembered, a little leaner, though his shoulders were so wide they strained the seams of his white cotton shirt. His black hair was a bit longer, she thought, but his tan was just as dark. Except for the slight weight loss, he didn't show any sign of having been shot only a little over two months earlier. His physical toughness was intimidating; *he* was intimidating. How could she have forgotten? She had remembered only his consideration, his passion, the tender care he'd given her, but he'd used no weapon other than his bare hands to kill that guard. While she had remembered his lethal competency and planned to use it on her own behalf, she had somehow forgotten that it was a prominent part of him, not a quality she could call up when she needed it and tuck away into a corner when the need was over. She would have to deal with this part of him on a regular basis and accept the man he was. He wasn't, and never would be, a tame house cat.

She liked house cats, but she didn't want him to be one, she realized.

She felt another jolt, this time of self-discovery. She needed to be safe now, because of the baby, but she didn't want to be permanently cosseted and protected. The grueling episode in Benghazi had taught her that she was tougher and more competent than she'd ever thought, in ways she hadn't realized. Her father would have approved if she'd married some up-and-coming ambassador-to-be, but that wasn't what she wanted. She wanted some wildness in her life, and Zane Mackenzie was it. For all that maddening control of his, he was fierce and untamed. He didn't have a streak of wildness; he had a core of it.

The strain between them unnerved her. She had dreamed of him finding her and holding out his arms, of falling into them, and when she had opened the door to him today she had expected, like a fool, for her dream to be enacted. Reality was much more complicated than dreams.

The truth was, they had known each other for about twenty-four hours total, and most of those hours had been over two months earlier. In those hours they had made love with raw, scorching passion, and he had made her pregnant, but the amount of time remained the same.

Perhaps he had been involved with someone else, but a sense of responsibility had driven him to locate her and find out if their lovemaking had had any consequences. He would do that, she thought; he would turn his back on a girlfriend, perhaps even a fiancée, to assume the responsibility for his child.

Again she was crashing into the brick wall of ignorance; she didn't know anything about his personal life. If she had known anything about his family, where he was from, she would have been able to find him. Instead, he must think she hadn't cared enough even to ask about his condition, to find out if he had lived or died.

He was coming back to the car now, his stride as smooth and effortlessly powerful as she remembered, the silent walk of a predator. His dark face was as impassive as before, defying her efforts to read his expression.

He opened the door and slid behind the wheel. "Transport will be here in a few minutes."

She nodded, but her mind was still occupied with their personal tangle. Before she lost her nerve, she said evenly, "I tried to find you. They took me back to Athens immediately, while you were still in surgery. I tried to get in touch with you, find out if you were still alive, how you were doing, what hospital you were in—anything. Dad had Admiral Lindley block every inquiry I made. He did tell me you were going to be okay, but that's all I was able to find out."

"I guessed as much. I tried to call you at the embassy a couple of weeks after the mission. The call was routed to your father."

"He didn't tell me you'd called," she said, the familiar anger and pain twisting her insides. Since she'd been forced off the *Montgomery,* those had been her two main emotions. So he *had* tried to contact her. Her heart lifted a little. "After I came home, I tried again to find you, but the Navy wouldn't tell me anything."

"The antiterrorism unit is classified." His tone was absent; he was watching in the mirrors as another car drove slowly past them, looking for an empty slot.

She sat quietly, nerves quivering, until the car had disappeared up the ramp to the next level.

"I'm sorry," she said, after several minutes of silence. "I know this is a lot to dump in your lap."

He gave her an unreadable glance, his eyes very clear and blue. "I wouldn't be here if I didn't want to be."

"Do you have a girlfriend?"

This time the look he gave her was so long that she blushed and concentrated her attention on her hands, which were twisting together in her lap.

"If I did, I wouldn't have made love to you," he finally said.

Oh, dear. She bit her lip. This was going from bad to worse. He was getting more and more remote, as if the fleeting moment of silent communication between them when he'd asked her to marry him had never existed. Her stomach clenched, and suddenly a familiar sensation of being too hot washed over her.

She swallowed hard, praying that the nausea that had so far confined itself to the mornings wasn't about to put in an unexpected appearance. A second later she was scrambling out of the car and frantically looking around for a bathroom. God, did parking decks *have* bathrooms?

"Barrie!" Zane was out of the car, striding toward her, his dark face alert. She had the impression that he intended to head her off, though she hadn't yet chosen a direction in which to dash.

The stairwell? The elevator? She thought of the people who would use them and discarded both options. The most sensible place was right there on the concrete, and everything fastidious in her rebelled at the idea. Her stomach had different ideas, however, and she clamped a desperate hand over her mouth just as Zane reached her.

Those sharp, pale eyes softened with comprehension. "Here," he said, putting a supporting arm around her. The outside barriers of the parking deck were waist-high concrete walls, and that was where he swiftly guided her. She resisted momentarily, appalled at the possibility of throwing up on some unsuspecting passerby below, but his grip was inexorable, and her stomach wasn't waiting any longer. He held her as she leaned over the wall and helplessly gave in to the spasm of nausea.

She was shaking when it was over. The only comfort she could find was that, when she opened her eyes, she saw there was nothing three stories below but an alley. Zane held her, leaning her against his supporting body while he blotted her perspiring face with his handkerchief, then gave it to her so she could wipe her mouth. She felt scorched with humiliation. The strict teachings of her school in Switzerland hadn't covered what a lady should do after vomiting in public.

And then she realized he was crooning to her, his deep voice an almost inaudible murmur as he brushed his lips against her temple, her hair. One strong hand was splayed over her lower belly, spanning her from hipbone to hipbone, covering his child. Her knees felt like noodles, so she let herself continue leaning against him, let her head fall into the curve of his shoulder.

"Easy, sweetheart," he whispered, once again pressing his lips to her temple. "Can you make it back to the car, or do you want me to carry you?"

She couldn't gather her thoughts enough to give him a coherent answer. After no more than a second, he evidently thought he'd given her enough time to decide, so he made the decision for her by scooping her up into his arms. A few quick strides brought them to the car. He bent down and carefully placed her on the seat, lifting her legs into the car, arranging her skirt over them. "Do you want something to drink? A soft drink?"

Something cold and tart sounded wonderful. "No caffeine," she managed to say.

"You won't be out of my sight for more than twenty seconds, but keep an eye out for passing cars, and blow the horn if anything scares you."

She nodded, and he hit the door lock, then closed the door, shutting her inside a cocoon of silence. She preferred the fresh air but understood why she shouldn't be standing outside the car, exposed to view—and an easy target. She leaned her head against the headrest and closed her eyes. The nausea was gone as swiftly as it had come, though her insides felt like jelly. She was weak, and sleepy, and a bit bemused by his sudden tenderness.

Though she shouldn't be surprised, she thought. She was pregnant with his child, and the possibility of exactly that was what had brought him in search of her. As soon as he'd realized she was nauseated, a condition directly related to her condition, so to speak, he'd shown nothing but tender concern and demonstrated once again his ability to make snap decisions in urgent situations.

His tap on the window startled her, because in her sleepy state she hadn't thought he'd been gone nearly long enough to accomplish his mission. But a green can, frosty with condensation, was in his hand, and suddenly she ferociously wanted that drink. She unlocked the door and all but snatched the can from him before he could slide into the seat. She had it popped open and was drinking greedily by the time he closed the door.

When the can was empty, she leaned back with a sigh of contentment. She heard a low, strained laugh and turned her head to find Zane looking at her with both amusement and something hot and feral mingled in his gaze. "That's the first time watching a woman drink a soft drink has made me hard. Do you want another? I'll try to control myself, but a second one might be more than I can stand."

Barrie's eyes widened. A blush warmed her cheeks, but that didn't stop her from looking at his lap. He was telling the truth. Good heavens, was he ever telling the truth! Her hand clenched with the sudden need to reach out and stroke him. "I'm not thirsty now," she said, her voice huskier than usual. "But I'm willing to go for a second one if you are."

The amusement faded out of his eyes, leaving only the heat behind. He was reaching out for her when his head suddenly snapped around, his attention caught by an approaching vehicle. "Here's our ride," he said, and once again his voice was cool and emotionless.

Chapter 10

She was marrying him because she wanted his protection. The thought gnawed at Zane during the long flight to Las Vegas. She sat quietly beside him, sometimes dozing, talking only if he asked her a question. She had the drained look of someone who had been under a lot of pressure, and now that it had eased, her body was giving in to fatigue. Finally she fell soundly asleep, her head resting against his shoulder.

The pregnancy would be taking a toll on her, too. He couldn't see any physical change in her yet, but his three older brothers had produced enough children that he knew how tired women always got the first few months—at least, how tired Shea and Loren had been. Nothing ever slowed Caroline down, not even five sons.

At the thought of the baby, fierce possessiveness jolted through him again. His baby was inside her. He wanted to scoop her onto his lap and hold her, but a crowded plane wasn't the place for what he had in mind. That would have to wait until after the marriage ceremony, when they were in a private hotel room.

He wanted her even more than he had before.

When she had opened the door and he'd looked down into her stunned green eyes, his arousal had been so strong and immediate that he'd had to restrain himself from reaching for her. Only the sight of her father bearing down on them had held him back.

He shouldn't have waited as long as he had. As soon as he'd been able to get around okay, he should have come after her. She had been living in fear, and handling it the same way she had in Benghazi, with calm determination.

He didn't want her ever to be afraid again.

Bunny's and Spooky's arrival at the parking deck, in Bunny's personally customized 1969 Oldsmobile 442, had been like a reunion. Barrie had tumbled out of the rental car with a happy cry and been enthusiastically hugged and twirled around by both SEALs. They were both discreetly armed, he'd noticed approvingly. They were wearing civilian clothes, with their shirts left loose outside their pants to conceal the firepower tucked under their arms and in the smalls of their backs. Normally, when they were off-duty, they didn't carry firearms, but Zane had explained the situation to them and left their preparations to their own discretion, since he wasn't their commanding officer any longer. In typical fashion, they had prepared for anything. His own weapon was still resting in a holster under his left armpit, covered by a lightweight summer jacket.

"Don't you worry none, ma'am," Spooky had reassuringly told Barrie. "We'll get you and the boss to the airport safe and sound. There's nothing outside of NASCAR that can keep up with Bunny's wheels."

"I'm sure there isn't," she'd replied, eyeing the car. It looked unremarkable enough; Bunny had painted it a light gray, and there wasn't any more chrome than would be on a factory job. But the deep-throated rumble from the idling engine didn't sound like any sound a factory engine would make, and the tires were wide, with a soft-looking tread.

"Bulletproof glass, reinforced metal," Bunny said proudly as he helped Zane transfer her luggage to the trunk of his car. "Plate steel would be too heavy for the speed I want, so I went with the new generation of body armor material, lighter and stronger than Kevlar. I'm still working on the fireproofing."

"I'll feel perfectly safe," she assured him.

As she and Zane crawled into the back seat of the two-door car, she whispered to him, "Where's Nascar?"

Spooky could hear a pin drop at forty paces. Slowly he turned around in the front seat, his face mirroring his incredulity. "Not where, ma'am," he said, struggling with shock. "*What.* NASCAR. Stock car racing." A good Southerner, he'd grown up with stock car racing and was always stunned when he encountered someone who hadn't enjoyed the same contact with the sport.

"Oh," Barrie said, giving him an apologetic smile. "I've spent a lot of time in Europe. I don't know anything about racing except for the Grand Prix races."

Bunny snorted in derision. "Play cars," he said dismissively. "You can't run them on the streets. Stock car racing, now that's real racing." As he was speaking, he was wheeling his deceptive monster out of the parking deck, his restless gaze touching on every surrounding detail.

"I've been to horse races," Barrie offered, evidently in an attempt to redeem herself.

Zane controlled a smile at the earnestness of her tone. "Do you ride?" he asked.

Her attention swung to him. "Why, yes. I love horses."

"You'll make a good Mackenzie, then," Spooky

drawled. "Boss raises horses in his spare time." There was a bit of irony in his tone, because SEALs had about as much spare time as albinos had color.

"Do you really?" Barrie asked, her eyes shining.

"I own a few. Thirty or so."

"Thirty!" She sat back, a slight look of confusion on her face. He knew what she was thinking: one horse was expensive to own and keep, let alone thirty. Horses needed a lot of land and care, not something she associated with an ex-Naval officer who had been a member of an elite antiterrorism group.

"It's a family business," he explained, swiveling his head to examine the traffic around them.

"Everything's clear, boss," Bunny said. "Unless they've tagged us with a relay, but I don't see how that's possible."

Zane didn't, either, so he relaxed. A moving relay surveillance took a lot of time and coordination to set up, and the route had to be known. Bunny was taking such a circuitous route to the airport that any tail would long since have been revealed or shaken. Things were under control—for now.

They made it to National without incident, though to be on the safe side Bunny and Spooky had escorted them as far as the security check. While Zane quietly handled his own armed passage through security, his two former team members had taken themselves off to collect the rental car and turn it in, though to the agency office at Dulles, not National, where he had rented it. Just another little twist to delay anyone who was looking for them.

Now that they were safely on the plane, he began planning what he would do to put an end to the situation.

The first part of it was easy. He would put Chance on the job of finding out what kind of mess her father was involved in; for her sake, he hoped it wasn't anything treasonous, but whatever was going on, he intended to put a stop to it. Chance had access to information that put national security agencies to shame. If William Lovejoy was selling out his country, then he would go down. There was no other option. Zane had spent his adult years offering his life in protection of his country, and now he was a peace officer sworn to uphold the law; it was impossible for him to look the other way, even for Barrie. He didn't want her to be hurt, but he damn sure wanted her to be safe.

Barrie slept until the airliner's wheels bounced on the pavement. She sat upright, pushing her hair away from her face, looking about with a slight sense of disorientation. She had never before been able to sleep on a plane; this sleepiness was just one more of the many changes her pregnancy was making in her body, and her lack of control over the process was disconcerting, even frightening.

On the other hand, the rest had given her additional energy, something she needed to face the immense change she was about to make in her life. This change was deliberate, but no less frightening.

"I want to shower and change clothes first," she said firmly. This marriage might be hasty, without any resemblance to the type of wedding ceremony she had always envisioned for herself, but while she was willing to forgo the pomp and expensive trappings, she wasn't willing—outside of a life-and-death situation—to get married wearing wrinkled clothes and still blinking sleep from her eyes.

"Okay. We'll check in to a hotel first." He rubbed his jaw, his callused fingers rasping over his beard stubble. "I need to have a shave anyway."

He had needed to shave that day in Benghazi, too. In a flash of memory she felt again the scrape of his rough chin against her naked breasts, and a wave of heat washed over her, leaving her weak and flushed. The cool air blowing from the tiny vent overhead was suddenly not cool enough.

She hoped he wouldn't notice, but it was a faint hope, because he was trained to take note of every detail around him. She imagined he could describe every passenger within ten rows of them in either direction, and when she'd been awake she had noticed that he'd shown an uncanny awareness of anyone approaching them from the rear on the way to the lavatories.

"Are you feeling sick?" he asked, eyeing the color in her cheeks.

"No, I'm just a little warm," she said with perfect truth, while her blush deepened.

He continued to watch her, and the concern in his eyes changed to a heated awareness. She couldn't even hide that from him, damn it. From the beginning it had been as if he could see beneath her skin; he sensed her reactions almost as soon as she felt them.

Slowly his heavy-lidded gaze moved down to her breasts, studying the slope and thrust of them. She inhaled sharply as her nipples tightened in response to his blatant interest, a response that shot all the way to her loins.

"Are they more sensitive?" he murmured.

Oh, God, he shouldn't do this to her, she thought wildly. They were in the middle of a plane full of people, taxiing toward an empty gate, and he was asking questions about her breasts and looking as if he would start undressing her any minute now.

"Are they?"

"Yes," she whispered. Her entire body felt more sensitive, from both her pregnancy and her acute awareness of him. Soon he would be her husband, and once again she would be lying in his arms.

"Ceremony first," he said, his thoughts echoing hers in that eerie way he had. "Otherwise we won't get out of the hotel until tomorrow."

"Are you psychic?" she accused under her breath.

A slow smile curved his beautiful mouth. "It doesn't take a psychic to know what those puckered nipples mean."

She glanced down and saw her nipples plainly beaded under the lace and silk of her bra and blouse. Her face red, she hastily drew her shirt over the betraying little nubs, and he gave a low laugh. At least no one else was likely to have heard him, she thought with scant comfort. He'd pitched his voice low, and the noise on board made it difficult to overhear conversations, anyway.

The flight attendants were telling them to remain in their seats until the plane was secured and the doors opened, and as usual the instructions were ignored as passengers surged into the aisles, opening the overhead bins and dragging down their carry-on luggage or hauling it out from under the seats. Zane stepped deftly into the aisle, and the movement briefly pulled his jacket open. She saw the holster under his left arm and the polished metal butt of the pistol tucked snugly inside it. Then he automatically shrugged one shoulder, and the jacket fell into place, a movement he'd performed so many times he didn't have to think about it.

She'd known he was armed, of course, because he'd informed the airport and airline security before they'd boarded the plane. During the boredom and enforced inactivity of the flight, however, she had managed to push the recent events from her mind, but the sight of that big automatic brought them all back.

He extended his hand to steady her as she stepped into the aisle ahead of him. Standing pressed like sardines in the line, she felt him like a warm and solid wall at her back, his arms slightly extended so that his hands rested on the seat backs, enveloping her in security. His breath stirred the hair on top of her head, making her realize anew exactly how big he was. She was of average height, but if she leaned back, her head would fit perfectly into the curve of his shoulder.

The man in front of her shifted, forcing her backward, and Zane curved one arm around her as he gathered her against his body, his big hand settling protectively over her lower belly. Barrie bit her lip as her mind bounced from worry to the pleasure of his touch. This couldn't go on much longer—either this exquisite frustration or the sharp darts of terror—or she would lose her mind.

The line of passengers began to shuffle forward as the doors were opened and they were released from the plane. Zane's hand dropped from her belly. As she began to move forward, Barrie caught the eye of an older woman who had chosen to remain in her seat until the stampede was over, and the woman gave her a knowing smile, her gaze flicking to Zane.

"Ma'am," Zane said smoothly in acknowledgment, and Barrie knew he'd caught the little byplay. His acute awareness of his surroundings was beginning to spook her. What if she didn't want him to notice everything? Most women would be thrilled to death with a husband who actually took note of details, but probably not to the extent that Zane Mackenzie did.

On the other hand, if the alternative was living without him, she would learn how to cope, she thought wryly. She'd spent over two months pining for him, and now that she had him, she wasn't about to get cold feet because he was alert. He was a trained warrior—an assassin, her father had called him. He wouldn't have survived if he hadn't been aware of everything going on around him, and neither would she.

That alertness was evident as they followed the signs to the baggage claim area. The airport was a shifting, flowing beehive, and Zane's cool gaze was constantly assessing the people around them. As he had more than once before, he kept himself between her and everybody else, steering her close to the wall and protecting her other side with his body. He'd already taken one bullet while doing that, she thought, and had to fight the sudden terrified impulse to grab him and shove *him* against the wall.

Before they reached the baggage claim, however, he pulled her to a halt. "Let's wait here a minute," he said.

She strove for calm, for mastery over the butterflies that suddenly took flight in her stomach. "Did you see anything suspicious?" she asked.

"No, we're waiting for someone." He looked at her, his cool gaze warming as he studied her face. "You're a gutsy little broad, Miss Lovejoy. No matter what, you hold it together and try to do the best you can. Not bad for a pampered society babe."

Barrie was taken aback. She'd never been called a broad before, or a society babe. If it hadn't been for the teasing glint in his eyes, she might have taken exception to the terms. Instead, she considered them for a moment, then gave a brief nod of agreement. "You're right," she said serenely. "I *am* gutsy for a pampered society babe."

He was surprised into a chuckle, a deliciously rich sound that was cut short when they were approached by a middle-aged man who wore a suit and carried a radio set in his hand. "Sheriff Mackenzie?" he asked.

"Yes."

"Travis Hulsey, airport security." Mr. Hulsey flashed his

identification. "We have your luggage waiting for you in a secure area, as requested. This way, please."

So he'd even thought of that, Barrie marveled as they followed Mr. Hulsey through an unmarked door. An attempt to grab her inside the airport would be tricky, given the security, so the most logical thing to do would be to wait at the ground transportation area, where everyone went after collecting luggage, then follow them to their destination and wait for a better opportunity. Zane had thwarted that; he must have made the arrangements when he'd gone forward to the lavatory.

The dry desert heat slapped them in the face as soon as they stepped through the door. Her three suitcases and his one garment bag, which he had collected from a locker at National, were waiting for them at a discreet entrance well away from the main ground transportation area. Also waiting for them was a car, beside which stood a young man with the distinctive austere military haircut, even though he wore civilian clothes.

The young man all but snapped to attention. "Sir," he said. "Airman Zaharias at your service, sir."

Zane's dark face lit with amusement. "At ease," he said. "I'm not my brother."

Airman Zaharias relaxed with a grin. "When I first saw you, sir, I wasn't sure."

"If he pulled rank and this is messing up your leave time, I'll get other transport."

"I volunteered, sir. The general did me a personal favor when I was fresh out of basic. Giving his brother a ride downtown is the least I can do."

Brother? *General?* Barrie raised some mental eyebrows. First horses, now this. She realized she didn't know anything about her soon-to-be husband's background, but the details she'd gleaned so far were startling, to say the least.

Zane introduced her with grave courtesy. "Barrie, Airman Zaharias is our safe transport, and he has donated his personal vehicle and time off for the service. Airman Zaharias, my fiancée, Barrie Lovejoy."

She solemnly shook hands with the young airman, who was almost beside himself in his eagerness to please.

"Glad to meet you, ma'am." He unlocked the trunk and swiftly began loading their luggage, protesting when Zane lifted two of the bags and stowed them himself. "Let me do that, sir!"

"I'm a civilian now," Zane said, amusement still bright in his eyes. "And I was Navy, anyway."

Airman Zaharias shrugged. "Yes, sir, but you're still the general's brother." He paused, then asked, "Were you really a SEAL?"

"Guilty."

"Damn," Airman Zaharias breathed.

They climbed into the air-conditioned relief of the airman's Chevrolet and were off. Their young driver evidently knew Las Vegas well, and without asking for instructions he ignored the main routes. Instead he circled around and took Paradise Road north out of the airport. He chattered cheerfully the entire time, but Barrie noticed that he didn't mention the exact nature of the favor Zane's general brother had done for him, nor did he venture into personal realms. He talked about the weather, the traffic, the tourists, the hotels. Zane directed him to a hotel off the main drag, and soon Airman Zaharias was on his way and they were checking in to the hotel.

Barrie bided her time, standing quietly to one side while Zane arranged for them to be listed in the hotel's computer as Glen and Alice Temple—how he arrived at those names she had no idea—and ignoring the clerk's knowing smirk. He probably thought they were adulterous lovers on a tryst, which suited her just fine; it would keep him from being curious about them.

They weren't alone in the elevator, so she held her tongue then, too. She held it until they were in the suite Zane had booked, and the bellman had been properly tipped and dismissed. The suite was as luxurious as any she had stayed in in Europe. A few hours before, she might have worried that the cost was more than Zane could afford, that he'd chosen it because he thought she would expect it. Now, however, she had no such illusion. As soon as he had closed and locked the door behind the bellman, she crossed her arms and stared levelly at him. "Horses?" she inquired politely. "Family business? A brother who happens to be an Air Force general?"

He shrugged out of his jacket, then his shoulder holster. "All of that," he said.

"I don't know you at all, do I?" She was calm, even a little bemused, as she watched him wrap the straps around the holster and deposit the weapon on the bedside table.

He unzipped his garment bag and removed a suit from it, then began unpacking other items. His pale glance flashed briefly at her. "You know *me*," he said. "You just don't know all the details of my family yet, but we haven't had much time for casual chatting. I'm not deliberately hiding anything from you. Ask any question you want."

"I don't want to conduct a catechism," she said, though she needed to do exactly that. "It's just..." She spread her hands in frustration, because she was marrying him and she didn't already know all this.

He began unbuttoning his shirt. "I promise I'll give you a complete briefing when we have time. Right now, sweetheart, I'd rather you got your sweet little butt in one shower while I get in the other, so we can get married and into this bed as fast as possible. About an hour after *that,* we'll talk."

She looked at the bed, a bigger-than-king-size. Priorities, priorities, she mused. "Are we safe here?"

"Safe enough for me to concentrate on other things."

She didn't have to ask what those other things were. She looked at the bed again and took a deep breath. "We could rearrange the order of these things," she proposed. "What do you think about bed, talk and then wedding? Say, to-morrow morning?"

He froze in the act of removing his shirt. She saw his eyes darken, saw the sexual tension harden his face. After a moment he pulled the garment free and dropped it to the floor, his movements deliberate. "I haven't kissed you yet," he said.

She swallowed. "I noticed. I've wondered—"

"Don't," he said harshly. "Don't wonder. The reason I haven't kissed you is that, once I start, I won't stop. I know we're doing things out of order—hell, everything's been out of order from the beginning, when you were naked the first time I saw you. I wanted you then, sweetheart, and I want you now, so damn bad I'm aching with it. But trouble is still following you around, and my job is to make damn sure it doesn't get close to you and our baby. I might get killed—"

She made a choked sound of protest, but he cut her off. "It's a possibility, one I accept. I've accepted it for years. I want us married as soon as possible, because I don't know what might happen tomorrow. In case I miscalculate or get unlucky, I want our baby to be legitimate, to be born with the Mackenzie name. A certain amount of protection goes with that name, and I want you to have it. Now."

Tears swam in her eyes as she stared at him, at this man who had already taken one bullet for her and was prepared to take another. He was right—she knew *him*, knew the man he was, even if she didn't know what his favorite color was or what kind of grades he'd made in school. She knew the basics, and it was the basics she had so swiftly and fiercely learned to love. So he wasn't as forthcoming as she might have wished; she would deal with it. So what if he was so controlled it was scary, and so what if those uncanny eyes noticed everything, which would make it difficult to surprise him on Christmas and his birthday? She would deal with that, too, very happily.

If he was willing to die for her, the least she could do was be completely honest with him.

"There's another reason I agreed to marry you," she said.

His dark brows lifted in silent question.

"I love you."

Chapter 11

He wore a dark gray suit with black boots and a black hat. Barrie wore white. It was a simple dress, ankle length and sleeveless, classic in its lines and lack of adornment. She loosely twisted up her dark auburn hair, leaving a few wisps hanging about her face to soften the effect. Her only jewelry was a pair of pearl studs in her ears. She got ready in the bath off the bedroom, he showered in the bath off the parlor. They met at the door between the two rooms, ready to take the step that would make them husband and wife.

At her blunt declaration of love, an equally blunt expression of satisfaction had crossed his face, and for once he didn't hide anything he was feeling. "I don't know about love," he'd said, his voice so even she wanted to shake him. "But I do know I've never wanted another woman the way I want you. I know this marriage is forever. I'll take care of you and our children, I'll come home to you every night, and I'll try my damnedest to make you happy."

It wasn't a declaration of love, but it was certainly one of devotion, and the tears that came so easily to her these days swam in her eyes. Her self-contained warrior *would* love her, when he lowered his guard enough to let himself. He had spent years with his emotions locked down, while he operated in tense, life-and-death situations that demanded cool, precise thoughts and decisions. Love was neither cool nor concise; it was turbulent, unpredictable, and it left one vulnerable. He would approach love as cautiously as if it was a bomb.

"Don't cry," he said softly. "I swear I'll be a good husband."

"I know," she replied, and then they had both gone to their separate bathrooms to prepare for their wedding.

They took a taxi to a chapel, one of the smaller ones that didn't get as much business and didn't have a drive-through service. Getting married in Las Vegas didn't take a great deal of effort, though Zane took steps to make it special. He bought her a small bouquet of flowers and gave her a bracelet of dainty gold links, which he fastened around her right wrist. Her heart beat heavily as they stood before the justice of the peace, and the bracelet seemed to burn around her wrist. Zane held her left hand securely in his right, his grip warm and gentle, but unbreakable.

Outwardly it was all very civilized, but from the first moment they'd met, Barrie had been acutely attuned to him, and she sensed the primal possessiveness of his actions. He had already claimed her physically, and now he was doing it legally. She already carried his child inside her. His air of masculine satisfaction was almost visible, it was so strong. She felt it, too, as she calmly spoke her vows, this linkage of their lives. During a long, hot day in Benghazi they had forged a bond that still held, despite the events that had forced them apart.

He had one more surprise for her. She hadn't expected a ring, not on such short notice, but at the proper moment he reached into the inside pocket of his jacket and produced two plain gold bands, one for her and one for him. Hers was a little loose when he slipped it over her knuckle, but their eyes met in a moment of perfect understanding. She would be gaining weight, and soon the ring would fit. She took the bigger, wider band and slid it onto the ring finger of his left hand, and she felt her own thrill of primal satisfaction. He was hers, by God!

Their marriage duly registered, the certificate signed and witnessed, they took another taxi to the hotel. "Supper," he said, steering her toward one of the hotel's dining rooms. "You didn't eat anything on the plane, and it's after midnight eastern time."

"We could order room service," she suggested.

His eyes took on that heavy-lidded look. "No, we couldn't." His tone was definite, a little strained. His hand was warm and heavy on the small of her back. "You need to eat, and I don't trust my self-control to last that long unless we're in a public place."

Perhaps feeding her was his only concern, or perhaps he knew more about seduction than most men, she thought as they watched each other over a progression of courses. Knowing that he was going to make love to her as soon as they reached the suite, anticipating the heaviness of his weight on her, the hard thrust of his turgid length into her…the frustration readied her for him as surely as if he was stroking her flesh. Her breasts lifted hard and swollen against the bodice of her dress. Her insides tightened with desire, so that she had to press her legs together to ease the throbbing. His gaze kept dropping to her breasts, and as before, she couldn't temper her response. She could feel her own moisture, feel the heaviness in her womb.

She was scarcely aware of what she ate—something bland, to reduce the chances of early-pregnancy nausea. She drank only water. But turnabout was fair play, so she lingered over each bite while she stared at his mouth, or in the direction of his lap. She delicately licked her lips, shivering with delight as his face darkened and his jaw set. She stroked the rim of her water glass with one fingertip, drawing his gaze, making his breath come harder and faster. Beneath the table, she rubbed her foot against the muscled calf of his leg.

He turned to snare their waiter with a laser glare. "Check!" he barked, and the waiter hurried to obey that voice of command. Zane scribbled their room number and his fictitious name on the check, and Barrie stared at him in amazement. It was hard to believe he could remember something like that when she could barely manage to walk.

For revenge, when he pulled her chair back so she could stand, she allowed the knuckles of one hand to brush, oh, so very lightly, against his crotch. He went absolutely rigid for a moment, and his breath hissed out between his teeth. All innocence, Barrie turned to give him a sweetly inquiring What's-wrong? look.

His darkly tanned face was even darker with the flush running under the browned skin. His expression was set, giving away little, but his eyes were glittering like shards of diamond. His big hand closed firmly around her elbow. "Let's go," he said in the soundless whisper she'd first heard in a dark room in Benghazi. "And don't do that again, or I swear I'll have you in the elevator."

"Really." She smiled at him over her shoulder. "How...uplifting."

A faint but visible shudder racked him, and the look he

gave her promised retribution. "Here I've been thinking you were so sweet."

"I am sweet," she declared as they marched toward the elevator. "But I'm not a pushover."

"We'll see about that. I'm going to push you over." They reached the bank of elevators, and he jabbed the call button with more force than necessary.

"You won't have to push hard. As a matter of fact, you can just blow me over." She gave him another sweet smile and pursed her lips, blowing a tiny puff of air against his chest to demonstrate.

The bell chimed, the doors opened, and they stood back to allow the car's passengers to exit. They stepped inside alone, and even though people were hurrying toward them to catch that car, Zane ruthlessly punched their floor number and then the door close button. When the car began to rise, he turned on her like a tiger on fresh meat.

She stepped gracefully out of his reach, staring at the numbers flashing on the digital display. "We're almost there."

"You're damn right about that," he growled, coming after her. In the small confines of the elevator she didn't have a chance of evading him, not that she wanted to. What she wanted was to drive him as crazy as he was driving her. His hard hands closed around her waist and lifted her; his muscled body pinned her to the wall. His hips pushed insistently at hers, and she gasped at how hard he was. Automatically her legs opened, allowing him access to the tender recesses of her body. He thrust against her, his hips moving rhythmically, and his mouth came down on hers, smothering, fiercely hungry.

The bell chimed softly, and the elevator gave a slight lurch as it stopped. Zane didn't release her. He simply turned with her still in his grasp and left the elevator, striding rapidly down the hall to their suite. Barrie twined her arms around his neck and her legs around his hips, biting back little moans as each stride he took rubbed his swollen sex against the aching softness of her loins. Pleasure arced through her like lightning with every step, and helplessly she felt her hips undulate against him in a mindless search for a deeper pleasure. A low curse hissed out from between his clenched teeth.

She didn't know if they passed anyone in the hall. She buried her face against his neck and gave in to the soaring hunger. She had needed him for so long, missed him, worried herself sick about him. Now he was here, vitally alive, about to take her with the same uncomplicated fierceness as before, and she didn't care about anything else.

He pushed her against a wall, and for one terrified, delirious moment she thought she had tempted him too much. Instead he unhooked her legs from around his waist and let her slide to the floor. He was breathing hard, his eyes dilated with a sexual hunger that wouldn't be denied much longer, but on one level he was still very much in control. Lifting one finger to his lips to indicate silence, he slipped his right hand inside his jacket. When his hand emerged, it was filled with the butt of that big automatic. He thumbed off the safety, dealt with the electronic lock on the door to their suite, depressed the door handle and slipped noiselessly inside. The door closed as silently as it had opened.

Barrie stood frozen in the hallway, sudden terror chasing away her desire as she waited with her eyes closed and her hands clenched into fists, all her concentration focused on trying to hear anything from inside the suite. She heard nothing. Absolutely nothing. Zane moved like a cat, but so did other men, men like him, men who worked best under cover of night and who could kill as silently as he had dispatched that guard in Benghazi. Her kidnappers hadn't possessed the same expertise, but whoever was behind her abduction wouldn't use Middle Eastern men here in the middle of the glitter and flash of Las Vegas. Perhaps this time he would hire someone more deadly, someone more interested in getting the job done than in terrifying a bound and helpless woman. Any thump, any whisper, might signal the end of Zane's life, and she thought she would shatter under the strain.

She didn't hear the door open again. All she heard was Zane saying, "All clear," in a calm, normal tone, and then she was in his arms again. She didn't think she moved; she thought he simply gathered her in, pulling her into the security of his embrace.

"I'm sorry," he murmured against her hair as he carried her inside. He paused to lock and chain the door. "But I won't take chances with your safety."

Fury roared through her like a brushfire. She lifted her head from the sanctuary of his shoulder and glared at him. "What about yours?" she demanded violently. "Do you have any idea what it does to me when you do things like that? Do you think I don't notice when you put yourself between me and other people, so if anyone shoots at me, you'll be the one with the bullet hole?" She hit him on the chest with a clenched fist, amazing even herself; she had never struck anyone before. She hit him again. "Damn it, I want you healthy and whole! I want our baby to have its daddy! I want to have more of your babies, so that means you have to stay alive, do you hear me?"

"I hear," he rumbled, his tone soothing as he caught her pounding fists and pressed them against his chest, stilling them. "I'd like the same things myself. That means I have to do whatever's necessary to keep you and Junior safe."

She relaxed against him, her lips trembling as she fought back tears. She wasn't a weepy person; it was just the hormonal roller coaster of pregnancy that was making her so, but still, she didn't want to cry all over him. He had enough to handle without having to deal with a sobbing wife every time he turned around.

When she could manage a steady tone, she said in a small voice, "Junior, is it?"

She saw the flash of his grin as he lifted her in his arms. "I'm afraid so," he said as he carried her to the bed. "My sister Maris is the only female the Mackenzies have managed to produce, and that was twenty-nine years and ten boys ago."

He bent and gently placed her on the bed and sat down beside her. His dark face was intent as he reached beneath her for the zipper of her dress. "Now let's see if I can get you back to where you were before you got scared, and we'll introduce Junior to his daddy," he whispered.

Barrie was seized by a mixture of shyness and uneasiness as he stripped the dress down her hips and legs, then tossed it aside. Since her kidnappers had stripped her in a deliberate attempt to terrorize her, to break her spirit, she hadn't been comfortable with being naked. Except for those hours hidden in the ruins in Benghazi, when Zane had finally coaxed her out of his shirt and she had lost herself in his lovemaking, she had hurried through any times of necessary nudity, such as when she showered, pulling on clothes or a robe as soon as possible. Once upon a time she had lingered after her bath, enjoying the wash of air over her damp skin as she pampered herself with perfumed oils and lotions, but for the past two months that luxury had fallen beneath her urgent need to be covered.

Zane wanted her naked.

Her dress was already gone, and the silk and lace of her matching bra and underpants weren't much protection. Deftly he thumbed open the front fastening of her bra, and the cups loosened, sliding apart to reveal the inner curves of her breasts. Barrie couldn't help herself; she protectively crossed her arms over her breasts, holding the bra in place.

Zane paused, his face still as his pale gaze lifted to her face, examining the helpless, embarrassed expression she wore. She didn't have to explain. He'd been there; he knew. "Still having problems with that shirt?" he asked gently, referring to the way she'd clung so desperately to his garment.

He'd switched on a single lamp. She lay exposed in the small circle of light, while his face was shadowed. She moistened her lips and nodded once, a slight acknowledgment that was all he needed.

"We can't undo things," he said, his face and tone serious. Using one finger, he lightly stroked the upper curves of her breasts, where they plumped above the protection of her crossed arms. "We can put them behind us and move on, but we can't undo them. They stay part of us, they change us inside, but as other things happen, we change still more. I remember the face of the first man I killed. I don't regret doing it, because he was a bomb-happy piece of scum who had left his calling card on a cruise ship, killing nine old people who were just trying to enjoy their retirement. Right then he was trying like hell to kill *me*...but I always carry his face with me, deep inside."

He paused, thinking, remembering. "He's a part of me now, because killing him changed me. He made me stronger. I know that I can do whatever has to be done, and I know how to go on. I've killed others," he said, as calmly as if he was discussing the weather, "but I don't remember their faces. Only his. And I'm glad I won."

Barrie stared at him, the shadows emphasizing the planes and hollows of his somber face, deepening the oldness in his eyes. Deep inside she understood, the realization going past thought into the center of instinct. Being kidnapped had changed her; she'd faced that before Zane had rescued her. She *was* stronger, more decisive, more willing to take action. When he'd shown up that afternoon, she had been preparing to take extraordinary measures to protect herself and the child she carried by disappearing from the comfortable life she'd always known. She'd been naked with Zane before—and enjoyed it. She would again.

Slowly she lifted one hand and stroked the precise line of the small scar on his left cheekbone. He turned his head a little, rubbing his cheek against her fingers.

"Take off *your* clothes," she suggested softly. Balance. If her nudity was balanced by his, she would be more comfortable.

His eyebrows quirked upward. "All right."

She didn't have to explain, but then, she'd known she wouldn't. She lay on the bed and watched him peel out of his jacket, then remove the shoulder holster, which once more carried its lethal cargo. This last was carefully placed on the bedside table, where it would be within reach. Then his shirt came off, and he dropped it on the floor, along with her dress and his jacket.

The new scar on his upper abdomen was red and puckered, and bisected by a long surgical scar where the ship's surgeon had sliced into him to stop the bleeding and save his life. She had seen the scar before, when he had removed his shirt before showering, but she had been under orders not to touch him then lest she make him forget his priorities. There was no such restriction now.

Her fingers moved over the scar, feeling the heat and vitality of the man, and she thought how easily all of that could have been snuffed out. She had come so close to losing him....

"Don't think about it," he murmured, catching her hand and lifting it to his lips. "It didn't happen."

"It could have."

"It didn't." His tone was final as he bent over to tug off his boots. They dropped to the floor with twin thuds, then he stood to unfasten his pants.

He was right. It hadn't happened. Pick yourself up, learn something, and go on. It was in the past. The future was their marriage, their child. The present was *now,* and as Zane swiftly stripped off his remaining clothes, a lot more urgent.

He sat beside her again, comfortable in his own skin. It was such wonderful skin, she thought a little dreamily, reaching out to stroke his gleaming shoulders and furry chest and rub the tiny nipples hidden among the hair until they stood stiffly erect. She knew she was inviting him to reciprocate, and her breath caught in her chest as she waited for him to accept.

He wasn't slow about it. His hands went to the parted cups of her bra, and his gaze lifted to hers. "Ready?" he asked with a slight smile.

She didn't reply, just shrugged one shoulder so that her breast slid free of the cup, and that was answer enough.

He glanced downward as he pushed the other cup aside, and she saw his pupils flare with arousal as he looked at her. His breath hissed out through parted lips. "I see our baby here," he whispered, gently touching one nipple with a single fingertip. "You haven't gained any weight, your stomach's still flat, but he's changed you here. Your nipples are darker, and swollen." Ever so lightly, his touch circled the aureola, making it pucker and stand upright. Barrie whimpered with the rush of desire, the familiar lightning strike from breast to loin.

He rubbed his thumb over the tip, then gently curved his

hand beneath her breast, lifting it so that it plumped in his palm. "How much more sensitive are they?" he asked, never looking up from his absorption with these new details in her body.

"Some—sometimes I can't bear the touch of my bra." she breathed.

"Your veins are bluer, too," he murmured. "They look like rivers running under a layer of white satin." He leaned down and kissed her, taking possession of her mouth while he continued to fondle her breasts with exquisite care. She melted with a purring little hum of pleasure, lifting herself so she could taste him more deeply. His lips were as hot and forceful as she remembered, as delicious. He took his time; the kiss was slow and deep, his tongue probing. Her pregnancy-sensitive breasts hardened into almost painful arousal, her loins becoming warm and liquid.

He bore her down onto the pillows, his hands slipping over her body, completely removing the bra and then disposing of her underpants. His eyes glittered hotly as he leaned over her. "I'm going to do everything to you I couldn't do before," he whispered. "We don't have to worry about being on guard, or making noise, or what time it is. I'm going to eat you up, Little Red."

She should have been alarmed, because his expression was so fierce and hungry she could almost take him literally. Instead, she reached out for him, almost frantic with the need to feel him covering her, taking her.

He had other ideas. He caught her hands and pressed them to the bed, as she had once done to him. He had trusted her with control, and now she returned the gift, arching her body up for whatever was his pleasure.

His pleasure was her breasts, with their fascinating changes. He took one distended nipple into his mouth, carefully, lightly. That was enough to make her moan, though not with pain; the prickles of sensation were incredibly intense. His tongue batted at her nipple, swirled around it, then pushed it hard against the roof of his mouth as he began suckling.

Her cry was thin, wild. Her breath exploded out of her lungs, and she couldn't seem to draw in any replacement air. Oh, God, she hadn't realized her breasts were *that* sensitive, or that he would so abruptly push her past both pleasure and pain into a realm so raw and powerful she couldn't bear it. She surged upward, and he controlled the motion, holding her down, transferring his mouth to her other nipple, which received the same tender care and enticement, then the sudden, deliberate pressure that made her cry out again.

He wouldn't stop. She screamed for him to, begged him, but he wouldn't stop. She heard her voice, frantic, pleading: "Zane—please. Oh, God, please. Don't—more. *More.*" And then, sobbing, *"Harder!"* And she realized she wasn't begging him to stop, but to continue. She writhed in his arms as he pushed her higher and higher, harder and harder, his mouth voracious on her breasts, and suddenly all her senses coalesced into a huge single throb that centered in her loins, and she came apart with pleasure.

When she could breathe again, think again, her limbs were weak and useless in the aftermath. She lay limply on the bed, her eyes closed, and wondered how she had survived the implosion.

"Just from sucking your breasts?" he murmured incredulously as he kissed his way down her stomach. "Oh, damn, are we going to have fun for the next seven months!"

"Zane...wait," she whispered, lifting one hand to his head. It was the only movement she had enough energy to make. "I can't—I need to rest."

He slid down between her legs and lifted her thighs onto his shoulders. "You don't have to move," he promised her in a deep, rich voice. "All you have to do is lie there." Then he kissed her, slowly, deeply, and her body arched as it began all over again, and he showed her all the things he hadn't been able to do to her before.

He brought her to completion once more before finally crawling forward and settling his hips between her thighs. She moaned when he filled her with a smooth, powerful thrust. She quivered beneath him, shocked by the thickness and depth of his penetration. How could she have forgotten? The discomfort took her by surprise, and she clung to him as she tried to adjust, to accept. He soothed her, whispering hot, soft words in her ear, stroking her flesh, which was already so sensitive that even the smooth sheet beneath her felt abrasive.

But, oh, how she had wanted this. *This.* Not just pleasure, but the sense of being joined together, the deep and intimate linkage of their bodies. This fed a craving within her that the climaxes he'd given her hadn't begun to touch. Her hips lifted. She wanted all of him, wanted him so deep that he touched her womb, ripening with his seed. He tried to moderate the thrusts that were rapidly pushing her toward yet another climax, but she dug her nails into his back, insisting without words on everything he had to give.

He shuddered, and with a deep-throated groan, gave her what she asked.

She slept then. It was long after midnight on the east coast, and she was exhausted. She was disturbed by the presence of the big, muscled man beside her in the bed, though, his body radiating heat like a furnace, and she kept waking from a restless doze.

He must sleep like a cat, she thought, because every time she woke and changed positions, he woke up, too. Finally he pulled her on top of him, settling her with her face tucked against his neck and her legs straddling his hips. "Maybe now you can rest," he murmured, kissing her hair. "You slept this way in Benghazi."

She remembered that, remembered the long day of making love, how he had sometimes been on top when they dozed, and sometimes she had. Or perhaps she had been the only one who dozed while he had remained alert.

"I've never slept with a man before," she murmured in sleepy explanation, nestling against him. "*Slept* slept, that is."

"I know. I'm your first in both cases."

The room was dark; at some time he had turned off the lamp, though she didn't remember when. The heavy curtains were drawn against the neon of the Las Vegas night, with only thin strips of light penetrating around the edges. It reminded her briefly of that horrible room in Benghazi, before Zane had taken her away, but then she shut out the memory. That no longer had the power to frighten her. Zane was her husband now, and the pleasant ache in her body told her that the marriage had been well and truly consummated.

"Tell me about your family," she said, and yawned against his neck.

"Now?"

"Mmm. We're both awake, so you might as well."

There was a twitch of flesh against her inner thigh. "I can think of other things to do," he muttered.

"I'm not ruling anything out." She wriggled her hips and was rewarded by a more insistent movement. "But you can talk, too. Tell me about the Mackenzie clan."

She could feel his slight shrug. "My dad is a half-breed American Indian, my mom is a schoolteacher. They live on a mountain just outside Ruth, Wyoming. Dad raises and trains horses. He's the best I've ever seen, except for my sister. Maris is magic with horses.''

"So the horses really are a family business."

"Yep. We were all raised on horseback, but Maris is the only one who went into the training aspect. Joe went to the Air Force Academy and became a jet jockey, Mike became a cattle rancher, Josh rode jets for the Navy, and Chance and I went to the Naval Academy and got our water wings. We can both fly various types of aircraft, but flying is just a means of getting us to where we're needed, nothing else. Chance got out of Naval Intelligence a couple of years ago."

Barrie's talent with names kicked in. She lifted her head, all sleepiness gone as she ran that list of names through her head. She settled on one, put the details together and gasped. "Your brother is General Joe Mackenzie on the Joint Chiefs of Staff?" Of course. How many Joe Mackenzies were Air Force generals?

"The one and only."

"Why, I've met him and his wife. I think it was the year before last, at a charity function in Washington. Her name is Caroline."

"You're right on target." He shifted a little, and she felt a nudging between her legs. She inhaled as he slipped inside her. Talk about right on target.

"Joe and Caroline have five sons, Michael and Shea have two boys, and Josh and Loren have three," Zane murmured, gently thrusting. "Junior will be the eleventh grandchild."

Barrie sank against him, her attention splintered by the pleasure building with each movement of his hips. "Don't talk," she said, and heard his quiet laughter as he rolled over and placed her beneath him...just where she wanted to be.

Chapter 12

Barrie awoke to nausea, sharp and urgent. She bolted out of bed and into the bathroom, barely reaching it in time. When the bout of vomiting was over, she sank weakly to the floor and closed her eyes, unable to work up enough energy to care that she was curled naked on the floor of a hotel bathroom, or that her husband of less than twelve hours was witness to it all. She heard Zane running water; then a wonderfully cool, wet washcloth was placed on her heated forehead. He flushed the toilet, something she hadn't been able to manage, and said, "I'll be right back."

As usual, she rapidly began to feel better after she had thrown up. Embarrassed, she got up and washed out her mouth and was standing in front of the mirror surveying her tousled appearance with some astonishment when Zane appeared with a familiar green can in his hand.

He had already popped the top. She snatched the can from him and began greedily drinking, tilting the can up like some college freshman guzzling beer. When it was empty, she sighed with repletion and slammed the can down on the countertop as if it was indeed an empty soldier of spirits. Then she looked at Zane, and her eyes widened.

"I hope you didn't go out to the drink machine like that," she said faintly. He was still naked. Wonderfully, impressively naked. And very aroused.

He looked amused. "I got it out of the minibar in the parlor." He glanced down at himself, and the amusement deepened. "There's another can. Want to go for it?"

Barrie drew herself up and folded a bold hand around his thrusting sex. "I'm not the kind of woman who loses her inhibitions after a couple of Seven-Ups," she informed him with careful dignity. She paused, then winked at him. "One will do."

Somehow she had expected they would make it back to the bed. They didn't. His hunger was particularly strong in the mornings, and after a tempestuous few moments she found herself on her knees, half bent over the edge of the bathtub while he crouched behind her. Their lovemaking was raw and fast and powerful, and left her once again lying weakly on the floor. She found some satisfaction in the fact that he was sprawled beside her, his long legs stretched under the vanity top.

After a long time he said lazily, "I'd thought I could wait until we were in the shower. I underestimated the effect of a soft drink on you, sweetheart...and what watching you drink it does to me."

"I think we're on to something," she reflected, curling nakedly against him and ignoring the chill of the floor. "We need to buy stock in the company."

"Good idea." He turned his head and began kissing her, and for a moment she wondered if the bathroom floor was going to get another workout. But he released her and rose lithely to his feet, then helped her up. "Do you want to have room service, or go down to a restaurant for break-fast?''

''Room service.'' She was already hungry, and with room service their breakfast should be there by the time she showered and dressed. She gave Zane her order, then, while he called it in, she selected the clothes she wanted. The silk dress was badly wrinkled, so she carried it into the bathroom with her to let the steam from her shower repair the damage.

She took her time in the shower, but even so, some wrinkles remained in the dress by the time she finished. She left the water running and turned it on hot to increase the amount of steam. On a hook behind the door hung a thick terry-cloth bathrobe with the hotel's logo stitched on the breast pocket. She pulled it on and belted it around her, smiling at the weight and size of the garment, and went out to see how long it would be before their breakfast arrived.

Zane wasn't in the bedroom; she could hear him talking in the parlor, and wondered if room service had been un-usually quick. But she heard only his voice as she walked to the open door.

He was on the phone, half-turned away from her as he sat on the arm of the couch. She had the impression that he was listening to the shower running even as he carried on his conversation.

''Keep the tail on her father, as well as on *his* tail,'' he was saying. ''I want to catch them all at one time, so I don't have to worry about any loose ends. When the dust settles, Justice and State can sort it out between them.''

Barrie gasped, all the color washing out of her face. Zane's head jerked around, and he stared at her, the blue mostly gone from his eyes, leaving them as sharp and gray as frost.

''Yeah,'' he said into the receiver, his gaze never wavering from hers. "Everything's under control here. Keep the pressure on." He hung up and turned fully to face her.

He hadn't showered yet, she noticed dully. His hair wasn't wet; there was no betraying dampness to his skin. He must have gotten on the phone as soon as she had begun her shower, setting in motion the betrayal that could send her father to jail.

"What have you done?" she whispered, barely holding herself together against the pain that racked her. "Zane, *what have you done?*"

Coolly he stood and came toward her. Barrie backed up, clutching the lapels of the thick robe as if it could protect her.

He flicked a curious glance toward the bathroom, where billows of steam were escaping from the half-open door. "Why is the shower still running?"

"I'm steaming the wrinkles out of my dress," she answered automatically.

His eyebrows lifted wryly. Though she didn't find the pun amusing, she had the thought that this was evidently a wrinkle he hadn't anticipated.

"Who were you talking to?" she asked, her voice stiff with hurt and betrayal and the strain of holding it all under control.

"My brother Chance."

"What does he have to do with my father?"

Zane watched her steadily. "Chance does intelligence work for a government agency; not the FBI or CIA."

Barrie swallowed against the constriction in her throat. Maybe Zane hadn't betrayed her father; maybe he'd already been under surveillance. "How long has he been following my father?"

"Chance is directing the tails, not doing them himself," Zane corrected.

"How long?"

"Since last night. I called him while you were showering then, too."

At least he didn't try to lie or evade. "How could you?" she whispered, her eyes wide and stark.

"Very easily," he replied, his voice sharp. "I'm an officer of the law. Before that, I was an officer in the Navy, in service to this country. Did you think I would ignore a traitor, even if it's your father? You asked me to protect you and our baby, and that's exactly what I'm doing. When you clean out a nest of snakes, you don't pick out a few of them to kill and leave the others. You wipe them out."

The edges of her vision blurred, and she felt herself sway. Oh, God, how could she ever forgive him if her father went to prison? How could she ever forgive herself? She was the cause of this. She had known the kind of man Zane was, but she had allowed herself to ignore it because she'd wanted him so desperately. Of course he'd turned her father in; if she'd been thinking clearly, instead of with her emotions, her hormones, she would have known exactly what he would do, what he had done. It didn't take a genius to predict the actions of a man who had spent his life upholding the laws of his country, and only a fool would ignore the obvious conclusion.

She hadn't even thought about it, so she guessed that made her the biggest fool alive.

She heard him say her name, his tone insistent, and then her vision was blocked by his big body as he gripped her arms.

Desperately she hung on to consciousness, gulping in air and refusing to let herself faint. "Let go of me," she protested, and was shocked at how far away her voice sounded.

"Like hell I will." Instead he swung her off her feet and

carried her to the bed, then bent to place her on the tumbled sheets.

As he had the night before, he sat beside her. Now that she was lying down, her head cleared rapidly. He was leaning over her, one arm braced on the other side of her hip, enclosing her in the iron circle of his embrace. His gaze never left her face.

Barrie wished she could find refuge in anger, but there was none. She understood Zane's motives, and his actions. All she could feel was a huge whirlpool of pain, sucking her down. Her father! As much as she loved Zane, she didn't know if she could bear it if he caused her father to be arrested. This wasn't anything like theft or drunken driving. Treason was heinous, unthinkable. No matter what conclusion her logic drew, she simply couldn't see her father doing anything like that, unless he was somehow being forced to do it. She knew *she* wasn't the weapon being used against him, although she had been drawn into it, probably when he had balked at something. No, she and Zane had both realized immediately that if she was being threatened and her father had nothing to hide, he would have had her whisked away by the FBI before she knew what was happening.

"Please," she begged, clutching his arm. "Can't you warn him somehow, get him out of it? I know you didn't like him, but you don't know him the way I do. He's always done what he thought was best for me. He was always there when I needed him, and b-before I left he gave me his blessing." Her voice broke on a sob, and she quickly controlled it. "I know he's a snob, but he isn't a bad person! If he's gotten involved in something he shouldn't, it was by accident, and now he doesn't know how to get out without endangering me! That *has* to be it. Zane, please!"

He caught her hand, folding it warmly within his. "I

can't do that," he said quietly. "If he hasn't done anything wrong, he'll be all right. If he's a traitor—" He shrugged, indicating the lack of options. He wouldn't lift a finger to help a traitor, period. "I didn't want you to know anything about it because I didn't want you to be upset any more than necessary. I knew I wouldn't be able to protect you from worry if he's arrested, but I didn't want you to find out about it beforehand. You've had enough to deal with these past couple of months. My first priority is keeping you and the baby safe, and I'll do that, Barrie, no matter what."

She stared at him through tear-blurred eyes, knowing she had collided with the steel wall of his convictions. Honor wasn't just a concept to him, but a way of life. Still, there was one way she might reach him. "What if it was *your* father?" she asked.

A brief spasm touched his face, telling her that she'd struck a nerve. "I don't know," he admitted. "I hope I'd be able to do what's right...but I don't know."

There was nothing more she could say.

The only thing she could do was warn her father herself.

She moved away from him, sliding off the bed. He lifted his arm and let her go, though he watched her closely, as if waiting for her to faint or throw up or slap him in the face. Considering her pregnancy and her state of mind, she realized, all three were possible, if she relaxed her control just a fraction. But she wasn't going to do any of them, because she couldn't afford to waste the time.

She hugged the oversize robe about her, as she had once hugged his shirt. "What exactly is your brother doing?" She needed as much information as possible if she was going to help her father. Maybe it was wrong, but she would worry about that, and face the consequences, later. She knew she was operating on love and blind trust, but that was all she had to go on. When she thought of her father as the man she knew him to be, she knew she had to trust both that knowledge and his honor. Despite their enormous differences, in that respect he was very like Zane, the man he'd scorned as a son-in-law: honor was a part of his code, his life, his very being.

Zane stood. "You don't need to know, exactly."

For the first time she felt the flush of anger redden her cheeks. "Don't throw my words back at me," she snapped. "You can say no without being sarcastic."

He studied her, then gave a curt nod. "You're right. I'm sorry."

She stalked into the bathroom and slammed the door. The small room was hot and damp with steam, the air thick with it. Barrie turned off the shower and turned on the exhaust fan. There wasn't a wrinkle left in the silk dress. Hurriedly she shed the robe and pulled on the underwear she'd carried into the bathroom, then pulled the dress on over her head. The silk stuck to her damp skin; she had to jerk the fabric to get it into place. The need to hurry beat through her like wings. How much time did she have before room service arrived with their breakfast?

The mirror was fogged over. She grabbed a towel and rubbed a clear spot on the glass, then swiftly combed her hair and began applying a minimum of makeup. The air was so steamy that it would be a wasted effort to apply very much, but she wanted to appear as normal as possible.

Oh, God, the exhaust fan was making so much noise she might not have heard their breakfast arriving. Hastily she cut it off. Zane would have knocked if their food was here, she assured herself. It hadn't arrived yet.

She tried to remember where her purse was, and think how she could get it and get out the door without Zane knowing. His hearing was acute, and he would be watching for her. But the room service waiter would bring their breakfast to the parlor, and Zane, being as cautious as he was, would watch the man's every move. That was the only time he would be distracted, and the only chance she would have to get out of the room undetected. Her window of opportunity would be brief, because he would call her as soon as the waiter left. If she had to wait for an elevator, she was sunk. She could always try the stairs, but all Zane would have to do was take the elevator down to the lobby and wait for her there. With his hearing, he probably heard the elevator every time it chimed, and that would give him an idea of whether she had been able to get one of the cars or had taken the stairs.

She opened the bathroom door a little, so he wouldn't be able to catch the click of the latch.

"What are you doing?" he called. It sounded as if he was standing just inside the double doors that connected the bedroom to the parlor, waiting for her.

"Putting on makeup," she snapped, with perfect truth. She blotted the sweat off her forehead and began again with the powder. Her brief flash of anger was over, but she didn't want him to know it. Let him think she was furious; a woman who was both pregnant and angry deserved a lot of space.

There was a brief knock on the parlor door, and a Spanish-accented voice called out, "Room service."

Quickly Barrie switched on the faucet, so the sound of running water would once again mask her movements. Peering through the small opening by the door, she saw Zane cross her field of vision, going to answer the knock. He was wearing his shoulder holster, which meant, as she had hoped, that he was on guard.

She slipped out of the bathroom, carefully pulled the door back to leave the same small opening, then darted to the other side of the bedroom, out of his line of sight if he glanced inside when he passed by the double doors. Her purse was lying on one of the chairs, and she snatched it up, then slipped her feet into her shoes.

The room service cart clattered as it was rolled into the room. Through the open parlor doors she could hear the waiter casually chatting as he set up the table. Zane's pistol made the waiter nervous; she could hear it in his voice. And his nervousness made Zane that much more wary of him. Zane was probably watching him like a hawk, those pale eyes remote and glacier-cold.

Now was the tricky part. She eased up to the open double doors, peeking through the crack to locate her husband. Relief made her knees wobble; he was standing with his back to the doors while he watched the waiter. The running faucet was doing its job; he was listening to it, rather than positioning himself on the other side of the table so he could watch both the waiter and the bathroom door. He probably did it deliberately, dividing his senses rather than diluting the visual attention he was paying to the waiter.

Her husband was not an ordinary man. Escaping him, even for five minutes, wouldn't be easy.

Taking a deep breath, she silently crossed the open expanse, every nerve in her body drawn tight as she waited for his hard hand to clamp down on her shoulder. She reached the bedroom door to the hallway and held the chain so it wouldn't clink when she slipped it free. That done, her next obstacle was the lock. She moved her body as close to the door as possible, using her flesh to muffle the sound, and slowly turned the latch. The dead bolt slid open with smooth precision and a snick that was barely audible even to her.

She closed her eyes and turned the handle then, concentrating on keeping the movement smooth and silent. If it made any noise, she was caught. If anyone was walking by in the hallway and talking, the change in noise level would alert Zane, and she was caught. If the elevator was slow, she was caught. Everything had to be perfect, or she didn't have a chance.

How much longer did she have? It felt as if she had already taken ten minutes, but it was probably no more than one. Crockery was still rattling in the parlor as the waiter arranged their plates and saucers and water glasses. The door opened, and she slipped through, then spent the same agonizing amount of time making sure it closed as silently as it opened. She released the handle and ran.

She reached the elevators without hearing him shout her name and jabbed the down button. It obediently lit, and remained lit. There was no welcoming chime to signal the arrival of the elevator. Barrie restrained herself from punching the button over and over again in a futile attempt to convey her urgency to a piece of machinery.

"Please," she whispered under her breath. *"Hurry."*

She would have tried calling her father from the hotel room, but she knew Zane would stop her if he heard her on the phone. She also knew her father's phone was tapped, which meant that incoming calls were automatically recorded. She would try to protect her father, but she refused to do anything that might endanger either Zane or their baby by leading the kidnappers straight to the hotel. She would have to call her father from a pay phone on the street, and a different street, at that.

Down the hall, she heard the room service cart clatter again as the waiter left their suite. Her heart pounding, she stared at the closed elevator doors, willing them to open. Her time was down to mere seconds.

The melodic chime sounded overhead.

The doors slid open.

She looked back as she stepped inside, and her heart nearly stopped. Zane hadn't yelled, hadn't called her name. He was running full speed down the hall, his motion as fluid and powerful as a linebacker's, and pure fury was blazing in his eyes.

He was almost there.

Panicked, she simultaneously pushed the buttons for the lobby and for the door to close. She stepped back from the closing gap as Zane lunged forward, trying to get his hand in the door, which would trigger the automatic opening sensor.

He didn't quite make it. The doors slid shut, and the box began to move downward. "God *damn* it," he roared in frustration, and Barrie flinched as his fist thudded against the doors.

Weakly she leaned against the wall and covered her face with her hands while she shook with reaction. Dear God, she'd never imagined anyone could be so angry. He'd been almost incandescent with it, his eyes all but glowing.

He was probably racing down the stairs, but he had twenty-one floors to cover, and he was no match for the elevator—unless it stopped to pick up passengers on other floors. This possibility nearly brought her to her knees. She watched the numbers change, unable to breathe. If it stopped even once, he might catch her in the street. If it stopped twice, he would catch her in the lobby. Three times, and he would be waiting for her at the elevator.

She would have to face that rage, and she'd never dreaded anything more. Leaving Zane had never been her intention. After she'd warned her father, she would go back to the suite. She didn't fear Zane physically; she knew instinctively that he would never hit her, but somehow that wasn't much comfort.

She had wanted to see him lose control, outside of that

final moment in lovemaking when his body took charge and he gave himself over to orgasm. Nausea roiled in her stomach, and she shuddered. Why had she ever wished for such a stupid thing? Oh, God, she never wanted to see him lose his temper again.

He might never forgive her. She might be forsaking forever any chance that he could love her. The full knowledge of what she was risking to warn her father rode her shoulders all the way to the lobby, one long, smooth descent, without any stops.

The rattle and clink of the slot machines never stopped, no matter how early or how late. The din surrounded her as she hurried through the lobby and out to the street. The desert sun was blindingly white, the temperature already edging past ninety, though the morning was only half gone. Barrie joined the tourists thronging the sidewalk, walking quickly despite the heat. She reached the corner, crossed the street and kept walking, not daring to look back. Her red hair would be fairly easy to spot at a distance, even in a crowd, unless she was hidden by someone taller. Zane would have reached the lobby by now. He would quickly scan the slot machine crowd, then erupt onto the street.

Her chest ached, and she realized she was holding her breath again. She gulped in air and hurried to put a building between herself and the hotel entrance. She was afraid to look back, afraid she would see her big, black-haired husband bearing down on her like a thunderstorm, and she knew she would never be able to outrun him.

She crossed one more street and began looking for a pay phone. They were easy to find, but getting an available one was something else again. Why were so many tourists using pay phones at this time of the morning? Barrie stood patiently, the hot sun beating down on her head, while a blue-haired elderly lady in support stockings gave detailed instructions to someone on when to feed her cat, when to feed her fish and when to feed her plants. Finally she hung up with a cheerful, "Bye-bye, dearie," and she gave Barrie a sweet smile as she hobbled past. The smile was so unexpected that Barrie almost burst into tears. Instead she managed a smile of her own and stepped up to the phone before anyone could squeeze ahead of her.

She used her calling card number because it was faster, and since she was calling from a pay phone, it didn't matter how she placed the call. *Please, God, let him be there*, she silently prayed as she listened to the tones, then the ringing. It was lunchtime on the east coast; he could be having lunch with someone, or playing golf—he could be anywhere. She tried to remember his schedule, but nothing came to mind. Their relationship had been so strained for the past two months that she had disassociated herself from his social and political appointments.

"Hello?"

The answer was so cautious, so wary sounding, that at first she didn't recognize her father's voice.

"Hello?" he said again, sounding even more wary, if possible.

Barrie pressed the handset hard to her ear, trying to keep her hand from shaking. "Daddy," she said, her voice strangled. She hadn't called him Daddy in years, but the old name slipped out past the barrier of her adulthood.

"Barrie? Sweetheart?" Life zinged into his voice, and she could picture him in her mind, sitting up straighter at his desk.

"Daddy, I can't say much." She fought to keep her voice even, so he would be able to understand her. "You have to be careful. You have to protect yourself. People *know*. Do you hear me?"

He was silent a moment, then he said with a calmness that was beyond her, "I understand. Are you safe?"

"Yes," she said, though she wasn't sure. She still had to face her husband.

"Then take care, sweetheart, and I'll talk to you soon."

"Bye," she whispered, then carefully hung the receiver in its cradle and turned to go to the hotel. She had taken about ten steps when she was captured in the hard grip she had been dreading. She didn't see him coming, so she couldn't brace herself. One second he wasn't there, the next second he was, surfacing out of the crowd like a shark.

Despite everything, she was glad to see him, glad to get it over with instead of dreading the first meeting during every dragging step to the hotel. The tension and effort had drained her. She leaned weakly against him, and he clamped his arm around her waist to support her. "You shouldn't be out in the sun without something on your head," was all he said. "Especially since you haven't eaten anything today."

He was in control, that incandescent fury cooled and conquered. She wasn't foolish enough to believe it was gone, however. "I had to warn him," she said tiredly. "And I didn't want the call traced to the hotel."

"I know." The words were brief to the point of curtness. "It might not make any difference. Las Vegas is crawling with a certain group of people this morning, and you may have been spotted. Your hair." Those two words were enough. Redheads were always distinctive, because there were so few of them. She felt like apologizing for the deep, rich luster of her hair.

"They're here?" she asked in a small voice. "The kidnappers?"

"Not the original ones. There's a deep game going on,

baby, and I'm afraid you just jumped into the middle of it."

The sun beat down on her unprotected head, the heat increasing by the minute. Every step seemed more and more of an effort. Her thoughts scattered. She might have plunged Zane and herself into the very danger she'd wanted to avoid. "Maybe I *am* a pampered society babe with more hair than brains," she said aloud. "I didn't mean—"

"I know," he said again, and unbelievably, he squeezed her waist. "And I never said you have more hair than brains. If anything, you're too damn smart, and it seems you have a natural talent for sneaking around. Not many people could have gotten out of that suite without me hearing them. Spook, maybe. And Chance. No one else."

Barrie leaned more of her weight against him. She was on his left side, and she felt the hard lump of the holster beneath his jacket. When he'd grabbed her, he'd instinctively kept his right hand free, in case he needed his pistol. What he *didn't* need, she thought tiredly, was having to support her weight and keep his balance in a firefight. She forced herself to straighten away from him, despite the way his arm tightened around her waist. He gave her a questioning look.

"I don't want to impede you," she explained.

His mouth curved wryly. "See what I mean? Now you're thinking of combat stuff. If you weren't so sweet, Mrs. Mackenzie, you'd be a dangerous woman."

Why wasn't he lambasting her? She couldn't imagine he'd gotten over his fury so fast; Zane struck her as the type of man who seldom lost his temper, but when he did, it was undoubtedly a memorable occasion—one that could last for years. Maybe he was saving it for when they were in the privacy of the suite, remaining on guard while they were in the street. He could do that, compartmentalize his anger, shove it aside until it was safe to bring it out.

She found herself studying the surging, milling, strolling crowd of tourists that surrounded them, looking for any betraying sign of interest. It helped take her mind off how incredibly weak she felt. This pregnancy was making itself felt with increasing force; though it had been foolish of her to come out into the sun without eating breakfast, and without a hat, normally she wouldn't have had any problem with the heat in this short amount of time.

How much farther was it to the hotel? She concentrated on her steps, on the faces around her. Zane maintained a slow, steady pace, and when he could, he put himself between her and the sun. The human shade helped, marginally.

"Here we are," he said, ushering her into the cool, dim cavern of the lobby. She closed her eyes to help them adjust from the bright sunlight and sighed with relief as the blast of air-conditioning washed over her.

The elevator was crowded on the ride up. Zane pulled her against the back wall, so he would have one less side to protect, and also to set up a human wall of protection between them and the open doors. She felt a faint spurt of surprise as she realized she knew what he was thinking, the motives behind his actions. He would do what he could to keep anything from happening, and to protect these people, but if push came to shove, he would ruthlessly sacrifice the other people in this elevator to keep her safe.

They got off on the twenty-first floor, the ride uneventful. A man and woman got off at the same time, a middle-aged couple with Rochester accents. They turned down the hallway leading away from the suite. Zane guided Barrie after them, following the couple until they reached their room around the corner. As they walked past, Barrie glanced inside the room as the couple entered it; it was untidy, piled with shopping bags and the dirty clothes they'd worn the day before.

"Safe," Zane murmured as they wound their way to the suite.

"They wouldn't have had all the tourist stuff if they'd just arrived?"

He slanted an unreadable look at her. "Yeah."

The suite was blessedly cool. She stumbled inside, and Zane locked and chained the door. Their breakfast still sat on the table, untouched and cold. He all but pushed her into a chair anyway. "Eat," he ordered. "Just the toast, if nothing else. Put jelly on it. And drink all the water." He sat down on the arm of the couch, picked up the phone and began dialing.

Just to be safe, she ate half a slice of dry toast first, eschewing the balls of butter, which wouldn't melt on the cold toast anyway. Her stomach was peaceful at the moment, but she didn't want to do anything to upset it. She smeared the second half slice with jelly.

As she methodically ate and drank, she began to feel better. Zane was making no effort to keep her from hearing his conversation, and she gathered he was talking to his brother Chance again.

"If she was spotted, we have maybe half an hour," he was saying. "Get everyone on alert." He listened a moment, then said, "Yeah, I know. I'm slipping." He said goodbye with a cryptic, "Keep it cool."

"Keep what cool?" Barrie asked, turning in her chair to face him.

A flicker of amusement lightened his remote eyes. "Chance has a habit of sticking his nose, along with another part of his anatomy, into hot spots. He gets burned occasionally."

"And you don't, I suppose?"

He shrugged. "Occasionally," he admitted.

He was very calm, unusually so, even for him. It was like waiting for a storm to break. Barrie took a deep breath and braced herself. "All right, I'm feeling better," she said, more evenly than she felt. "Let me have it."

He regarded her for a moment, then shook his head—regretfully, she thought. "It'll have to wait. Chance said there's a lot of activity going on all of a sudden. It's all about to hit the fan."

Chapter 13

They didn't have even the half hour Zane had hoped for.

The phone rang, and he picked it up. "Roger," he said, and placed the receiver into its cradle. He stood and strode over to Barrie. "They're moving in," he said, lifting her from the chair with an implacable hand. "And you're going to a different floor."

He was shoving her out of harm's way. She stiffened against the pressure of his hand, digging in her heels. He stopped and turned to face her, then placed his hand over her belly. "You have to go," he said, without a flicker of emotion. He was in combat mode, his face impassive, his eyes cold and distant.

He was right. Because of the baby, she had to go. She put her hand over his. "All right. But do you have an extra pistol I could have—just in case?"

He hesitated briefly, then strode into the bedroom to his garment bag. The weapon he removed was a compact, five-shot revolver. "Do you know how to use it?"

She folded her hand around the butt, feeling the smoothness of the wood. "I've shot skeet, but I've never used a handgun. I'll manage."

"There's no empty chamber, and no safety," he said as he escorted her out the door. "You can pull the hammer back before you fire, or you can use a little more effort and just pull the trigger. Nothing to it but aiming and firing. It's a thirty-eight caliber, so it has stopping power." He was walking swiftly toward the stairs as he talked. He opened the stairwell door and began pushing her up the stairs, their steps echoing in the concrete silo. "I'm going to put you in an empty room on the twenty-third floor, and I want you to stay there until either Chance or I come for you. If anyone else opens the door, shoot them."

"I don't know what Chance looks like," she blurted.

"Black hair, hazel eyes. Tall. So good-looking you start drooling when you see him. That's what he says women do, anyway."

They reached the twenty-third floor. Barrie was only slightly winded, Zane not at all. As they stepped into the carpeted silence of the hallway, she asked, "How do you know which rooms are empty?"

He produced one of the electronic cards from his pocket. "Because one of Chance's people booked the room last night and slipped me the key card while we were eating supper. Just in case."

He always had an alternate plan—just in case. She should have guessed.

He opened the door to room 2334 and ushered her inside, but he didn't enter himself. "Lock and chain the door, and stay put," he said, then turned and walked swiftly toward the stairwell. Barrie stood in the doorway and watched him. He stopped and looked at her over his shoulder. "I'm waiting to hear the door being locked," he said softly.

She stepped back, turned the lock and slid the chain into place.

Then she stood in the middle of the neat, silent room and quietly went to pieces.

She couldn't stand it. Zane was deliberately walking into danger—*on her account*—and she couldn't join him. She couldn't be there with him, couldn't guard his back. Because of the baby growing inside her, she was relegated to this safe niche while the man she loved faced bullets for her.

She sat on the floor and rocked back and forth, her arms folded over her stomach, keening softly as tears rolled down her face. This terror for Zane's safety was worse than anything she'd ever felt before, far worse than what she'd known at the hands of her kidnappers, worse even than when he'd been shot. At least she'd *been* there then. She'd been able to help, able to touch him.

She couldn't do anything now.

A sharp, deep report that sounded like thunder made her jump. Except it wasn't thunder; the desert sky was bright and cloudless. She buried her face against her knees, weeping harder. More shots. Some lighter, flatter in tone. A peculiar cough. Another deep thundering, then several in quick succession.

Then silence.

She pulled herself together and scrambled to the far corner of the room, behind the bed. She sat with her back against the wall and her arms braced on her knees, the pistol steady as she held it trained on the door. She didn't see how anyone other than Zane or Chance could know where she was, but she wouldn't gamble on it. She didn't know what any of this was about, or who her enemies were, except for Mack Prewett, probably.

Time crawled past. She didn't have her wristwatch on,

and the clock radio on the bedside table was turned away from her. She didn't get up to check the time. She simply sat there with the pistol in her hand and waited, and died a little more with each passing minute of Zane's absence.

He didn't come. She felt the coldness of despair grow in her heart, spreading until it filled her chest, the pressure of it almost stopping her lungs. Her heartbeat slowed to a heavy, painful rhythm. *Zane.* He would have come, if he'd been able. He'd been shot again. Wounded. She wouldn't let herself even think the word *dead,* but it was there, in her heart, her chest, and she didn't know how she could go on.

There was a brief knock on the door. "Barrie?" came a soft call, a voice that sounded tired and familiar. "It's Art Sandefer. It's over. Mack's in custody, and you can come out now."

Only Zane and Chance were supposed to know where she was. Zane had said that if anyone else opened the door, to shoot them. But she'd known Art Sandefer for years, known and respected both the man and the job he did. If Mack Prewett had been dirty, Art would have been on top of it. His presence here made sense.

"Barrie?" The door handle rattled.

She started to get up and let him in, then sank back to the floor. No. He wasn't Zane and he wasn't Chance. If she had lost Zane, the least she could do was follow his last instructions to the letter. His objective had been her safety, and she trusted him more than she had ever trusted anyone else in her life, including her father. She definitely trusted him more than she did Art Sandefer.

She was unprepared for the peculiar little coughing sound. Then the lock on the door exploded, and Art Sandefer pushed the door open and stepped inside. In his hand was a pistol with a thick silencer fitted onto the end of the barrel. Their eyes met across the room, his weary and cynical and acutely intelligent. And she knew.

Barrie pulled the trigger.

Zane was there only moments, seconds, later. Art had slumped to a sitting position against the open door, his hand pressed to the hole in his chest as his eyes glazed with shock. Zane kicked the weapon from Art's outstretched hand, but that was all the attention he paid to the wounded man. He stepped over him as if he wasn't there, rapidly crossing the room to where Barrie sat huddled in the corner, her face drawn and gray. Her gaze was oddly distant and unfocused. Panic roared through him, but a swift inspection didn't reveal any blood. She looked unharmed.

He hunkered down beside her, gently brushing her hair from her face. "Sweetheart?" he asked in a soft tone. "It's over now. Are you all right?"

She didn't answer. He sat down on the floor beside her and pulled her onto his lap, holding her close and tight against the warmth of his body. He kept up a reassuring murmur, a gentle sound of reassurance. He could feel the thud of her heartbeat against him, the rhythm hard and alarmingly slow. He held her tighter, his face buried against the richness of her hair.

"Is she all right?" Chance asked as he, too, stepped over Art Sandefer and approached his brother and new sister-in-law. Other people were coming into the room, people who tended to the wounded man. Mack Prewett was one of them, his eyes sharp and hard as he watched his former superior.

"She'll be fine," Zane murmured, lifting his head. "She shot Sandefer."

The brothers' eyes met in a moment of understanding. The first one was tough. With luck and good care, Sandefer would survive, but Barrie would always be one of those who knew what it was like to pull that trigger.

"How did he know which room?" Zane asked, keeping his voice calm.

Chance sat down on the bed and leaned forward, his forearms braced on his knees. His expression was pleasant enough, his eyes cool and thoughtful. "I must have a leak in my group," he said matter-of-factly. "And I know who it is, because only one person knew this room number. I'll take care of it."

"You do that."

Barrie stirred in Zane's grip, her arms lifting to twine around his neck. "Zane," she said, her voice faint and choked, shaking.

Because he'd felt the same way, he heard the panic in her voice, the despair. "I'm okay," he whispered, kissing her temple. "I'm okay."

A sob shook her, then was quickly controlled. She was soldiering on. Emotion swelled in his chest, a huge golden bubble of such force that it threatened to stop his breathing, his heartbeat. He closed his eyes to hold back the tears that burned his lids. "Oh, God," he said shakily. "I thought I was too late. I saw Sandefer walk in before I could get off a round at him, and then I heard the shot."

Her arms tightened convulsively around his neck, but she didn't say anything.

Zane put his hand on her belly, gulping in air as he fought for control. He was trembling, he noticed with distant surprise. Only Barrie could make mincemeat of his nerves. "I want the baby," he said, his voice still shaking. "But I didn't even think about it then. All I could think was that if I lost you—" He broke off, unable to continue.

"Baby?" Chance asked, politely inquiring.

Barrie nodded, her head moving against Zane's chest.

Her face was still buried against him, and she didn't look up.

"Barrie, this is my brother Chance," Zane said. His tone was still rough, uneven.

Blindly Barrie held out her hand. Amused, Chance gently shook it, then returned it to Zane's neck. He had yet to see her face. "Glad to meet you," he said. "I'm happy about the baby, too. That should deflect Mom's attention for a while."

The room was filled to overflowing: hotel security, Las Vegas police, medics, not to mention Mack Prewett and the FBI, who were quietly controlling everything. Chance's people had pulled back, melting into the shadows where they belonged, where they operated best. Chance picked up the phone, made one brief call, then said to Zane, "It's taken care of."

Mack Prewett came over and sat down on the bed beside Chance. His face was troubled as he looked at Barrie, clutched so tightly in Zane's arms. "Is she all right?"

"Yes," she said, answering for herself.

"Art's critical, but he might make it. It would save us a lot of trouble if he didn't." Mack's voice was flat, emotionless.

Barrie shuddered.

"You were never meant to be involved, Barrie," Mack said. "I began to think Art was playing both sides, so I asked your father to help me set him up. The information had to be legitimate, and the ambassador knows more people, has access to more inside information, than can be believed. Art went for the bait like a hungry carp. But then he asked for something really critical, the ambassador stalled, and the next thing we knew, you'd been snatched. Your dad nearly came unglued."

"Then those bastards in Benghazi knew we were coming in," Zane said, his eyes going cold.

"Yeah. I managed to shuffle the time frame a little when I gave the information to Art, but that was the most I could do to help. They weren't expecting you as early as you got there."

"I couldn't believe it of him. Art Sandefer, of all people," Barrie said, lifting her head to look at Mack. "Until I saw his eyes. I thought *you* were the dirty one."

Mack smiled crookedly. "It rocked me that you figured out anything was going on at all."

"Dad tipped me off. He acted so frightened every time I left the house."

"Art wanted you," Mack explained. "He was playing it cool for a while, or we would have had this wrapped up weeks ago. But it wasn't just the information. Art wanted *you.*"

Barrie was stunned by what Mack was saying. She glanced at Zane and saw his jaw tighten. So that was why she hadn't been raped in Benghazi; Art had been saving her for himself. He could never have released her, of course, if she had seen his face. Perhaps he would have drugged her, but more likely he would simply have raped her, kept her for himself for a while, then killed her. She shuddered, turning her face once more against Zane's throat. She was still having trouble believing he was safe and unharmed; it was difficult to drag herself out of the black pit of despair, even though she knew the worst hadn't happened. She felt numb, sick.

But then a thought occurred to her, one she would have had sooner if concern for Zane hadn't wiped everything else from her mind. She looked at Mack again. "Then my father's in the clear."

"Absolutely. He was working with me from the get-go."

He met her gaze and shrugged. "Your dad can be a pain in the rear, but his loyalty was never in question."

"When I called him this morning—"

Mack grimaced. "He was relieved to know you loved him enough to call, despite the evidence against him. Your leaving the hotel stirred up a hornet's nest, though. I thought we had everything under control."

"How?"

"Me," Chance interjected, and for the first time Barrie looked at her brother-in-law. She didn't drool, but she had to admit that his good looks were startling. Viewed objectively, he was the most handsome man she'd ever seen. However, she far preferred Zane's scarred, somber face, with its ancient eyes.

"I checked into another hotel under Zane's name," Chance explained. "You weren't listed at all, but Art knew you were with Zane, because he'd checked the license plate on that rental car and traced the rental to Zane's credit card. We didn't want to make it too obvious for him, we wanted him to have to work to find us, so he wouldn't be suspicious. When he found out you'd married Zane, though, he stopped being so cautious." Chance grinned. "Then you went for a walk this morning, and fubar happened. The pay phone you chose was right across the street from the hotel where I'd checked in, and Art's people spotted you immediately."

Across the room, the medics finally had Art Sandefer ready for transport to a hospital. Zane watched the man being carried out, then cut his narrowed gaze to Mack. "If I'd known about you a little sooner, most of this could have been avoided."

Mack didn't back down from that glacial stare. "As far as that goes, Commander, I didn't expect you to have the contacts you have—" he glanced at Chance "—or to move as fast as you did. I'd been working on Art for months. You made things happen in one day."

Zane stood, effortlessly lifting Barrie in his arms as he did so. "It's over now," he said with finality. "If you gentlemen will excuse me, I need to take care of my wife."

Taking care of her involved getting a third room, because the suite was in bad shape and he didn't want her to see it. He placed her on the bed, locked the door, then stripped both her and himself and got into bed with her, holding their naked bodies as close together as possible. They both needed the reassurance of bare skin, no barriers between them. He got hard immediately, but now wasn't the time for lovemaking.

Barrie couldn't seem to stop trembling, and, to her astonishment, neither could Zane. They clung together, touching each other's faces, absorbing the smell and feel of each other in an effort to dispel the terror.

"I love you," he whispered, holding her so close her ribs ached from the pressure. "God, I was so scared! I can't keep it together where you're concerned, sweetheart. For the sake of my sanity, I hope the rest of our lives are as dull as dishwater."

"They will be," she promised, kissing his chest. "We'll work on it." And tears blurred her eyes, because she hadn't expected so much, so fast.

Then, finally, it was time for more. Gently he entered her, and they lay entwined, not moving, as if their nerves couldn't stand a sharp assault now, even one of pleasure. That, too, came in its own time...her pleasure, and his.

Epilogue

"Twins," Barrie said, her voice still full of stunned bewilderment as she and Zane drove along the road that wound up the side of Mackenzie's Mountain. "Boys."

"I told you how it would be," Zane said, glancing at the mound of her stomach, which was much too big for five months of pregnancy. "Boys."

She gave him a glassy stare of shock. "You didn't," she said carefully, "say they would come in pairs."

"There haven't been twins in our family before," Zane said, just as carefully. In truth, he felt as shaky as Barrie did. "This is a first."

She stared out the window, her gaze passing blindly over the breathtaking vista of craggy blue mountains. They lived in Wyoming now; with Zane's two-year tenure as sheriff in Arizona over, he had declined to run for election, and they had moved closer to the rest of the family. Chance had been after him for those two years to join his organization—though Barrie still wasn't certain exactly what that organization *was*—and Zane had finally relented. He wouldn't be doing fieldwork, because he didn't want to risk the life he had with Barrie and Nick and now these two new babies who were growing inside her, but he had a rare knack for planning for the unexpected, and that was the talent he was using.

The entire family, including her father, was gathered on the mountain to celebrate the Fourth of July, which was the next day. Zane, Barrie and Nick had driven up two days before for an extended visit, but today had been her scheduled checkup, and he'd driven her into town to the doctor's office. Given the way her waistline had been expanding, they should have expected the news, but Zane had simply figured she was further along in her pregnancy than they'd thought. Seeing those two little fetuses on the ultrasound had been quite a shock, but there hadn't been any doubt about it. Two heads, two tails, four arms and hands, four legs and feet—and both babies definitely male. Very definitely.

"I can't think of two names," Barrie said, sounding very near tears.

Zane reached over to pat her knee. "We have four more months to think of names."

She sniffed. "There's no way," she said, "that I can carry them for four more months. We'll have to come up with names before then."

They *were* big babies, both of them, much bigger than Nick had been at this stage.

"After Nick, it took a lot of courage just to think of having another baby," she continued. "I'd geared myself up for one. *One*. Zane, what if *they're both like Nick?*"

He blanched. Nick was a hellion. Nick had a good shot at turning the entire family gray-haired within another year. For a very short person with a limited vocabulary, their offspring could cause an unbelievable uproar in a remarkably short period of time.

They reached the crest of the mountain, and Zane slowed the car as they neared the large, sprawling ranch house. A variety of vehicles were parked around the yard—Wolf's truck, Mary's car, Mike and Shea's Suburban, Josh and Loren's rental, Ambassador Lovejoy's rental, Maris's snazzy truck, Chance's motorcycle. Joe and Caroline and their five hooligans had arrived by helicopter. Boys seemed to be everywhere, from Josh's youngest, age five, to John, who was Joe's oldest and was now in college and here with his current girlfriend.

They were adding two more to the gang.

They got out and walked up the steps to the porch. Zane put his arm around her and hugged her close, tilting her face up for a kiss that quickly grew heated. Barrie glowed with a special sexuality when she was pregnant, and the plain truth was he couldn't resist her. Their love play was often extended these days, now that pregnancy had once again made her breasts as sensitive as they had been when she'd carried Nick.

"Stop that!" Josh called cheerfully from inside the house. "That's what got her in that condition in the first place!"

Reluctantly Zane released his wife, and together they went into the house. "That isn't exactly right," he told Josh, who laughed.

The big television was on, and Maris, Josh and Chance were watching some show-jumping event. Wolf and Joe were discussing cattle with Mike. Caroline was arguing politics with the ambassador. Mary and Shea were organizing a game for the younger kids. Loren, who was often an oasis of calm in the middle of the Mackenzie hurricane, gave

Barrie's rounded stomach a knowing look. "How did the checkup go?" she asked.

"Twins," Barrie said, still in that numb tone. She gave Zane a helpless, how-did-this-happen look.

The whirlwind of activity came to a sudden stop. Heads lifted and turned. Her father gasped. Mary's face suddenly glowed with radiance.

"Both boys," Zane announced, before anyone could ask.

A sigh almost of relief went around the room. "Thank God," Josh said weakly. "What if it was another one—or *two*—like Nick!"

Barrie's head swiveled around as she began searching for a particular little head. "Where *is* Nick?" she asked.

Chance bolted upright from his sprawled position on the couch. The adults looked around with growing panic. "She was right here," Chance said. "She was dragging one of Dad's boots around."

Zane and Barrie both began a rapid search of the house. "How long ago?" Barrie called.

"Two minutes, no more. Just before you drove up." Maris was on her knees, peering under beds.

"Two minutes!" Barrie almost moaned. In two minutes, Nick could almost single-handedly wreck the house. It was amazing how such a tiny little girl with such an angelic face could be such a demon. "Nick!" she called. "Mary Nicole, come out, come out, wherever you are!" Sometimes that worked. Most times it didn't.

Everyone joined in the search, but their black-haired little terror was nowhere to be found. The entire family had been ecstatic at her birth, and she had been utterly doted on, with even the rough-and-tumble cousins fascinated by the daintiness and beauty of the newest Mackenzie. She really did look angelic, like Pebbles on the old *Flintstones* cartoons. She was adorable. She had Zane's black hair; slanted, deceptively innocent blue eyes; and dimples on each side of her rosebud mouth. She had sat up by herself at four months, crawled at six, walked at eight, and the entire family had been on guard ever since.

They found Wolf's boot beneath Mary's glassed-in collection of angels. From the scuff marks on the wall, Zane deduced his little darling had been trying to knock the collection down by heaving the boot at it. Luckily the boot had been too heavy for her to handle. Her throwing arm wasn't well developed yet, thank God.

She had a frightful temper for such a little thing, and an outsize will, too. Keeping her from doing something she was determined to do was like trying to hold back the tide with a bucket. She had also inherited her father's knack for planning, something that was eerie in a two-year-old. Nick was capable of plotting the downfall of anyone who crossed her.

Once, when Alex, Joe's second oldest, had seen her with a knife in her hand and swiftly snatched it away before she could harm anyone or anything, Nick had thrown a howling temper tantrum that had been halted only when Zane swatted her rear end. Discipline from her adored daddy made her sob so heartbrokenly that everyone else got a lump in their throats. That, and making her sit down in her punishment chair, were so far the only two things they'd discovered that could reduce her to tears.

When she had stopped sobbing, she had pouted in a corner for a while, all the time giving Alex threatening looks over one tiny shoulder. Then she had gone to Barrie for comfort, crawling into her mother's lap to be rocked. Her next stop had been Zane's lap, to show him that she forgave him. She'd wound her little arms around his neck and rubbed her chubby little cheek against his rough one. She'd even taken a brief nap, lying limply against his broad shoulder. She'd woken, climbed down and darted off to the kitchen, where she'd implored Mary, whom she called Gamma, for a "dink." She was allowed to have soft drinks without caffeine, so Mary had given her one of the green bottles they always kept in store especially for Nick. Zane and Barrie always shared a look of intimate amusement at their daughter's love for Seven-Up, but there was nothing unusual about seeing her clutching the familiar bottle in her tiny hands. She would take a few sips, then with great concentration screw the top onto the bottle and lug it around with her until it was finally empty, which usually took a couple of hours.

On this occasion, Zane had happened to be watching her, smiling at her blissful expression as her little hands closed on the bottle. She had strutted out of the kitchen without letting Mary open the bottle for her and stopped in the hallway, where she vigorously shook the bottle with so much vigor that her entire little body had been bouncing up and down. Then, with a meltingly sweet smile on her face, she had all but danced into the living room and handed the bottle to Alex with a flirtatious tilt of her head. "Ope' it, pees," she'd said in her adorable small voice... and then she'd backed up a few steps.

"No!" Zane had yelled, leaping up from his chair, but it was too late. Alex had already twisted the cap and broken the seal. The bottle spewed and spurted, the sticky liquid spraying the wall, the floor, the chair. It hit Alex full blast in the face. By the time he'd managed to get the cap securely back on the bottle, he was soaked.

Nick had clapped her hands and said, "Hee, hee, hee," and Zane wasn't certain if it was a laugh or a taunt. It didn't matter. He had collapsed on the floor in laughter, and there was an unbreakable law written in stone somewhere that you couldn't punish youngsters if you'd laughed at what they'd done.

"Nick!" he called now. "Do you want a Popsicle?" Next to Seven-Ups, Popsicles were her favorite treat.

There was no answer.

Sam tore into the house. He was ten, Josh and Loren's middle son. His blue eyes were wide. "Uncle Zane!" he cried. "Nick's on top of the house!"

"Oh, my God," Barrie gasped, and rushed out of the house as fast as she could. Zane tore past her, his heart in his throat, every instinct screaming for him to get to his child as fast as possible.

Everyone spilled into the yard, their faces pale with alarm, and looked up. Nick was sitting cross-legged on the edge of the roof, her little face blissful as she stared down at them. "Hi," she chirped.

Barrie's knees wobbled, and Mary put a supporting, protective arm around her.

It was no mystery how Nick had gotten on the roof—a ladder was leaning against the house, and Nick was as agile as a young goat. The ladder shouldn't have been there; in fact, Zane would have sworn it hadn't been when he and Barrie had arrived, no more than five minutes earlier.

He started up the ladder, his gaze glued on his daughter. A scowl screwed her small features together, and she scrambled to her feet, perilously close to the edge of the roof. "No!" she shrieked. "No, Daddy!"

He froze in place. She didn't want to come down, and she was absolutely fearless. She paid no more heed to her danger than if she'd been in her bed.

"Zane," Barrie whispered, her voice choked.

He was shaking. Nick stomped one little foot and pointed a dimpled finger at him. "Daddy down," she demanded.

He couldn't get to her in time. No matter how fast he

moved, his baby was going to fall. There was only one thing to do. "Chance!" he barked.

Chance knew immediately. He ambled forward, not making any swift movements that would startle her. When he was directly below her, he grinned at his cherubic niece, and she grinned at him. He was her favorite uncle.

"Dance," she crowed, showing all her tiny white teeth.

"You little Antichrist," he said fondly. "I'm really going to miss you when you're in prison. I give you...oh, maybe to the age of six."

Benjy, Josh's youngest, piped up behind them, "Why did Uncle Chance call her Dannychrist? Her name's Nick."

Nick spread her arms wide, bouncing up and down on her tiptoes. Chance held up his arms. "Come on, cupcake," he said, and laughed. "Jump!"

She did.

He deftly snagged her in midair, and hugged the precious little body to his chest. Barrie burst into tears of relief. Then Zane was there, taking his daughter in his arms, pressing his lips to her round little head, and Barrie rushed over to be enveloped in his embrace, too.

Caroline looked at Joe. "I forgive you for not having any female sperm," she announced, and Joe laughed.

Josh was frowning sternly at Sam. "How did the ladder get there?" he demanded.

Sam looked at his feet.

Mike and Joe began to frown at their boys.

"Whose bright idea was it to play on top of the house?" Mike asked of the seven boys who hadn't been inside, and thus absolved of blame.

Seven boys scuffed their shoes on the ground, unable to look up at the three fathers confronting them.

Josh took down the ladder, which was supposed to be in the barn. He pointed to the structure in question. "March," he said sternly, and two boys began their reluctant walk to the barn—and their retribution. Benjy clung to Loren's leg, blinking at his two older brothers.

Mike pointed to the barn. His two boys went.

Joe raised an eyebrow at his three youngest. They went.

The three tall, broad-shouldered brothers followed their sons to the barn.

Nick patted Barrie's face. "Mommy cwy?" she asked, and her lower lip quivered as she looked at Zane. "Fix, Daddy."

"I'll fix, all right," he muttered. "I'll fix some glue to your little butt and stick you on a chair."

Barrie giggled through her tears. "Everyone wished for a girl," she said, hiccuping as she laughed and cried at the same time. "Well, we got our wish!"

Wolf reached out and plucked his only granddaughter from his son's brawny arms. She beamed at him, and he said ruefully, "With luck, it'll be thirty years before there's another one. Unless..." His dark eyes narrowed as he looked at Chance.

"No way," Chance said firmly. "You can turn that look on Maris. I'm not getting married. I'm not reproducing. They're starting to come by the bunches now, so it's time to call a halt. I'm not getting into this daddy business."

Mary gave him her sweet smile. "We'll see," she said.

DEFENDING HIS OWN
by Beverly Barton

* * *

To several very special ladies
whose friendships have meant so much to me
over the past few years. Thank y'all for your support
and encouragement: Jean Tune, JoAnn Courtney,
Helen Everett and Marsha Hunt.

Dear Reader,

Defending His Own is very special to me for several reasons. For one thing, it is the first book in my popular Intimate Moments series, THE PROTECTORS. Too, the setting is Sheffield, Alabama, a sister city to my hometown.

This book has elements of mystery and suspense interwoven with a classic romance story and secret-child theme, with a twist. The hero, Ashe Laughlin, was not only the first official Dundee Private Security and Investigation Agency bodyguard, but he was a former poor kid from the wrong side of the tracks. This is one of my favorite types of heroes—the redeemable bad boy. Since many readers have recently discovered THE PROTECTORS series, I'm delighted that Silhouette is reprinting this first book.

I hope you enjoy this book, as well as the many new stories coming in THE PROTECTORS series.

All the best,

Beverly Barton

Prologue

She must have taken the wrong turn off Cotton Lane. There was nothing out here but a bunch of cotton fields and an endless stretch of dirt road, apparently leading nowhere except in and out of the fields.

Deborah Vaughn slowed her dark blue Cadillac to a stop, shifted the gears into Park and picked up the piece of paper on which she'd written the directions. Despite the protection of her sunglasses, Deborah squinted against the sun's blinding glare. Holding up her hand to shield her eyes, she glanced down at the map and instructions she'd brought along to help her find the new development property her real estate firm had just purchased. Damn! She had turned off too soon.

Glancing around, she didn't see anywhere to make a turn, and she certainly had no intention of backing her car all the way to Cotton Lane. She'd just have to go a little farther and find some place to turn around.

Shifting the gears into Drive, she drove on. Within a few minutes she spotted what appeared to be the burned-out remains of an old shack. A wide, weed-infested path, marred with deep ruts, ran straight from the dirt road to where a shiny black Ford pickup had parked in knee-high grass behind the still-standing brick chimney.

Loud, pulse-pounding country music blared from the truck's radio.

Deborah assumed the truck belonged to the farmer who had planted the acres of cotton. She drove her Cadillac onto the path, intending to back up and head out the way she had come. The sun's glare blocked her vision, allowing her only partial vision of the open truck door. A man jumped out of the driver's side, and yelled a warning. She glanced toward the back of the truck where two men stood, one holding a gun to the other's head.

Sunshine reflected off the metal on the gun in the killer's hand. The gun fired. The wail of a steel guitar blasted from inside the truck. Deborah screamed. Blood splattered from the dead man's head. The killer turned abruptly and stared at the Cadillac, at the woman inside, then released his hold on the body. His victim slumped to the ground.

Deborah recognized the killer from his picture in the paper. She couldn't remember his name, but she knew he was somehow connected to that outlaw gang headed by Buck Stansell.

The man who'd leaped out of the truck pointed toward Deborah's car.

Dear God, she had to get away! Shifting the car into reverse, she backed out of the bumpy path and then headed the Cadillac toward Cotton Lane. She heard the truck's engine roar to life. Glancing back she saw the killer aim his gun out the window.

The Caddy sped down the dirt road, the black truck in hot pursuit. While the driver veered the truck off the side of the dirt road, partially into the open field, the killer aimed his gun toward Deborah. The truck closed in on the car, the truck's hood parallel to the Cadillac's left rear bumper. The killer fired; the bullet shattered the outside mirror. Deborah cried out, but didn't slow her escape, didn't take her eyes off the road ahead of her.

A cloud of dust flew up behind the Cadillac, providing a thin veil of protection between her and the men determined to overtake her. The truck picked up speed just as Deborah saw Cotton Lane ahead of her. Another bullet ripped through the driver's door.

They intended to kill her. She had no doubt in her mind. She'd seen the killer's face, the man who had murdered another in cold blood. She could identify him. And he knew it.

The minute she turned the Caddy onto Cotton Lane, she sped away from the truck. She had to escape. Had to find help. But who? Where? The police!

She didn't dare slow down enough to use her cellular phone. She had to make it to the police station before her pursuers caught her.

Where the hell was the police station in Leighton? *Think, dammit, Deborah! Think!*

She crossed Highway 72, paying little attention to whether or not traffic was coming from the other direction. The sleepy little town of Leighton, Alabama lay straight ahead. The truck breathed down her neck like a black dragon, the killer's gun spitting deadly lead fire.

A bullet sailed through the back glass, embedding itself in the dashboard. Deborah ran the Caddy straight through the town's one red light. The black truck slowed, but continued following her.

Deborah brought her car to a screeching halt at the side of the police station, a small metal building on the right side of the narrow street. Glancing behind her, she saw the black truck creep by. Lying down in the front seat, she eased open the door, crawled out and made a mad dash to safety.

A young officer jumped up from behind a metal desk when Deborah ran inside the station. "What the hell's going on, lady? You look like the devil's chasing you."

"He is." Deborah panted, wiping the perspiration from her face with the palm of her hand. She grabbed the approaching officer's shoulders. "I just witnessed a murder."

"You what?" The young officer's face paled. "Come on in and sit down."

"I don't want to sit down," Deborah screamed. "They're out there. Two of them. The killer and the man who was driving the truck. They followed me all the way into town. They shot at me. They were trying to kill me!"

"Good God!" He shoved Deborah aside, drew his 9mm handgun and rushed outside.

The female officer who'd been listening to the conversation rushed over to Deborah and followed her when she headed for the door. Looking up and down the street, Deborah didn't see the truck. She leaned against the doorpost.

"Are you all right?" the woman officer asked.

"I will be."

The male officer let out a long, low whistle when he saw Deborah's Cadillac. "Good thing they didn't get a lucky shot or you'd be dead, ma'am."

"They're gone, aren't they?" Deborah asked, realizing they wouldn't have hung around, making it easy for the police to arrest them.

"Yes, ma'am, looks that way." He walked toward her, shaking his head. "Just where did this murder take place?"

"Out past some cotton fields, somewhere off Cotton Lane."

"Don't suppose you recognized either man in the truck or the man you say they murdered?"

"I only recognized one of them," Deborah said. "The killer. He's one of Buck Stansell's gang. I remember seeing his picture in the paper when he went to trial a few months ago on drug-related charges."

"Lon Sparks?" the officer asked. "You saw Lon Sparks kill a man?"

"Yes, if that's his name...I saw him kill a man. Shot him in the head. Blood everywhere. All over the dead man. All over the killer." Deborah trembled, her hands shaking uncontrollably.

"Damn, ma'am, I sure wouldn't want to be in your shoes. Lon Sparks is a mean bastard, if you'll pardon me saying so." The officer returned his gun to his holster.

"Shut up, Jerry Don, can't you see she's already scared out of her wits." Putting an arm around Deborah's shoulder, the female officer led her back inside the station. "We'd better get hold of the chief and then call the sheriff. If the killing took place out past Cotton Lane, then it's a county matter."

"Everything will be all right," Jerry Don said. "You're safe here with us, Miss...er... Miss...?"

"Deborah Vaughn."

"Come on over and sit down, Miss Vaughn, and tell me exactly what happened," The female officer said.

"May I use your phone first?" Deborah picked up the telephone on the officer's desk. "I'm expected at home for dinner and my mother will worry if I'm late."

Her hands trembled as she dialed the number. "Mother, I'm afraid I'll be running a little late. You and Allen go ahead and have dinner without me. No. No, everything's all right. I just ran into a little car trouble out here in Leighton. Nothing I can't handle.''

Nothing she couldn't handle. That's right, Deborah. You're tough, aren't you? You can handle anything that's thrown your way. You don't need anyone to take care of you. You've been taking care of everyone else for so long, you wouldn't know how it felt to admit you needed someone.

Well, it looked like the time had come. If the police wanted her to live long enough to testify against a cold-blooded killer, someone was going to have to protect her from Buck Stansell's outlaws.

Chapter 1

He had sworn he'd never come back to Sheffield, Alabama. But never say never. Ashe McLaughlin had discovered that anyone so absolutely certain often wound up eating his own words. And in his case, the taste was mighty bitter.

He had been gone eleven years, and little had changed. Except him. He had changed. He was older. Smarter. Harder.

He chuckled to himself. Harder? Hell, folks in northwest Alabama had considered him a real bad boy, one of those McLaughlins from Leighton, his daddy nothing but a white trash outlaw. But Ashe hadn't been as tough as everyone thought. He had hated the legacy of poverty and ignorance his family had given him. He'd wanted more. He'd fought long and hard to better himself. But Wallace Vaughn had destroyed Ashe's dreams of being accepted in Colbert County.

Eleven years ago he'd been told to leave town or else—or else he would have done jail time.

Now, here he was returning to a town that hadn't wanted his kind. He couldn't help wondering if anyone other than his grandmother would welcome him home. He supposed Carol Allen Vaughn would be glad to see him. After all, she'd been the one who'd asked him to take this job. He was probably a fool for agreeing to act as Deborah's bodyguard.

Deborah Vaughn. No amount of time or distance had been able to erase her from Ashe's memory.

He parked his rental car in the circular drive in front of the old Allen home, a brick Greek Revival cottage on Montgomery Avenue. His grandmother had once been the housekeeper here for the Vaughn family.

Walking up to the front door, he hesitated before ringing the bell. He'd never been allowed to enter the house through the front door but had always gone around to the back and entered through the kitchen. He remembered sitting at the kitchen table doing his homework, sharing milk and cookies with Deborah, and sometimes her older cousin Whitney. That had been a lifetime ago.

He rang the doorbell. What the hell was he doing here? Why had he allowed Carol Vaughn's dare to goad him into returning to a town he hated? *Deborah needs you,* she'd said. *Are you afraid to see her again?* she had taunted him.

He was not afraid to see Deborah Vaughn again. After ten years as a Green Beret, Ashe McLaughlin was afraid of nothing, least of all the girl who had betrayed him.

A plump, middle-aged woman opened the door and greeted him with a smile. "Yes, sir?"

"I'm Ashe McLaughlin. Mrs. Vaughn is expecting me."

"Yes, please come inside. I'll tell Miss Carol you're here."

Ashe stepped into the gracious entrance hall large enough to accommodate a grand piano as well as a large mahogany and gilt table with an enormous bouquet of fresh flowers in the center. A sweeping staircase wound upward on the left side of the room.

"If you'll wait here, please." The housekeeper scurried down the hall toward the back of the house.

He'd been summoned home. Like a knight in the Queen's service. Ashe grinned. Better a knight than a stable boy, he supposed. Why hadn't he just said no? *I'm sorry, Mrs. Vaughn, but whatever trouble Deborah has gotten herself into, you'll have to find someone else to rescue her.*

God knows he had tried to refuse, but once he'd heard that Deborah's life was in real danger, he had wavered in his resistance. And Carol Vaughn had taken advantage of the weakness she sensed in him.

"Ashe, so good of you to come, dear boy." The voice still held that note of authority, that hint of superiority, that tone of Southern gentility.

He turned to face her, the woman he had always thought of as the personification of a real lady. He barely recognized the woman who stood before him. Thin, almost gaunt, her beautiful face etched with faint age lines, her complexion sickly pale. Her short blond hair was streaked with gray. She had once been full-figured, voluptuous and lovely beyond words.

She couldn't be much more than fifty, but she looked older.

Caught off-guard by her appearance, by the drastic change the years had wrought, Ashe stared at Carol Vaughn. Quickly recovering his composure, he took several tentative steps forward and held out his hand.

She clasped his big, strong hand in her small, fragile one and squeezed. "Thank you for coming. You can't imagine how desperately we need your help."

Ashe assisted Carol down the hallway and into the living room. The four-columned entry permitted an unobstructed view of the room from the foyer. The hardwood floors glistened like polished metal in the sunlight. A blend of antiques and expensive reproductions bespoke of wealth and good taste.

"The sofa, please, Ashe." She patted his hand. "Sit beside me and we'll discuss what must be done."

He guided her to the sofa, seated her and perched his big body on the edge, not feeling comfortable in her presence. "Does Deborah know you sent for me?"

"I haven't told her," Carol said. "She's a stubborn one, that girl of mine. She's always had a mind of her own. But she's been a dutiful daughter."

"What if she doesn't agree to my being here?" He had known Deborah when she was seventeen, a plump, pretty girl who'd had a major crush on him. What would she look like now? And how did she feel about him after all these years?

"Mazie, please bring us some coffee," Carol instructed the housekeeper who stood at the end of the hallway. "And a few of those little cakes from the bakery. The cinnamon ones."

"Refreshments aren't necessary, Mrs. Vaughn. Really." Ashe felt ill at ease being entertained, as if his visit were a social call. "I'm here on business. Remember?"

"Mazie, go ahead and bring the coffee and the cakes, too." Carol turned her attention to Ashe. "Times change, but good manners don't. Of course my mother would be appalled that I had welcomed a gentleman, unrelated to me and not a minister, into my home when I am quite alone."

"Coffee will be fine, Mrs. Vaughn."

"You used to call me Miss Carol. I much prefer that to the other. Your calling me Mrs. Vaughn makes us sound like strangers. And despite your long absence from Sheffield, we are hardly strangers, are we, Ashe?"

"No, ma'am, we're not strangers."

"Mazie has prepared you a room upstairs. I want you with Deborah at all times." Carol blushed ever so lightly. "Or at least close by."

"Has she received any more threats since we spoke two days ago?"

"Mercy, yes. Every day, there's a new letter and another phone call, but Charlie Blaylock says there's nothing more he can do. And I asked him why the sheriff was incapable of protecting innocent citizens."

"Has a trial date been set for Lon Sparks?" Ashe asked.

"Not yet. It should be soon. But not soon enough for me. I can't bear the thought of Deborah being in danger."

"She just happened to be in the wrong place at the wrong time." Ashe knew what that was like. And he knew as well as anyone in these parts just how dangerous Buck Stansell and his band of outlaws could be. For three generations, the Stansell bunch, along with several other families, had cornered the market on illegal activities. Everything from prostitution to bootlegging, when the county had been dry. And nowadays weapons and drugs dominated their money-making activities.

"She insists on testifying." Carol glanced up when she saw Mazie bringing the coffee. "Just put it there on the table, please."

Mazie placed the silver service on the mahogany tea table to the left of the sofa, asked if there would be anything else and retreated to the kitchen when told all was in order.

"Do you prefer your coffee black?" Carol asked.

"Yes, ma'am. Thank you." When his hostess poured the coffee and handed it to him, Ashe accepted the Haviland cup.

"I will expect you to stay in Sheffield until the trial is over and Deborah is no longer in danger."

"I've already assured you that I'll stay as long as is necessary to ensure Deborah's safety."

"And I will send the sum we agreed upon to your agency in Atlanta on a weekly basis."

"You and I have come to an agreement on terms," Ashe said. "But unless Deborah cooperates—"

"She will cooperate."

Ashe widened his eyes, surprised by the vigor of Carol Vaughn's statement. Apparently her fragile physical condition had not extinguished the fire in her personality.

The front door flew open and a tall, gangly boy of perhaps twelve raced into the living room, tossing a stack of schoolbooks down on a bowfront walnut commode.

"I made a hundred on my math test. See. Take a look." He dashed across the room, handed Carol his paper and sat down on the floor at her feet. "And guess what else, Mother? My team beat the hel...heck out of Jimmy Morton's team in PE today."

Carol caressed the boy's blond hair, petting him with deep affection. "I'm so proud of you, Allen."

The boy turned his attention to Ashe, who stared at the child, amazed at his striking resemblance to Deborah. Ashe's grandmother had mentioned Allen from time to time in her letters and phone calls. He'd always thought it odd that Wallace and Carol Vaughn had had another child so late in life. When Wallace Vaughn had run Ashe out of town eleven years ago, the Vaughns had had one child—seventeen-year-old Deborah.

"Who's he?" Allen asked.

"Allen, this is Mr. McLaughlin. He's an old friend. He and Deborah went to school together."

"Were you Deborah's boyfriend?" Allen scooted around on the floor until he situated himself just right, so he could prop his back against the Queen Anne coffee table.

"Allen, you musn't be rude." Carol shook her index finger at the boy, but she smiled as she scolded him.

"I wasn't being rude. I was just hoping Mr. McLaughlin was here to ask Deborah for a date. She never goes out unless it's with Neil, and she told me that he isn't her boyfriend."

"I must apologize for Allen, but you see, he is very concerned that Deborah doesn't have a boyfriend," Carol explained. "Especially since he's going steady himself. For what now, Allen, ten days?"

"Ah, quit kidding me." Allen unlaced his shoes, then reached up on top of the tea table to retrieve a tiny cinnamon cake. He popped it into his mouth.

Ashe watched the boy, noting again how much he looked like Deborah as a young girl. Except where she had been short and plump with small hands and feet, Allen was tall, slender and possessed large feet and big hands. But his hair was the same color, his eyes an almost identical blue.

"Hey, what do we know about Mr. McLaughlin? We can't let Deborah date just anybody." Allen returned Ashe's penetrating stare. "If he gets serious about Deborah, is he the kind of man who'd make her a good husband?"

The front door opened and closed again. A neatly attired young woman in a navy suit and white blouse walked into the entrance hall.

"Now, Allen, you're being rude again," Carol said. "Besides, your sister's love life really isn't any of our business, even if we did find her the perfect man."

"Now what?" Deborah called out from the hallway, not even looking their way. "Mother, you and Allen haven't found another prospect you want me to consider, have you? Just who have you two picked out as potential husband material this time?"

Carrying an oxblood leather briefcase, Deborah came to an abrupt halt when she looked into the living room and saw Ashe sitting beside her mother on the sofa. She gasped aloud, visibly shaken.

"Come in, dear. Allen and I were just entertaining Ashe McLaughlin. You remember Ashe, don't you, Deborah?"

"Was he your old boyfriend?" Allen asked. "Mother won't tell me."

Ashe stood and took a long, hard look at Deborah Vaughn...the girl who had proclaimed her undying love for him one night down by the river, eleven years ago. The girl who, when he gently rejected her, had run crying to her rich and powerful daddy.

The district attorney and Wallace Vaughn had given Ashe two choices. Leave town and never come back, or face statutory rape charges.

"Hello, Deborah."

"What are you doing here?"

She had changed, perhaps even more than her pale, weak mother. No longer plump but still as lovely as she'd been as a teenager, Deborah possessed a poise and elegance that had eluded the younger, rather awkward girl. She wore her long, dark blond hair tucked into a loose bun at the nape of her neck. A pair of small golden earrings matched the double gold chain around her neck.

"Your mother sent for me." Ashe noted the astonished look on her face.

Deborah, still standing in the entrance hall, gazed at her mother. "What does he mean, you sent for him?"

"Now, dear, please come in and let's talk about this matter before you upset yourself."

"Allen, please go out in the kitchen with Mazie while I speak with Mother and Mr. McLaughlin."

"Ah, why do I have to leave? I'm a member of this family, aren't I? I shouldn't be excluded from important conversations." When his sister remained silent, Allen looked pleadingly at his mother, who shook her head.

"Do what Deborah says." Carol motioned toward the hallway. "This is grown-up talk and although you're quite a young man, you're still not old enough to—"

"Yeah, yeah. I know." Allen jumped up and ran out of the room, his eyes downcast and his lips puckered into a defiant pout.

"What's going on?" Deborah marched into the living room, slamming her briefcase down atop Allen's books on the antique commode. She glared at Ashe. "What are *you* doing here?"

"As Ashe said, I sent for him." Tilting her chin upward, Carol straightened her thin shoulders.

"You what?"

"Calm yourself," Carol said.

"I am calm." Deborah spoke slowly, her teeth clenched tightly.

"Ashe works for a private security firm out of Atlanta." Carol readjusted her hips on the sofa, placing her hand down on the cushion beside her. "I've hired him to act as your bodyguard until the trial is over and you're no longer in any danger."

"I can't believe what I'm hearing." Deborah scowled at Ashe.

"You've brought this man back into our lives. Good God, Mother, do you have any idea what you've done?"

"Don't speak to me in that tone of voice, Deborah Luellen Vaughn! I've done what I think is best for everyone concerned."

"And you?" Deborah looked directly at Ashe. "Why would you come back to Sheffield after all these years? How on earth did my mother persuade you to return?" Deborah's rosy cheeks turned pale, her lips quivered. "What—what did she tell you?"

"I told him that your life had been threatened. I explained the basic facts." Carol turned to Ashe. "This is what he does for a living, and I'm paying him his usual fee, isn't that right, Ashe?"

"This is strictly a business arrangement for me," Ashe replied. "My services are for hire to anyone with enough money to afford me."

Where was the sweet girl he'd once known? The laughing, smiling girl who'd been his friend long before she'd become his lover one hot summer night down by the river. He had never regretted anything as much as he had regretted taking Deborah's virginity. He'd been filled with rage and half drunk. Deborah had been with him that night, trying to comfort him, and he had taken advantage of her loving nature. But she'd paid him back.

"I don't want you here. Keep a week's salary for your trouble." Deborah nodded toward the door. "Now, please leave."

"No!" Reaching out, Carol grabbed Ashe by the arm. "Please, don't leave. Go in the kitchen and have some cookies with Allen."

"Mother! Think what you're saying."

"Please, Ashe. Go out into the kitchen for a few minutes while I speak with Deborah."

Ashe patted Carol on the hand, then pulled away from her. "I won't leave, Miss Carol. It would take an act of congress to get me out of Sheffield."

He smiled at Deborah when he walked past her, halting briefly to inspect her from head to toe, then proceeding down the hallway and through the door leading to the kitchen.

Heat and cold zigzagged through Deborah like red-hot and freezing blue shafts of pain. Ashe McLaughlin. Here in Sheffield. Here in her home. And he'd seen Allen!

"He can't stay."

"Come over here, dear." Carol patted the sofa seat. "You've

needed him for such a long time, Deborah, but now more than ever. You know I disagreed with your father's assessment of Ashe, but I loved your father and never would have gone against his wishes. But once Wallace died, I begged you to let me contact Ashe. He's kept in touch with Mattie all these years. We could have asked him to come home at any time.''

"He kept in touch with his grandmother, not with us. He left this town and didn't look back. He never once called me or wrote me or..." Deborah crossed the room, slumped down on the sofa beside her mother and folded her hands in her lap. "I need to phone the office and let them know I won't be back in this afternoon. I had planned to just drop Allen off, but I saw the car in the drive and wondered who... I don't want Ashe McLaughlin here.''

"But I do." Carol's blue eyes met her daughter's blue eyes, stubborn, determined and equally strong. "We both know that I'm only in remission. The cancer could worsen at any time and I'll have to go in for more surgery. I could die without ever seeing you happy.''

"You honestly think Ashe McLaughlin can make me happy? Get real, Mother." Deborah lowered her voice to a snarling whisper. "The man seduced me when I was seventeen, dropped me like a hot potato and left town two months later, never bothering to find out whether or not he'd gotten me pregnant.''

"I think you should know that—"

"If you're convinced I need a bodyguard then have the private security agency send someone else. Tell them we want someone older or younger or... Hell! Tell them anything, but get rid of Ashe.''

"I believe he still cares about you." Carol smiled, deepening the faint lines in her face.

"Mother!"

"It's been eleven years, Deborah, and you haven't had one serious relationship in all that time. Doesn't that tell you anything about your own feelings?''

"Yes. It tells me that I'm a smart girl. I learn from my mistakes.''

"It tells me that you've never gotten over Ashe McLaughlin, that somewhere deep down, in your heart of hearts, you're still in love with him.''

Deborah couldn't bear it. Her mother's words pierced the protective wall she had built around her heart. She didn't love Ashe McLaughlin. She hated him. But she knew only too well how fine a line there was between love and hate.

"I've hardly had time to date, let alone find the man of my dreams. Have you forgotten that I was in my senior year of college when Daddy died and I had to complete my courses for my degree and step in at Vaughn & Posey?" Deborah paused, waiting for her mother to comment. Carol said nothing.

"Then I had to earn my Realtors' license and work damn hard to fill Daddy's shoes at the firm," Deborah said. "Over the last few years while other firms have floundered, I've kept Vaughn & Posey in the black, making substantial gains each year. Over the last five years, we've been involved in two different subdivision developments."

Carol held up her hand, signaling acquiescence. "I know what a busy young woman you've been. But other people lead busy lives and still find time for romance."

"I don't need any romance in my life. Have you also forgotten how my foolishly romantic illusions about love nearly destroyed my life eleven years ago?"

"Of course I haven't forgotten. But there's more at stake than my desire to see you and Ashe settle things between you. Your life is in danger—real danger. Charlie Blaylock can only do so much. You need twenty-four-hour-a-day protection, and Ashe is highly qualified to do the job I've hired him to do."

"What makes him so highly qualified?"

"He was a Green Beret for ten years and joined, what I am told, is the best private security agency in the South. If you won't agree to his staying here for any other reason, do it for me. For my peace of mind."

"Mother, really. You're asking a great deal of me, aren't you? And you're putting Allen at risk. What if Ashe were to suspect the truth? Do we dare take that kind of chance? How do you think Allen would react if he found out that everything we've told him is a lie?"

Tears gathered in the corners of Deborah's eyes. She blinked them away. No tears. Not now. She cried only when she was alone, where no one could see her. Where no one would know that the strong, dependable, always reliable Deborah Luellen

Vaughn succumbed to the weakness of tears. Since her father died, she had learned to be strong—for her mother, for Allen, for those depending upon Vaughn & Posey for their livelihoods.

"Even if Ashe learns the truth, he would never tell Allen."

"How can you be so sure?"

"Intuition."

Deborah groaned. Sometimes her mother could be incredibly naive for a fifty-five-year-old woman. "I don't want Ashe Mc-Laughlin to become a part of our lives."

"He's always been a part of our lives." Carol glanced up at the oil painting of Allen at the age of three, hung over the fireplace beside the portrait of a three-year-old Deborah. "All I ask is that you allow him to stay on as your bodyguard until after Lon Sparks's trial. If you feel nothing for Ashe except hatred, then his being here should do nothing more than annoy you. Surely you can put up with a little annoyance to make your dying mother happy."

"You aren't dying!"

"Please, dear, just talk to Ashe."

Sighing deeply, Deborah closed her eyes and shook her head. How could she say no to her mother? How could she explain what the very sight of Ashe McLaughlin had done to her? Wasn't she already going through enough, having to deal with testifying against a murderer, having to endure constant threats on her life, without having to put up with Ashe McLaughlin, too?

"Oh, all right, Mother. I'll talk to Ashe. But I'm not promising anything."

"Fine. That's all I ask." Gripping the arm of the sofa for support, Carol stood. "I'll go in the kitchen and see how Ashe and Allen are getting along, then I'll send Ashe out to you."

Standing, Deborah paced the floor. Waiting. Waiting to face the man who haunted her dreams to this very day. The only man she had ever loved. The only man she had ever hated. Stopping in front of the fireplace, she glanced up at Allen's portrait. He looked so much like her. Their strong resemblance had made it easy to pass him off as her brother. But where others might not see any of Ashe in Allen's features, she could. His coloring was hers, but his nose was long and straight like Ashe's, not short and rounded like hers. His jaw tapered into a square chin unlike her gently rounded face.

Now that Allen was ten, it was apparent from his size that he would eventually become a large man, perhaps as big as Ashe, who stood six foot three.

But would Ashe see any resemblance? Would he look at Allen and wonder? Over the years had he, even once, asked himself whether he might have fathered a child the night he had taken her virginity?

"Deborah?"

She spun around to face Ashe, who stood in the hallway. Had he noticed her staring at Allen's portrait?

"Please come in and sit down."

He walked into the living room, but remained standing. "I came back to Sheffield as a favor to your mother." *And because she dared me to face the past.* "She sounded desperate when she called. My grandmother told me about Miss Carol's bout with cancer. I—"

"Thank you for caring about my mother."

"She was always good to Mama Mattie and to me. Despite what happened between the two of us, I never blamed your mother."

What was he talking about? What reason did he have to blame anyone for anything? He'd been the one who had left Sheffield, left an innocent seventeen-year-old girl pregnant.

"Mother has gotten it into her head that I need protection, and I don't disagree with her on that point. I'd be a fool to say I'm not afraid of Buck Stansell and his gang. I know what they're capable of doing. I saw, firsthand, how they deal with people who go against them."

"Then allowing me to stay as your bodyguard is the sensible thing to do."

How was it, he wondered, that years ago he'd thought Whitney Vaughn was the most beautiful, desirable creature on earth, when all along her little cousin Deborah had been blossoming into perfection? Although Whitney had been the woman he'd wanted, Deborah was the woman he'd never been able to forget.

"I would prefer your agency send another representative. That would be possible, wouldn't it? Surely, you're no more eager than I am for the two of us to be thrown together this way."

"Yes, it's possible for the Dundee Agency to send another

agent, but your mother wants me. And I intend to abide by her wishes."

Deborah glared at him, then regretted it when he met her gaze head-on. She didn't like the way he was looking at her. As if...as if he found her attractive.

"You could speak to Mother, persuade her to agree to another agent."

"Yes, I could speak to your mother, but I don't think anything I say will dissuade her from having me act as your personal body-guard." Ashe took a tentative step toward Deborah. She backed away from him. "Why is it that I get the feeling Miss Carol would like to see something romantic happen between you and me?"

Deborah turned from him, cursing the blush she felt creeping into her cheeks. When he placed his hands on her shoulders, she jerked away from him, rushing toward the French doors that opened up onto a side patio. She grasped the brass handle.

"I'm not interested in forming any kind of relationship with you other than employer and employee," Ashe said. "I agreed to act as your bodyguard because a fine, dear lady asked me to, as a personal favor to her. That's the only reason I'm here. You don't have to worry that I'll harass you with any unwanted atten-tion."

Deborah opened the French doors, walked outside and gazed up at the clear blue sky. Autumn sky. Autumn breeze. A hint of autumn colors surrounded her, especially in her mother's chrys-anthemums and marigolds that lined the patio privacy wall.

Why should Ashe's words hurt her so deeply? It wasn't as if she still loved him. She had accepted the fact, long ago, that she had meant nothing to him, that Whitney had been the woman he'd wanted. Why would she think anything had changed?

Ashe followed her out onto the side patio. "It wasn't easy for me to come back. I never wanted to see this place again as long as I lived. But I'm back and I intend to stay to protect you."

"As a favor to my mother?"

"Partly, yes."

She wouldn't face him; she couldn't. "Why else would you come back to Sheffield?"

"Your mother asked me if I was afraid to face the past. She dared me to come home."

"And were you afraid to face the past?"

"I'm here, aren't I? What does that tell you?"

"It tells me that you have a soft spot in your heart for my mother because she was kind to your grandmother and you and your cousin, Annie Laurie. And it tells me that you're the type of man who can't resist a dare."

"If I'm willing to come back to Sheffield, to act as your personal bodyguard because it's what Miss Carol wants, then it would seem to me that you should care enough about her to agree to her wishes. All things considered." He moved over to where Deborah stood near the miniature waterfall built into the privacy wall.

Turning her head slightly, she glanced at him. He had changed and yet he remained the same. Still devastatingly handsome, a bit cocky and occasionally rude. The twenty-one-year-old boy who'd made love to her had not completely vanished. He was there in those gold-flecked, green eyes, in that wide, sensuous mouth, in those big, hard hands. She jerked her gaze away from his hands. Hands that had caressed her intimately. Hands that had taught her the meaning of being a sexual woman.

How could she allow him to stay in her home? How could she endure watching him with Allen, knowing they were father and son?

Was there some way she could respect her mother's wishes and still keep the truth from Ashe?

"Let's understand something up front," Deborah said, facing him, steeling herself not to show any emotion. "I don't want you here. I had hoped I'd never see you again as long as I lived. If I agree to your acting as my bodyguard until the end of the the trial, to please Mother, you must promise me, here and now, that once I am no longer in any danger, you'll leave Sheffield and never return."

"Do you honestly think I'd want to stay?"

"Promise me."

"I don't have to promise you anything. I don't owe you anything." He glared at her, into those bright, still innocent-looking blue eyes and wanted to grab her and shake her until her teeth rattled. Who the hell did she think she was, giving him orders, demanding promises from him?

"You're still as stubborn, as bullheaded, as aggravating as you ever were," she said.

"Guilty as charged." He wanted to shout at her, to tell her she seemed to be the same little girl who wanted her own way. But this time she couldn't go running to Daddy. This time Wallace Vaughn couldn't force him to leave town. Nobody could. Most certainly not Deborah.

"We seem to be at an impasse."

"No, we're not. Once I settle in, pay a few visits on family and get the lay of the land, so to speak, you're stuck with me for the duration." When she opened her mouth to protest, he shook his head. "I won't promise you anything, but I can tell you this, I don't intend to stay in Alabama one day longer than necessary. And while I'm here, you don't have anything to fear from me. My purpose is to protect you, not harm you."

They stared at each other, face-to-face, two determined people, neither giving an inch. Finally Deborah nodded, then looked away.

"Dinner is at six-thirty, if you care to join us," she said.

"Fine. I'll be back from Mama Mattie's before then." Ashe hesitated momentarily, overwhelmed with a need to ask Deborah why. Why had she gone running to her daddy eleven years ago? Had his rejection made her hate him that much?

"I'll have Mazie prepare you a room, if Mother hasn't already seen to it."

"Thanks." There was no reason to wait, no reason to keep looking at her, to continue wondering exactly what it was about this woman that had made her so unforgettable. He tried to smile, but the effort failed, so he turned and walked back inside the house.

Deborah balled her hands into fists. Taking and releasing a deep breath, she said a silent prayer, asking God to keep them all safe and to protect Allen from the truth. A truth she had kept hidden in her heart since the day he was born, since the day she agreed to allow her son to be raised as her brother.

Chapter 2

As Ashe drove his rental car up Montgomery Avenue, into the downtown area of Sheffield, he noticed the new businesses, mostly restaurants—Louisiana, Milestones and New Orleans Transfer. Come what may, Southerners were going to eat well. Mama Mattie's homespun philosophy had always been that if folks spent their money on good food, they wouldn't need to spend it on a doctor.

Mama Mattie. How he loved that old woman. She was probably the only person he'd ever truly loved. The only person who had ever really loved him. He could barely remember a time during his growing up years when he hadn't lived with her. He had faint memories of living in a trailer out in Leighton. Before he'd started school. Before his daddy had caught his mama in bed with another man and shot them both.

The courts had sentenced JoJo McLaughlin to life in prison, and that's where he'd died, seven years later.

Mama Mattie had tried to protect Ashe from the ugly truth, from the snide remarks of unthinking adults and the vicious taunts of his schoolmates. But his grandmother had been powerless to protect him from the reality of class distinction, from the social snobbery and inbred attitudes of elite families, like the Vaughns, for whom she worked.

If he'd had a lick of sense, he would have stayed in his place and been content to work at the service station during the day and at the country club as a busboy on weekend nights. But no, Ashe McLaughlin, that bad boy who'd come from white trash outlaws, had wanted to better himself. It didn't matter to anyone that he graduated salutatorian of his high school class or that he attended the University of North Alabama on an academic scholarship. He still wasn't good enough to associate with the *right people*.

He had thought Whitney Vaughn cared about him, that their passionate affair would end in marriage. He'd been a fool. But he'd been an even bigger fool to trust sweet little Deborah, who professed to be his friend, who claimed she would love him until the day she died.

Crossing the railroad tracks, Ashe turned off Shop Pike and drove directly to Mama Mattie's neat frame house.

When he stepped out of the car, he saw her standing in the doorway, tall, broad-shouldered, her white hair permed into a halo of curls around her lean face.

He had sent her money over the years. Wrote her occasionally. Called her on her birthday and holidays. Picked up special gifts for her from around the world. She had asked him to come home a few times during the first couple of years after he joined the army, but she'd finally quit asking.

She wrote him faithfully, once a month, always thanking him for his kindness, assuring him she and Annie Laurie were well. Sometimes she'd mention that Miss Carol had dropped by for a visit, and told him what a precious little boy Allen Vaughn was. But she never mentioned Deborah. It was as if she knew he couldn't bear for her name to be mentioned.

Mattie Trotter opened the storm door, walked out onto the front porch and held open her arms. Ashe's slow, easy gait picked up speed as he drew closer to his grandmother. Taking the steps two at a time, he threw his arms around Mama Mattie, lifting her off her feet.

"Put me down, you silly boy! You'll throw out your back picking me up." All the while she scolded, she smiled, that warm, loving smile Ashe well remembered from his childhood.

Placing her on her feet, he slipped his arm around her waist, hugging her to his side. She lacked only a few inches being as tall as he was. "It's so good to see you again, Mama Mattie."

"Come on inside." She opened the storm door. "I've made those tea cakes you always loved, and only a few minutes ago, I put on a fresh pot of that expensive coffee you sent me from Atlanta."

Ashe glanced around the living room. Small, not more than twelve by fourteen. A tan sofa, arms and cushions well-worn, sat against the picture window, a matching chair to the left. The new plaid recliner Ashe had sent her for Christmas held a fat, gray cat, who stared up at Ashe with complete disinterest.

"That's Annie Laurie's Mr. Higgins. She's spoiled him rotten," Mattie said. "But to be honest, I'm pretty fond of him myself. Sit down, Ashe, sit down."

He sat beside her on the sofa. She clasped his hands. "There were times when I wondered if I'd ever see you again. I'm an old woman and only God knows how much longer I'm going to be in this world."

"Don't talk like that. You'll live to be a hundred."

Releasing his hands, she looked directly into his eyes. "Have you seen Deborah?"

"Yeah, Mama Mattie, I've seen Deborah Vaughn."

"She turned out to be a beautiful woman, didn't she?"

"She was always beautiful, just not...not finished."

"Miss Carol looks bad, doesn't she?" Mattie shook her head sadly. "That bout she had with cancer a while back took its toll on her. She's in remission now, but we all live in fear she'll have a relapse."

"She aged more than I'd expected," Ashe said, recalling how incredibly lovely Carol Vaughn had once been. "But nothing else has changed about her. She's still a very kind lady."

"So is Deborah."

"Don't!" Ashe stood abruptly, turning his back on his grandmother, not wanting to hear her defend the woman who had been responsible for having him run out of town eleven years ago.

Mattie sighed. "I still say you judged her wrong. She was just a child. Seventeen. You rejected all that sweet, young love she felt for you. If she went to her daddy the way you think she did, then you shouldn't hold it against her. My God, boy, you took her innocence and then told her you didn't want her."

"It wasn't like that and you damn well know it." Ashe needed to hit something, smash anything into a zillion pieces. He hated remembering what he'd done and what his stupidity had cost him.

"Don't you swear at me, boy." Mattie narrowed her eyes, giving her grandson a killing look.

"I'm sorry, Mama Mattie, but I didn't come by to see you so we could have that old argument about Deborah Vaughn." Ashe headed toward the kitchen. "Where are those tea cakes?"

Mattie followed him, busying herself with pouring coffee into brown ceramic mugs while Ashe devoured three tea cakes in quick succession. He pulled out a metal and vinyl chair and sat down at the table.

"They taste just the same. As good as I remember."

He would never forget walking into the Vaughns' kitchen after school every day, laying his books on the table and raiding Mama Mattie's tea cake tray. More often than not, he and Annie Laurie rode home with Miss Carol when she picked up Deborah and Whitney from school.

Whitney had ignored him as much as possible, often complaining to her aunt that she thought it disgraceful they had to be seen with *those children*. He supposed her haughty attitude had given him more reason to want to bring her down to his level, and eventually he'd done just that. He hadn't been Whitney's first, but he hadn't cared. She'd been hot and eager and he'd thought she really loved him.

All the while he'd been drooling over Whitney, he hadn't missed the way Deborah stared at him, those big blue eyes of hers filled with undisguised adoration.

"Thinking about those afternoons in the Vaughn kitchen?" Mattie asked.

"What is it with you and Miss Carol? Both of you seem determined to resurrect some sort of romance between Deborah and me." Ashe lifted the coffee mug to his lips, sipped the delicious brew and held his mug in his hand. "Deborah and I were never sweethearts. We weren't in love. I liked her and she had a big teenage crush on me. That's all there ever was to it. So tell me what's going on?"

"Neither one of you has ever gotten married."

"Are you saying you'd like to see me married to Deborah?" Ashe's laughter combined a snicker, a chuckle and a groan. "It's never going to happen. Not in a million years. Wherever did you get such a crazy idea?''

"You came back home when Miss Carol called and told you that Deborah was in trouble, that her life was in danger," Mattie said. "In eleven years nothing I've said or done could persuade you to return. And don't try to tell me that you came back because of Miss Carol. You could have sent another man from that private security place where you work. You didn't have to come yourself and we both know it."

"Miss Carol asked for me, personally. I knew how sick she'd been. You've told me again and again that you were afraid she might die."

"So knowing Buck Stansell is probably out to stop Deborah from testifying didn't have anything to do with your coming home? You don't care what happens to her?"

"I didn't say I don't care. I wouldn't want anything to happen to her." When Miss Carol had first telephoned him and explained the situation, his blood had run cold at the thought of anyone harming Deborah. Despite what she'd done to him, he couldn't help remembering the sweet, generous, loving girl he'd known since she was a small child. He had thought she didn't matter to him, that he didn't even hate her anymore. But he'd been wrong. He cared. He cared too damned much. Now that he'd seen Deborah again, he was worried that he couldn't act as her bodyguard and keep their relationship on a purely business level. And that could be dangerous for both of them. If he was smart, he'd call Sam Dundee and tell him to put another agent on the first available flight out of Atlanta.

But where Deborah Vaughn was concerned, he'd never been smart. Not when he had ignored her to pay court to her older cousin. Not when he'd accepted her comfort and love when Whitney had rejected him. And not when he'd been certain she would never betray him to anyone, least of all her father.

Mattie poured herself a second cup of coffee, broke a tea cake in two and popped half into her mouth. Chewing slowly, she watched Ashe. When he turned around and caught her staring at him, he smiled.

"All right. I admit it. Part of the reason I agreed to Miss Carol's request was because I don't want to see anything happen to Deborah. There. I said it. Are you satisfied?"

Mattie grinned, showing her perfect, white dentures. "You ought to go have a talk with Lee Roy and Johnny Joe. They're working for Buck Stansell, you know."

"Yeah, I figured as much, since their daddy and mine were both part of that gang years ago, along with Buck's daddy."

"Well, I don't trust Johnny Joe, but I always saw something in Lee Roy that made me think he was a mite better than that bunch of trash he came from."

"Hey, watch what you're saying, Mama Mattie. You're talking about my family." Ashe grinned.

"Your daddy's family, not mine, and not yours. I think Johnny Joe took after his daddy and his Uncle JoJo, where Lee Roy reminds me a bit of your daddy's sister. She wasn't such a bad girl. She and your mama always got along."

"You think Lee Roy and Johnny Joe know something about the threats against Deborah?" Ashe asked.

"Can't nobody prove nothing, but folks know that Buck Stansell was behind that killing Deborah witnessed. Whoever's been sending her those notes and making those phone calls, you can bet your bottom dollar that Buck's behind it all."

"What do you know about this Lon Sparks? I don't remember him."

"No reason you should. He showed up around these parts a few years back. I hear he come up from Corinth with a couple of other guys that Buck recruited when he expanded his drug dealings."

"How do you know so much, old woman?" Ashe laid his hand over his grandmother's where it rested beside her coffee cup.

"Everybody hears things. I hear things. At the beauty shop. At the grocery store. At church."

"After I've settled in and made my presence known, I'll take a ride out to Leighton and see how my cousins are doing."

"You be careful, Ashe. Buck Stansell isn't the kind of man to roll over and play dead just because Deborah's got herself a bodyguard."

"Don't you worry. I'm not stupid enough to underestimate Buck. I remember him and his old man. I've come up against their type all over the world."

"While you're taking care of Deborah and Miss Carol and that precious little Allen, make sure you take care of yourself, too.'' Mattie squeezed her grandson's big hand.

The back door swung open and a tall, thin young woman in a sedate gray pantsuit walked in and stopped dead still when she saw Ashe.''

"Oh, my goodness, it's really you!" Annie Laurie threw herself into Ashe's arms. "Mama Mattie said you'd come home, but I wasn't so sure. You've been away forever and ever."

Mr. Higgins sneaked into the kitchen, staring up at Annie Laurie, purring lightly.

Ashe held his cousin at arm's length, remembering the first time he'd seen her. She'd been a skinny eight-year-old whose parents had been killed in an automobile accident. Mama Mattie, Annie Laurie's mother's aunt, had been the child's closest relative and hadn't hesitated to open her home and heart to the girl, just as she had done for Ashe. "Here, let me have a good look at you. My, my. You sure have grown. And into a right pretty young lady."

Blushing, Annie Laurie shoved her slipping glasses back up her nose. "You haven't seen me since I was thirteen."

Hearing a car exit the driveway, Ashe glanced out the window in time to see a black Mercedes backing up, a familiar looking redheaded guy driving.

"Your boyfriend bring you home from work?" Ashe asked.

Annie Laurie's pink cheeks flamed bright red. She cast her gaze down toward the floor, then bent over, picked up Mr. Higgins and held him in her arms.

"Stop teasing the girl," Mattie said.

"He's not your boyfriend?" Ashe lifted her chin.

"He's my boss."

"Your boss?"

"That was Neil Posey," Mattie said. "You remember him. He's Archie Posey's son. He's partners with Deborah in their daddies' real estate firm."

"You work for Vaughn & Posey Real Estate?" Ashe asked. "I guess Mama Mattie told me and I'd just forgotten."

"I'm Neil's...that is Mr. Posey's secretary. And he's not my boyfriend. He's Deborah's...I mean, he likes her."

"What?" Ashe laughed aloud. Neil Posey was Deborah's boyfriend? That short, stocky egghead with carrot red hair and trillions of freckles.

"I've tried to tell Annie Laurie that Deborah isn't interested in Neil just because he follows her around like a lovesick puppy dog." Mattie shook her head, motioning for Ashe to let the subject drop. "Are you staying for supper? I've got some chicken all thawed out. It won't take me long to fry it up."

"Sorry, Mama Mattie, I'm expected for dinner at the Vaughns', but I'm looking forward to some of your fried chicken while I'm home."

"You be sure and tell Deborah and Miss Carol I asked about them," Mattie said. "And, here, take Allen some of my tea cakes. He loves them as much as you used to when you were his age."

Ashe caught an odd look in his grandmother's eyes. It was as if she knew something she wanted him to know, but for some reason didn't see fit to tell him. He shook off the notion, picked up his coffee mug and relaxed, enjoying being home. Back in his grandmother's house. Back with the only real family he'd ever known.

Deborah checked her appearance in the cheval mirror, tightened the backs of her pearl earrings and lifted the edge of her neckline so that her pearl necklace lay precisely right. Ashe McLaughlin's presence at their dinner table tonight had absolutely nothing to do with her concern about her appearance, she told herself, and knew it was a lie. Her undue concern *was* due to Ashe, and so was her nervousness.

Didn't she have enough problems without Ashe reappearing in her life after eleven years? How could her mother have thought that bringing that man back into their lives could actually help her? She'd almost rather face Buck Stansell alone than have to endure weeks with Ashe McLaughlin at her side twenty-four hours a day.

Of course, her mother had been right in hiring a personal bodyguard for her. She had to admit that she'd considered the possibility herself. But not Ashe!

Ever since she had inadvertently driven up on the scene of Corey Looney's execution, she had been plagued by nightmares. Both awake and asleep. Time and again she saw the gun, the blood, the man's body slump to the ground. Even in the quiet of her dark bedroom, alone at night, she could hear the sound of the gun firing.

Shivers racked Deborah's body. Chill bumps broke out on her arms. The letters and telephone calls had begun the day the sheriff arrested Lon Sparks. At first she had tried to dismiss them, but when they persisted, even the local authorities became concerned.

Colbert County's sheriff and an old family acquaintance, Charlie Blaylock, had assigned a deputy to her before and during the preliminary hearing, but couldn't spare a man for twenty-four-hour-a-day protection on an indefinite basis. Charlie had spoken to the state people, the FBI and the DEA, hoping one or more of the agencies' interest in Buck Stansell's dealings might bring in assistance and protection for Deborah.

But there was no proof Buck Stansell was involved, even though everyone knew Lon Sparks worked for Stansell. The federal boys wanted to step in, but murder in Colbert County was a local crime. They'd keep close tabs on the situation, but couldn't become officially involved.

Charlie had been the one to suggest hiring a private bodyguard. Deborah had agreed to consider the suggestion, never dreaming her mother would take matters into her own hands and hire Ashe McLaughlin.

Closing the door behind her, Deborah stepped out into the upstairs hallway, took a deep breath and ventured down the stairs. When she entered the foyer, she heard voices coming from the library, a room that had once been her father's private domain. Her mother had kept the masculine flavor of the room, but had turned it into a casual family retreat where she or Deborah often helped Allen with his homework. The old library was more a family room now.

She stood in the open doorway, watching and listening, totally unnoticed at first. Her mother sat in a tan-and-rust floral print chair, her current needlepoint project in her hand. She smiled, her gaze focused on Allen and Ashe, who were both sitting on the Tabriz rug, video-game controls in their hands as they fought out a battle on the television screen before them.

"You're good at this," Allen said. "Are you sure you don't have a kid of your own you play with all the time?"

Deborah sucked in a deep breath, the sting of her son's words piercing her heart. She couldn't bear the way Allen looked at Ashe, so in awe of the big, friendly man he must never know was his father.

"I don't have any kids of my own." Ashe hadn't thought much about having a family. His life didn't include a place for a wife and children, although at one time, a family had been high on his list of priorities—eleven years ago when he'd thought he would marry Whitney Vaughn and carve a place for himself in local society. Hell, he'd been a fool in more ways than one.

"You should be thinking about a family, Ashe," Carol Vaughn said, laying aside her needlework. "You're how old now, thirty-two? Surely you've sowed all the wild oats a man would need to sow."

Ashe turned his head, smiled at Carol, then frowned when he caught sight of Deborah standing in the doorway. "I haven't really given marriage a thought since I left Sheffield. When a man puts his trust in the wrong woman, more than once, the way I did, it makes him a little gun-shy."

Deborah met his fierce gaze directly, not wavering the slightest when he glared at her with those striking hazel eyes...gold-flecked green eyes made even more dramatic since they were set in a hard, lean, darkly tanned face.

Ashe realized that he could not win the game of staring her down. Deborah Vaughn had changed. She was no longer the shy, quiet girl who always seemed afraid to look him in the eye. Now she seemed determined to prove to him how tough she was, how totally immune she was to him.

With that cold, determined stare she told him that he no longer had any power over her, that the lovesick girl she'd once been no longer existed. Her aversion to him came as no great surprise, but what did unsettle him was her accusatory attitude, as if she found him at fault.

All right, he had taken her innocence when he'd had no right to touch her, but he'd told her he was sorry and begged her to forgive him. He had rejected her girlish declaration of love as gently as he'd known how. If he'd been a real cad, he could have taken advantage of her time and again. But he'd cared about Deborah, and his stupidity in taking her just that one time had made him heartsick.

But he had not ruined her life. It had been the other way around.

She had almost ruined his a couple of months later by running to her daddy. Why had she done it? Had she hated him that much? Did she still hate him?

Carol glanced at her daughter. "Deborah, come join us. Mazie tells me dinner will be ready promptly at six-thirty."

"She's always punctual. Dinner's at six-thirty every night," Deborah said.

"She's prepared Allen's favorite. Meat loaf with creamed potatoes and green peas," Carol said.

"Hey, pal, that's my favorite, too." Ashe elbowed Allen playfully in the ribs.

Allen leaned into Ashe, toppling the big man over onto the rug. Within seconds the two were wrestling around on the floor.

Deborah looked from father and son to her mother. Nervously she cleared her throat. When no one paid any heed to her, she cleared her throat again.

"Come sit down." Carol gestured toward the tufted leather sofa. "Let the boys be boys. They'll tire soon enough."

When Deborah continued staring at Allen and Ashe rolling around on the floor, both of them laughing, Carol stood and walked over to her daughter.

"Allen needs a man in his life." Carol slipped her arm around Deborah's waist, leading her into the room. "He'll soon be a teenager. He's going to need a father more than ever then."

"Hush, Mother! They'll hear you."

Carol glanced over at the two rowdy males who stopped abruptly when their roughhousing accidently knocked over a potted plant.

"Uh-oh, Allen, we'll be in trouble with the ladies now." Rising to his knees, Ashe swept up the spilled dirt with his hands and dumped it back into the brass pot.

"Don't worry about it," Carol said. "I'll ask Mazie to run the vacuum over what's left on the rug."

Deborah glanced down at her gold and diamond wristwatch. "It's almost six-thirty. I'll check on dinner and tell Mazie about the accident with the plant."

The moment Deborah exited the room, Allen shook his head, stood up and brushed off his hands. "What's the matter with Deborah? She's acting awful strange."

"She's nervous about the upcoming trial, but you know that,

Allen.'' Carol smiled, first at Allen and then at Ashe. ''Our lives have been topsy-turvy for weeks now.''

''No, I'm not talking about that.'' Allen nodded toward Ashe. ''She's been acting all goofy ever since Ashe showed up here today.'' He turned to Ashe. ''Nobody ever answered my question about whether you and Deborah used to be an item.''

''Allen—'' Carol said.

''Deborah and I were good friends at one time.'' Ashe certainly couldn't say anything negative about his sister to the boy. ''I'm four years older, so I dated older girls.''

''Deborah had a crush on Ashe for years,'' Carol said.

When Ashe glanced at Carol, she stared back at him, her look asking something of him that Ashe couldn't comprehend.

''She liked you, but you didn't like her back?'' Allen asked. ''Boy, were you dumb. Deborah's pretty and about the nicest person in the world.''

''Yeah, Allen, I was pretty dumb all right. I'm a lot smarter now.''

''Well, if Deborah gives you a second chance this time, you won't mess things up, will you?'' Allen looked at him with eyes identical to Deborah's, the purest, richest blue imaginable.

''I'm not here to romance your sister,'' Ashe said. ''I'm here to protect her, to make sure—''

Carol cleared her throat; Ashe realized he was saying too much, that they wanted the boy protected from the complete, ugly truth.

''Ashe is here to act as Deborah's bodyguard. You know, the way famous people have bodyguards to protect them from their overzealous fans. Well, Ashe is going to make sure the reporters and people curious about the trial don't interfere with her life in any way.''

''The kids at school say Buck Stansell will try to kill Deborah if she tells in court what she saw that man do,'' Allen said, looking directly to Ashe for an explanation. ''Is that true?''

''No one is going to hurt Deborah while I'm around.'' Ashe placed his hand on the boy's shoulder. ''And I'll be here until after the trial, maybe a little longer.''

Carol Vaughn sighed. Ashe glanced at the doorway. Deborah had returned and was looking straight at him, her eyes filled with pain and fear and something indiscernible. Longing? Ashe wondered. Or perhaps the remembrance and regret of longing?

Deborah willed herself to be strong, to show no sign of weakness in front of Allen and her mother or in Ashe's presence. She'd heard Ashe say that no one would hurt her while he was around. For one split second her heart had caught in her throat. He had sounded so determined, so protective, as if he truly cared what happened to her.

"Dinner is ready." Damn, her voice shouldn't sound so unsteady. She had to take control. "Is everything all right?"

"Fine," Carol and Ashe said in unison.

Rushing across the room, Allen threw his arms around Deborah. "I'll help Ashe protect you. You'll have two men in your life now, and we'll make sure nobody bothers you."

Deborah hugged her son to her, threading her fingers through his thick blond hair. "I feel very safe, knowing that I have you two guys looking out for me."

Carol Vaughn steered Allen and Ashe into the hall. "You two wash up and meet us in the dining room." She slipped her arm around Deborah's waist. "Come, dear."

Carol managed to keep the conversation directed on Allen during the meal, telling Ashe about the boy's exploits since early childhood. Deborah wished her mother didn't have her heart set on reuniting them all. There was no way it would ever happen. She and Ashe didn't even like each other. She certainly had good reason not to like Ashe, and it seemed he thought he had reason to dislike her.

"I told Mazie to save the apple pie for tomorrow night's dinner," Carol said. "Ashe brought us some of Mattie's delicious homemade tea cakes."

"I love Mama Mattie's tea cakes," Allen said.

Jerking his head around, Ashe stared at Allen. Had he heard correctly? Had Allen Vaughn referred to Ashe's grandmother as Mama Mattie?

"Mattie insisted Allen call her Mama Mattie." Carol laid her linen napkin on the table. "She said that she liked to think of Allen as a grandchild."

Deborah strangled on her iced tea. Lifting her napkin to her mouth, she coughed several times. Her faced turned red. She glared at her mother.

"Let's have Mazie serve the tea cakes in the library with coffee for us and milk for Allen.'' Easing her chair away from the table, Carol stood.

Allen followed Carol out of the dining room, obviously eager for a taste of Mattie Trotter's tea cakes. Deborah hesitated, waiting for Ashe. He halted at her side as he walked across the room.

"You look lovely tonight," he said. What the hell had prompted that statement? He'd thought it, and made the remark before thinking.

"Thank you."

She wore blue silk, the color of her eyes. And pearls. A lady's jewel. Understated and elegant.

"We've tried to protect Allen from the complete truth," she said. "He's so young. And he and I are very close. He was only four when Daddy died, and he tries to be our little man."

"He knows more than you think." Ashe understood her need to protect the boy; on short acquaintance he felt an affinity with Deborah's brother and a desire to safeguard him. "Anything made public, he's bound to hear sooner or later. You're better off being up front with him."

"Just what do you know about ten-year-old boys?"

"I know they're not babies, that a boy as smart as Allen can't be fooled."

"It's not your place to make decisions where—"

The telephone rang. Deborah froze. Ashe wished he could erase the fear he saw in her eyes, the somber expression on her face. "Have you had your number changed? Unlisted?"

"Yes." She swallowed hard.

"It's for you, Miss Deborah." Mazie stood in the doorway holding the portable phone. "It's Mr. Posey."

Letting out a sigh, Deborah swayed a fraction. Ashe grabbed her by the elbow.

"Are you all right?" he asked.

Deborah took the phone from Mazie, placed her hand over the mouthpiece and looked at Ashe. "Go ahead and join Mother and Allen in the library."

"Neil Posey?" Ashe asked. "Has he changed any or do his buddies still call him Bozo?"

Deborah widened her eyes, glaring at Ashe as if what he'd said had been sacrilege. *Go away. Now.* She mouthed the words. Grinning, Ashe threw up his hands in a what-did-I-say gesture, then walked out of the room.

"Neil?"

"I thought perhaps you'd like to take a drive," he said. "It's such a lovely autumn night. We could stop by somewhere for coffee later."

"Oh, that's such a sweet thought, but I'm afraid... Well, tonight just isn't good for me. We...that is, Mother has company tonight."

"I see. I'm disappointed of course, but we'll just make it another night."

"Yes, of course."

"See you tomorrow," Neil said. "Yes. Tomorrow." Deborah laid the phone down on the hall table.

Before she took three steps, the telephone rang again. She eyed it with suspicion. *Don't do this to yourself. Answer the damned thing. It's not going to bite you.*

"Hello. Vaughn residence."

"Deborah?" the man asked.

"Yes."

"Telling the sheriff what you saw was your first mistake. Testifying in court will be your last mistake."

"Who is this?" Sheriff Blaylock had put a tap on their telephones, the one in her bedroom and the one in the library. *Damn, why hadn't she remembered not to answer the portable phone?*

"This is someone concerned for your safety."

"How did you get our number?" She gripped the phone with white-knuckled ferocity.

"Change it as many times as you want and we'll still keep calling."

"Leave me alone!" Deborah's voice rose.

Ashe appeared before her, grabbed the phone out of her hand and shoved her aside. She stared at him in disbelief.

"Ms. Vaughn won't be taking any more phone calls." He ended the conversation, laid the phone on the hall table, then grabbed Deborah by the arm. "From now on, you're not to answer the phone. Mazie or I will screen all the incoming calls."

The touch of his big hand on her arm burned like fire. He was hard, his palm warm. She looked up at him, saw the genuine concern in his eyes and wanted nothing more than to crumple into his arms. It would be so easy to give in to the fear and uncertainty that had plagued her since she had witnessed Corey Looney's death. Ashe was big and strong, his shoulders wide enough to carry any burden. Even hers. She wanted to cry out to him "Take care of me," but she couldn't. She had to be strong. For herself. For her mother and Allen.

"Please, don't mention the phone call to Mother. It will only worry her needlessly."

"Needlessly?" Ashe grabbed Deborah by the shoulders. "You're so cool and in control. You're not the girl I used to know. She would have been crying by now. What changed you so much?"

You did. The words vibrated on the tip of her tongue. They would be so easy to say, so difficult to explain. "I grew up. I took on the responsibilities Daddy left behind when he died so suddenly."

Ashe ran his hands up and down her arms. She shivered. For one instant he saw the vulnerable, gentle girl he'd once liked, the Deborah who had adored him. "You won't answer the telephone, at home or at work."

"All right."

"And I won't mention this call to Miss Carol."

"Thank you."

He could barely resist the urge to kiss her. She stood there facing him, her defiant little chin tilted, her blue eyes bright, her cheeks delicately flushed. God, but she was beautiful. But then she always had been. Even when he'd fancied himself in love with Whitney, he hadn't been immune to Deborah's shy, plump beauty.

"If you ever need to let down your defenses for a few minutes, to stop being strong all the time for your mother and brother, I'll be around." He released her, but continued looking directly at her.

She nodded her head, turned and walked away from him.

He didn't want to care about her. Dammit! All these years he'd never been able to forget her. Or the fact that she had betrayed him to her father. Or that she had been a virgin and he had taken advantage of her. And he could never forget when she'd told him she loved him that night, he had seen a depth of emotion on her face he'd never seen again.

He waited in the entrance hall for a few minutes, wondering how the hell he was going to do his job protecting Deborah from the bad guys, when what she desperately needed was protection from him.

Chapter 3

"Mother had Mazie put your bag in here," Deborah said. "One of the guest rooms. It's right across the hall from mine."

"I'm sure it'll be fine." Ashe followed her into the room. Over the years he had stayed in some fancy places. It wasn't as if the finer things in life impressed him the way they once had. But even now, after all these years, he couldn't suppress the satisfaction of knowing he'd be sleeping in a guest room at the Vaughns' house.

Deborah flipped on the overhead light, revealing a room done tastefully in shades of tan and green. The antique oak bedroom suite, masculine in its heavy lines and massive size, would have overwhelmed a smaller room.

"Mother's room is to the right." Deborah returned to the hall. Ashe stood in the doorway. "And that's Allen's room." She pointed to the open door from which a blast of loud music came, then quieted. "He forgets and plays it too loud sometimes, but he's trying to be more considerate, for Mother's sake."

"I suppose it's been difficult for her trying to raise a young boy, alone, especially at her age." Ashe caught a glimpse of Allen darting around in his room, apparently straightening things.

"Mother is an incredible lady, but she hasn't been alone in

raising Allen. I've been with her, taking as much responsibility for him as I possibly could.''

"I'm sure you have. I just meant she's raised him without a father, without a man around to help her."

Deborah noticed Ashe watching their son. No! She had to stop thinking that way. Allen Vaughn was her brother.

"He's picking up because he plans to invite you in. He has a lot of questions to ask you about being a bodyguard.''

"He's quite a boy, isn't he?" Ashe looked at Deborah. "He reminds me of you. Same coloring. Same quick mind.''

"Yes, Allen and I are very much alike." But there are things about him that remind me of you, she wanted to say. Even before Ashe had come back into their lives, she had found similarities between Allen and the man who had fathered him. Now that they'd be together all the time, would those similarities become even more apparent?

"He's big for his age, isn't he?" Ashe asked. He'd thought it strange that Allen was so tall for a ten-year-old. Deborah couldn't be more than five-four, about the same height as Miss Carol; and Wallace Vaughn had been short and stocky.

"Yes." She smiled, thinking about how Ashe had looked as a boy of ten. He had been a part of her life for as long she could remember. He'd come to live with Mattie Trotter when he was only six, right after his mother's death. Deborah had grown up accustomed to seeing Ashe in the kitchen and out in the garden, during the summers and after school, until he'd grown old enough for part-time jobs.

"What are you thinking about?" Ashe couldn't quite discern that faraway look in her eyes. Whatever thoughts had captured her, they must have been pleasant.

"I was thinking about when we were kids. You and little Annie Laurie, Whitney and I." She could have lied, but why should she? They could not change the past, neither the good nor the bad. What had happened, had happened.

"How is Whitney?"

Deborah hadn't thought Ashe's interest in her cousin would create such a sharp pain inside her heart. *Don't do this to yourself! It doesn't matter any more. Whitney is not your rival. You don't love Ashe McLaughlin.*

"She's as well as anyone could be married to George Jamison III."

"What does that mean, exactly?"

"It means that George is quite content to live off Whitney's money, and the two of them have never had children because Whitney is too busy trying to raise the little boy she married."

"I'd say Whitney got what she deserved, wouldn't you?" He could remember a time when he had longed to make Whitney Vaughn his wife. He'd been a fool. She had wanted Ashe for one thing and one thing only. She had enjoyed the sense of danger and excitement she found having an affair with a bad boy her friends considered beneath them.

"She could have married you, couldn't she? You never would have deserted *her*. And you wouldn't have lived off her inheritance." Deborah turned toward her room.

Ashe gripped her by the elbow, pulling her toward him. Jerking her head around, she glared at him. "Your cousin didn't want to marry me. Remember?" he said. "She thought I wasn't good enough for her. But you didn't think that, did you, Deborah?"

He said her name all soft and sexy and filled with need. The way he'd said it that night. She tried to break away, to force herself into action, to terminate the feelings rising within her. No, she had never thought she was too good for Ashe. She had adored him for as long as she could remember and held her secret love in her heart until the night he'd turned to her for comfort.

He had taken the comfort she'd offered—and more. He'd taken all she had to give. And left her with nothing.

No, that wasn't true. He had left her with Allen.

"Did you change your mind, later? After—" Ashe began.

"No, I... The difference in our social positions isn't what kept us apart and we both know it."

"What about now?" he asked.

"What do you mean?" She looked at him, questioning his statement, daring him to ask her what she thought of the man who had come back into her life after deserting her eleven years ago.

"I'm the hired help around here." His lips were so close that his breath mingled with hers. "Would Miss Deborah ever fool around with the hired help?"

"You're being offensive." She tried to pull away from him; he held fast. Her heartbeat drummed in her ears.

They stared at each other. Defiant. Determined. Neither backing down.

"Hey, Ashe, come in my room and let me introduce you to Huckleberry," Allen called out from down the hallway.

Allen's interruption immediately broke the tense spell. Deborah breathed a sigh of relief; Ashe loosened his hold on her arms.

"Allen, does Mother know you've brought Huckleberry inside?" Deborah asked as she eased her body away from Ashe.

A large tan Labrador retriever stood beside Allen, the dog's tongue hanging out, his tail wagging as the boy stroked his back.

Ashe grinned. "Where does Huckleberry usually stay?"

"Outside," Deborah said. "But occasionally Mother allows Allen to bring him inside."

"Come on." Allen waved at Ashe. "I want to show you my room. Deborah helped me redo the whole thing last year. It's a real guy's room now and not a baby's room anymore."

"Is your mother having a difficult time letting Allen grow up?" Ashe asked.

"Yes, I suppose she is. But he is the baby, after all."

"Come on, Ashe." Allen motioned with his hand.

"Coming?" Ashe asked Deborah.

"Yes, in a minute. You go ahead."

Ashe gave Huckleberry a pat on the head when he entered Allen's domain. He'd speak to Deborah and Miss Carol about allowing the dog to remain inside. A dog as big as Huckleberry could act as a deterrent to anyone foolish enough to break into the house.

Allen's room was indeed a *real guy's room*. Posters lined one wall. Dark wooden shutters hung at the windows. A sturdy antique bed, covered in blue-and-green plaid, and a huge matching dresser seemed to be the only antique items in the room. A color television, a CD player, a VCR and a tape recorder filled a wall unit beside a desk that held a computer, monitor and printer.

"This is some room, pal. I'd say your sister made sure you had everything a guy could want."

"Yeah, she let me get rid of everything babyish." Allen grabbed Ashe by the hand. "Come take a look at these. This is one of my hobbies."

Allen led Ashe over to a shiny metal trunk sitting at the foot of his bed. Lying atop the trunk were two brown albums.

"What have you got here?"

"My baseball card collection."

Deborah stood in the hallway, listening, waiting. How was she going to protect Allen from Ashe McLaughlin when she was finding it difficult to protect herself from him? The moment he'd pulled her close, the moment he'd said her name in that husky, sexy voice of his, she'd practically melted. No other man had ever made her feel the way Ashe did.

Damn him! Damn him for having the same dizzying effect on her he'd always had. Eleven years hadn't changed the way she wanted him. If she thought she would be immune to Ashe's charms, then she'd been a total fool. If she wasn't careful, she'd wind up falling in love with him all over again.

She couldn't let that happen. And she couldn't allow Ashe to find out that Allen was his son.

Deborah walked down the hall, stopping in the doorway to Allen's bedroom. Ashe and Allen sat on the bed, Huckleberry curled up beside them, his head resting on a pillow. A lump formed in Deborah's throat.

Please, dear Lord. Don't let anyone else notice what I see so plainly—the similarities in boy and man.

"How long were you a Green Beret?" Allen asked.

"Ten years."

"Wow, I'll bet that's one exciting job, huh? Did you ever kill anybody?"

Deborah almost cried out, not wanting Ashe to discuss his life in the special forces with their ten-year-old son. She bit her lip and remained silent, waiting for Ashe's reply.

"Yes, Allen, I've killed. But it isn't something I like to talk about. It was my job get rid of the bad guys, but killing is never easy."

"That's what you're here in Sheffield to do, isn't it?" Allen asked. "You're here to protect Deborah against the bad guys, and if you have to, you'll kill them, won't you?"

"I hope it doesn't come to that," Ashe said. "But, yes, I'll do whatever it takes to keep Deborah safe."

"How long have you been a bodyguard?"

"I started working for Sam Dundee last year, right after I left the army."

"Why'd you leave the Green Berets?"

Deborah cleared her throat, stepped inside Allen's room and gave him a censuring stare. "I think you've asked Ashe enough questions for one night. Save a few for later."

"Ah, Deborah, can't he stay just a little while longer?" Allen whined in a typical childlike manner. "I was going to ask him about the two of you when you were kids." Allen turned his attention to Ashe. "Did you ever kiss Deborah when you two were teenagers?"

"Allen!" Deborah scolded, her voice harsher than she had intended.

"Yes, I kissed Deborah." Ashe watched her closely, noting that she wouldn't look at him, that she had balled her hands into fists and held them rigidly at her hips.

"I knew it! I knew it!" Allen bounced up and down on the bed. "You two were a thing, weren't you?"

"No, Allen." Deborah trembled inside, and prayed the shivers racing through her body didn't materialize externally. "Stop jumping up and down on the bed."

"You sure are being a grouch." Settling back down on the side of the bed, Allen glanced back and forth from Deborah to Ashe. "What's the big secret about you two being an item when you were teenagers? Is it a big deal that Ashe was your boyfriend?"

"We've told you that Ashe wasn't my boyfriend," Deborah said. No, he'd never been her boyfriend, just her lover for one night. One night that had changed her life forever. "We were friends."

"Then why did he kiss you?" Allen asked.

Deborah looked to Ashe, her gaze pleading with him, then she glanced away quickly. "Sometimes an occasion arises when a friend might kiss another friend," Deborah said.

The look on Allen's face plainly said he didn't believe a word of it.

"Deborah and I were friends all our lives," Ashe explained. "Then not long before I left Sheffield, we thought we could be more than friends. That's when I kissed her. But it didn't work out. So you see, Allen, your sister was never actually my girlfriend."

"Do you have a girlfriend now?"

"Allen!" Rolling her eyes heavenward, Deborah shook her head in defeat. "Enough questions for one night."

Ashe laughed. "I remember being the same way when I was his age. I used to drive Mama Mattie nuts asking her so many questions. I guess it's the age. The whole world is a mystery when you're ten."

"I guess it's a guy thing, huh, Ashe?"

Allen looked at Ashe McLaughlin with such adoration in his eyes that Deborah almost cried. There had been a time when she, too, had adored Ashe. It was so easy to fall under his spell, to succumb to his charm. Maybe her son had inherited her weakness.

"Curiosity isn't a guy thing," Ashe said. "I remember a time when your sister's curiosity got the minister in big trouble."

"What?" Allen grinned, stole a quick glance at Deborah and burst into laughter. "Deborah did something she wasn't supposed to do? I can't believe it. She always does the right thing."

"Well, she made the mistake of walking in on Reverend Bently and the new choir director, a very attractive lady," Ashe said.

"I asked Mother, right in the middle of her study club meeting, why Reverend Bently would kiss Miss Denise." Deborah smiled, remembering the utter horror on her mother's face and the loud rumble of ladies' voices rising in outrage as they sat in Carol Vaughn's garden, dropping their finger sandwiches and spilling their tea.

"How'd you know, Ashe? Were you there? Did you see it happen?"

"Allen, that's enough questions," Deborah said. "You've got school tomorrow and I have work. Besides, Ashe hasn't even settled in yet. Save the rest of your million and one questions for another day."

"Ah...ahh... All right."

"Deborah told me all about it when I stopped by to pick up Mama Mattie that evening after I got off from work. Your sister was only twelve then, and at that age she used to tell me everything."

Not everything, Deborah thought. Not then, not later, and certainly not now. She never told him how much she loved him. Not until that night by the river. But he'd known she had a crush on him, just as he was aware, now, that she was afraid of him, afraid of how he made her feel.

"Deborah's right, pal. It's getting late." Ashe ruffled the boy's thick blond hair, hair the exact shade Deborah's had been as a child. "I'll be around for several weeks. You'll have a chance to ask me a lot more questions."

Deborah waited in the hallway until Ashe walked past her and toward his own room. He hesitated in the doorway.

"You were always special to me," he said. "I trusted you in a way I didn't trust another soul."

She stood in the hall, staring at his back as he entered his room and closed the door. She shivered. What had he meant by that last statement? Was he accusing her of something? He had trusted her. Well, she had trusted him, too. And he had betrayed her. He had taken her innocence, gotten her pregnant and left town.

Whatever had gone wrong between them hadn't been her fault. It had been his. He hadn't loved her. He'd used her. And afterward, when she'd poured out her heart to him, he'd said he was sorry, that he never should have touched her.

Ashe McLaughlin had regretted making love to her. She could never forget the pain that knowledge had caused her. Even if she could forgive him, she could never forget what he'd said to her eleven years ago... *But I don't love you, Deborah. Not that way. What we did tonight shouldn't have happened. I'm sorry. It was all my fault. Forgive me, honey. Please forgive me.*

Tears gathered in the corners of her eyes. She walked the few steps to her open bedroom door, crossed the threshold, closed the door quietly and, once alone, wiped away her tears.

"All of Ms. Vaughn's calls are to be screened. That means the caller must identify him or herself and must be someone Ms. Vaughn knows. Otherwise the call will be directed to me. Is that understood?"

Ashe McLaughlin issued orders to the office staff of Vaughn & Posey, the men obviously intimidated, the women enthralled. Standing six-foot-three, broad-shouldered and commanding in his gray sport coat, navy slacks and white shirt, Ashe was the type of man to whom no one dared utter a word of protest.

Listening to Ashe give orders, Deborah waited in her office doorway, Neil Posey at her side. When the staff, one by one, turned their heads in her direction, she nodded her agreement with Ashe. He'd made it perfectly clear to her before they arrived at work that he would be in charge of her life, every small detail, until she was no longer in danger.

Ashe turned to Annie Laurie, who had worked as Neil's secretary for the past five years, and was doing double duty as Deborah's secretary while hers was out on maternity leave. "Carefully check all of Deborah's mail. Anything suspicious, bring to me. And I'll open all packages, no matter how innocent looking they are. Understand?"

"Of course, Ashe." Despite her mousy brown hair and out-of-style glasses, plain little Annie Laurie had grown into a lovely young woman.

Deborah tried not to stare at Ashe, but she found herself again inspecting him from head to toe as she had done at breakfast this morning. No wonder all the females in the office were practically drooling. Although his clothes were tailored to fit his big body, on Ashe they acquired an unpretentious casualness. He wore no tie and left the first two buttons of his shirt undone, revealing a tuft of dark chest hair.

"Who does he think he is coming in here issuing orders right and left?" Neil Posey whispered, his tone an angry hiss. "When you introduced him as your bodyguard, I assumed you would be giving him orders, not the other way around."

"Ashe can't do the job Mother hired him to do unless I cooperate." Deborah patted Neil on the shoulder. "Ashe is here to protect me. He's a trained professional."

"He hasn't changed. He's as damn sure of himself as he ever was." Neil took Deborah's hand in his. "I don't like the idea of that man living in your house, sleeping across the hall from you."

"He could hardly protect me if he stayed at a motel."

"Why Ashe McLaughlin? Good grief, Deb, you were in love with the guy when we were in high school." Neil's eyes widened. He stared directly at Deborah. "You don't still...the man doesn't mean anything to you now, does he?"

"Lower your voice." She had told Neil time and again that she couldn't offer him more than friendship. She'd never led him on or made him any promises. Perhaps it was wrong of her to go out with him from time to time, but he was such a comfortable, nonthreatening date.

"I'm sorry," Neil said. "It's just I'd hate to see him break your heart. You mooned around over him for years and all he could see was Whitney."

"Yes, Neil, I know. Can we please change the subject?"

Deborah caught a glimpse of Ashe going from desk to desk, speaking personally to each Vaughn & Posey employee. Ashe looked up from where he was bent over Patricia Walden's desk and smiled at Deborah. He'd seen her staring at him, watching while Patricia fluttered her long, black eyelashes at him. Deborah forced a weak smile to her lips.

"Look at him flirting with Patricia, and her a married woman!" Neil sucked in his freckled cheeks, making his long, narrow face appear even more equine than usual.

"Neil, close the door, please. We need to discuss the Cotton Lane Estates. I'm afraid we've allowed my situation to interfere in our moving ahead on this project."

Neil closed the door, followed Deborah across the room, waited until she sat, then seated himself. "We have the surveyor's report. No surprises there. I've had Annie Laurie run a check on the deed. Everything is in order. Mr. and Mrs. McCullough have agreed to our last offer. I'd say, despite your problems, things are moving ahead quite smoothly."

"We should have had this deal wrapped up a week ago. Have Mr. and Mrs. McCullough come in today and let's get everything signed, sealed and delivered. We've still got several months of good weather, so if we can give Hutchinson the go-ahead, he can move his crews in there and cut the roads we'll need before we divide the land into one-acre lots."

"I'll give the McCulloughs a call. Since he's retired, they shouldn't have any problem driving down from Decatur this afternoon."

"Fine. And thanks for handling things while my life has been turned upside down lately."

Neil smiled, that widemouthed grin that showed all his teeth. "You know I'd do anything for you, Deb. Anything."

The door opened and Ashe McLaughlin walked in, making no apologies for interrupting. "Make time at lunch to go with me to see Sheriff Blaylock. I want to arrange for one of his men to keep an eye on you tomorrow while I do a little investigating on my own."

"I don't think that's necessary," Neil said. "Whenever you

need to do your *investigating,* I'll be more than happy to stay with Deborah.

"Neil—" Deborah wanted to caution her friend, but she didn't get the chance.

"Look, Posey, I appreciate the fact you're Deborah's friend, but you're a realtor. I'm a professional bodyguard. If I can't be at Deborah's side, I want another professional to be there. One of the sheriff's deputies."

"I can assure you that I'd die to protect Deborah."

"That may be so, but once they kill you, what would keep them from killing her?" Ashe ignored Deborah's pleading look that said not to crush Neil Posey's ego. But Ashe didn't give a damn about Posey's ego. He simply wanted to make sure the man understood he wasn't equipped to play hero. "Do you own a gun? Do you carry it with you? Have you ever killed a man?"

"No, I don't own a gun and I most certainly have never killed another human being." Neil shuddered, obviously offended at the thought.

"It's all well and good to be willing to die to protect Deborah, but it's just as important to be willing to kill, or at least maim an assailant, in order to protect her."

"I'll arrange to go with you to see Charlie Blaylock," Deborah said, her tone sharp. She wanted Ashe to know how displeased she was with him. There had been no need to humiliate Neil. "Thank you for your offer, Neil. I'd feel completely safe with you, but..." She nodded in Ashe's direction. "Mother is paying Mr. McLaughlin a small fortune, so I plan to get our money's worth out of him."

"Yes, well...I understand." With shoulders slumped, Neil slinked out of Deborah's office like a kicked dog.

She marched across the room, slammed shut the door and turned on Ashe. "How dare you make Neil feel less than the man he is! What gave you the right to humiliate him that way?"

"My intention wasn't to humiliate Neil. Hell, I have no reason to dislike the man, to want to hurt him. My intention was to show him that he's useless as a bodyguard."

"Did you have to do it in front of me?" She looked down at her feet. "Neil has a crush on me."

Ashe laughed. "That must be the reason Annie Laurie can't get to first base with him."

Deborah snapped her head up, her eyes making direct contact with Ashe's. She smiled. "I've done everything but offer to pay for their wedding to get Neil interested in Annie Laurie. He can't seem to see past me to take notice of what a wonderful girl Annie Laurie is and how much she adores him."

Ashe stared at Deborah, his expression softening as he remembered another stupid man who had been so blinded by his passion for one woman that he'd allowed a treasure far more rare to slip through his fingers. Unrequited love was a bitch.

"I'm sorry if you think I was too rough on Neil. Annie Laurie had told me he liked you, but I had no idea he fancied himself in love with you. I'll tread more lightly on his ego from now on."

"Thank you, Ashe. I'd appreciated it."

A soft knock sounded at the door, breaking the intensity of Deborah's and Ashe's locked stares.

"Yes?"

Annie Laurie cracked open the door, peeked inside and held out a bundle of mail. "I've checked through these. The one I put on top looks odd to me. Whoever sent it used one of Deborah's business cards as a mailing label."

"Hand me that letter and place the others on the desk," Ashe said.

Annie Laurie obeyed Ashe's command. Deborah glanced from Annie Laurie's worried face to the letter in Ashe's hand. She waited while he turned the envelope over, inspecting it from every angle. He held it up to the light.

"Does this look pretty much like the other letters you've received?" he asked.

"The others were typed," Deborah said. "This is the first time they've used my business card."

Ashe walked over to Deborah's desk, picked up her letter opener and sliced the envelope along the spine. Lifting out a one-page letter, he laid the opener down, spread apart the white piece of stationery and read aloud the message, which had been typed.

"Don't show up in court. If you do, you'll be sorry."

Deborah glanced at Annie Laurie who seemed to be waiting for something. "Is there something else?" she asked.

Tilting her head to one side and casting her gaze downward, Annie Laurie smiled. "Megan stopped by to see you. She's got Katie with her."

"Oh." Deborah returned Annie Laurie's smile. "I suppose everyone's passing Katie around as if she were a doll. Tell Megan I'll be out in just a minute."

Annie Laurie slipped out of the office, silently closing the door behind her.

"What was that all about? Who are Megan and Katie?"

"Megan is my secretary. She's on maternity leave. Katie is her two-week-old baby girl."

Ashe shook his head. "You've just received another threatening letter and you're concerned with coochie-cooing over your secretary's new baby?"

"I've received a letter very similar to the one you hold in your hand every day since Lon Sparks was arrested," Deborah said. "And I get at least one threatening phone call a day. But it isn't every day that Katie goes for her two-week checkup and Megan brings her by to see us."

Ashe grinned. God bless her, Deborah hadn't really changed. Not nearly as much as he thought she had. And certainly nowhere near as much as she tried to make everyone think. Underneath all that tough, career woman exterior lay the heart of the sweet, caring girl she'd been years ago. He supposed he should have realized that Deborah was perfectly capable of handling both roles, that sophistication and success didn't exclude the more nurturing qualities that made Deborah such a loving person.

"You go visit with mother and baby," Ashe said. "I'll phone Sheriff Blaylock and let him know we'll be stopping by around noon. We'll let him add this letter to his collection."

"It won't do any good." Deborah opened the door. "There are never any fingerprints, nothing unique about the stationery. They're all mailed from Sheffield. And the typewriter isn't much of a clue. Hundreds of people in this area have access to the same brand."

"Whoever's doing this is experienced. He's no amateur."

"Buck Stansell may be a redneck outlaw, but he's a professional redneck outlaw."

"Yeah, his family's been in the business for several generations." Ashe glanced around Deborah's office. "Kind of like the Vaughns have been in real estate for three generations."

"Don't assume that I'm taking the threats lightly," she said, her hand on the doorpost. "I'm shaking in my boots. But I have a business to run, people who count on Vaughn & Posey for their livelihoods. And I have a mother who's in bad health and a ch...a brother who's only a child.''

"Who has access to your business cards?"

"What?"

"Could just anybody get one of these cards?" Ashe waved the envelope in the air.

"Oh, yes, anybody could get one." Deborah walked into the outer office. "Megan, we're so glad you stopped by. Who's got Katie? Come on, Helen, give her to me."

Ashe stood in the doorway, watching Deborah hold her secretary's baby. She looked so natural, as if cuddling a baby in her arms was something she did all the time. Why wasn't she married, with children of her own? A woman like Deborah shouldn't be single, still living at home with her mother and little brother. She should be hustling a pack of kids off to school and baseball games and cheerleader practice. She should be holding her own child in her arms.

Ashe didn't mean to eavesdrop, but when Megan pulled Deborah aside into the corner near her office, he remained standing just behind the partially closed door.

"I want to thank you again for the bonus you gave me," Megan said. "Bennie is so proud, he would never have accepted the money if you hadn't convinced him it was a bonus and that Mr. Posey had given the same amount to his secretary. Annie Laurie even went along with our little fib."

"It was a bonus," Deborah said. "A baby bonus. I think every baby should have a fully equipped nursery."

"We could never have afforded everything without that bonus. And after that, you didn't have to bring another gift to the hospital." Megan looked down at the pink-and-white ruffled dress her daughter wore. "It looks beautiful on her, don't you think?"

Ashe closed the door. Still the do-gooder. Still the tenderhearted pushover. No, Deborah hadn't changed. She was older, more beautiful, more experienced and certainly more sophisticated. But she was still the girl he'd considered his friend, the girl with whom he would have trusted his soul.

Was it possible that she had no idea what her father had done to him? Had he misjudged her all these years? Maybe she hadn't run to Wallace Vaughn and cried rape. But even if she hadn't falsely accused him, she'd still told her father that the two of them had made love. Surely she would have known how her father would react.

Even after Ashe had left town, Wallace Vaughn had slandered him. It had become public knowledge that Deborah's father had run Ashe McLaughlin out of Sheffield.

All the old feelings came rushing back, bombarding him with their intensity. All the love, the hate, the fear and the uncertainty. Maybe Carol Vaughn had been right. He hadn't returned to Sheffield before now because he was afraid to face the past, to find out the truth, to confront Deborah and Whitney.

But he was back now, and there was no time like the present to meet the ghosts of his past head-on.

Chapter 4

Charlie Blaylock had been a friend of her father and Deborah suspected he'd always had a soft spot in his heart for her mother. He asked about Carol every time he ran into Deborah, and his concern certainly seemed a bit more than neighborly.

Deborah tried to relax as she sat in Charlie's office listening to him explain the details of the Lon Sparks case to Ashe, and exactly what he could and could not do to protect Deborah against Buck Stansell and his bunch of outlaws.

"When Carol asked my advice about hiring a private body-guard for Deborah, I was all for it." Charlie gazed out the window that overlooked the parking area. He moved with a slow, easy stride, all six feet five inches, three hundred pounds of him. "We don't have a smidgen of proof that Buck and his boys are involved in the threats Deborah's been receiving. If we had any proof, we could make a move to stop them. But even if we caught the guy who's making the phone calls, Buck would just have somebody else take up where he left off."

"I'm planning on paying a visit to Lee Roy and Johnny Joe." Ashe stood, walked across the room, and stopped at Charlie's side. "I want you to have one of your men stay with Deborah while I drop in on my cousins."

Charlie lifted his eyebrows. "When were you planning on visiting the Brennan brothers?"

"Tomorrow. Bright and early."

"I've tried to tell Ashe that I've survived for a couple of weeks now without his constant protection." Deborah squirmed around in the uncomfortable straight-back chair in which she sat. "I'll be perfectly all right at the office for a couple of hours."

"I'll have somebody stop by the house around seven in the morning and stay with Deborah until you finish your business and get back to Sheffield." Charlie laid his big hand on Ashe's shoulder, gripping him firmly. "I was surprised when Carol told me she was hiring you. Last I'd heard, you were still in the army. The Green Berets, wasn't it?"

"I left over a year ago." Ashe looked down at Charlie's hand resting on his shoulder, all friendly like.

Ashe figured Charlie Blaylock knew exactly what his old friend, Wallace Vaughn, had done to him eleven years ago. Although Charlie had been sheriff even then, Wallace had brought the district attorney with him when he'd had his little talk with Ashe. And Sheffield's chief of police had been waiting right outside the door, waiting to arrest Ashe if he hadn't agreed to leave town and never return. But Charlie would have known what Wallace had been up to, perhaps had even given him a little advice on how to get rid of that white trash boy who had dared to violate Wallace's precious daughter.

Charlie gave Ashe's shoulder another tight squeeze, then released him. "Carol wants you here. She's convinced herself that nobody else can protect Deborah. I'll do everything I can to cooperate with you."

"I'll keep that in mind."

Removing the most recent threatening letter from his coat pocket, Ashe dropped it on Charlie's desk. "You might want to have this examined, but I'd say it's clean."

"Another one?" Charlie asked. "This has become a daily occurrence, hasn't it?"

"I expect you'll notify the big boys, keep them informed on every detail. Let them know that I've arrived, if you haven't already called them." Walking across the room, Ashe held out his hand to Deborah. "Let's go get a bite of lunch."

Deborah started to take his hand, then hesitated when Charlie spoke.

"What makes you think anybody else is involved in this case?" Charlie picked up the envelope from his desk, glancing at it casually as he turned it over.

"Buck Stansell has the drug market cornered in this county. And if Corey Looney's death was drug related, the DEA is already unofficially involved." Ashe dropped the hand he'd been holding out to Deborah.

She glanced back and forth from Charlie's flushed face to Ashe's cynical smile. The big boys? The DEA? No one had told her that Corey Looney had been executed because of a drug deal.

"What are y'all—" Deborah began.

"I don't know what you're talking about." Charlie laid the envelope on his desk, rested his hand on the back of his plush leather chair and looked Ashe straight in the eye.

"My boss is a former agent," Ashe said. "All Sam Dundee had to do was make a phone call. I know everything you know, Blaylock. Everything."

"Stop it, both of you!" Deborah jumped up, slammed her hands down on her hips and took a deep breath. "I have no idea what y'all are talking about, but I'm tired of you acting as if I'm not in the room. I'm the person whose life is in danger. *I'm* the one who should know *everything!*"

Ashe grabbed her by the elbow, forcing her into action as he practically dragged her out of Charlie's office. "I'll tell you whatever you need to know at lunch."

"Whatever I need to know!" She dug in her heels in the hallway.

Ashe gave her a hard tug. She fell against him and he slipped his arm around her. "It's a beautiful fall day. Let's pick up something and take it down to Spring Park for a picnic."

Deborah jerked away from him. She couldn't bear being this close to him. Despite their past history, she could not deny the way Ashe made her feel—the way no other man had ever made her feel.

"What was all that between you and Charlie?" Deborah stood her ground, refusing to budge an inch, her blue eyes riveted to Ashe's unemotional face. "For a minute there I thought he wanted to take a punch at you."

Ashe glanced around the corridor, listening to the sound of voices from the adjoining offices. "This isn't the time or the place."

"Just tell me this, is the DEA involved in this case?"

"Unofficially." Ashe grabbed her by the arm again. "Come on. We'll get lunch, go to the park and talk."

"All right." She followed his lead, outside and into the parking lot.

She didn't resist his manhandling, macho jerk that he was. Ashe's brutally masculine qualities had fascinated her as a teenager. Now they irritated and annoyed her. Yet she had to admit, if she was totally honest with herself, that she couldn't imagine any other bodyguard with whom she'd feel more secure.

There was a strength in Ashe that went beyond the normal male quality. It had been there, of course, years ago, but she recognized it now for what it was. Primitive strength that came from the core of his masculinity, the ancient need to beat his chest and cry out a warning to all other males.

Deborah shivered. Everything male in Ashe called to all that was female within her. If he claimed her, as he once had done, would she be able to reject him? A need to be possessed, protected and cherished coursed through her veins like liquid fire, heating her thoughts, warming her femininity.

When he opened the passenger door of his rental car and assisted her inside, she glanced up at him. Her heartbeat roared in her ears. Ashe hesitated just a fraction of a second. He looked at her lips. She resisted the urge to lick them.

"Where's a good place to get take-out close by?" He shut the door, walked around the hood of the car and got in on the driver's side.

"Stephano's on Sixth Street has good food." She clutched her leather bag to her stomach. "It's on the left side of the street, so you may want to turn off on Fifth and make the block."

When she returned home this evening, she'd tell her mother that this wasn't going to work, having Ashe as her bodyguard. Even if he kept her safe from Buck Stansell, another few weeks of being near Ashe would drive her insane.

Ashe picked up a couple of meatball subs, colas and slices of sinfully rich cheesecake. Gazing down into the bag, Deborah shook her head.

"This is too much food. I can't eat all of this. I have to watch my..." She left the sentence unfinished. She'd been about to tell Ashe McLaughlin that she had to watch her weight. Of course she had no need to tell him; he could well remember what a plump teenager she'd been.

"Splurging one day won't spoil that knockout figure of yours." Ashe kept his gaze focused on the road as he turned the car downward, off Sixth Street, and into the park area beneath the hill.

He thought she had a knockout figure? Was that the reason he couldn't seem to take his eyes off her all morning? Why he watched every move she made at the office? The thought of Ashe approving of her figure sent pinpricks of excitement rushing through her. Idiot! She chastised herself. You shouldn't care what he thinks. You shouldn't care what any man thinks, least of all Ashe. He didn't want you when you were a plump teenager, and you don't want him now. So there.

Liar! Good or bad. Right or wrong. You still want Ashe McLaughlin. You've never wanted anyone else.

"Is there a woman in your life back in Atlanta?" She heard herself ask, then damned herself for being such a fool. How could she have asked him such a question?

Ashe parked the car in the shade, opened his door and turned to take their lunch bag from Deborah. "No one special," Ashe said. "Women come and go, but there's been no one special in my life since I left Sheffield eleven years ago."

Whitney, Deborah thought. Her cousin had been the only special woman in Ashe's life. Jealousy and pity combined to create a rather disturbing emotion within Deborah. Both feelings constituted an admission that she still cared about Ashe.

And she didn't want to care. God in heaven, she didn't dare care. He had taken her innocence, broken her heart and left her pregnant. What woman in her right mind would give a man like that a second chance?

But then, Ashe hadn't said or done anything to indicate he wanted a second chance.

"This place hasn't changed much, has it?" Ashe looked around Spring Park, a small area of trees, playground equipment and picnic tables surrounding a small lake fed by an ancient underground spring.

"It's a bit lonely this time of day and this late in the season. Most of the activity takes place over there—" Deborah pointed to the south of the park "—at the golf course."

Ashe chose a secluded table on the west side of the park, near a cove of hedge apple trees, their bare branches dotted with mistletoe. The spring's flow meandered around behind them on a leisurely journey toward Spring Creek. Laying down the paper sack, Ashe removed the white napkins and spread out their lunch. He handed Deborah a cup and straw. She avoided touching his hand when she accepted the offering.

"Are you afraid of me?" he asked, swinging his long legs under the picnic table.

Deborah sat across from him, gripping the plastic container of food as she placed the cola on the concrete table. "Why should I be afraid of you? You're here to protect me, aren't you?"

"I wasn't asking if you were afraid that I might physically harm you. We both know that's ridiculous. I'm asking why your hands tremble whenever you think I might touch you. And why you have a difficult time looking directly at me. Your eyes give you away, honey."

She undid the plastic covering her meatball sandwich. "I feel awkward around you, Ashe. I guess I'm just not as sophisticated as the women you're accustomed to these days. Maybe what happened between us in the past didn't affect your life the way it did mine."

No, Ashe didn't suppose what had happened between them had affected his life the way it had hers. She had gone on as if nothing had happened, secure in her family's love and support and Wallace Vaughn's money. Maybe she'd suffered a broken heart for a while until she'd found another boyfriend. But he had paid a high price for their night of passion. He had lost his dream. His big plans of becoming one of the area's movers and shakers had turned sour.

"You don't look like you've fared too badly." Ashe surveyed her from the top of her golden blond hair, all neatly secured in a fashionable bun at the nape of her neck, to the length of shapely legs partially hidden beneath the picnic table. "You're successful, beautiful and rich."

Did he actually have no idea what he'd done to her? Of course he didn't know about the child they had created together, but how could he have forgotten his adamant rejection, his cruel words of regret, his deliberate avoidance of her in the days and weeks following their lovemaking?

"Whenever we're together, I can't seem to stop thinking about... I suppose it's true what they say about a woman never forgetting her first lover."

Her words hit him like a hard blow to the stomach. He sucked in air. Why did she sound so innocent, so vulnerable? After all this time, why did the memories of that night haunt him? Why did the thought of a young girl's passionate cries still echo in his mind? "And a guy never forgets what its like to take a virgin, to be her first. I never meant for it to happen. One minute you were comforting me and the next minute—"

"You don't have to tell me again that you wished it hadn't happened, that you regretted making love to me the minute it was over. You made that perfectly clear eleven years ago! Do you think I don't know that you were pretending I was Whitney all the while you were..."

Deborah lifted her legs, swung them around and off the concrete bench and jumped up, turning her back to Ashe. The quivering inside her stomach escalated so quickly it turned to nausea.

Dammit! Is that what she actually thought? That he had pretended she was Whitney? Yes, he'd thought he was in love with Whitney, but the minute she announced her engagement to George Jamison III, there at the country club where he worked, he'd begun to doubt his love. And when she had laughed in his face and told him he'd been a fool to think she'd ever marry a loser like him, all the love inside him had died. Murdered by her cruelty.

Ashe got up and walked over to Deborah. He wanted to touch her, to put his arms around her and draw her close. She stood there, her shoulders trembling, her neck arched, her head tilted upward. Was she crying? He couldn't bear it if she was crying.

"Deborah?"

She couldn't speak; unshed tears clogged her throat. Shaking her head, she waved her hands at her sides, telling him to leave her alone.

"I did not pretend you were Whitney." He reached out to touch her, but didn't. He dropped his hand to his side. "I might've had a few drinks to dull the pain that night, but I knew who you were and I knew what I was doing."

"You were—" she gasped for air "—using me."

How could he deny the truth? He had used her. Used her to forget another woman's heartless rejection. Used her to salve his bruised male ego. Used her because she'd been there at his side, offering her comfort, her love, her adoration.

"Yeah, you're right. I used you. And that's what I regretted. I regretted taking advantage of you, of stealing your innocence. But I didn't regret the loving."

The unshed tears nearly choked her. The pain of remembrance clutched her heart. He didn't regret the loving? Was that what he'd just said?

He grabbed her shoulders in a gentle but firm hold. She tensed, every nerve in her body coming to full alert. She couldn't bear for him to touch her, yet couldn't bring herself to pull away.

"I told you I was sorry for what happened, that I regretted what I'd done." Ashe couldn't see Deborah's face; she kept her back to him. But in his mind's eye he could see plainly her face eleven years ago. There in the moonlight by the river, her face aglow with the discovery of sexual pleasure and girlish love, she had crumpled before his very eyes when he'd begged her to forgive him, told her that what happened had been a mistake. She had cried, but when he'd tried to comfort her, she had lashed out at him like a wildcat. He'd found himself wanting her all over again, and hating himself for his feelings.

"I've never felt so worthless in my life as I did that night." Deborah balled her hands into fists. She wanted to hit Ashe, to vent all the old bitterness and frustration. She wanted to scream at him, to tell him that he'd left her pregnant and she hated him for not caring, for never being concerned about her welfare or the child he had given her.

He turned her around slowly, the stiffness in her body unyielding. She faced him, her chin lifted high, her eyes bright and glazed with a fine sheen of moisture.

"When I took you, I knew it was you. Do you understand? I wanted you. Not Whitney. Not any other woman."

"But you said...you said—"

"I said it shouldn't have happened. It shouldn't have. I didn't love you, not like I should have. I couldn't offer you marriage. What I did was wrong."

She quivered from head to toe, clinching her jaws tightly, trying desperately not to cry. She glared at him, her blue eyes accusing him.

Dear God, he had hurt her more than he'd ever known. After all these years, she hadn't let go of the pain. Was that why she'd gone to her father? Is that why she'd accused him of raping her? Or had she accused him? Was it possible that the rape charges had been Wallace's idea? The thought had crossed his mind more than once in the past eleven years.

"Neither of us can change the past," he said. "We can't go back and make things right. But I want you to know how it really was with me. With us."

"It doesn't matter. Not any more." She tried to pull away from him; he held her tight.

"Yes, it does matter. It matters to me and it matters to you."

"I wish Mother had never brought you back." Deborah closed her eyes against the sight of Ashe McLaughlin, his big hands clasping her possessively.

"She's doomed us both to hell, hasn't she?" Ashe jerked Deborah into his arms, crushing her against him. "I would have made love to you a second time that night and a third and fourth. I wanted you that much. Do you understand? I never wanted anything as much as I wanted you that night. Not Whitney. Not my college degree. Not being successful enough to thumb my nose at Sheffield's elite."

Her breathing quickened. Her heart raced wildly. She wanted to run. She wanted to throw her arms around Ashe. She wanted to plead with him to stop saying such outrageous things. She wanted him to go on telling her how much he'd wanted her, to tell her over and over again.

"Why...why didn't you tell me? That night? All you kept saying was that you were sorry." Deborah leaned into him, unable to resist the magnetic pull of his big body.

"You wanted me to tell you I loved you. I couldn't lie to you, Deborah. I'd just learned that night that I didn't know a damned thing about love."

"Ashe?"

He covered her lips with his own. She clung to him, returning his kiss with all the pent-up passion within her. The taste of her was like a heady wine, quickly going to his head. It had been that way eleven years ago. The very touch of Deborah Vaughn intoxicated him.

He thrust his tongue into her mouth, gripped the back of her head with one hand and slipped the other downward to caress her hip. He grew hard, his need pulsing against her. She wriggled in his arms, trying to get closer. Their tongues mated in a wet, daring dance. A prelude to further intimacy.

When they broke the kiss to breathe, Ashe dropped his hand to her neck, circling the back with his palm. His moist lips sought and found every sweet, delicious inch of her face.

Deborah flung her head back, exposing her neck as she clung to him, heat rising within her, setting her aflame. Ashe delved his tongue into the V of her blouse, nuzzling her tender flesh with his nose. Reaching between them, he undid the first button, then the second, his lips following the path of his fingers.

A loud blast rent the still autumn air. Ashe knocked Deborah to the ground, covering her body with his as he drew his 9mm out of his shoulder holster.

"Keep down, honey. Don't move."

"Ashe? What happened? Did—did someone shoot at us?" She slipped her arms around his waist.

Lifting his head, Ashe glanced around and saw nothing but an old red truck rounding the curve of the road, a trail of exhaust smoke billowing from beneath the bed. He let out a sigh of relief, but didn't move from his position above Deborah. He waited. Listening. Looking in every direction, lifting himself on one elbow to check behind them.

"Ashe, please—"

"It's all right." After returning his gun to its holster, he lowered himself over her, partially supporting his weight with his elbows braced on the ground. "I'm pretty sure the noise was just a truck backfiring."

"Oh." She sighed, then looked up into Ashe's softening hazel eyes. Eyes that only a moment before had been clear and trained on their surroundings. Now he was gazing down at her with the same undisguised passion she'd seen in them when he had unbuttoned her blouse.

Her diamond hard nipples grazed his chest. His arousal pressed against her. She needed Ashe. Needed his mouth on her body.

Needed him buried deep inside her. Needed to hear him say that he wanted her more than he'd ever wanted anything or anyone.

"It's safe for us to get up now, isn't it?" She heard her own breathless voice and knew Ashe would realize how needy she was.

"I don't think it's safe for us anywhere, honey. We're in danger from each other here on the ground or standing up."

When he lowered his mouth, brushing her lips with his, she turned her head to the side. But she still held him around the waist, her fingers biting into his broad back.

"Eleven years ago, you weren't much more than a girl. What you felt was puppy love. And I was a confused young man who didn't have the foggiest idea what love was all about. But I was older and more experienced. I take the blame for everything." Ashe kissed her cheek, then drew a damp line across to her ear. "We're both all grown up now. Whatever happens between us, happens between equals. No regrets on either side. No apologies. I want you. And you want me."

She shook her head, needing to deny the truth. If she admitted she wanted him, she would be lost. If they came together again, for him it would be sex, but for her it would be love. Just like last time. She couldn't have an affair with Ashe and just let him walk out of her life after the trial. She couldn't give herself to him and risk having her heart broken all over again.

"Please, let me get up, Ashe. I'm not ready for this." She shoved against his chest. He remained on top of her, unmoving, his eyes seeking the truth of her words.

Nodding his head, he lifted himself up and off her, then held out his hand. She accepted his offer of assistance, taking his hand and allowing him to pull her to her feet. She brushed the blades of grass and crushed leaves from her dress, redid the open buttons and straightened the loose strands of her hair.

"I need to get back to work," she said, not looking directly at him. "Let's take this food back to the office with us. We'll be safer there. We won't be alone."

Without a word, Ashe gathered up their sandwiches, returning them to the paper bag. She was right. They'd both be a lot safer if they weren't alone. He intended to do everything in his power to protect Deborah, to make sure no harm came to her. But could he protect her from what they felt for each other? From the power of a desire too powerful to resist?

Later that day Ashe stood in the doorway of Allen's room watching Deborah help the boy with his homework. She played the part of his mother convincingly. He wondered how long she had substituted for Miss Carol. Ever since illness had sapped Miss Carol's strength and she lived in constant fear the cancer would return?

No one seeing Deborah and Allen together could deny the bond between sister and brother. Her whole life seemed to revolve around the boy, and he so obviously adored her.

While Allen struggled with the grammar assignment, he eased his right hand down to stroke Huckleberry's thick, healthy coat.

"Remember, Allen, it's rise, rose, risen," Deborah said. "Do this one again."

Nibbling on the tip of his pencil eraser, Allen studied the sentence before him. "Hmm-hmm."

Ashe remembered how Deborah had struggled with algebra. When he had tutored her, downstairs at the kitchen table, she'd sat there nibbling on her eraser, a perplexed look on her face identical to Allen's. Ashe had been the one who'd had trouble with grammar, and Deborah had helped him write more than one term paper.

Gripping his pencil in his left hand, Allen scribbled the sentence across the sheet of notebook paper, then looked up at Deborah. "Is that right?"

Checking his work, she smiled. "Yes, it's right. Now go on to the next one." She glanced up and saw Ashe. Her smile vanished. Standing, she moved her chair from Allen's right side to his left, shielding him from Ashe's view.

Why had she moved? he wondered. It was as if she were protecting Allen. But from what? Surely not from him.

Ashe walked into the room. Huckleberry lifted his head from the floor, gave Ashe a quick glance, recognized him as no threat and laid his head back down, his body pressed against Allen's foot.

"Hey, Ashe." Allen looked up from his homework paper. "I'm

almost finished here, then we can play a video game on the computer.''

''Maybe Ashe doesn't want to play,'' Deborah said, standing up, placing her body between Ashe and her brother. ''We've had a long day. Maybe he wants to read or watch TV alone for a while.''

''I'm alone all the time in my apartment in Atlanta,'' Ashe said. ''I like being part of a family. Allen and I are pals. I think we enjoy doing a lot of the same things.''

''Oh. I see.'' Did he spend all his time in his Atlanta apartment alone? She doubted it. A man like Ashe wouldn't be long without a woman. She pictured the entrance to his apartment. The thought of a revolving door flashed through her mind.

''Your sister used to have a problem with algebra,'' Ashe said, walking around Deborah to sit down in the chair she had vacated. ''English grammar seems to be your downfall just like it was mine. I guess guys have a difficult time choosing the right words, huh?'' Ashe glanced up at Deborah, who glared down at him.

''I don't have to sweat making good grades in anything except this.'' Allen punched his paper with the tip of his pencil. ''I've got three more sentences to go, then watch out, Indiana Jones!''

Allen leaned over his desk, reading from his book. He jotted down the sentence, choosing the correct verb tense. Ashe watched the way his untutored handwriting spread across the page, like so much hen scratch. The boy's penmanship was no better than his own. Another shortcoming a lot of guys had in common.

Ashe noticed a crossword puzzle book lying on the edge of the desk. He loved working the really tough ones, the ones that often stumped him and stimulated his mind. He'd been a dud at English grammar, but he was a whiz at figuring out puzzles, even word puzzles.

Ashe picked up the book. ''Have you got an extra pencil?''

Allen opened his desk drawer, retrieved a freshly sharpened number two and handed it to Ashe. ''You like crossword puzzles, too?''

''Love 'em.'' Taking the pencil and sticking it behind his ear, Ashe opened the book, found the most complicated puzzle and studied it.

He felt Deborah watching him. What the hell was the matter

with her? "Are you planning on hanging around and cheering us on while we play Indiana Jones and the Last Crusade?"

"No. I just want to make sure Allen finishes his homework."

"I'll make sure he does. Go wash out your lingerie or something. Read a good book. Call your boyfriend." Ashe's expression didn't alter as he named off a list of alternatives to standing guard over her brother.

"I told you Deborah doesn't have a boyfriend. She won't give any guy the time of day." Allen never looked up from his paper.

Ashe glanced down at the puzzle. "What's another word for old maid?"

Allen smothered his laughter behind his hand, sneaking a peek at Deborah out of the corner of his eye.

"Try the word *smart*," Deborah said. "As in any smart woman dies an old maid, without having to put up with a man trying to run her life."

"Spinster." Ashe acted as if he hadn't heard Deborah's outburst. Jerking the pencil from behind his ear, he printed the letters into the appropriate boxes.

"Hey, you're left-handed just like me," Allen said, his face bursting into a smile.

Deborah's heart sank. No. She mustn't panic. A lot of people were left-handed. There was no reason for Ashe to make the connection.

"We seem to have a lot in common." Ashe couldn't explain the rush of emotion that hit him. Like a surge of adrenaline warning him against something he couldn't see or hear, touch, taste or feel. Something he should know, but didn't. And that sense of the unknown centered around Allen Vaughn. Ashe found himself drawn to the boy, in a way similar yet different from the way he'd been drawn to Deborah when they'd been growing up together.

"Ashe, I... We need to talk," Deborah said.

He glanced up at her. Her face was pale. "Can't it wait until later? Allen and I are looking forward to our game."

"This won't take long." She nodded toward the hallway.

He laid down the puzzle book and pencil, stood up and patted Allen on the back. "You finish your homework while I see what Deborah wants that's so important it can't wait."

"Hurry," Allen said. "I'm almost through."

Deborah led Ashe out into the hallway, closing Allen's bedroom door behind him. "Please don't let Allen become too fond of you. He's at an age where he wants a man around, and he seems to idolize you. He thinks you're something special."

"So what's the problem?" Ashe asked. "I like Allen. I enjoy spending time with him. Do you think I'm a bad influence on him?"

"No, that isn't it."

"Then what is it?"

"If you two become close—too close—it'll break his heart when you leave Sheffield. He's just a little boy. I don't want to see him hurt."

Ashe pinched her chin between his thumb and forefinger, tilting her downcast eyes upward, making her look directly at him. "Who are you afraid will get too close to me? Who are you afraid will be brokenhearted when I leave? Who, Deborah? You or Allen?"

She hardened her stare, defying him, standing her ground against the overwhelming emotions fighting inside her. "You won't ever break my heart again, Ashe McLaughlin. I know you aren't here to stay, that you're in Sheffield on an assignment, just doing your job. But Allen is already forming a strong attachment to you. Don't encourage him to see you as a...a...big brother."

"A father figure, you mean, don't you? Allen needs a father. Why hasn't Carol ever remarried and given him a father? Or why haven't you married and given him a brother-in-law?"

"I don't think my personal affairs or my mother's are any of your business."

"You're right." He released her chin.

"Please don't spend so much time with Allen. Don't let him start depending on you. You aren't going to be around for very long."

"What should I do to entertain myself at night?" he asked. "Should I play bridge with your mother and her friends? Should I watch the Discovery channel on TV downstairs in the library? Should I invite a lady friend over for drinks and some hanky-panky in the pool house? Or should I come to your bedroom and watch you undress and see your hair turn to gold in the moonlight? Would you entertain me to keep me away from Allen?"

Her hand itched to slap his face. She knotted her palm into a fist, released it, knotted it again, then repeated the process several times.

"If you hurt my...my brother, I'll—"

He jerked her into his arms, loving the way she fought him, aroused by the passion of her anger, the heat of her indignation. "I'm not going to hurt Allen. You have my word."

Ceasing her struggles, she searched his face for the truth. "And I don't want to hurt you, Deborah. Not ever again. No matter what we've done to each other in the past, we don't have to repeat our mistakes."

"You're right," she said breathlessly. "Do your job. Act as my bodyguard until the trial is over and the threats stop. There's no need for you to become a temporary member of the family. None of us need a temporary man in our lives."

Was that what he was? Ashe wondered. A temporary man. Never a permanent part of anything. Just there to do a job. It hadn't mattered before, that he didn't have a wife or children. That his life held so little love, so little commitment. Why had being back in Sheffield changed all that? Being around families again, his family and Deborah's, brought to mind all his former hopes and dreams. Dreams of living in one of the big old houses in Sheffield, of becoming a successful businessman, of showing this town how far he'd come—from the depths of white trash, from the McLaughlins of Leighton. And the biggest part of his dream had been the society wife and the children she'd give him. Children who would never know the shame he'd felt, would never face the prejudice he'd fought, would never be looked at as if they were nothing.

"I'll do my job. I'll be careful not to let Allen become too attached to me. And I won't come into your bedroom and make slow, sweet love to you. Not unless you ask."

He didn't give her a chance to say a word. Turning, he marched down the hall, opened Allen's door and walked in, never once looking back at Deborah.

"Hell will freeze over, Ashe McLaughlin, before I ever ask you to make love to me again!" she muttered under her breath.

Chapter 5

A passel of hounds lay in the dirt yard surrounding the double-wide trailer. A brand-new cherry red Camaro, parked beside an old Ford truck, glistened in the morning sun. A long-legged, large-breasted brunette with a cigarette dangling from her lips flung open the front door and ushered three stair-step-size children onto the porch. Her voice rang out loud and clear.

"Get your rear ends in the car. I ain't got all morning to get you heathens to school."

The children scurried toward the Camaro. The woman turned around, surveyed Ashe from head to toe and grinned an I'd-like-to-see-what-you've-got-in-your-pants-honey kind of grin.

Ashe leaned against the hood of the rented car he had parked several feet off the gravel drive leading to Lee Roy Brennan's home. He eyed the smiling woman.

"Well, hello." She gave the youngest child a shove inside the car, never taking her eyes off Ashe. "You here to see Lee Roy?"

"Yeah. Is he around?"

"Could be." She ran her hand down her hip, over the tight-fitting jeans that outlined her shapely curves. "Who wants to know?"

"How about you go tell Lee Roy that Ashe McLaughlin wants to see him?"

"Well, Mr. Ashe McLaughlin, you sure do look like you're everything I ever heard you were." She stared directly at his crotch, then moved her gaze up to his face. "Lee Roy says you been in the army. One of them Green Berets. A real tough guy."

Ashe glanced at the three children in the Camaro. People like this didn't care what they said or did in front of their kids. He had vague memories of his old man cursing a blue streak, slapping his mother around and passing out drunk. Yeah, Ashe knew all about the low-class people he'd come from and had spent a lifetime trying to escape.

"Go tell Lee Roy his cousin wants to see him," Ashe said.

The woman's smile wavered, her eyes darting nervously from Ashe to the trailer. "Yeah, sure. He heard you was back in these parts."

Ashe didn't move from his propped position against the hood of his car while Lee Roy's wife went inside the trailer. Three pairs of big brown eyes peered out the back window of the Camaro. Ashe waved at the children. Three wide, toothy smiles appeared on their faces.

"Hey, cousin. What's up?" Lee Roy Brennan stepped out onto the wooden porch connected to his trailer, his naked beer belly hanging over the top of his unsnapped jeans.

"Just paying a social call on my relatives." Ashe lowered his sunglasses down on his nose, peering over the top so that his cousin could see his eyes. Ashe had been told that he possessed a look that could kill. Maybe not kill, he thought, but intimidate the hell out of a person.

"You run them kids on to school, Mindy." Lee Roy swatted his wife's round behind.

She rubbed herself against the side of his body, patting him on his butt before she sauntered off the porch and strutted over to the car. She gave Ashe a backward glance. Although he caught her suggestive look in his peripheral vision, he kept his gaze trained on Lee Roy.

"Come on in and have a cup of coffee. Johnny Joe just got up. He's still in his drawers, but he'll be glad to see you."

Standing straight and tall, Ashe accepted his cousin's invitation.

Lee Roy slapped Ashe on the back when they walked inside the trailer.

"Didn't think I'd ever see you around these parts again. Not after the way old man Vaughn run you out of the state."

Ashe removed his sunglasses, dropped them into the inside pocket of his jacket and glanced over at the kitchen table where Johnny Joe, all five feet eight inches of him, sat in a wooden chair. Swirls of black hair covered his stocky body, making him look a little like an oversize chimpanzee.

"Heard you was back. What the hell ever made you agree to hire on as a bodyguard for that Vaughn gal?" Johnny Joe picked up a mug with the phrase Proud to be a Redneck printed on it. "I figured you wouldn't have no use for that bunch."

Lee Roy wiped corn flake crumbs out of a chair, then turned to lift a mug off a wooden rack. "Have a seat. You still like your coffee black?"

"Yeah." Ashe eyed the sturdy wooden chair, a few crumbs still sticking to the side. Sitting down, he placed his hands atop the table, spreading his arms wide enough apart so that his cousins could get a glimpse of his shoulder holster.

Lee Roy handed Ashe a mug filled with hot, black coffee, then sat down beside his brother. "You're working for some fancy security firm in Atlanta now, huh? Got your belly full of army life?"

"Something like that," Ashe said. "And private security work pays better, too."

The brothers laughed simultaneously. Ashe didn't crack a smile.

"You bleeding old lady Vaughn dry?" Johnny Joe asked. "After what her old man almost did to you, I figure you got a right to take 'em for all you can get."

Ashe glared at Johnny Joe, the hirsute little weasel. He hadn't taken after the McLaughlin side of the family in either size, coloring or temperament. No, he was more Brennan. Little, dark, smart-mouthed and stupid.

"Shut up, fool." Lee Roy swatted his younger brother on his head. "Ashe wouldn't have come back to take care of Deborah Vaughn just for the money."

"You doing her again, Ashe?" Johnny Joe snickered.

Lee Roy slapped him up side his head again, a bit harder.

"What the hell was that for?" Johnny Joe whined.

"Don't pay no attention to him." Lee Roy looked Ashe square in the eye. "It's good to see you again. We had some fun together, back when we was kids. You and me and Evie Lovelady."

"Yeah, we had some good times." Ashe had liked Lee Roy better than any of his McLaughlin relatives and the two of them had sowed some pretty wild oats together. Fighting over Evie Lovelady's favors. Getting drunk on Hunter McGee's moonshine in the backseat of Lee Roy's old Chevy. Getting into fights with Buck Stansell when he cheated at cards.

Another life, a lifetime ago.

"This ain't just a social call to get reacquainted with relatives," Lee Roy said. "Spit it out, whatever it is you come here to say."

"I understand you two are working for Buck Stansell. Is that right?"

Johnny Joe opened his mouth to respond, but shut it quickly when his older brother gave him a warning stare.

"Buck took over the business when his old man died a few years back." Lee Roy picked up his coffee mug, took a swig, then wiped his mouth with the back of his big hand. "Our old man and yours both worked for Buck's daddy."

"I know who my daddy worked for and what he did for a living," Ashe said, laying his palms flat on the table. "I've chosen to work on the other side of the law. And right now, my main concern is Deborah Vaughn's safety."

"I see." Lee Roy studied the black liquid in his mug.

"She ain't in no danger as long as she keeps that pretty little mouth of hers shut," Johnny Joe said.

"Dammit, man, you talk too much." Lee Roy turned to Ashe. "You ought to stay out of things that ain't none of your business. What happens to Deborah Vaughn shouldn't be your concern."

Ashe leaned over the table, glanced back and forth from one brother to the other, finally settling his hard stare on Lee Roy. "Deborah Vaughn is very much my concern, and what happens to her is my personal business."

"Are you saying that there's still something between the two of you? Hell, man, I'd have figured—"

"I will take it personally if anything happens to her. If one hair on her head is harmed, I'll be looking for the guy who did it. Do I make myself clear?"

"Why are you telling us?" Lee Roy asked.

"I'm asking you to relay the message." Ashe shoved back the chair and stood, towering over his seated cousins. "Tell Buck Stansell that Deborah Vaughn is my woman. She's under my protection. This isn't just another job to me."

"You sure you want to tangle with ol' Buck?" Johnny Joe grinned, showing his crooked teeth, three in a row missing on the bottom.

"I've trapped and gutted meaner bastards than Buck Stansell, and you can tell him that. Buck and his friends don't want to tangle with me. If I have to come after them, I will."

"You sure do talk big," Johnny Joe said. "But then you always did. Just 'cause you been in the Green Berets—"

"Shut up!" Lee Roy said.

"I know that the local, state and federal authorities would all like to see Buck behind bars." Ashe walked toward the door. "So would I. But you tell him that my only interest in him and his business is my woman's safety. If he leaves her alone, I'll leave him alone. Pass that advice along."

"Yeah, I'll do that," Lee Roy said. "Can't say whether or not Buck will take the advice, but it's possible that whoever's out to get Deborah Vaughn might listen. Her being your woman just might make a difference. To certain people."

Ashe smiled then, nodded his head and walked out the door. He'd bet money that before he was halfway back to Sheffield, Lee Roy and Johnny Joe would be on their way to see Buck Stansell.

Ashe parked his rental car in the lot adjacent to Vaughn & Posey Real Estate. Walking up the sidewalk, he almost laughed aloud when he saw the sheriff's deputy pacing back and forth just inside the office entrance. The fresh-faced kid looked like a posted sentry marching back and forth.

When Ashe opened the door, the deputy spun around, taking a defensive pose, then relaxed when he recognized Ashe.

"No problems here, Mr. McLaughlin. Not even a phone call or a letter."

"Good. Tell Sheriff Blaylock that I said you did a fine job.

Thanks—'' Ashe glanced at the boy's name tag "—Deputy Regan.''

The young man grinned from ear to ear. "Ms. Vaughn's taking care of some personal business right now, but she agreed to keep her door open so she wouldn't be out of my sight.''

Ashe slapped the deputy on the back. "I'll take over now. I appreciate your diligence in keeping Ms. Vaughn safe for me.''

Ashe noticed Deborah in her office, standing to the side of another woman, whose back was to him. Deborah glanced at him, her face solemn.

The young deputy backed out of the office like a servant removing himself from the presence of his king. Ashe nodded a farewell to the boy, then focused all his attention on Deborah and the other woman.

He heard a rather loud hiss, then someone cleared their throat. Looking around, he saw Annie Laurie motioning for him to come to her.

"What's up?''

"Shh...shh.'' She flapped her hands in the air and shook her head. "Whitney Jamison—'' Annie Laurie pointed to Deborah's office "—is in there right now. She came prancing in here with her nose in the air, looking all over the place for you.''

Ashe sat down on the edge of Annie Laurie's desk, leaned over and whispered, "What makes you think she was looking for me?''

"She said so, that's how I know.'' Annie Laurie kept her voice low. "She took one look at the deputy and asked what he was doing here. Deborah told her he was on temporary guard duty. Then Whitney asked what was the problem, had you already deserted her? Then that bitch laughed. I wish Deborah had slapped her face.''

"Aren't you overreacting just a little?''

"No, I don't think I am. Do you suppose for one minute that Whitney will let Deborah forget that you once asked Whitney to marry you and she dumped you, that she made you look like a fool?''

"Maybe I'd better go on in there and make sure there's not a catfight.'' Ashe grinned.

"Wipe that stupid grin off your face,'' Annie Laurie said. "Deborah Vaughn is not the type of lady to get into a catfight over any man, not even you, cousin dear.''

Ashe laughed, but took note of Annie Laurie's words. She was right. Deborah wasn't the catfight type by any stretch of the imagination. But if she was, and she did choose to go one-on-one with Whitney, he'd place all his money on Deborah.

Ashe walked into Deborah's office, stopping directly behind Whitney, who was obviously unaware of his presence.

"It's going to be a delightful evening. Simply everyone will be there. You must come. If you don't, I'll never forgive you. After all, George's fortieth birthday celebration should be something for him to remember."

"Of course I'll be there," Deborah said. "I wouldn't miss it."

Deborah looked over her cousin's shoulder, making direct eye contact with Ashe, who couldn't seem to erase the lopsided grin off his face. The very sound of Whitney's voice grated on his nerves. Why had he never noticed how whiny she sounded?

"You mean we'll be there, don't you?" Ashe stepped to one side, placing himself beside Deborah's desk.

Whitney spun around, a cascade of long black curls bouncing on her shoulders, settling against her pink silk blouse. "Ashe!"

She stared at him, her eyes hungry, her mouth opening and then closing as she bit down on her bottom lip. Whitney Vaughn Jamison was still beautiful, erotically beautiful with her dark hair and eyes and slender, delicate body.

Over the years there had been a few times when he'd wondered how he'd feel if he ever saw her again. Now he knew. He didn't feel a damned thing. Except maybe grateful she'd rejected him. Despite her beauty, there was a noticeable hardness in her face, a lack of depth in those big, brown eyes. He'd been too young and foolish to have seen past the surface eleven years ago.

"Whitney, you haven't changed a bit." It was only a small lie, a partial lie. She'd grown older, harder, hungrier.

"Well, darling, you've certainly changed. You've gotten bigger and broader and even better looking." Rushing over to him, she slipped her arms around his neck and kissed him boldly on the mouth.

She all but melted into him. Ashe did not return her kiss. He eased her arms from around his neck, held her hands in his for a brief moment, then released her and took a step over toward Deborah.

"What's this big event you've invited Deborah and me to attend? Something special for ol' George's birthday?" Ashe took another step in Deborah's direction.

"His fortieth birthday." Whitney pursed her lips into a frown. "And he's being a beast about getting older. I think it really bothers him that I'm so much younger."

"Not that much younger," Ashe said. "If I recall, you're thirty-four."

Whitney gasped, then smiled and purred as she gave Ashe another hungry look. "Of course you'd remember. You probably remember a lot of things about me, don't you, Ashe?"

"Not really, Whitney. To be honest, I haven't given you more than a passing thought over the years."

Ashe slipped his arm around Deborah's waist. Glaring at him, she opened her mouth to protest. He tightened his hold on her. She wriggled, trying to free herself.

"Deborah, on the other hand, I never forgot." He pulled her close to his side, smiled at her and barely kept himself from laughing out loud when he saw the stricken look on her face.

"Well, don't tell me you were cheating on me with my little cousin behind my back." Whitney pasted a phony smile on her heavily made-up face.

"Sort of like the way you cheated on me with George?" Ashe asked.

"That was years ago. Surely you don't still hold that against me?" Whitney fidgeted with the shoulder strap on her beige leather purse.

"Whitney, I appreciate your stopping by to invite me—" Deborah gasped when Ashe squeezed her around the waist "—us to George's birthday party." She glared at Ashe. "We'll be there."

"I'll be looking forward to seeing you again, Ashe. The party's at the country club." Whitney's genuine smile returned with a vengeance.

When she didn't receive the reaction from Ashe she'd hoped to evoke, she waved at him with her index finger. "Until next Saturday night."

The moment Whitney exited the office, Deborah jerked out of Ashe's embrace, stormed across the room and slammed the door.

"Just what was that all about?" Deborah anchored her hands on her hips.

"I think your cousin was coming on to me. What do you think?"

"Of course, she was coming on to you. My God, I expected her to drag you down on my desk and jump on top of you at any minute."

Ashe chuckled, then coughed and covered his mouth when he noticed Deborah's face reddening and her eyes widening.

"I was not referring to the way Whitney threw herself at you," Deborah said. "I was talking about your dragging me into your arms, accepting her invitation on *our* behalf and telling her that I was the one you never forgot."

"Oh, that."

"Yes, that!"

"You had already accepted her invitation when I walked in, hadn't you? All I did was let Whitney know that you didn't go anywhere without me these days."

"I could have, and would have, explained to her that as my bodyguard, you'd have to accompany me." Deborah dropped her hands to her sides. "That doesn't explain your manhandling me in front of Whitney or your reason for saying what you did."

"I put my arm around you because I wanted Whitney to think that there's more than a business arrangement between the two of us."

"But there isn't."

"Of course there is. Do you honestly think I came back to Sheffield, to a town I swore had seen the last of me, to lay my life on the line for a woman who pretends she hates me, simply as a favor to a woman who was once kind to me and my grandmother?"

"Yes. That's what you told me."

"Doing a favor for Miss Carol was only part of my reason for accepting this job." Ashe realized that he'd been lying to himself as well as Deborah about his reasons for accepting Carol Vaughn's dare. "I wasn't lying when I told Whitney that you were the one I never forgot."

Deborah's vision blurred. Her ears rang with the pounding of her heart. "Don't—" she threw up her hands in front of her as if to ward him off "—please, don't. Whitney was the one. You loved her. Don't you dare lie to me!"

"You and I need to have a long talk and get a few things

straight, but I doubt this is the time or the place.'' Ashe heard the phones in the outer office ringing and the buzz of voices. ''Whitney doesn't mean a damn thing to me. You, on the other hand, do. I'm here to protect you. And you'll be a lot safer if everyone thinks you're—''

A loud knock on the outer office door interrupted Ashe midsentence. Opening the door, Annie Laurie walked in with a package in her hands.

''This just came for Deborah. There's no return address.'' Annie Laurie held the square box out in front of her. ''Something inside there is ticking!''

Deborah stood deadly still staring at the box. Ashe took the package out of Annie Laurie's hands. Listening, he heard the steady *tick, tick, tick* coming from inside the cardboard container.

''Don't panic, and don't scare the others in the office,'' Ashe said. ''Go back to your desk and call the Sheffield police. Talk to Chief Burton. Tell him to send whatever kind of bomb squad he has over here, pronto.''

''You think it's a bomb?'' Annie Laurie gulped, then started backing out of the office. ''What do we do?''

''You and Deborah get everyone outside. Tell them you'll explain once you're out. Walk them across the street. And make sure everyone stays there.''

''What about you?'' Deborah asked.

''I'm going to set this box down on your desk and follow you all outside.''

Deborah shoved a stricken Annie Laurie out of the office, then rounded all her employees together and ushered them outside, while Annie Laurie phoned the police. Deborah started into Neil's office, but Annie Laurie reminded her that Neil was in Florence at a realtor's brunch.

Ashe set the ticking box down on Deborah's desk. His gut instincts told him that this wasn't a bomb, but his instincts had been wrong a few times and it had nearly cost him his life. He didn't take chances anymore. Not with other people's lives. Certainly not with Deborah's life.

Within five minutes Chief Burton and his bomb squad arrived. The employees of Vaughn & Posey stood across the street in front of the bank, their evacuation and the presence of several police vehicles garnering attention from passersby. A small crowd of spectators gathered on the corner.

Ashe stayed beside Deborah, who stood ramrod straight, her vision focused on her office building. She gripped Ashe's hand tightly, but he was certain she had no idea what she was doing.

A member of the bomb squad walked through the front door, holding the open box in his hands. "Somebody's got a real warped sense of humor, Chief. Take a look at this."

Ashe held on to Deborah's hand as she dashed across the street.

"Everybody can go back to work," Chief Burton said. "There's no bomb."

"What was ticking?" Deborah asked.

The chief held out the box. "Take a look, Ms. Vaughn."

Inside the hand-delivered package lay an ordinary alarm clock, tightly wound. Positioned on all four sides of the box, surrounding the ticking clock, were unlit sticks of dynamite. A small white card was stuck to the face of the clock, the message typed. "Next time, boom!"

Ashe could almost hear a man's insidious laughter. Buck Stansell's crazy, sharp laugh. Ashe remembered the man's diabolical sense of humor. Buck had not meant to harm Deborah, only to frighten her. If Buck had wanted Deborah dead, he would have killed her before Ashe had come into the picture.

But what would happen if Deborah couldn't be scared off, if she showed up in court to testify against Lon Sparks? With a man like Buck Stansell, anything was possible. All Ashe knew was that whatever happened, he was going to take care of Deborah.

"A clock!" Deborah balled her hands into fists. "A stupid alarm clock!"

"Looks like another warning," Chief Burton said. "I'll see that Charlie's people get a look at this. I doubt we'll be able to trace it to anybody, but we'll see what we can do. Maybe somebody at the messenger service will remember who sent it, but I've got my doubts. Anybody could've paid a kid off the street to run a package by the office."

"It's not going to stop, is it?" Deborah looked to Ashe for an answer. He grasped her by the shoulders. She trembled.

"I'm not going to lie to you," he said. "The phone calls and letters aren't going to stop. But I'm screening them. You don't have to deal with them at all. And from now on, any UPS deliveries will come directly to me, too. You don't even have to know about them.''

"Unless you think it's another bomb and we have to evacuate the office again." Deborah wanted to walk into Ashe's arms, to lay her head on his chest and cry. Instead she pulled away from him, turning to her employees, still standing around outside on the sidewalk. "Let's get back to work." Then she held out her hand to Chief Burton, thanked him for arriving so promptly and took one last look at the gag gift she'd been sent.

She walked back into the building, her head held high. At that moment Ashe didn't think he'd ever been as enthralled by a woman's show of strength. He knew she'd been scared to death, had felt her trembling beneath his hands, but despite her anger and uncertainty, she was not defeated.

Ashe waited around outside for a few minutes until the police left and the crowd cleared. He found Deborah in her office, alone, her elbows propped up on her desk, her hands covering her face.

He closed the door behind him. Dropping her hands, she stared up at him, her eyes damp but without any real tears.

He walked over, knelt down beside her swivel chair and took her hands into his. "It's all right if you want to cry or scream or hit something. Nobody can be strong all the time."

"I have to be," she said, her voice flat and even, masking her emotions. She looked down at her lap where he held her hands. "Mother and Allen have no one else but me. If I fall apart...if I..." Pausing, she swallowed. "I have to keep Vaughn & Posey going. So many people depend on this business. And since Mother's illness, she's become very fragile emotionally."

"Then put up a brave front for Miss Carol and Allen. Even let your employees go on thinking you're superwoman. But I've got some broad shoulders, Deborah. And they're here for you to lean on any time you feel the need."

She looked at him, her blue eyes softening just a fraction. "Part of the job, Mr. McLaughlin? I thought you were supposed to protect me. Giving comfort is extra, isn't it? How much more will that cost me?"

He stood and jerked her up into his arms in one swift move. She gasped as she fell against him and he trapped her body, holding her securely in his arms. He lowered his head until their breaths mingled.

She closed her eyes, blocking out the sight of him, telling herself she was a fool to succumb to his easy charm.

"The comfort is free, Ms. Vaughn." He whispered the words against her lips. "If you're woman enough to accept it."

Sucking in a deep breath, she opened her eyes. He released his hold on her and gave her a slight push away from him. Turning his back on her, he headed for the door.

"Ashe?"

"I'm just going to get a cup of coffee. I'm not leaving you, even if right now I'd like nothing better than to walk out that door and not come back."

"No one is stopping—"

He pivoted around, glaring at her. "No, that's not true. I don't want to walk out on you and never come back. What I want, more than anything, is to shove all that stuff off your desk, lift you up on it and—"

"I think you're confusing me with Whitney," Deborah said.

"No, honey, that's something I've never done. It's your legs I'd like to slide between and your body I'd like to claim, not your cousin's."

Ashe turned, walked out of the office and closed the door behind him.

Deborah stood beside her desk, trembling. Visions of her lying on top of her desk flashed through her mind. She shook her head trying to dislodge the thoughts of Ashe McLaughlin leaning over her body, lifting her hips and burying himself inside her.

She covered her mouth with her hand to still her cry, then bit down on the side of her finger as shivers of desire rippled through her.

Chapter 6

Deborah had thought about making a fire in her sitting room fireplace, but had neither the strength nor the determination. Although the October night was chilly, it wasn't really cool enough for a fire. She'd simply thought a cosy glowing fire would be soothing. Instead she had settled for a nice warm bath and a cup of cinnamon tea.

She curled up on the huge padded window seat beneath the stained glass window in her sitting room alcove. Her room was her haven. Since early childhood, she had escaped into this luxurious old room with its high ceilings and aged wooden floors. Many days she had sat where she sat now, watching the way the sun turned the colors in the stained glass window to sparkling jewels.

She had written silly, girlish poems about love and life and Ashe McLaughlin. She had long ago burned those poems. Even now she could feel the tears on her face, the tears she had shed the night she'd tossed those hopeless professions of love into the fireplace and watched her youthful dreams go up in smoke.

She shouldn't be dwelling on the past, not with so many problems facing her in the present. Between the constant harassing threats and Ashe's presence, her nerves were raw. She wanted to scream, to cry, to break something—anything—into a thousand pieces.

She wanted Ashe to go away; she wanted Ashe to never leave her. She fantasized about telling Ashe that Allen was his son; she lived in fear Ashe would discover the truth.

Deborah set her teacup on the mahogany tea table beside the window bench, pulled the cream crocheted afghan over her legs and rested her head against the window frame. She should have been in bed an hour ago, but she knew she wouldn't be able to sleep. The simple, orderly life she had worked out for herself had suddenly and irrevocably fallen apart. She had turned off on the wrong road, witnessed a murder and her life would never be the same again. Not only was her life being threatened by the most notorious hoodlums in the state, but the very man determined to protect her posed the greatest threat of all. How ironic, she thought, that she should fear Ashe McLaughlin even more than she feared Buck Stansell.

She heard a soft rap on her door. Her mother? Had she taken ill? Or Allen, who usually slept soundly the whole night through? No. Not her mother. Not Allen.

Ashe.

Dropping the afghan to the floor, she walked across the room, her heart hammering away in her chest. Just before opening the door, she readjusted her silk robe, tightening the belt around her waist.

Ashe McLaughlin stood in the hallway, one big hand braced against the doorpost. He still wore his charcoal gray slacks and his dove gray linen shirt, but the shirt was completely unbuttoned and the hem hung loose below his hips.

"May I come in? We need to talk."

"It's late, Ashe. After midnight. I'm tired." She didn't want him in her room, didn't want to be alone with him. "Can't this wait until morning?"

"It could, but since we're both awake, I see no reason to postpone our conversation." He dropped his hand from the doorpost, leaned toward her and looked her over from head to toe. "Are you going to let me in?"

If she said no, he would think she was afraid of him, that he still held some kind of power over her. She couldn't let him think she cared, that he... Oh, who was she kidding? Any fool could see that Ashe McLaughlin made her act like a silly, lovesick schoolgirl.

"Come on in." She stepped back, allowing him entrance.

He followed her into the sitting room, glancing around, taking note of the lush femininity of the room. All muted cobalt blues and faded rose colors with splashes of rich cream. Ruffles and lace and dainty crocheted items whispered "Lady."

"Won't you sit down?" She indicated the antique rocker covered in a vibrant floral pattern.

Ashe eyed the delicate chair, wondering if it would hold his weight. Deborah sat on the wide, plush window seat. Without asking permission, he walked over and sat down beside her. She jumped, then glared at him.

"I was afraid I'd break that little rocker," he said, smiling.

"You could have sat in the arm chair, there by the fireplace." She indicated the wing chair, a wide-brimmed, lace hat hanging from one wing.

"I'd rather sit beside you." He knew he made her nervous, and he thought he knew why. No matter what had happened between them eleven years ago, no matter how betrayed either of them felt, the spark that had ignited a blazing fire between them that one night down by the river still burned inside both of them.

"Fine, sit beside me." She glanced over at the tea service. "Would you care for some cinnamon tea?"

"No, thanks."

"What was so urgent that you couldn't wait until tomorrow to discuss it with me?" Feeling her robe slipping open across her thigh, she grabbed the blue silk and held it in place.

"Are you all right, Deborah?" he asked. "I mean really all right. You've had a rough day, and you barely said ten words at dinner. Miss Carol is worried. So is Allen."

"I'm fine, and I'll make sure Mother and Allen both know it. Now, if that's all you came to say—" she started to rise.

"Sit down."

She eased back down onto the bench.

"As you know, I paid a visit to Lee Roy and Johnny Joe, a couple of my cousins who work for Buck Stansell."

Her eyes, wide and overly bright, looked right at him. Damn her, she was working hard at being brave, at pretending she wasn't slowly falling apart. And he figured having him around wasn't helping her any. But he couldn't leave, couldn't let Sam Dundee send another agent to protect her. Deborah was his responsibility, his to protect, his to defend against whatever harm came her way.

"What happened?" Deborah asked. "I'm sure they didn't admit that Buck Stansell was harassing me, trying to convince me that he'd have me killed if I testify against Lon Sparks."

"No, the boys didn't admit to anything. They didn't have to. I know my cousins. I know their kind. My father was one of them. They're what I came from."

Without hesitating, without thinking, Deborah touched his hand. Comforting. Caring. So much like the Deborah he'd known and liked.

"You were never anything like those people. You didn't get into any real trouble when you were a teenager. Everything you did, you did to improve your life, to get away from your roots."

He laid his open palm atop her small hand, trapping it between his big, hard hands. "You never looked down on me, never thought you were better than I was, like so many people did. Even though you were just a kid, you seemed to understand what I wanted, what I needed."

Deborah shivered, her stomach quivering, warmth spreading through her like the morning sunshine slowly bathing the horizon with its life-giving light. She couldn't bear feeling this way, longing to put her arms around Ashe, to tell him that she had loved him so dearly, had wanted nothing more than for him to return her love. She'd been a foolish girl; he'd been in love with her cousin.

She pulled her hand out of his gentle clasp. "So, your...you..." Her voice cracked. She cleared her throat. "...your visit to your cousins didn't accomplish anything."

Dear God, how he wanted to kiss her. Here in the feminine confines of her sitting room, surrounded by all her frills and lace. The smell of her fresh and lightly scented from her bath. Her skin glowing. Soft. Begging for his touch.

"No, you're wrong," he said. "The visit did accomplish a few things. I made contact with the enemy camp. I found out Lee Roy and I still have a connection. And I sent a warning to Buck Stansell." He reached out; she retreated. He reached out farther and touched her cheek. She trembled, but didn't pull away from him.

"I laid claim to you. I told them that Buck should know you are my woman, and if he harms you, I'll seek revenge."

"You...you...*claimed* me?" She widened her eyes, staring at him in disbelief.

He ran the tips of his fingers down her cheek, caressing her throat, then circled her neck, urging her forward. "I know Buck and his type. They're wild, they're ruthless, but they aren't stupid. The one thing they respect and understand is brute force. Another man's strength. They know who I am, the life I've lived. And they know that if I say I'll come after them if they harm you, I mean it."

"But Ashe, I don't—"

"For as long as I'm your bodyguard, we will pretend to be a couple. We're old friends who have become lovers. As far as Buck Stansell and the whole state of Alabama is concerned, you're my woman, and this isn't a job anymore. This is personal. In taking care of you, I'm simply defending my own against any harm. Do you understand what I'm saying?"

Yes, she understood. She understood only too well. Not only would she have to endure constant threats on her life and Ashe's daily presence in her life, but she would have to put on an act, playing the part of Ashe's lover.

"I can't do it," she said, trying to pull away from him.

He held her in his gentle yet firm grip, raking his thumb up and down the side of her neck. "Why can't you?"

"I can't lie about something that important. I can't pretend with Mother and with Allen."

"Tell your Mother the truth, and I don't think Allen will care if you have a boyfriend. He seems to think you need one." Ashe continued stroking the side of her neck.

"You had no right to tell anyone that I'm your woman! I'm not. I never have been and I never will be."

He jerked her up against him, his lips a whisper away from hers. "This pretense just might save your life or at least make Buck think twice about harming you. I don't give a damn about your objections—I'm more concerned about saving your life. From this moment on, for all intents and purposes, you're mine. Do I make myself clear?"

Deborah swallowed hard, then closed her eyes to block out the sight of Ashe's face. She couldn't pretend to be his woman. Dear

Lord, didn't he understand anything about her? Years ago she had lived in a fantasy world where she dreamed Ashe would leave Whitney and come to her, claiming her, making her his. And on that one night, the night she conceived Allen, she had given herself to the man she loved, and afterward he had told her he didn't want her.

"You can't order me around. You can't make me do something I don't want to do." She clenched her teeth and stared him straight in the eye.

"You're so damned stubborn."

His lips covered hers with hot, demanding urgency, the need to override her objections forefront in his mind. But his body's needs overcame his intention to bend her to his will. He didn't want to force her to do anything; he wanted her compliance.

Deborah fought the kiss for a few brief seconds, then succumbed to the power of his possession, giving herself over to the feel of his arm around her, pulling her closer and closer, his fingers threading through her hair, capturing her head in the palm of his hand.

Her breasts pressed against his hard chest. His tongue delved into her mouth. Slipping her arms around inside his shirt, she clung to him, her nails biting into the muscles of his naked back. Deborah and Ashe sought to appease the hunger gnawing inside them, their lips tasting the sweetness, their tongues seeking, their hands laying claim to the feast of their aroused bodies.

Ashe felt hard and hot as Deborah ran her hands over his chest, across his tiny, pebble hard nipples, lacing her fingers through his dark chest hair.

Ashe reached between their bodies, separating the folds of her silk robe, feeling for her breast. He eased the robe off her shoulder, then the thin strap of her gown, exposing her left breast, lifting it in his hand.

When he rubbed his fingers across her jutting nipple, she cried out. He took the sound into his mouth, deepening their kiss. She curled against him. He dragged her onto his lap, lowered his head and covered her nipple with his mouth, sucking greedily. All the while he stroked a fiery path down her back, stopping to caress her hip.

The taste of her filled him, urging him to sample more and more of her soft, sweet flesh. He hadn't meant for things to get so out of hand, but once he'd touched her, he couldn't stop himself, couldn't seem to control his desire.

Deborah's breath came in strong, fast pants as she clung to his shoulder with one hand and held his head to her breast with the other.

They wriggled and squirmed, arms embracing, hands caressing, lips savoring, legs entwined. Losing their balance in the fury of their passion, they toppled off the window bench and onto the floor. Ashe's leg rammed against the mahogany tea table, knocking it over, sending the tea service crashing onto the Oriental carpet.

Breathing erratically, Deborah glanced away from Ashe to the wreckage on the floor beside them. Reality intruded on the erotic dream. She shoved against Ashe's chest.

He wanted her to ignore everything around them, to concentrate on recapturing the raw, wild need that had claimed them, but he saw the hazy look of longing clear from her eyes.

She pulled up her gown to cover her breast and lifted herself into a sitting position on the floor. Ashe rose to his feet, offered her his hand and lifted her, pulling her back into his arms.

"You're Ashe McLaughlin's woman. I think we just proved that it won't be difficult for us to carry off the masquerade for as long as it's necessary."

He brushed her lips with his, then released her. Deborah staggered on her feet, but found her footing quickly, determined not to give in to the desire to scratch Ashe's eyes out.

Damn the man! He had gotten his way. He had proved that she was just as vulnerable to him as she'd been at seventeen.

"I'd like for you to go now," she said. "I'll explain things to Mother and I'll tell Allen what I think will pacify his curiosity."

"There's less than two weeks until the trial. I think we can pretend for that long. Then for another week or so, if Buck Stansell decides to retaliate for your testifying against Lon Sparks."

"I suppose there's always that possibility, isn't there? If that happens, then this nightmare could go on forever."

"Let's take it one day at a time. We'll get you through the trial, then worry about what might or might not happen afterward."

Deborah nodded. Ashe glanced down at the overturned table, the scattered tea service, the spilled tea.

"I'll clean up this mess," he said.

"No, please." She looked at him and wished she hadn't. His gaze said he still wanted her. "I'll take care of it. I'd like for you to leave. Now."

He walked out of her bedroom. She stood there trembling with unshed tears choking her. *I will not cry. I will not cry.* She knelt down on the floor, righted the tea table and picked up the silver service. A dark stain marred the blue-and-cream perfection of the rug. She jumped up and ran into the bathroom, wet a frayed hand towel and glanced into the mirror above the sink.

Dear Lord. Her hair was in disarray, the long strands fanned out around her face. Her cheeks were flushed, her eyes overly bright. Her lips were swollen. A pink rash covered her neck and the top of her left breast, a result of Ashe's beard stubble. She looked like a woman who'd been ravished. Suddenly she felt like a woman who'd been ravished.

Tears gathered in her eyes. She laid her head against the mirror and cried.

In the week since they had begun their pretense, Ashe hadn't kissed her again, indeed he'd barely touched her, except in front of others—a part of their performance as lovers. In another week Lon Sparks's trial would begin. But when it ended, would the threats end, too, or would they turn deadly? Ashe screened all of Deborah's calls and her mail. The daily threats continued, meaningless threats since Deborah never heard the messages or read the letters. Two more little *gifts* had arrived, both of these delivered by unknown messenger to her home. One, a green garden snake, Ashe had taken outside and released. The other had been more ominous, one he'd made sure neither Deborah nor Miss Carol saw. A newspaper photograph of Deborah, singed around the edges, a book of matches laid on top and the words "Your house might catch on fire" scrawled in red ink across the newspaper.

Nerve-racking threats to be sure, harassment to say the least, but not once had Deborah's life actually been in jeopardy. Was Buck Stansell playing some sort of sick game or was he trying to throw them off guard, waiting to act at the last moment?

"It's been a long time since you've been in the country club."

Carol Vaughn slipped her arm through Ashe's. He looked away from the living room window where he'd been staring sightlessly outside while he waited for Deborah. He smiled at Miss Carol. "Eleven years."

"The night Whitney announced her engagement to George." Carol patted Ashe on his forearm. "She was such a selfish girl, but always so bubbly. Now she's a very sad, selfish woman."

"Are you trying to warn me about something, Miss Carol?"

"Do I need to warn you?"

"I haven't been carrying a torch for Whitney all these years, if that's what's troubling you."

"No, I didn't think you had. You wouldn't look at my daughter as if she were you favorite meal and you hadn't eaten in a long time, if you were in love with another woman."

Had he been that obvious? So apparent in his desire for Deborah that even her own mother had noticed? "Why, Miss Carol, what big eyes you have."

"And sharp teeth, too. If for one minute I thought you'd hurt Deborah again, I'd have no qualms about chewing you up into little pieces."

"And you could do it, too." Taking her hand in his, he walked her across the room and seated her on the sofa. "I never meant to hurt Deborah. I made a mistake, but I tried to keep from making an even bigger mistake. I was honest with her, and I paid dearly for that honesty."

"My husband adored Deborah. She was our only child. I didn't agree with what he did to you, and I told him so at the time. But Wallace could not be reasoned with on any subject, and certainly not when he felt Deborah had been wronged."

"I never made Deborah any promises eleven years ago, and I won't make any to her now. None that I can't keep." Ashe heard Deborah's and Allen's voices coming from the upstairs landing. "I'm attracted to Deborah and she's attracted to me. We're both adults now. If things become complicated, we'll deal with them."

Carol nodded meekly. Ashe couldn't understand the wary look in her blue eyes, that sad expression on her face. What was Miss Carol so afraid would happen?

Allen rushed down the stairs and into the living room. "Come see," he said. "Deborah's beautiful. She looks like one of those models on TV."

Ashe helped Miss Carol to her feet and they followed Allen into the hallway. All three of them looked up to the top of the stairs where Deborah stood.

For one split second Ashe couldn't breathe. He didn't think he'd ever seen anything as lovely as the woman who walked slowly down the stairs, the diamonds in her ears and around her throat dimmed by her radiance.

Allen glanced up at Ashe, then punched him in the side. "See, what'd I tell you?"

"You're right, pal. She's beautiful."

Deborah descended the staircase, butterflies wild in her stomach. How many times had she dreamed of a real date with Ashe McLaughlin? Now, it was a reality. Now, eleven years too late.

He stood at the bottom of the stairs, Allen to his left. The sight of her son at his father's side tugged at Deborah's heart. What would Ashe say if she told him the truth about Allen? Would he be glad? Or would he be sorry?

Ashe looked at Deborah, seeing her as if for the first time, all sparkling and vibrant, beautiful beyond description. How could any man see her and not want her?

The royal blue satin draped across her shoulders in a shawl collar, narrowing to her tiny waist and flaring into a full, gathered skirt, ankle-length gown. Her satin shoes matched the dress to perfection, and when she stopped at the foot of the stairs, Ashe noticed that the deep rich color she wore turned her blue eyes to sapphires.

"You look lovely, my dear." Carol Vaughn kissed her daughter's cheek. "Please give my regrets to Whitney. I'm sure she'll understand that I'm not quite up to these late-night social affairs."

Deborah hugged her mother close. Her beautiful, brave mother, whose bout with cancer had taken its toll on all of them. "I dread going," Deborah whispered so low that only Carol heard her words. "I have no idea what Whitney will do. She's bound to make a play for Ashe."

Pulling out of Deborah's arms, Carol smiled. "You two run along now and have a wonderful time." Carol glanced at Ashe who hadn't taken his eyes off Deborah. "And don't feel that you need to come home early."

Allen rushed out of the hallway and into the library, returning quickly with a gold foil-wrapped gift. "Don't forget George's birthday present.'' Allen shook the small package. ''What is it anyway?''

''It's a fourteen-karat gold money clip.'' Deborah took the gift. ''Whitney mentioned that George had misplaced his money clip.''

''Hocked it, no doubt.'' Carol nudged Ashe in the center of his back. ''I do believe you've taken Ashe's breath away with your loveliness.''

''Yeah, he looks like somebody hit him in the head.'' Allen laughed. ''Hey, man, have you got it bad or what?''

Ashe jabbed Allen playfully in the ribs, lifted him up off the floor with one arm and rubbed his fist across the top of the boy's head before placing him back on his feet. ''You wouldn't make fun of a guy for mooning over his girl, would you?''

''Naw, as long as you don't kiss her in front of me.'' Putting his hand on his hip, Allen stood up straight and gave Ashe a hard look. ''If I catch you kissing her, then, as the man of the house, I'd have to ask you what your intentions are, wouldn't I?''

''Yes, Allen, I suppose you would,'' Ashe said. ''So, I'll tell you what, I'll try to make sure I kiss Deborah when you're not around.''

''Will you two stop this.'' Deborah tried to hug Allen, but he wriggled away from her. ''What's the matter? Have you gotten too big to give me a hug and a kiss?''

''No, that's not it.'' Grinning, Allen swiped his hand in front of him in a negative gesture. ''I'm just afraid your boyfriend will get jealous and sock me.''

Allen broke into peals of boyish laughter. Ashe chuckled. Carol covered her mouth to hide her giggle. Deborah shook her head in mock disgust.

''Let's go now, Ashe, before I wind up socking Allen,'' Deborah said.

Taking the long satin jacket from where Deborah carried it across her arm, Ashe wrapped it around her shoulders. He slipped his arm about her waist and escorted her out to her repaired and newly painted Cadillac waiting in the drive.

When he opened the door, he turned and lifted her hand to his lips. ''You're the most beautiful thing I've ever seen.''

He kissed her wrist. Chills shivered through her. She looked into his eyes. ''Thank you.''

He helped her into the car, rounded the Caddy and got behind the wheel. "No matter what happens tonight, there are a few things I want you to keep in mind."

"Such as?" Deborah smoothed the gathers in her skirt, her fingers gliding nervously over the heavy satin. She didn't look at Ashe.

"Such as I didn't come back to Sheffield to protect Whitney. I wouldn't have, for any amount of money. And I'm not staying in town because of her or issuing threats to dangerous men because of her."

"Did she hurt you so badly back then that you hate her now? You know they say there's only a fine line between love and hate. Maybe you still care about her more than you'd like to admit. After all, she was your first love and—"

Ashe grabbed Deborah so quickly that she didn't have time to think of resisting. His kiss came so hard and fast that it obliterated every thought from her mind, filling her with the heat of his anger, the determination of his desire. His mouth devoured hers, the kiss turning from bold strength to gentle power. Her hands crept up around his neck. He stroked her waist. The satin jacket fell from her shoulders leaving them bare. Ashe allowed his lips to retreat from hers, as he nibbled at her bottom lip and tasted her chin. He lowered his head to her shoulder, his mouth closing over her soft flesh.

Shutting her eyes and tossing back her head, Deborah moaned. "Ashe..."

"Don't ever try to tell me how I feel." Lifting his head, he stared into her blue eyes. "Whitney wasn't my first anything. I'd had a dozen girls before her. You should remember all the girls I dated. And as far as my being in love with her, I wasn't. I was infatuated with what she represented. She represented a dream. That night at the country club when she announced her engagement, I saw my dream come to an end."

"Neither of us has ever been able to forget that night, have we? But for different reasons."

He gripped her chin between his thumb and forefinger. "If you think I've ever forgotten what it was like making love to you, then you're wrong."

"I suppose you remember all of them, don't you? Whitney, the dozen before her, and God only knows how many since."

Ashe fell backward against the soft leather of the seat, shook his head and laughed. "You're jealous! You are honest-to-goodness jealous."

"I am not!" Deborah jerked the satin jacket up around her shoulders.

"Somewhere deep down inside, Deborah Vaughn, you're the one who still cares. I still mean something to you, don't I?"

Yes, she wanted to scream. Yes, you mean something to me. You are my first and only lover. You are the father of my child, the child I can never claim as my own. Oh, yes, Ashe McLaughlin, you most definitely still mean something to me.

"I think you're taking the part of playing my lover far too seriously." Deborah turned around in the seat, focusing her attention on the front porch lights. "We are pretending to care about each other. That's all."

"That's not all," Ashe said. "You asked me if I remember all the women I've had sex with. Well, yes, I do remember. Some more than others. But I didn't have sex with you, Deborah." There in the darkness his voice sounded deeper and darker and more sensuous than ever. "I made love to you. I took all that sweet, innocent passion you offered and I drowned myself in your love. I had never been in so much pain, and I had never needed a woman's unselfish love the way I needed yours that night. Don't you think I know that I did all the taking and you did all the giving."

"Please, Ashe, I don't want—"

"What? You don't want to hear the truth? You don't want to hear how much I wanted to keep on taking what you offered? How much guts it took for me to reject you? Hell, I knew I couldn't give a girl like you what you should have. I knew the best thing I could do for you was to get out of your life and stay out."

"And that's exactly what you did." Deborah cringed at the accusatory tone of her own voice. "You couldn't even stay in the same town with me, could you? You couldn't hang around long enough to find—"

Dear God, she'd been about to say *find out if you'd gotten me pregnant!*

"None of this matters now, does it?" Pulling the shoulder harness across her, she snapped the seat belt in place. "If we don't leave for the country club right now, we're going to be more than fashionably late.''

"Sooner or later we'll have to finish this conversation," Ashe said. "I think we both have quite a lot to get off our chests."

"It'll have to be later."

"Fine." He turned on the overhead lights. "You might want to check your makeup. I think most of your lipstick is on my mouth." Pulling a handkerchief from his pocket, he wiped his face.

Deborah opened her evening bag, took out her lipstick and glanced in the mirror to see how much repair was needed. She worked quickly, trying not to notice that she looked like a woman who'd just been thoroughly kissed.

"I'm ready," she said.

Ashe backed the Cadillac out of the drive and headed toward the country club.

"Ashe McLaughlin, you old dog. I never thought I'd see you back in Sheffield."

Keeping his arm firmly around Deborah's waist, Ashe jerked his head around, seeking the familiar voice. "Peanut Haygood?"

The skinny teenage boy who'd lived down the street from Ashe's grandmother had turned into a heavyset, bearded man wearing a uniform and carrying a gun. By the looks of old Peanut, Ashe figured he was part of the private security for George Jamison's big birthday bash.

"Peanut? Man, you've changed since the last time I saw you."

"Yeah, well, a guy grows up and fills out," Peanut said. "I heard you were in town." He nodded politely to Deborah. "Nice to see you, Ms. Vaughn. Sorry to hear about all your problems. One of these days we're going to get the goods on Buck Stansell and put him away for life."

"Are you on the police force?" Deborah asked.

"Yes, ma'am. Over in Muscle Shoals." Peanut slapped Ashe on the back. "Looks like you and me wound up in the same business, huh? You a Green Beret and me a policeman. Now you're a private security agent and I moonlight as a guard for these fancy shindigs at the country club."

"Ashe, if you'll excuse me, I need to go to the ladies' room and then check my wrap.'' Forcing a smile, Deborah nodded toward the rest room.

"I'll be waiting right outside." Ashe followed her down the corridor, Peanut right behind him keeping up a steady stream of conversation.

From where he stood, Ashe could see the entrance to the ballroom. He spotted Whitney immediately. Her loud laughter echoed out into the hallway. She had her arm draped around a young man who seemed utterly fascinated by her.

"Who'd ever thought Deborah Vaughn would turn into such a looker, huh?" Peanut jabbed Ashe in the ribs. "You two were always friends, weren't you? Rumor was her daddy had you run out of town."

"Rumors aren't always reliable," Ashe said.

"Well, Ms. Vaughn sure got herself into a mess with ol' Buck and his bunch of roughnecks. It's too bad she come up on Lon Sparks shooting Looney. Neither one of those boys was worth a cuss."

"Do you think Buck would kill to protect Sparks or seek revenge if he goes to the pen?"

"I'd say Buck would be more likely to have Lon Sparks killed to keep him from talking than he would to kill Ms. Vaughn. Sparks is a liability to them now. Me and some of the boys at work have got us a theory." Peanut stretched his five feet nine inches and placed his hand atop the gun holster resting on his hip.

"What's your theory?"

"We think Buck is putting on an act of trying to scare Ms. Vaughn, trying to make Lon Sparks think he's protecting him. You get my drift?"

"Yeah, I get it. Buck always was one for playing games." Ashe knew he should be comforted at the thought that it was possible Buck Stansell had no intention of killing Deborah, but Ashe's gut instincts told him that he should take nothing for granted. No matter what Buck's intentions were, the man was dangerous, a highly explosive bad boy, who was capable of anything.

Ashe caught a glimpse of Whitney coming his way. She swayed her narrow hips, encased in silver lamé, as she sauntered out of the ballroom.

"Now there's a real piece of work," Peanut said. "Sexy as

hell and so gorgeous she gives a man ideas. But not worth the cost of the lead it'd take to shoot her.''

"You seem to know an awful lot about Whitney Jamison.'' Ashe watched his old lover flirting outrageously with every man in her path as she made her way through the influx of late arrivals congested in the hallway.

"Hey, I've been moonlighting on this job for a good many years and I've seen quite a bit of Mrs. Jamison. She really works these social occasions, and I've rarely seen her leave with her husband, if you know what I mean.''

Ashe grinned. "Not the faithful type?''

"Can't say I blame her, married to a loser like George Jamison. The man hasn't held a job in years. They live off her inheritance, you know. Her shares in that real estate firm Ms. Vaughn runs. And Georgie Porgie likes to gamble. They're always flying off to Vegas and Atlantic City and down to Biloxi.''

Whitney walked up to Ashe, slipped her arms around his neck and kissed him soundly on the mouth. Still draped around him, she smiled. "Come dance with me, darling. If I remember correctly, you were a marvelous dancer.''

"You were the marvelous dancer,'' Ashe said. "I just followed your lead.''

Whitney's throaty laughter rumbled from her chest. Her almost naked chest, Ashe noted. Her strapless silver lamé dress crisscrossed over her full breasts, just covering her tight nipples. "It's been a long time, hasn't it?'' Whitney sighed. "Come on, let's see if we're still good together.'' She rubbed herself intimately against Ashe.

Peanut cleared his throat. Ashe stared at him. The guard gave his head a few sharp jerks in the direction of the ladies' room. Glancing over his shoulder, Ashe saw Deborah watching him.

Grasping Whitney's arms, he pulled them from around his neck and stepped backward, putting some distance between them. Whitney's gaze followed Ashe's. She laughed again, an almost hysterical giggle.

"You'll have to find yourself another partner,'' Ashe said. "I'm afraid my dance card is filled.''

Whitney leaned over and whispered in Ashe's ear, "If you think my little cousin is going to give you what you need, then you'd better think again. She doesn't know the first thing about men, and most certainly nothing about a man like you.''

"That's where you're wrong, Mrs. Jamison.'' Ashe walked over to Deborah, slipped his arm around her rigid body and pulled her up against his side. "Would you like to dance, honey?'' he asked Deborah.

Unsmiling, every nerve in her body tense, Deborah glared at Ashe. "Perhaps, after I've wished George a happy birthday and given him his present.'' She held up the shiny golden gift.

When Ashe guided Deborah past Whitney, Deborah paused. "You look lovely tonight, Whitney. But then I'm sure you already know that. No doubt every man at the party has told you at least once.''

Whitney grinned, a rather shaky grin, one that didn't reach her eyes, one that didn't begin to compare with the smile spreading across Deborah's face.

"And you look adorable,'' Whitney said, giving Deborah a quick hug. "And aren't you the lucky one, having Ashe McLaughlin as your escort. But then, I suppose Aunt Carol is paying him extra, isn't she?''

"And he's worth every cent.'' Deborah tugged on Ashe's arm. She led him away from her cousin, down the hallway and into the ballroom.

Ashe and Deborah heard Peanut Haygood's hardy chuckle, but neither turned around to see Whitney's reaction.

"When did you learn to play hardball?'' Ashe asked.

"When my father died and I had to take responsibility for his business as well as my mother and Allen.''

"Let's find George and give him his present.'' Ashe ran his hand up and down Deborah's arm. "I want to dance with you.''

Deborah wasn't quite sure what she thought or how she felt. A mixture of anger and exhilaration rioted along her nerve endings. All the old jealousies she'd felt for her cousin had come racing to the forefront when she'd walked out of the ladies' room and seen Whitney wrapped around Ashe. But when she had won their verbal sparring match, she'd felt as if she were walking on air.

She couldn't help wondering what would happen if she spent the night in Ashe's arms, dancing with him here at the country club? Perhaps the safest course of action would be to give George his present, stay long enough to appease her social set's curiosity and make a quiet, discreet exit. If Whitney indulged in her usual weakness for champagne, there was a chance she might make a scene later on. And Deborah wanted to avoid a real confrontation that would put her in the spotlight.

The whole town knew she was the prosecution's star witness, and that her life was in danger. And she had no doubt that Ashe McLaughlin's constant presence at her side had set tongues wagging. What would they say once Ashe had shown everyone that their relationship was intimate?

She didn't give a damn what *they* would say. She never had. She'd always been a lot like her mother. Carol Allen Vaughn had known who she was—an Allen—and had never considered herself subject to the rules and regulations of the society biddies. And no one had ever dared question Carol's judgment or suggest her actions were inappropriate. In that respect, Deborah was her mother's daughter.

But Carol had given in to Wallace Vaughn's authority, always the dutiful wife. If only her mother had gone against her father's wishes. If only—

"Deborah, such a smashing dress!" George Jamison III smiled his widemouthed, white-toothed smile and gave his cousin-in-law a peck on the cheek. "For me?" George eyed the gold foil-wrapped gift.

"Oh, yes. This is for you." Deborah hadn't realized that while she'd been thinking, Ashe had led her straight to the birthday boy. Although boy was hardly the appropriate word for a balding man of forty. Then again, perhaps boy was the correct word to describe George, who, in many ways, was far more immature than Allen.

"I'll just put it here with my other goodies." George laid the gift on top of a stack of presents arranged on the table behind him. "I suppose Whitney greeted y'all at the door. She's such a marvelous hostess. And she does love a good party."

"Yes, she met us in the hallway, actually," Deborah said.

Ashe tightened his hold around Deborah's waist. "Happy birthday, George."

George glanced at Ashe, his long, thin nose slightly tilted upward. He made no move to offer Ashe his hand. "McLaughlin." George's pale gray eyes met Ashe's vibrant hazel glare. "I was surprised to hear you'd come back to Sheffield to act as Deborah's bodyguard. Of course, we're all pleased that someone is looking out for her. I understand that you're highly qualified to handle brutes like Buck Stansell. Then, of course, it must be a help that you've had ties to those people all your life."

"Yes, it is a help." Ashe lifted the corners of his mouth just enough to hint at a smile, but he knew George Jamison would recognize the look in his eyes for what it was. Contempt. Dislike. Disgust.

"We can't stay too long," Deborah said. "I don't like to leave Mother alone."

"I quite understand." Glancing across the room, George waved at someone. "Do enjoy yourselves. I'm sure this is a bit of a treat for you, McLaughlin. Finally getting to come to the country club through the front door. Rather different from the last time you were here, isn't it?"

"George, you're being—" Deborah said.

"You're right." Catching sight of Whitney dancing with the young man she had cornered earlier, Ashe nodded in her direction. "Eleven years ago you and I were the only two guys Whitney was seeing."

"How dare you!" George's thin, white cheeks flushed pink.

Ashe led Deborah away from George, quickly ushering her through the crowd and onto the dance floor.

"That was a horrible thing to say to George," Deborah said.

"I was justified, don't you think?" Ashe pulled her close, leaning over to nuzzle her neck with his nose.

She gulped in a deep breath of air. "Yes, you were most definitely justified. George always has been a little snot! He's so immature."

"A little snot?" Ashe chuckled. "I guess that does aptly describe George, doesn't it?"

Deborah loved the feel of Ashe's arms around her, the security of his strength, the sensuality of his nearness. She didn't know what she had expected to happen tonight. Between Ashe and Whitney. Between Ashe and George. But she certainly hadn't expected to feel so light and free and thoroughly amused.

It suddenly hit her that neither she nor Ashe were the same two people who had left this country club eleven years ago. They had both grown up.

Ashe was no longer in awe of the wealthy social set that ruled the county. His dreams weren't wrapped up in a sexy package called Whitney Vaughn. He wasn't an angry, outraged, spurned lover.

And Deborah no longer saw herself as a wallflower beside her exquisite cousin. Any residue of leftover jealousy she might have once felt disappeared completely. She was strong. She was successful. She was attractive.

And Ashe McLaughlin wanted her!

They moved to the music, giving themselves over to the bluesy rendition of an old Glenn Miller song. They spent nearly an hour on the dance floor, wrapped in each other's arms. Occasionally Deborah noticed some curious stares and heard a few whispered innuendoes. None of it mattered, she told herself. She and Ashe were presenting themselves to the world as lovers. She could not allow herself to think otherwise. When the danger to her life ended, Ashe would be gone.

But during the duration of his stay, they could become lovers. She didn't doubt for one minute that Ashe wanted her. He had made that abundantly clear. The question was did she dare risk giving herself to him? Did she dare risk falling in love with him all over again? How could she become his lover and continue lying to him about Allen?

"Are you about ready to leave?" Ashe whispered, then kissed her ear.

Deborah shivered. "Yes. I think everyone has seen us and drawn their own conclusions."

"We don't have to go back to your house." Ashe ran his hand up and down her back. "We could find some place to be alone."

"No. I'm not... Just take me home. I can't handle a repeat performance of that night eleven years ago when we left the country club together."

"It wouldn't be the same. We aren't the same," he said. "We'd both know what we were getting into this time."

"That's the problem, isn't it? At least for me."

The music came to a end. Couples left the dance floor, while others waited for the next set to begin. Deborah pulled away from Ashe, intending to make a quick exit. Ashe jerked her into his arms, grasped the back of her head with his hand and kissed her, long, hard and devouring. Every rational thought went out of her head.

When she was weak and breathless, he ended the kiss, draped

his arm around her shoulders and escorted her off the dance floor, past a glaring Whitney and her openmouthed guests.

"Every person in this room knows you're mine," he whispered as they walked out into the hall. "And since they're aware of my reputation, no one will doubt that I'm the kind of man who'd kill to defend his own."

Chapter 7

Deborah folded the blueprints and laid them aside. She couldn't seem to concentrate on the plans for Cotton Lane Estates, although she had promised Vaughn & Posey's backers a detailed report on their present subdivision project.

She lifted the cup of warm coffee to her lips and downed the sweet liquid. Clutching the coffee mug in her hands, she closed her eyes. In a few days, Lon Sparks's trial would begin and she'd be called on to testify. The waiting had been almost unbearable, not knowing what might or might not happen. She couldn't give in to her fears and allow the likes of Buck Stansell to frighten her into backing down from doing what she knew was right. But sometimes she wondered what her mother and Allen would do if anything happened to her. Her mother's health was so precarious, and Allen was still so young. What if he lost both her and her mother?

Ashe McLaughlin had a right to know he had a son. That's what her mother had told Deborah's father years ago and that's what she kept telling Deborah now. If anything were to happen to the two women in Allen's life, he would still have his father.

But how could she tell Ashe the truth? She and her mother had kept the true circumstances of Allen's birth a secret for ten years.

What would Allen do if he suddenly discovered that the two people he loved and trusted most in the world had been lying to him his whole life?

No, she didn't dare risk losing Allen's love by telling Ashe the truth. She had no way of knowing how Ashe would react and whether or not he'd tell Allen everything.

Her mother had warned her that sooner or later Ashe would have to be told. Deborah had decided that it must be later, much later. She had to be strong. Just a little while longer. Ashe wouldn't stay in Sheffield if she wasn't in danger. He would walk out of their lives and never look back, the way he'd done eleven years ago. She could trust him with her life, but not with her heart—and not with Allen's future.

When she heard a soft knock at the door, Deborah opened her eyes. "Yes?"

Annie Laurie eased the door open. "Mr. Shipman's on the phone. He says it's urgent he speak to you."

"Mr. Shipman? The principal at Allen's school?"

"Yes, that Mr. Shipman."

"Okay. Thanks, Annie Laurie." Deborah picked up the telephone and punched the Incoming Call button. "Hello, Mr. Shipman, this is Deborah Vaughn. Is something wrong?"

Ashe slipped by Annie Laurie and into Deborah's private office, closing the door behind him. Deborah glanced at him.

"Ms. Vaughn, you need to come to school and pick up Allen," Mr. Shipman said. "I'm afraid there's been a problem on the playground during PE class."

"Has Allen been in a fight?" Deborah asked.

Ashe lifted his eyebrows and shrugged his shoulders as if saying "Boys will be boys."

"Oh, no Ms. Vaughn, I didn't mean to imply that Allen had gotten himself into any trouble. Quite the contrary. It seems that when the fifth graders were playing softball during PE, a stranger approached Allen. Your brother won't tell us what the man said to him, but Allen seems terribly upset. I thought it best to phone you immediately."

"Yes, yes, you did the right thing, Mr. Shipman. I'll be right over." Deborah's heartbeat throbbed loudly in her ears, obliterating every other sound, even Ashe's voice. "Please, don't leave

Allen alone. Make sure someone is with him until I pick him up.'' Deborah returned the phone to its cradle.

When Deborah didn't respond to his questions, Ashe grabbed her by the shoulders, shaking her gently. ''What's going on? Has something happened to Allen?''

''A strange man approached Allen on the playground during PE. Mr. Shipman said the man upset Allen.'' Deborah clutched the lapels of Ashe's jacket. ''What if— Oh, God, Ashe, what if Buck Stansell sent someone to hurt Allen?''

''Did anyone besides Allen get a good look at this man? Did they see whether he was on foot or driving?''

''I didn't think to ask, dammit.'' Releasing her hold on Ashe, Deborah walked around to the front of her desk. Yanking open the bottom drawer, she lifted out her leather bag and threw the straps over her shoulder. ''I have to pick up Allen and take him home. I have to make sure he's all right. If anyone dares harm him, I'll—''

''I'll take care of anyone who threatens Allen, in the same way I'll handle anyone who threatens you.'' Ashe held out his hand. ''Give me the keys to your Caddy. I'll drive. On the way over to the school, pull yourself together. Allen doesn't need to see how upset you are.''

Deborah took a deep breath. ''You're right. It's just that, in the back of my mind, I kept wondering if and when Buck Stansell would target Mother or Allen. Oh, Ashe, I can't let anything happen to Allen.''

''Nothing is going to happen to Allen.'' He took her hand in his. ''I promise.''

Within five minutes they marched side by side into Richard Shipman's office where Allen sat, silent and unmoving, in a corner chair. The minute he saw Deborah, he ran into her open arms.

''Give us a few minutes alone with Allen,'' Ashe said to the principal, who immediately nodded agreement and exited his office.

''What happened, sweetheart?'' Deborah asked, bending on her knees, hugging her child close, stroking his thick blond hair. ''Tell us everything.''

Allen clung to Deborah for several moments, then glanced over at Ashe. ''You can't let them do anything to hurt her.''

"Allen, will you tell me what happened?" Ashe reached down and patted Allen on the back.

Allen shook his head, released his tenacious hold on Deborah, but still clung to her hand as she stood. "He walked up to me on the playground. I was waiting my turn at bat. He said he knew my sister and that he wanted me to give her a message."

"Oh, Ashe!" Deborah clenched her teeth tightly together in an effort not to cry in front of Allen.

Laying his hand on Deborah's shoulder, Ashe gave her a reassuring squeeze. "Had you ever seen this man before?"

"No," Allen said.

"Come on, let's go sit down over here on the sofa." Deborah led Allen across the room to the small, leather sofa situated against the back wall between two oak filing cabinets. "I want you to answer all of Ashe's questions. He's here to help us. Do you understand?"

"What—what do you want to know?" Allen looked at Ashe.

"Would you recognize the man if you ever saw him again? Can you tell me what he looked like?"

"Yeah, I'd recognize him, all right. He was big and ugly and he smelled bad."

"Sounds like somebody Buck would sent around to frighten a child," Ashe said.

"He didn't scare me." Allen tightened his hold on Deborah's hand. "I told him off. If you don't believe me, just ask Tripper Smith. He heard me telling that guy he'd better leave my sister alone."

Ashe knelt down in front of Allen. "I know you're brave and that you'd fight for your sister."

Deborah forced a smile when she looked at Allen's pale little face. "Did the man try to hurt you?"

"Naw, he just said to give my sister a message. He said to tell you that if you show up in court Monday, you'll be very sorry. And I told him that nothing he said or did would keep you from testifying against that murderer. And he said if you did, you were stupid. That's when I tried to hit him, but he just laughed and walked away."

"Did your teacher see the man, or any of the other kids beside this Tripper Smith?" Ashe asked.

"My teacher didn't see nothing, but several of the kids saw

him. Tripper's the one who went and told Coach Watkins what had happened.''

''Okay, Allen, why don't you and Deborah go do whatever is necessary to get you checked out of school for the day. I'll make a couple of phone calls and then we'll be ready to leave.'' Ashe wished he had the big, bad-smelling stranger in front of him right now. He'd teach Buck Stansell's messenger that it wasn't nice to go around frightening little boys, especially not a child under his protection.

''Are we going home?'' Allen asked. ''Do we have to tell Mother what happened? She'll just worry.''

''We aren't going home,'' Ashe said. ''I think you and Deborah and I should go somewhere for burgers and fries and then do something fun together this afternoon. How does that sound to you, Allen?''

''Sounds great to me.'' Allen looked at Deborah. ''Can I really play hooky for the rest of the day?''

''You bet you can.'' Deborah stood. Allen jumped up beside her. ''We'll go get Allen checked out of school and wait for you in the office.''

''I'll only be a few minutes.'' Ashe picked up the telephone and dialed the police department. ''Allen, I know you don't want to worry your mother, but we'll have to tell her what happened when we go home.''

Allen nodded. Deborah ushered him out of the principal's office, thankful that Ashe McLaughlin was taking charge of the situation, thankful that she hadn't had to face this alone. The thought that they had come together like a family—a mother, a father and their child—flashed through Deborah's mind. She couldn't allow herself the indulgence of such thoughts. Thinking of the three of them as a family could be dangerous.

''I can't eat another bite.'' Ashe shoved a French fry into Deborah's mouth. She slapped his hand away.

''I want one of those sundaes, don't you, Ashe?'' Allen read the list of desserts off the wall sign behind the counter. ''I want caramel with nuts.''

''That's my favorite, too.'' Ashe slid out from behind the booth. ''I'll order us both one. What do you want, Deborah?''

"Nothing! I've eaten enough for a couple of meals."

"Ah, she's just worried she'll get fat," Allen said. "She used to be sort of plump a long time ago. Hey, you already know that. You knew Deborah even before I did."

"So I did." Ashe sauntered off to order their desserts, coming back with two caramel sundaes and a small chocolate ice-cream cone, which he handed to Deborah.

"Chocolate used to be your favorite," he said.

"It still is," she admitted, taking the cone and napkin he handed her. During the last months of her pregnancy, she had craved chocolate ice cream. Maybe that was the reason Allen hated the stuff. She'd gorged him on it before he'd been born.

She didn't realize she'd been sitting there smiling, a dazed look in her eyes until Ashe waved his hand in front of her face.

"Where did you go?" he asked. "You're a million miles away."

"Just thinking about chocolate ice cream," she said.

"Well, you'd better eat it before it melts." Allen lifted a spoonful of his sundae to his mouth. "Thanks for getting extra nuts, Ashe."

"Nothing's too good for us, pal." Ashe didn't think he'd ever felt about a kid the way he felt about Allen. He didn't understand it, couldn't explain it, but he felt connected to Allen Vaughn. Maybe it was because of his past history with the family, his respect for Miss Carol, his friendship with Deborah. Whatever the cause, he found himself wondering what it would be like to have a child of his own, a boy like Allen.

"Now who's gathering moss?" Deborah wondered what Ashe was thinking. The man was such a mystery to her. Once she'd thought she knew him, but she'd been wrong. He'd never been the man she thought he was.

"What can folks do on a weekday afternoon around here for fun?" Ashe asked. "How about a movie?"

"No matinees except on the weekend," Deborah said.

"What about miniature golf?" Allen wiped his mouth with his paper napkin. "I think it's still open every afternoon until Thanksgiving."

"How about it, Deborah, are you game for a round of golf?" Ashe smiled at her and she returned his smile. "You should do that more often, you know."

"What?" she asked.

"Smile like that. A guy would agree to anything you wanted if you smiled at him like that." The warmth of her smile brought back memories of the way she'd smiled at him, lying in his arms in the moonlight, down by the river. He had never forgotten that beautiful smile or the way it had made him feel just looking at her.

"Aw, are you getting all mushy?" Allen shook his head. "Save all that love talk for when you're alone with her. I'm too young to hear stuff like that."

"Allen!" Deborah rolled her eyes heavenward.

"Eat your sundae," Ashe said. "And I'll keep in mind that you aren't old enough to learn from a master just yet. But in a few more years, you'll be begging me to share my secrets of seduction with you."

"Ashe! Of all things to say to a ten-year-old."

"Ah, lay off Ashe." Allen spoke with his mouth half full of sundae. He swallowed. "You just don't understand guy stuff."

"Oh, well, excuse me." Grinning, Deborah licked the dripping ice cream from around the edge of her cone. She glanced over at Ashe, who watched her intently, his vision focused on her mouth. She licked a circle around the chocolate ice cream, all the while watching Ashe watch her. This was a grown-up game she was playing, a subtle sexual game that Allen wouldn't notice. But Ashe noticed. He knew precisely what she was doing and why.

His jaw tightened. His eyes shone with the intensity of their gaze, fixed on her mouth, on her tongue. He gripped the edge of the table with one hand and laid his tightly clenched fist beside his half-eaten sundae.

She was arousing him and she knew it. She liked the sense of power he gave her by his display of desire. If they were alone, instead of sitting in a fast-food restaurant with Allen, she wasn't sure she'd have the nerve to tempt Ashe.

"Are you any good at playing miniature golf?" Allen tossed his plastic spoon into his empty sundae bowl. "Hey, Ashe, are you listening to me?"

"What did you say, pal?"

"Are you good at playing miniature golf?" Allen repeated. "Deborah and Mother play real golf and they take me along.

They're teaching me how to play. But right now, I still like miniature golf better.''

"I can't say I've ever played miniature golf before," Ashe said. "Today you'll have to be my teacher."

"I like that idea. I don't think I've ever taught anybody anything before." Allen beamed with pleasure.

Deborah relaxed and finished off her ice-cream cone, thinking how easily a child can adapt, how quickly Allen had gone from a frightened, worried little boy into a secure, happy kid looking forward to a new experience.

Would he adapt so easily if someday she told him the truth—that she was his mother and Ashe was his father?

"Straight upstairs and into the bathtub for you, young man." Deborah gave Allen a gentle push up the stairs, then dropped down on the bottom step. When Allen dashed off, galloping up the stairs and down the hall, Ashe propped his foot on the step beside Deborah and leaned over, kissing the tip of her nose.

She stared up at him, bewilderment in her eyes. "What was that for?"

"For being so cute. Your hair is an absolute mess." He twirled a loose strand around his index finger. "Your shoes are ruined and you've got chocolate stains on your blouse."

They both glanced down to the dark circle on the silk that lay over the rise of her left breast. "I need to get out of this blouse and soak it before the stain sets in any worse than it already has."

Ashe released her hair, ran his finger down the side of her neck and over into the V of her blouse. "Need any help?"

Carol Vaughn cleared her throat. Ashe straightened. Deborah looked up at her mother who walked from the living room into the hallway.

"Is Allen all right?" Carol asked. "He didn't seem upset."

"He's practically forgotten about what happened," Deborah said. "Thanks to Ashe. We've eaten hamburgers and fries twice today, played God only knows how many rounds of miniature golf, went to see that ridiculous dog movie and bought Allen a brand-new computer game."

"Should we take Allen out of school until the trial is over?" Carol asked.

"No, that would only make matters worse for him." Getting up, Deborah walked over to her mother and placed her arm around her frail shoulders. "I think Ashe should act as Allen's bodyguard from now on instead of mine."

"Oh, Deborah, no. Do you think Allen really is in danger?"

"Miss Carol, there's no way to know whether Allen is in real danger, but we don't dare take any chances," Ashe said. "I called the police, and Chief Burton has assured me that they'll send a patrol car around every day during Allen's PE time. And I spoke to Sheriff Blaylock, gave him a description of the man who confronted Allen on the playground."

"Do you think there's any chance of catching the man?" Carol slipped her thin arm around her daughter's waist.

"I doubt it," Ashe said. "My bet is that Buck got somebody from out of town and the guy's long gone by now."

"I didn't want to think that Allen might be in danger," Carol said. "But it did cross my mind that these people might try to get to Deborah through her...her brother."

"You could also be in danger, Miss Carol, especially when you're outside the house. With the security system we have in place now, it would be difficult for anyone to break in." Anyone who wasn't a highly trained professional, Ashe thought. He doubted any of Buck's local boys had the know-how to get past a sophisticated system, but it was possible.

"I'm not worried about myself, only my children. You must keep Deborah and Allen protected no matter what."

"Mother, don't fret this way. It isn't good for you."

"With your permission, Miss Carol, I'd like to bring in another man to guard Allen," Ashe said.

"Someone else from Dundee Security?" Carol asked.

"Yes, ma'am."

"Do you think that's necessary?" Carol looked to Deborah, who nodded and squeezed her mother's hand.

"All right, you do what you think best." Carol allowed Deborah to help her up the stairs. Pausing on the landing, she looked down at Ashe. "You have no idea how reassured I am by your presence here, Ashe McLaughlin, knowing that you have taken responsibility for Deborah and Allen."

Deborah's gaze met Ashe's. Looking away quickly, she assisted her mother to her room. Ashe couldn't quite figure out that strange look in Deborah's eyes, almost pleading. And sad. And even afraid. This wasn't the first time he'd sensed Deborah feared him, but he couldn't understand why. Not unless she still loved him. Dear God, was it possible? Of course not, no one kept loving someone eleven years after they'd been rejected.

Ashe went into the library, closed the door and dialed Simon Roarke's private number. Dundee himself would have been Ashe's first choice, but Sam seldom took on private cases any more. His other top choices were J.T. Blackwood, who was already involved in another case, and Simon Roarke.

He'd known Simon for nearly a year, had met him when he'd first hired on with Dundee Security. The two had liked each other immediately, finding they had enough in common to form a friendship. A couple of former career soldiers who'd been born and raised in Southern poverty.

"Roarke here." His voice sounded like gravel being dumped onto sheet metal.

"This is McLaughlin. I need you on the first plane out of Atlanta. Tonight if possible."

"What's up?"

"The woman I'm protecting has a ten-year-old brother. Today a stranger approached him on the school playground and gave him a message for his sister."

"The bastard!" Roarke said, the sound possessing the depth of a rottweiler's bark. "He didn't hurt the kid, did he?"

"Allen's fine. I just want to make sure he stays that way." Ashe knew that if Simon Roarke had one weakness, it was children. His only child had died years ago, and Simon had never fully recovered, had never escaped the demons of pain.

"I'll let Sam know where I'll be. He can fax me all the information on your case," Roarke said. "And I'll see you first thing in the morning."

Ashe stayed in the den for nearly thirty minutes after he finished talking to Roarke. He stood by the window, looking out into the darkness, not seeing what lay before him, only envisioning Deborah's smile. He wanted her to smile at him again the way she'd smiled at him that night so long ago. He hadn't realized how much he needed someone to love him.

Hell! He was a fool. Deborah didn't love him. She might desire him the way he desired her, but she wasn't a seventeen-year-old girl anymore. She didn't look at him through the eyes of love and see her Prince Charming. And he had no one to blame but himself. He had been the one to destroy her fairy-tale dreams.

She had offered him everything. And he'd been too young and stupid to realize what he was rejecting.

He made his way upstairs, turning off lights as he went. Allen's bedroom door stood open. The sound of his and Deborah's voices floated down the hall. Strange, how quickly he'd come to feel at home in the Vaughn household, how quickly he had come to think of Miss Carol and Allen, and yes, dammit, Deborah, as his own family.

He stood several feet away from Allen's room, looking through the open door. Deborah, fresh from a bath and wearing a navy blue silk robe, sat on the edge of Allen's bed. She pulled the covers up around his chest, then patted the edges into place. Lifting her hand, she reached out and touched Allen's face, the gesture so filled with love that it hit Ashe in the pit of his stomach with knockout force.

"We're going to be just fine, you know," Deborah said, cradling Allen's cheek with her hand. "I've been taking care of us for a long time now and haven't done such a bad job. Now Ashe is here, and he won't let anything happen to you or me or Mother."

"I like Ashe a lot, don't you? He's the kind of man any guy would like for a father." Allen threw his arms around Deborah, giving her a bear hug.

Deborah hugged him fiercely. Ashe noticed her shoulders trembling. He wanted to go to them, put his arms around Deborah and Allen and become a part of the love they shared. He wanted to tell them that he'd die to protect them.

Allen fell back into the bed, his eyes drooping as he yawned. "Since Ashe is too young for Mother, you could marry him. He'd make a pretty great brother-in-law."

"I'll keep that in mind, but don't expect anything. Ashe is our friend, but he has a life in Atlanta. Once the trial is over and things gets back to normal, Ashe will be leaving."

"I wish he would stay forever." Allen yawned, then closed his eyes. "Don't you wish he'd stay forever?"

Deborah kissed Allen on the forehead, turned out the lamp on the bedside table and walked out of Allen's room, leaving the door partially open. She saw Ashe standing in the hallway, staring directly at her, the oddest expression on his face.

"You didn't answer him," Ashe said. "Do you wish I'd stay forever?"

"Is anything forever, Ashe?" She walked toward him, then lowered her eyes and passed him, turning to go into her room.

Reaching out, Ashe grabbed her by the wrist. She halted. "I didn't use to think so. Now, I'm not so sure."

Deborah pulled her wrist out of his loose grasp. "Let me know when you're sure, Ashe." She went into her bedroom and closed the door.

Chapter 8

Completing the jury selection had taken all morning, so Deborah had remained at work until noon, then gone home for lunch with her mother. Ashe had told her there was no need for her to make an appearance in court until she was called on to testify, but she had insisted on going.

Now she wished she hadn't. Local and state newspaper and television reporters swarmed around her like agitated bees, each person trying their best to zero in on the prosecution's eye witness. Ashe shielded her with his body, practically carrying her past the horde of reporters and crowd of spectators. She clung to her protector, closing her eyes against the sight of clamoring people, the din of voices rising higher and higher.

Seating her near the back of the courtroom, Ashe stood at her side, like a guardian angel wielding a flaming sword to keep danger at bay and the unwanted from trespassing on her private space. When Judge Williams entered the courtroom, Deborah stood, taking Ashe's hand in hers. She sought and found comfort in his presence. His power and strength nourished her own, helping her face what lay ahead.

There had been no question in her mind that she would attend this first day of Lon Sparks's trial. She thought it necessary to show the world, by her presence, that she would not be intimidated by Buck Stansell and his gang of hoodlums. Of course, none of them were in attendance. They would stay away, keeping up the pretense that they were not involved, when the whole county knew they were.

One by one, the prosecution called their witnesses. First, the Leighton police, then Charlie Blaylock and two of his deputies. The day's proceedings moved along quickly, Deborah sitting tensely, Ashe at her side. At five o'clock, the court session ended, the judge announcing a recess until the following morning. Would they get to her that soon? Deborah wondered. Would the trial actually come to an end in a week's time? Unless the defense dragged things out, Deborah couldn't imagine the trial lasting much longer.

When Ashe touched her, she jumped. Standing, he offered her his hand. "I'll get you to the car as quickly as possible. Just stay right by my side. Don't look at or respond to the reporters."

"Some of them kept watching me during the trial proceedings." She accepted Ashe's assistance. "I saw them looking at me during the testimony. Especially when Jerry Don Lansdell told how I came running into the Leighton police station that day. The defense lawyer, that Mr. Prater, had Jerry Don practically admitting that I was too hysterical to know what I was talking about, that I was a raving lunatic."

"Don't worry about it. The jurors aren't stupid. They saw through what Sparks's lawyer was trying to do." Ashe slipped his arm around her. "When you're on the stand, you'll convince the jurors that you saw Lon Sparks murder Corey Looney. These people are not going to doubt your word, Deborah. You're a respected citizen with nothing to gain by lying."

Deborah glanced at her diamond-studded wristwatch. "It's too late to make Allen's soccer game. It should be ending about now."

"Then let's go home and let him tell us all about the game." Ashe led Deborah out of the crowded courtroom.

In the hallway, the same horde of insistent reporters swarmed around her. Deborah squared her shoulders. Ashe kept her protected, holding her close to his side.

"Ms. Vaughn, are you disturbed by the defense's accusation that you were too traumatized by the murder you witnessed to make a proper identification of the killer?'' A lanky young reporter stuck a microphone into Deborah's face.

Ashe pierced the man with a sharp look, then shoved his way through the semicircle of inquisitors. They followed in hot pursuit. When Ashe and Deborah reached the stairs, he halted, turning around sharply.

"Ms. Vaughn has no comment, ladies and gentlemen, other than she will be in court to testify when called upon.''

Ashe hurried her down the stairs, the reporters following, bombarding them with questions—everything from "Is it true Ms. Vaughn's ten-year-old brother had been attacked by a stranger on the school playground?'' to "Is she romantically involved with her bodyguard?''

By the time Ashe and Deborah made their way to her Cadillac, parked across the street in the adjacent parking lot, Deborah wanted to scream. How on earth did celebrities endure their every move being a media event?

Ashe drove the Caddy out of the parking lot and headed up Water Street, making a right turn onto Main Street. Laying her head against the back of the leather seat, Deborah closed her eyes and let out a deep breath. Her face would be spread across the morning newspapers and appear on the evening newscasts. Right then and there, she decided not to turn on the television or even look at the paper.

A train caught them before they entered Sheffield. Ashe shifted the car into Park and glanced at Deborah. She looked like she was ready to scream or cry, maybe both. If only she had taken his advice and not gone to court today. Maybe now she would wait until time for her testimony before returning. She was so damn stubborn, so determined to show him and the rest of the world what a strong woman she was.

"When is Allen's next soccer game?'' he asked.

"What?'' She opened her eyes. "Oh. Day after tomorrow.''

"If you're not on the witness stand, I think we should go to Allen's game.''

"I try to make it to as many of his games as I possibly can. Except when she was very sick, Mother's never missed one. She's Allen biggest supporter.''

"You haven't been worrying about Allen, have you?'' Ashe noticed the last train car pass and the guard rails lifting. "I can assure you that Simon Roarke will guard him and your mother with his life. He's a good man, and highly trained.''

''I'm sure you're right.'' Deborah rubbed her forehead with her fingertips. ''But even good men who are highly trained can be taken out. No one, not even you, Ashe, is invincible.''

Shifting the gears into Drive, Ashe followed the line of backed up traffic over the railroad tracks and up Montgomery Avenue. ''It's all right, you know, if you want to cry or scream or hit something. I won't think you're weak if you do.''

''Thanks for your permission, but I don't need to do anything except get home and show my mother and my...my brother that I'm fine.''

''Hey, they already know you're strong and capable and in control. You don't have to try to be a paragon for them. My God, Deborah, what are you trying to prove by this woman of steel routine? And to whom?''

To you, she wanted to scream. To you, Ashe McLaughlin. I want you to know that I'm not the same silly little girl who threw herself at your feet. I want you to see me for the woman I am now. The woman your rejection helped create. A woman in charge of her own life. A woman capable of caring for others, without any help from a man.

Ashe turned into the Vaughn driveway and saw Simon Roarke pulling Carol Vaughn's silver Mercedes in right beside them. He parked in the three-car garage behind the house. The moment Deborah emerged from her Cadillac, Allen, in his gold-and-blue soccer uniform, raced around the cars and directly toward Deborah and Ashe.

''We won. I scored the winning goal.'' Allen jumped up and down in a boyish frenzy of triumph. ''Tell them, Mr. Roarke. Tell them, Mother. I was awesome, wasn't I? You should have been there.''

''Yes, I should have been,'' Deborah said. ''Ashe and I will be at Wednesday's game if I don't have to testify that day.''

Deborah caught the quick exchange of glances between Ashe and Simon Roarke. She wanted to ask them what was going on, but didn't dare in front of her mother and son. Besides, it might have meant nothing more than a coded recognition that all was well.

"Allen is quite an athlete," Roarke said in his gravelly voice. "They wouldn't have won the game without him."

"See. See." Full of youthful exuberance, Allen bounced around in the driveway. "Boy, Ashe, I wish you could have seen me make that goal."

A twinge of guilt tugged on Deborah's heartstrings. How was she going to handle Allen's growing dependency on Ashe? How would she be able to keep Ashe from disappointing their son? And that's the way she thought of Allen—as their son.

"Miss Carol should have videotaped it for us." Ashe winked at Carol, who stood near the entrance to the side patio.

"Oh, I could never watch the game and videotape it at the same time. I get too excited at these games," Carol said. "I'd end up dropping the videocamera and breaking it."

"Hey, what's Mazie fixing for supper tonight?" Allen asked, running around the side of the garage, Roarke following him. "I'm starving."

"Pork chops, I think," Carol said, opening the gate to the side patio.

"I gotta go get Huckleberry out of the backyard now that we're home. I'll bet he's hungry, too." Allen bounded out of sight, Roarke on his heels.

Ashe and Deborah followed Carol through the gate and onto the side patio. A cool evening breeze swirled around them. Carol shivered.

"I think autumn weather is here to stay," she said.

"Yes, it seems—" Deborah said.

A loud scream pierced the evening stillness. Allen's scream!

"Allen!" Deborah cried, gripping Ashe by the sleeve, then breaking into a run.

Ashe grabbed her by the arm, stopping her. "You and Miss Carol go into the house and lock the patio door. I'll see what's wrong."

Deborah nodded agreement, then led her mother inside, locking the door behind them. "Sit down in here and rest, Mother. I'll go see what's happened."

Once she had seated her mother on the sofa, Deborah raced through the house, meeting Mazie coming down the stairs.

"What was that screaming all about?" Mazie asked. "It sounded like Allen."

"It was," Deborah said. "Go see about Mother. She's in the living room."

Deborah rushed through the kitchen, flung open the back door and ran into the fenced backyard. Roarke stood facing Deborah, but his attention was riveted to the boy and man and dog on the ground. Deborah's heart stopped, her lungs filling with air as she sucked in a terrified breath.

Huckleberry lay on the ground, Allen on his knees beside him, trying to hug the big dog in his arms. Ashe hovered over Allen, his hand on Allen's shoulder as he talked in a low voice.

In the throes of a spasm, Huckleberry jerked. His spine arched, his head leaned backward, his legs twitched.

"What—what happened?" Deborah walked forward slowly.

"Looks like the dog's been poisoned," Roarke said.

"He's vomited," Ashe said, nodding toward the foul-smelling evidence. "If he has been poisoned, vomiting is a good sign. There's hope a vet might save him."

Tears streamed down Allen's face. He glanced up at Deborah. "Why would anybody want to hurt Huckleberry?"

Why indeed? Ashe looked at Deborah and she knew. This was another warning from Buck Stansell.

"Come on, Allen." Ashe pried the boy's arms from around his dog, lifting him to his feet. "Go inside and get a quilt to wrap Huckleberry in. He's still alive. If we hurry we might be able to help him."

Allen nodded in numb silence, then flew through the open back door.

"Roarke, get the vet's phone number from Miss Carol and call and tell him to meet us." Kneeling, Ashe hoisted the big, stiff-legged Lab into his arms. "Deborah, go get the car started. Allen and I will bring Huckleberry around."

Deborah had the car ready when Allen opened the door and helped Ashe place Huckleberry on the backseat. Father and son leaped into the backseat beside the dog, Ashe pulling Allen onto his lap.

"Let's go," he said.

Deborah drove like a madman, running several red lights as she flew down Second Street. She prayed that nothing would prevent them from making it to Dr. Carradine's Pet Hospital in Muscle Shoals. She heard Ashe talking to Allen, reassuring him without giving him false hope.

"Talk to Huckleberry, son. Tell him we're taking care of him. Tell him he's a fine dog."

Tears gathered in Deborah's eyes. She swatted them away with the back of her left hand while she kept her right hand on the steering wheel. It was so unfair for this to happen to Huckleberry. He was an innocent animal, a child's pet. The rage inside her boiled. If she could have gotten her hands around Buck Stansell's neck, she didn't doubt that, at this precise moment, she had the strength to strangle the man.

When she swerved into Carradine's Pet Hospital, Dr. Carradine rushed out the front door and over to the car. Ashe got out, pulling Allen with him. Dr. Carradine leaned over inside the car.

"I'd say from the looks of Huckleberry that he has been poisoned. My guess is strychnine." Dr. Carradine lifted Huckleberry, straining himself in the process, his small, slender arms barely able to manage the dog's weight.

Ashe took Huckleberry from the vet the moment he emerged from the car.

"Bring him inside quickly. I'll anesthetize him. It'll stop the spasms."

Deborah took Allen's hand and they followed Ashe into the veterinary clinic. When they entered the lobby, Ashe turned to Deborah.

"You and Allen stay out here."

"No, I want to go with Huckleberry," Allen cried.

"You can help Huckleberry by letting me take care of him," Dr. Carradine said.

Allen clung to Deborah, tears pouring from his eyes, streaking his face, falling in huge drops from his nose and chin.

Ashe laid the big Lab on the examining table. Huckleberry panted wildly, then went into another spasm. Ashe watched while the doctor filled a syringe and plunged it deep into the dog's body. Poor animal. The veterinarian refilled the syringe and administered a second injection.

"What now?" Ashe wondered if there was any hope of saving Allen's pet.

"Wait and pray," Dr. Carradine said. "I've given him enough anesthesia to put him in a deep sleep. If we can keep him this way, he has a slight chance of pulling through. But I have to be honest with you. It doesn't look good.''

"Huckleberry had been vomiting when we found him." Ashe looked down at the short, slender young veterinarian. "It's possible he didn't completely digest all the poison."

"Good. It's the best possible sign, and that's what we'll tell Allen. There's nothing to do now but wait. If Allen and Deborah want to come on back here and be with him, it'll be all right."

The moment they saw Ashe in the doorway leading to the examining room, Deborah and Allen hurried toward him.

"Huckleberry is resting," Ashe said. "He's sound asleep. Dr. Carradine says that since Huckleberry vomited, there's a good chance his body hasn't absorbed enough poison to kill him. We have hope he'll pull through."

Allen flung his arms around Ashe's waist. Ashe laid his hand on Allen's head, then leaned down and picked him up into his arms and carried him into the examining room. Deborah followed behind them, tears blurring her vision.

"Huckleberry needs to rest," Dr. Carradine said. "I'll continue to give him injections to keep him peaceful. We'll hope for the best."

Ashe set Allen on his feet beside the examining table, keeping his hand on the boy's shoulder. Allen reached out, stroking his pet's back.

"Y'all can go on home and I'll call if there's any change," the vet said.

"No, I can't leave Huckleberry. What if he wakes up and I'm not here?" Allen threw his arms around the comatose animal."

Ashe pulled Allen away from the dog, turned the child to face him and knelt down on one knee. "We aren't going anywhere until Huckleberry wakes up. You and Deborah and I will keep watch over him."

Deborah gulped down the sobs when she saw the tentative little smile trembling on Allen's lips as he nodded his head.

Ashe glanced over at Dr. Carradine. "I'll bring in some chairs from the waiting room."

The doctor smiled. "I'll help you."

For what seemed like endless hours to Deborah, she and Ashe and Allen waited at Huckleberry's side, rising in fear each time the dog showed signs of going into another spasm. Dr. Carradine kept him medicated, and as the hours wore on, Deborah almost wished she, too, could be given an injection that would ease her pain. Watching the way Allen suffered tore at her heart the way nothing ever had. To watch her child hurting and know she could do nothing to ease his pain became unbearable.

Standing quickly, Deborah paced the floor. Allen had fallen asleep, his head resting in Ashe's lap. Deborah walked into the waiting room and looked out the windows. Evening had turned to night. The bright lights along Woodward Avenue sparkled like Christmas tree decorations. She glanced down at her watch. Ten-thirty.

Turning around, she walked back to the examining room, stopping in the doorway. Ashe was in the process of removing his jacket. He raised his leg just a fraction to give Allen's head a slight incline, then draped his jacket over the sleeping child. Covering her face with one hand, Deborah closed her eyes and said a silent prayer, asking God to save Huckleberry.

Ashe felt a hot fury rising inside him. A killing rage. Buck Stansell had no respect for animal life and little for human life. Buck's kind thought of animals as unfeeling, worthless creatures. Killing a dog would mean no more to him than flicking ashes off his cigarette.

Ashe adjusted his jacket around Allen, amazed how much he'd grown to care about Deborah's young brother. He had never been around children, had never allowed himself to think much about what it would be like to be a father. But he couldn't help wondering about how it would feel to have a son like Allen. The boy was intelligent and inquisitive and filled with a joy for life. He was sensitive and caring. In so many ways, Allen reminded Ashe of the young Deborah he had known and loved. Perhaps that was the reason he felt so close to Allen, so connected. Because he was so very much like Deborah.

Odd thing was, the boy reminded him of himself, too. Tall and lanky, with hands and feet almost too big for his body. He'd been the same as a kid. And cursed with being left-handed himself, he understood the adjustments Allen had had to make.

Ashe felt a twinge of sadness. Eleven years ago, he'd been thankful he hadn't gotten Deborah pregnant, but being around Allen so much these days had made him wonder if a child of theirs wouldn't have been a lot like Deborah's little brother.

For a couple of months after their passionate night down by the river, Ashe had worried about not having used any protection. But it had been an unfounded worry. By the time Wallace Vaughn had had him run out of town, Deborah would have known whether or not she was pregnant. And if she'd been carrying his child, she would have told him. Deborah had loved him, and she would have known that a child could have bound them together forever.

Deborah came in and sat down beside Ashe. Reaching out, he draped her shoulders with his arm and drew her close. She sighed.

"It's going to be all right, honey," Ashe said. "No way is God going to let that dog die and break Allen's heart."

She couldn't reply; instead she nodded and tried to smile. Closing her eyes, she relaxed against him.

Ashe sat there in the veterinarian's examining room, one arm holding Deborah possessively, the other laid protectively over Allen. As the hours passed, his leg fell asleep and his arms became stiff, but he didn't readjust his position. Both Allen and Deborah slept, as did Huckleberry.

Ashe closed his eyes for a few minutes, resting, then reopened them quickly when he heard movement from the examining table. Huckleberry opened his eyes and raised his head. No longer was his big body grossly contorted, but lay relaxed on the table.

Ashe gave Deborah a gentle shake. Opening her eyes, she glanced up at him. "Huckleberry's awake. Take a look."

"Oh, my God!" She jumped up out of the chair and ran toward the dog, taking his huge face in her hands. "Hey, there, big boy. You sure had us worried."

Ashe shook Allen, who groaned in his sleep. Ashe shook him again.

"What?"

"Wake up, son. Huckleberry wants to see you." Ashe lifted Allen in his arms and carried the boy across the room, sitting him down on the examining table beside his dog. "Go get Dr. Carradine," Ashe told Deborah.

She rushed out of the room. Allen hugged Huckleberry, who, though still groggy, raised his head and tried to sit up. "He's going to be all right!" Allen repeated the words several times, as if to convince himself.

Deborah returned with Dr. Carradine, who took a good look at

Huckleberry and smiled. "Looks like we got lucky. I think Huckleberry will soon be as good as new."

The dog struggled to get up. Ashe lifted him off the table and set him on the floor. He staggered around slowly, like a drunken sailor. Sitting on the floor, Allen called his pet to him. The Lab padded over to the boy, who threw his arms around the big dog and hugged him.

"Why don't you folks go on home and get some rest," Dr. Carradine said. "Leave Huckleberry here until—" he glanced down at his watch "—it's after midnight. Well, I was going to say until tomorrow afternoon. Pick him up anytime after 2:00 p.m. today."

"If he's all right, why can't I take him home now?" Allen asked.

"Because Huckleberry needs some rest and so do you, young man." Dr. Carradine glanced at Deborah. "And so does your sister and Mr. McLaughlin. I have a feeling that if you take Huckleberry home now, all three of you would stay up the rest of the night with him."

"Come on, pal." Ashe leaned down to give Huckleberry a pat on the head. "Let's go home. Huckleberry is in good hands with Dr. Carradine. And I promise we'll pick him up at two o'clock."

Allen agreed reluctantly, giving Huckleberry a farewell hug before leaving.

Ashe carried Allen, who'd gone to sleep on the drive home, from the car into the house. The boy roused from his sleep and smiled at Ashe.

Allen yawned. "I'm not a baby. I can walk."

"Sure you can, pal," Ashe said.

He set Allen on his feet, then he and Deborah followed the child upstairs and into his room. Deborah spread back the covers. Allen's eyelids drooped. Curling up in the middle of the bed, he made no objections when Deborah removed his shoes, jeans and shirt. By the time she had stripped him down to his white cotton briefs, he had fallen fast asleep.

"He's all tired out," Ashe said. "He's been through almost as much as Huckleberry."

Deborah pulled up the covers, then sat down on the side of the bed. Allen was the dearest, most precious thing in her life. There wasn't a day that passed when she didn't want to tell him she was his mother, to claim him as her own. But she had agreed to this charade when she'd been eighteen and not strong enough to stand up to her father. He had told her she had two choices, either give Allen up for adoption or allow him to be raised as her brother.

If only she'd had the strength to tell her father to go to hell. If only she'd taken her child and found Ashe McLaughlin and forced him to face his responsibility as a father. But she'd done what was expected of her. She'd taken what others would consider the easy way out.

Deborah smoothed the loose strands of Allen's thick blond hair away from his face. Leaning over, she kissed his forehead, then stood.

Ashe watched her, the way she looked at Allen, the way she touched him. No one could doubt the depth of her love for the boy. If he didn't know better, he'd swear she was his mother instead of his sister. But then motherly love was not limited to mothers. Indeed his grandmother had loved and cared for him in a way his own mother never had.

But what if Deborah was Allen's mother? Was it possible? No, don't even consider the possibility, he warned himself. Idiotic thoughts like that could be dangerous to his sanity. He was letting his imagination run away with him.

Allen was Deborah's brother, Miss Carol's change-of-life baby. Any other explanation was out of the question. There was no way Deborah could have been pregnant and not told him. She wouldn't have kept something that important a secret.

Deborah, although lovely beyond words, looked tired. Drained. Sad. On the verge of renewed tears.

"Come on, honey, you need to get some rest." Turning off the light, he guided her out of Allen's room and down the hall.

"I need a bath before I go to bed," she said. "I'm filthy."

He walked her into her sitting room and gently shoved her down in the rocking chair. "Sit still and rest. I'll get your bath ready for you."

When she started to protest, Ashe laid his index finger over her lips, silencing her. She stared up at him, her eyes filled with such deep emotion that Ashe wanted to lift her into his arms. But he didn't. Instead he entered her bathroom and turned on the gold taps, letting the warm water flow into her claw-foot bathtub. Rummaging around in the antique chest beside the vanity, he found some perfumed bath oil and splashed it into the water flow. He laid out two huge, fluffy, blue towels and a crochet-edged wash cloth.

In Deborah's bedroom, he turned down her bed and then found her gown, neatly folded in a top dresser drawer. Pale pink silk, spaghetti straps, heavy white lace across the bodice and hem. After spreading the gown out across the foot of her bed, he flung the matching robe over his arm.

When he returned to the sitting room, she was rocking back and forth slowly, her eyes opening and closing, her chin nodding farther and farther toward her chest.

Before she could protest, he lifted her out of the rocker and into his arms. Her eyes flew open. She grabbed him around the neck to balance herself.

"What are you doing?" She stared at him, wide-eyed.

"Taking you to the bathroom."

"I'm perfectly capable of walking, you know."

"I like carrying you," he said. "It gives me an excuse to hold you in my arms."

She relaxed, allowing him to carry her. She felt completely safe and secure wrapped in Ashe's strong arms. When they passed through her bedroom, she noticed he had turned down her bed and laid out her gown. The gesture touched her, making her feel cherished and cared for in a way she couldn't remember being cared for since she was a child.

"Ashe?"

"Hmm?"

"Thank you for being so wonderful with Allen."

"It was easy. Allen is a great kid. He reminds me so much of you, Deborah. The way you were at his age."

And he reminds me of you, she wanted to say. Every time I look at him, I see you. The way he smiles. The way he rests the side of his face in his hand when he's pondering something. The expression on his face when he's trying to talk me into allowing him to do something he knows is against the rules.

Once in the bathroom, Ashe lowered Deborah to her feet, sliding her slowly down his body, his big hands holding her hips in place against him.

She felt his arousal, knew he wanted her. And heaven help her, she wanted him.

She pulled away, turning her back to him. "Thank you for everything." Bending over the tub, she turned off the faucet. "I can handle things from here on out. Good night, Ashe."

He whirled her around. She gasped when she saw the look of longing in his eyes. "Are you sending me away?"

"Yes, please, Ashe. Go."

"All right. If you're sure that's what you want."

"Yes, I'm sure." She really didn't want him to leave. She wanted him to stay, to undress her, to bathe her, to dry her damp skin and carry her to her bed.

Ashe ran the tip of his index finger down her cheek, then stepped back. "If you need me, you know where I'll be." He laid her pink silk robe on the vanity stool.

Looking down at the bathtub, she nodded. Ashe turned and left her alone. She closed the door behind him, and took a deep breath. She undressed quickly, throwing her clothes into a heap on the floor, then stepped into the bathtub and buried herself in the soft, scented water. Leaning her head back against the wall behind the tub, she closed her eyes and picked up the washcloth. Soaping the cloth, she ran it over her face, then rinsed by splashing water in her face. She slid the cloth down one arm and then the other. Lowering the soapy cloth to her breasts, her hand froze when the material made contact with her nipple, which jutted out to a peak.

She was aroused and aching. Aching to be with Ashe. Aching to open her arms and her body and take him in. But she didn't dare. For if she opened her heart to him, she would be lost.

Hurriedly, she bathed, washed her hair and dried off, praying she would be able to find forgetfulness in sleep.

Chapter 9

Ashe stood at the window of his bedroom that looked down over the patio. The moonlight illuminated the autumn flowers and shrubs so lovingly cared for by the Vaughns' weekly gardener. Ashe sloshed around the brandy in his glass, took a sip and set the liquor down on the ornate antique table to the left of the window. He scratched his naked chest, then ran his hand across his stomach.

He couldn't remember the last time he'd ached so badly for a woman, and certainly not for one particular woman. Deborah Vaughn had insinuated herself into his mind so firmly that he couldn't shake her. She had become his first thought in the morning and his last thought at night. Not Deborah Vaughn his client, but Deborah the woman.

He'd made a mistake coming back to Sheffield, seeing Deborah again. He had walked away from her once, rejected her because he hadn't loved her the way she'd loved him. Now he wanted her as he had never wanted another woman. He burned with the need to possess her.

Ashe slipped on his leather loafers. Buttoning his open shirt, he walked out into the hall. He'd tried for nearly an hour to relax, to stop thinking about Deborah, to quit remembering how she'd felt in his arms when he'd carried her to her bath. But he couldn't forget.

He walked down the hallway, stopping at Allen's open door. Looking inside, he saw the boy sleeping soundly, his upper body uncovered. Ashe crept silently into the room and pulled the sheet and blanket up to cover Allen's shoulders. The little fellow had been through quite an ordeal. Ashe balled his hands into fists. Buck Stansell didn't deserve to live. But his kind always landed on their feet, always found a way to slip through the cracks in the legal system.

After leaving Allen's room, Ashe eased the door to Miss Carol's room ajar and peered inside. She slept peacefully. Deborah had told him that often her mother had to rely on sleeping pills in order to rest.

He opened Deborah's bedroom door. More than anything he wanted to find her awake, waiting for him, her arms open, imploring him to come to her. What he found was an empty bed, Deborah nowhere in sight. Where the hell was she?

He made his way down the stairs, checking each room, one by one, until he entered the library. A table lamp burned softly, casting gentle shadows over the woman sitting alone on the leather sofa, her feet curled beneath her. When he stepped inside the room, she turned her head and looked at him.

"Couldn't you sleep, either?" she asked.

"No."

Did she have any idea how beautiful she was, how irresistible she looked? Like a porcelain figure, all flawless creamy skin and pink silk clinging to her round curves, her long blond hair cascading down her back and over her shoulders.

He grew hard just looking at her, just smelling the scent of her bath oil clinging to her skin. He stood inside the open door. Waiting. Wanting. Needing.

"I can't believe I'm still wide awake." She looked at him with hunger in her eyes, and wondered if he realized how much she wanted him. "I'm exhausted and yet I feel as if I've had an extra dose of adrenaline."

"Yeah, me, too."

She stretched her back, leaning into the sofa. Ashe caught his breath, the sight of her almost more than he could bear. Her firm breasts strained against the silk of her gown. Her full hips pressed into the soft leather cushions.

"I fixed myself a drink." She nodded to the partially full glass on the end table. "It didn't help."

"I did the same thing," he said. "I came down about thirty minutes ago and swiped some of your brandy."

"Obviously it didn't help you go to sleep." She clenched her hands, then unclenched them, repeating the process several times. She wished he hadn't come downstairs and found her alone and restless. He'd know she couldn't stop thinking about him, couldn't make herself forget the feel of his arms around her, the strength of his arousal pressing against her.

"Since neither of us can sleep, how about taking a ride?" Holding his breath, he waited for her reply.

"A ride?" She scooted to the edge of the sofa, knowing there was more at stake than just a moonlight drive. "That sounds like a great idea." Standing, she smiled at him, then rushed past him and out into the hallway. "Give me a minute to put on some clothes," she said softly, then ran up the stairs.

He checked his back pocket for his wallet, then thought about his gun and holster lying on his nightstand. He hurried upstairs, retrieved his gun and put on his jacket, then walked down the hall to Simon Roarke's bedroom. He knocked softly. Within seconds Roarke cracked the door and peered out at him.

"What's up?"

"Deborah and I are going for a ride," Ashe said. "I wanted you to know I'd be out of the house for a while."

"Yeah, sure. No problem." Simon grinned, something the man didn't do often.

"Don't go reading anything into this." Ashe turned to leave.

Opening the door, Roarke laid his hand on Ashe's shoulder, gripping him firmly. "She's the one, isn't she?"

Ashe stiffened at his friend's words. "The one what?"

"The one you told me about that night six months ago when we both got stinking drunk and wound up crying all over each other."

Ashe didn't like to remember that night; he'd thought Roarke would never remind him. "Yeah, she's the one."

Pulling away, Ashe ran his hand through his hair, straightened his jacket and headed downstairs. He paced the marble-floored entrance hall until Deborah descended the stairs wearing a pair of olive green cotton twill pants and a baggy cotton sweater in an olive-and-cream stripe.

"Let's go," she said, her chest rising and falling with quick, panting little breaths.

"You want to take your Caddy or my rental car?"

She tossed him a set of keys. "The Caddy."

He slipped his arm around her waist and they rushed outside, the cool night air assaulting them the minute they opened the door.

"I should get you a set of keys to the Caddy," she said as he helped her inside.

He leaned down, giving her a quick kiss, then closed the passenger door and raced around to the other side of the car.

He knew where he was going to take her; he'd known the minute he'd suggested the ride. It hadn't been a premeditated idea, just something that hit him in a flash. In the dark confines of the car, he could hear her breathing, could smell that heady scent of flowery bath oil mixed with the musty scent of woman. He started the Caddy and backed out of the drive.

She waited for him to ask her where she wanted to go. He didn't ask. It didn't take her long to realize the direction in which he was headed. Dear God, no! Surely he wasn't taking her there. Was he that insensitive? Didn't he realize she'd never been back since that night?

The road leading down to the river was dark, lonesome and flanked on both sides by heavily wooded areas. Deborah closed her eyes, shutting out the sight, clenching her teeth in an effort not to scream. How could he do this to her!

"Please take me home." Her voice wavered slightly.

"I thought you wanted to take a ride." He kept his gaze focused on the view ahead of him.

"I don't want to go down to the river."

"Why not?"

"You know damn well why not."

"I want you to tell me." He glanced at her and wished he hadn't. Her face was barely visible in the moonlight, but he could feel the tension in her body and make out the anger etched on her features.

"Take me home, Ashe. Now!"

He continued driving toward the river. "It's time we talked.

Really talked. We need to clear up a few things before we make love.''

"Before we make... Why, you arrogant bastard! You think you're going to take me down to the river and screw me again and then walk out of my life and never look back. Well, you'd better think again. I'm not some lovesick teenager who believes in fairy tales.''

"No, you're not." He pulled the Cadillac off the road and onto a narrow dirt lane surrounded by trees. "You're a woman who wants to be made love to very badly, and I'm the man who is dying to love you.''

When he reached out to touch her, she jerked away from him. "Don't. I don't want you. Do you hear me? I *do not* want you.''

"Honey, stop lying to yourself. Do you think I like knowing I'm so hung up on you I can't think about anything else? Do you honestly think you're the only one with bad memories about that night?''

"Oh, I know all about your bad memories!" Whipping around in the seat, she faced him. "You let your anger with Whitney and your need for a woman overcome your better judgment, and you screwed me. Then afterward you were filled with regret.''

He jerked her into his arms, lowered his head and whispered against her lips. "Stop saying I screwed you, dammit! It wasn't like that and you know it. I made love to you, Deborah.''

Struggling to free herself, she laughed in his face. "You didn't make love to me, you sc—''

He kissed her hard and fast, adeptly silencing her. She pulled away as much as he would allow and glared at him.

"Maybe I wasn't in love with you," he admitted. "But I did love you. I'd loved you since we were kids. You were one of my best friends.''

The tears welled up inside her; her chest ached from restraint. This was what she didn't want—what she couldn't bear. "All right. We made love. But you regretted it. You said it could never happen again.''

"I cared too much about you to hurt you by pretending there could be more for us. I felt like a heel, but I did what I thought was best for you.''

She took a deep breath. "I hated you after that night, you know.

But all the while I swore to myself I despised you, I kept praying you'd come and tell me you loved me. I was such a fool.''

"And when two months went by and I didn't come to you, you decided to get revenge. All that love turned to hate so quickly.''

"What are you talking about? I admit I thought about how I'd like to toss you into a pool of piranhas, but that's as far as my seeking revenge went.'' She scooted away from him when he loosened his hold on her. "Besides, you didn't stick around long enough for me to plot any elaborate revenge schemes.''

"You don't call siccing your daddy on me revenge?''

Her eyes widened. She opened her mouth on a silent gasp, then shook her head. "What—what do you mean, siccing my daddy on you?''

"Are you pretending you've forgotten or are you trying to tell me you honestly don't know what I'm talking about?''

"I have no idea what you're talking about,'' she said.

"Then let me refresh your memory.'' Turning sideways, Ashe leaned his back against the door, crossed his arms over his chest and rested his head on the side window. "About two months after our night down here—'' moving his head from side to side, he glanced out at the starlit sky, the dark waters of the Tennessee River and the towering trees tipped with moonlight ''—the police chief hauled my rear end downtown. And who do you think was waiting for us when we got to the police station?''

Deborah's stomach did a nervous flip-flop. "Daddy?''

"Bingo! Wallace Vaughn himself, fit to be tied and ready to string me up for raping his little girl.''

"Raping!'' The blood soared through Deborah, her heartbeat wild, the pounding beat deafening to her own ears.

"Yeah, that was my reaction,'' Ashe said, uncertain whether to accept Deborah's shock at face value or remain suspicious. "But the D.A. was there with your daddy and he assured me that they weren't kidding. They were accusing me of rape, and when I told them that the charge would never stick, they both laughed in my face.''

"I had no idea Daddy could have done anything so—''

"You didn't go crying to your Daddy?'' All these years he had been so sure Deborah had lied to her father, that she had made him believe that, at the very least, Ashe had seduced her, and at the worst, had taken her by brute force.

"I didn't tell my father anything." Deborah scooted to the far side of the car, her back up against the door, she and Ashe glaring at each other in the semidarkness.

"Why the hell lie to me now?" He wanted to shake her until her teeth rattled. God, help him, he never thought he would feel such bitter anger again, that confronting her with what she'd done would resurrect the hatred he'd felt—for Wallace Vaughn, for the whole town of Sheffield, and, yes, for Deborah herself.

Deborah lifted her feet up on tiptoes, tensing her legs as she ran her hands up and down the tops of her thighs. "I never told Daddy about our...about our making love that night. I told my mother." *I had to tell her. I was seventeen and pregnant by a man who didn't love me or want me. I didn't know what else to do.*

"You told Miss Carol?"

"I needed someone to talk to about what had happened." *About the fact that I was carrying your child.* "Who else would I have gone to other than my own mother?"

"Did you tell your mother that I'd forced you?" Cold shivers covered Ashe like a blanket of frost spreading across the earth on a winter night.

"No. I told my mother the truth, all of it. She'd known, of course, that I'd left the country club with you that night and she knew why."

"I'm surprised your father didn't hunt us down."

"He didn't know I was with you. He didn't see me leave," Deborah said. "Mother told him I was spending the night with a girlfriend after the engagement party."

"I know Miss Carol often kept the complete truth from your father in order to maintain peace, so why did she feel it necessary to tell him about what had happened between you and me that night?"

Because I was pregnant! "I was very upset, very unhappy. Mother thought she was doing the right thing by telling Daddy. She couldn't have known what he'd do. And I never knew anything about what he did. Obviously, Daddy realized what a mistake he'd made. You were never arrested. If you had been, I would have told the truth. I would have made them understand that what happened that night was my fault, not yours.''

''Deborah?''

''Well, it was, wasn't it? I mean, I did throw myself at you and practically beg you to make love to me, didn't I?''

''If I'd been more of a man and less a boy that night, I'd have turned you down and saved us both a lot of misery.''

''And that's what the memory of that night has been for you, hasn't it, a misery?'' Deborah shut her eyes, capturing her tears beneath closed lids.

Dear God, no! The results had been a misery, but not that night. Never that night! ''No, honey, that's not true. The memory of that night is bittersweet for me.''

''More bitter than sweet.'' Swallowing her tears, she lowered her head, wrapped one arm across her stomach and cupped the side of her face in her other hand. ''That's why you left town, wasn't it? To get away from me?''

''I left town because your father and the D.A. gave me no other choice.'' Ashe slid across the seat, grabbed Deborah by the shoulders and shook her gently several times. ''Look at me, dammit.'' With her head still bowed, she raised her eyes to meet his. ''Your father told me that if I didn't leave town and never come back, he'd make sure I did time for rape. He wanted me out of your life for good.''

''No, he wouldn't have... He knew. Oh, Ashe, he knew.''

''He knew what?'' Ashe gripped her shoulders, tightening his hold when she didn't immediately respond.

''He knew I was—'' She'd almost said *pregnant with your baby*. ''He knew I loved you, that I would never have testified against you, that I would have made a fool of myself to protect you.''

A searing pain ripped through Ashe, the hot, cauterizing pain of truth, killing the festering infection of lies and suspicions, preventing him from clinging to past resentments.

''Dear God, Deborah. All these years I've thought...'' He pulled her into his arms. She trembled, and he knew she was on the verge of tears, that she was holding them in check, being strong. He stroked her back; she laid her head on his chest.

She had not betrayed him. She hadn't even told her father, only her mother. She had never accused him of forcing her or seducing her. Lies. All lies. Wallace Vaughn's lies to force Ashe out of Deborah's life. Had the old man been that afraid that sooner or later Ashe would destroy Deborah's life?

Ashe found himself kissing the side of her face, along her hairline, one hand continuing to stroke her back while he threaded the fingers of his other hand through her hair, caressing her tenderly.

"Have you hated me all these years, Ashe?" she asked, her voice a whisper against his chest.

"I've hated you. I've hated myself. Hell, I've hated just about everyone and everything associated with my past." When she gazed up at him, he dotted her forehead with kisses. "But I never hated what we shared that night, the feelings inside me when we made love. It had never been like that for me before." He swallowed hard. "And it's never been that way for me again. Not ever."

"Oh, Ashe." She slipped her arms around him, burrowing her body into his, seeking and finding a closer joining.

He took her mouth like a dying man clinging to life, as if without the taste of her he could not go on. She accepted the kiss, returning it full measure, her hands clawing at his back, inching their way up beneath his jacket, yanking his shirt from his slacks, making contact with his naked flesh. Ashe thrust his tongue deeper into her mouth, their tongues mating furiously.

Breathless, their lips separated, but they clung to each other, Deborah unbuttoning Ashe's shirt, Ashe lifting Deborah's sweater up and over her arms.

"I've wanted you since that first day I came back to town." He nuzzled her neck with his nose as he lifted his hand to her lace-covered breast. "I've called myself every kind of fool, but nothing's eased this ache inside me."

She curled her index finger around a swirl of dark chest hair, then leaned over to kiss one tiny nipple. Ashe groaned. "I hated you for making me want you again," she said. "I swore no one would ever hurt me the way you did, and here I am throwing myself at you again as if I were seventeen."

"No, honey, no." He took her face in both his hands, looking deep into her eyes, smiling his irresistible smile. "This works both ways. I want you and you want me. Neither of us are kids. We're two responsible adults who are as frustrated as hell."

She laughed. "Ashe, I don't know if I can handle this, what I'm feeling. It scares me. It scares me more now than it did when I was seventeen." She circled his neck with her arms, pressing her cheek against his. "When I was seventeen I was so in love with you that nothing we did seemed wrong. I didn't know the first thing about sex. Now...well, now I'm aching with wanting you. It's different now. It's—"

"It's right this time, honey," he said against her lips. "No fairy tales, no declarations of undying love, just a man and a woman who want each other desperately. Mutual desire."

"Yes." She nodded. "Mutual desire." *You're wrong, she wanted to shout. It isn't all that different now. I'm still in love with you and you still don't return that love.*

"Let's vanquish all those bad memories," he said. "Let's lay the past to rest. Tonight."

His kiss was less frantic this time, more tender and giving, yet as hot and needy as the one before. There was no way to make him understand that she could never lay the past to rest, that Allen was the embodiment of that night so long ago when a young and foolish girl had given herself to a man who didn't love her.

Ashe held her in his arms, burying his face in her neck, breathing in the sweet fragrance of her hair. "We can't make love back at your house and I know you don't want to make love here, in the car, the way we did that night. Where can we go, honey? A motel room seems cheap and I want this night to be special for you—for us."

"You're wrong about my not wanting to make love here and now, in the car," she said. "I do."

"Why would you want to—"

"I'm not sure I can explain how I feel, but... Well, it would somehow validate that first time. I know it sounds crazy, but... I need for us to make love here, now, in the car, the way we did that night when... Please, Ashe, make love to me."

"That's exactly what you said to me that night." And damn his rotten soul, he hadn't been able to resist her. She had been the sweetest temptation he'd ever known—and she still was.

"I guess I'm still begging." A lone tear escaped her eye and trickled down her cheek.

Ashe kissed the teardrop. "No, Deborah, I'm the one doing the begging this time. I'm the one who'll die if I can't have you. I'm the one willing to do anything to make you happy, to see you smile, to make your forget.''

He actually remembered every word she'd said to him that night when she'd told him she wanted to make him happy, wanted to make him forget Whitney, wanted to make him smile again. She had pleaded with him to make love to her, saying she'd die if he didn't.

"You remember what I said."

"Every word." He lifted her sweater up and off, tossing it into the back seat, then unhooked her bra and eased it off her shoulders. "And I remember how you looked and how you felt." He covered both breasts with his hands and planted a row of kisses from her collarbone to her shoulder. "And the smell of you. My sweet, innocent Deborah."

He licked the tip of her breast; she moaned. He unsnapped and unzipped her slacks; she shoved his jacket off his shoulders. Ashe removed his shoulder holster, laying it on the dashboard before removing his shirt.

She kissed his chest, tiny, loving nicks. He tugged her slacks down and off her legs, throwing them on top of her sweater. She shivered when he dipped his hand beneath the elastic of her silky panties and cupped her buttocks, lifting her up and over him as he slid down onto the seat, his head braced against the armrest on the door.

While he suckled at her breasts, his fingers delved between the delicate folds of her body, finding the sensitive, hidden peak. She unzipped his trousers and reached inside to cover his arousal with the palm of her hand. Their kisses grew hotter, harder, longer, as they moved to the rhythm of nature's mating music, their bodies straining for closer and closer contact.

Lifting his hips, Ashe removed his wallet, then tugged his trousers downward and kicked them into the floorboard. "I'm dying," he groaned. "I wanted to wait, to take more time, to—"

Leaning over him, she covered his mouth, silencing him with the fury of her kiss. He ran his hands up and down, over her shoulders, down her back, pulling at her panties until she helped him remove them. He eased her over and onto her back, drawing her body beneath his as he ripped off his briefs, sheathed himself and positioned her for his possession.

"Now, honey? Now!" He was fast losing control.

"Yes, now!"

He plunged into her, lifting her hips, delving deep and hard. She gripped his shoulders, rising to meet his demands. Sliding her legs up his until she reached his hips, she whispered his name over and over, telling him with the tone of her voice and little moans of pleasure that she was near the brink. He didn't want this to end, wanted it to go on forever, but knew he couldn't last much longer. The pleasure was too great, too intense to slow the upward spiral toward completion.

"It's too good, honey. Too good."

He felt her tightening around him. She clasped him like a tight fist. Crying out, she quivered in his arms as spasm after spasm of fulfillment racked her body. His release came hard and fast, shaking him to the core of his being.

He cried out, losing himself in her, kissing her as they shivered from the aftershocks of such a powerful loving.

Lifting himself, Ashe pulled Deborah up off the seat and into his arms, holding her against him, listening to her rapid breathing.

"I want to make love to you again," he told her. "Tonight. Tomorrow. The day after tomorrow."

She didn't say anything; she couldn't. She knew he was telling her that, this time, there would be no rejection and no regrets. She lifted her face to him, glorying in the feel of his arms around her, the passion in his consuming kiss.

Dawn spread a honeyed pink glow across the horizon. When Ashe parked the Caddy in the driveway, Deborah awoke. Lifting her head from his shoulder, she smiled.

"It's 5:40," he said. "Mazie is going to be up and about any time now."

"Think she'll catch us sneaking in?"

"Would you care if she does?" Ashe opened the car door and assisted Deborah. Wrapping his arm around her, he led her to the front door.

"She'd probably be shocked. She's not used to me sneaking into the house at all hours."

Ashe unlocked the door. They walked into the entrance hall, arm in arm. "What do you usually do, stay overnight at your lover's house?"

Shadowy morning light coming through the windows illuminated the stairs. Deborah stopped dead still in the middle of the staircase.

"I haven't had any lovers," she said, then pulled out of Ashe's arms and ran up to the landing.

He caught her just as she flung open her sitting room door, whirling her around to face him, pulling her into his arms. "What do you mean you haven't had any lovers?"

"There's never been anyone else. Only you." Lowering her head, she looked down at the floor.

He lifted her chin in the curve of his thumb and forefinger. "Honey, I—"

"I never fell in love again, that's all. I hoped that sooner or later the right guy would come along and I'd be ready, but it just didn't happen."

"Just Mr. Wrong again, huh?"

"No, Ashe, not Mr. Wrong. Just not Mr. Right." She slipped her arms around his neck and kissed him, then stepped back and smiled. "This time we're lovers. Remember? Mutual desire?"

"You'd better get in your room and lock me out or we'll be right in the middle of some mutual desire any minute now."

"Good night, then." She laughed. "Or should I say good morning."

"Next time, we're going to have to find some place else to make love." He rubbed the small of his back. "I'm too old to do it in a car, even a big Caddy."

"Next time," she whispered to herself. Next time. She knew she would never be able to resist him and that for him this was only an affair. But not for her. She was already so in love with Ashe McLaughlin she couldn't bear for him to leave her.

He kissed her with a passion that told her that even if he wasn't in love with her, leaving her was as difficult for him as it was for her. Releasing her, he shoved her into her room and closed the door. She took a deep breath, turned and raced into her bedroom, falling in a heap on her bed. Hugging herself, she rolled into a ball and closed her eyes.

This was what she had dreaded since the moment she'd walked in and saw Ashe talking to her mother in the living room. And, if she was honest with herself, this was what she had wanted to happen. No matter how hard she had tried to deny it, she still loved Ashe McLaughlin. She had never truly stopped loving him.

What on earth was she going to do now? She had rushed headlong into an affair with her son's father. How could she continue lying to Ashe, keeping the truth about his child from him? The longer she waited to tell him, the more difficult it would be—for both of them. But did she dare tell him? Would he understand? Or would he hate her for keeping his son from him all these years?

Chapter 10

"Please, tell us, Ms. Vaughn, what happened when you took that wrong turn off Cotton Lane?" the district attorney asked.

"I realized I'd gotten off on the wrong road and was looking for a place to turn around." Deborah sat straight, her hands folded in her lap. "I noticed a truck pulled off the road. One man jumped out of the truck, but I couldn't see his face. There were two other men behind the truck, one holding a gun to the other's head."

Deborah's stomach tightened into a knot; she gripped her damp hands together. Glancing out into the courtroom she sought Ashe. Their gazes met and held. She took a deep breath.

"Are you all right, Ms. Vaughn?" District Attorney Jim Bitterman spoke softly, his voice a light tenor, a distinct contrast to his rugged, almost ugly face and wiry, muscular body.

"Yes." Deborah kept her vision focused on Ashe for several seconds longer, gaining strength from his presence.

"Will you continue, please?"

"The man holding the gun was Lon Sparks."

"Objection, your honor," the defense attorney, Leland Prater shouted, rising from his seat and moving his short, rotund body around the desk. "Ms. Vaughn was not acquainted with Mr. Sparks and therefore could hardly have recognized him."

"Ms. Vaughn later identified Mr. Sparks from a photograph, your honor," Jim Bitterman said.

"Overruled," Judge Heath said.

"Please continue." District Attorney Bitterman stood directly in front of Deborah. "Tell the jury what you saw."

"Lon Sparks shot the man in the head." Deborah closed her eyes momentarily, the memory of that dreadful sight closing in around her, filling her with the sense of fear she'd known in those horrific seconds when she'd witnessed the murder.

Jim Bitterman allowed her to continue recalling the events at her own pace. Leland Prater, long known as an old bag of wind and one of the most crooked lawyers in the area, objected every chance he got, deliberately unnerving Deborah as much as possible. But she did not waver in her testimony, not even when Prater cross-examined her.

She'd been warned, by Jim and by Ashe, that Prater's strategy would be to bring her to tears, show her to be a highly emotional, hysterical woman, who had allowed her hysteria and fear to wrongly identify Lon Sparks.

Not one tear fell from her eyes. Not one shrill word escaped her lips. When her nerves rioted, she took deep breaths and looked to Ashe, seeking and finding the strength she needed to do the job she and she alone could do.

When she was dismissed, Deborah stepped down and walked slowly toward Ashe, who stood and waited for her. He slipped his arm around her and led her out of the courtroom. Even the bevy of reporters flinging questions at her did not disturb the serenity she felt as Ashe led her downstairs and out of the courthouse.

Neither of them said a word until they were safely inside Deborah's car. Ashe buckled her seat belt, kissed her on the nose and smiled at her.

"It's over." She sighed. "It's really over."

"Yeah, honey, it's over." But Ashe wasn't sure. Not one incident of harassment had occurred since Huckleberry's poisoning two days ago, and that made Ashe all the more suspicious. Buck Stansell should have escalated his threats the closer the day came for Deborah to testify. But he hadn't. He hadn't done anything. Did that mean he was waiting to take revenge? Hell!

Deborah checked her watch. "We have time to make the last half of Allen's soccer game, don't we?"

"That's where I'm headed." Ashe maneuvered the Caddy out of the parking lot and onto Water Street.

Leaning against the cushioned headrest, Deborah closed her eyes. Ashe reached out and took her hand, squeezing it tightly. She smiled, but didn't open her eyes or speak. She felt such a great sense of relief.

She had done the right thing, despite being afraid. She had faced the devil—and won! Now, all she had to face were her own personal demons, the biggest lie in her life. She'd had the courage to stand up against Buck Stansell and his gang, but did she have the guts to tell Ashe the truth about Allen? She knew now that she'd been wrong to keep his son's existence a secret from him all these years. Despite her own feelings, her deep sense of betrayal and rejection, she should have contacted Ashe long ago. Mama Mattie would have given her his phone number or address if only she'd asked.

But what would telling Ashe the truth now do to their new relationship? Although he had promised her nothing permanent, had made no commitment to her, she knew he truly cared about her. She, and she alone, was the woman he wanted. Would it be so wrong to wait, to take what time she had left with Ashe and savor the joy she felt, the mutual passion and desire?

"Are you sure you're up to this?" Ashe parked the Cadillac behind a row of cars lined up along the shoulder of Avalon Avenue, west of the railroad tracks that separated Muscle Shoals from Tuscumbia and Sheffield.

"The worst is over. Right? There's no reason why I can't resume my normal activities, is there?"

"Deborah..." Dear God, he didn't want to tell her that he thought the worst might not be over, that the worst might be yet to come. But he would not lie to her. "We can't be sure what Buck Stansell might do if Lon Sparks is convicted."

"You're saying it isn't over." She clutched her shoulder bag to her stomach. "You think he might try to kill me after the trial ends, don't you?"

"There's no way to know." Ashe grasped her shoulder, urging her to turn to him. "But my guess is that you're safe until the jury reaches a verdict."

She leaned toward him, wanting to fall into his arms, wanting and needing his comfort and reassurance. But this was hardly the time or the place. "Then I'm going to try not to think about it, for now. I don't know how much more Mother and Allen can take. I can't bear to think what it would have done to Allen if Huckleberry had died."

"Don't think about it. Huckleberry is as good as new," Ashe said. "Come on, let's go cheer for the home team."

Deborah and Ashe joined Carol Vaughn and Simon Roarke on the sidelines of a tense soccer game between two sets of ten-to twelve-year-olds. Carol had built herself a comfortable nest around her folding lawn chair. She sat with a plaid blanket wrapped about her legs, a thermos of hot coffee at her side. Roarke stood directly behind her chair, his gaze moving around the crowd, then back to the soccer game where Allen Vaughn raced down the field, his long, strong legs moving with agile grace.

Roarke stepped aside when Deborah laid her hand on her mother's shoulder. Ashe nodded, motioning to Roarke.

"How's the game going?" Deborah asked.

"We're ahead," Carol said. "Two to one."

Deborah glanced at the sky. "It's getting cloudy and the wind's up. I hope it doesn't start raining."

"Where's your coat?" Carol asked.

"I didn't wear one today. Just my suit. But don't worry, I'm fine."

"Mothers worry."

"I'm okay. Really. Everything is going to be all right."

Ashe and Roarke moved away from the crowd, close enough to keep an eye on everyone and yet far enough away to have a private discussion.

"We're going to be staying for at least another couple of weeks," Ashe said. "If we're lucky, this will be over when the trail ends, but my gut instincts tell me not to count on it."

"A man could do a lot worse than living around here, spending the rest of his life in a small town." Roarke's dark gaze came to a halt on Allen Vaughn as the boy kicked the ball past the goalie and scored a point for his team.

Ashe slapped Roarke on the back. "Did you see that? Damn that boy's good. He's big and fast and strong and a real fighter.

Look at his face. Good God, how I know that feeling. He's light-headed from the victory.''

"He reminds me of you," Roarke said.

"What?"

"Allen Vaughn reminds me of you."

"Hell, he's just like Deborah. They could be twins."

"I know he looks like Deborah, but the more I'm around the kid, the more he reminds me of you."

"What the hell are you talking about?" Ashe watched Allen, seeing nothing except his blond hair, his blue eyes, his strong physical resemblance to Deborah.

"When did you leave Sheffield and join the army?"

"When did I... Eleven years ago."

"When exactly?"

"In July."

Grunting, Roarke nodded. "Allen Vaughn was born in February. Seven months after you left town."

"So?"

"Has it never once crossed your mind that you might have gotten Deborah pregnant, that Allen could be your son?"

Ashe's body rebelled, tensing every muscle, bringing every nerve to full alert, knotting his stomach painfully. "She would have told me. Deborah never would have kept something like that from me. She was in love with me. If she'd been pregnant with my child, she would have come running to me."

"Are you sure?"

"Yes, dammit, I'm sure!"

"Then forget I said anything."

"I sure as hell will." Ashe glared at his friend, a man he had come to like and respect since their first meeting over a year ago. Roarke stood eye to eye with Ashe, the two equal in height and size, broad-shouldered, long-legged. Roarke, like Ashe himself, a former warrior, still in his prime.

"You want me to give Sam a call tonight and let him know we'll be staying...indefinitely?" Roarke asked.

"No. This is my case. I'll call Sam." Ashe watched Allen, inspecting his every move with an analytical eye, searching for evidence to substantiate Roarke's suspicion. "I'll let him know we could be here for a few more weeks. Once I know Deborah is safe, we'll head back to Atlanta."

Dammit! Why couldn't Roarke have kept his suspicions to himself? They were totally unfounded. They had to be! Not getting Deborah pregnant that long-ago night was the one and only thing Ashe hadn't had to feel guilty about all these years. Allen Vaughn was Deborah's brother, not her son. Most certainly not *his* son. No way in hell!

Dinner had been a double celebration. Deborah's court appearance was over and Allen Vaughn had once again scored the winning goal that led his team to victory.

Deborah and Ashe had allowed her family to believe the danger was over; indeed, Deborah convinced herself that there was hope all the threats and harassment had come to an end.

She had sensed a tension in Ashe she hadn't noticed before tonight. He kept watching Allen and his close scrutiny unnerved her. Did he suspect something? Or was he simply worrying that Buck Stansell still posed a threat to her family, that Allen might be the target of the man's revenge?

But then Ashe would look at her and his eyes would warm, his expression telling her plainly that he was remembering their lovemaking in the early morning hours. Yesterday. Less than forty-eight hours ago.

"I'm afraid I must say good-night." Carol rose from her chair in the library. "Come along, Allen. It's a half hour past your bedtime."

"How about coming up with me, Ashe?" Allen asked. "You said you wanted to see my science test."

"You bet I do. I want to see what you did to get 105% on that test instead of just a plain old 100%." Ashe laid his hand on Allen's shoulder and the two followed Miss Carol.

"Are you staying down here for a while?" Carol asked her daughter.

"Yes, I think I'll fix myself a drink and relax a bit before I come up."

"Don't forget to say good-night," Allen called out from the hallway.

"I won't forget."

Alone in the library, Deborah kicked off her shoes and tucked her feet up on the sofa. Suddenly she felt the man's presence before she heard him clear his throat. Jerking her head around, she saw Simon Roarke standing in the doorway.

"Come on in, Mr. Roarke," Deborah said. "Would you care for a drink?"

"No, thanks." He walked over to the liquor cart. "May I fix something for you?"

"Just a little brandy."

Roarke poured the liquor and handed it to Deborah. "This about right?"

"Perfect." Deborah looked up at Simon Roarke, thinking, and not for the first time, that there was a hint of sadness in his eyes. "Please, sit down and talk to me."

"What do you want to talk about, Ms. Vaughn?"

"Call me Deborah. And I'd like to ask you about your friendship with Ashe."

Roarke sat in the wing chair to Deborah's left. "We've known each other a year. We have similar backgrounds and found we worked well together and enjoyed spending some of our off time together."

"You were in the army, too?"

"Yeah."

"How long have you worked for the Dundee Agency?"

"Over two years."

"You aren't married?"

"No."

"Girlfriend?" Deborah asked.

"Neither Ashe nor I are in a committed relationship, if that's what you're asking. I'm sure he's told you that."

Deborah smiled. "I'm not very good at this, am I? Cross-examining you to get information about Ashe isn't something I'd ordinarily do, but—"

"But you're curious about Ashe. Why don't you just ask him what you want to know?"

"Yes, that would be the logical thing to do, wouldn't it?" Deborah slid her feet off the sofa and back into her shoes. "Did he tell you that we knew each other, years ago?"

"Yes."

"You aren't making this easy for me, Mr. Roarke."

"Just Roarke," he said. "I'm afraid I can't tell you what you want to know. I'm not sure Ashe can tell you. He probably doesn't even know himself.''

"Is it that obvious?" Deborah clasped her knees with her fingertips. "I made a mistake about the way Ashe felt about me once, and I don't want to make another mistake."

"You're talking to the wrong man. I can't speak for Ashe." Roarke grunted, then chuckled softly. "Hell, I'm a failure when it comes to figuring out the way other people feel and think. I'm thirty-five. I'm alone, and I'll be alone the rest of my life. Ashe is different. He's not so far gone, the right woman couldn't save him."

Deborah took a sip of the brandy, then set the glass aside. "I like you, Roarke. I—"

"Allen is waiting for you to come up." Ashe stood in the doorway, a rather comical look of jealousy on his face.

Deborah couldn't suppress a gurgle of laughter from escaping.

Standing, Roarke took a couple of steps, leaned over, lifted Deborah's hand and kissed it. "I like you, too, Deborah." He walked past Ashe without glancing his way.

"What the hell was that all about?" Ashe asked.

"I was pumping Roarke for information about you."

"That's not what it sounded like when I walked in. Sounded more like a mutual admiration society."

Deborah stood and walked over to Ashe, slipped her arm around his neck and pressed her body into his. "I like your friend Roarke." She rubbed herself against Ashe. "But not the same way I like you."

Ashe jerked her up against him and his lips covered hers, claiming her with demanding possession. Breathing hard, they ended the kiss, but held each other close.

"I want to make love to you," he said. "Is there any way we can slip off somewhere? Anywhere?"

"Let me go up and say good night to Allen, then I'll meet you in the pool house in thirty minutes."

"The pool house? Out back?"

"Yes. We'll have all the privacy we want out there."

Ashe laughed. "I don't know if I can wait thirty minutes."

"Let's make it twenty minutes," she said, pulling out of his arms.

"You aren't afraid someone will find us out, using the pool house as a rendezvous?"

"I really don't care, do you?"

"No, honey, I don't give a damn who knows we're lovers."

Deborah saw the light in the pool house from where she stood on the back patio. Soft, shimmering light. Candles? Had Ashe found the candles left over from the last pool party they'd given back in the summer, the one for her mother's garden club friends?

She straightened her green satin robe, readjusted the quilted lapels and tightened the sash belt. She told herself not to be nervous, that she had no reason to be. After all, it wasn't as if she were a seventeen-year-old virgin.

Who was she kidding? She might not be a totally inexperienced teenager, but she was hardly accustomed to late night rendezvous in the pool house with a virile, amorous lover. She couldn't believe she was actually going to do this. But then she had never dreamed that she and Ashe would become lovers. Truly lovers.

She walked slowly toward the pool house, her heart hammering, her nerves quivering, her body filled with anticipation. Music met her as she hesitated in the doorway. An instrumental version of "The Shadow of Your Smile" surrounded her. Apparently he'd found the tape player and the stack of her mother's favorite tunes on cassettes. He stood inside waiting for her, two glasses of wine in his hand. He held out one to her when she entered the small octagon-shaped shelter, centered directly behind the swimming pool.

Ashe had changed into a pair of faded jeans and a zippered fleece jacket. He looked incredible. All muscle and firm flesh, tanned and lean and waiting for her.

She accepted the wine. He nodded toward the padded poolside chaise longue that had been stored for the winter. Seating herself, she glanced around inside the twelve-by-twelve-foot room. A dozen fat pink and yellow candles, half consumed on a previous occasion, circled the inner perimeter, casting a mellow, romantic glow over the room.

"To the most beautiful woman in the world." Ashe saluted her with his glass.

Her smile wavered, but she managed to keep it in place after she took a sip of the white wine. "You're beautiful, too, you know. You always were. The most beautiful boy, the most beautiful man. I never could see anyone else except you."

Hurriedly she downed the remainder of the wine. The tune changed to "What Are You Doing for the Rest of Your Life?" She'd heard her mother hum these old tunes for as long as she could remember. They were such romantic songs, meant to be shared by lovers.

Ashe took her empty glass. "Want a refill?"

"No." She looked up at him. "I don't dare drink any more. I'm already drunk from just looking at you."

He set their glasses on a small round glass and metal table, then took Deborah's hands and lifted her to her feet. Drawing her into his arms, he rubbed his cheek against hers and danced her slowly around the room.

"You don't have any idea what your honesty does to me, do you?" He caught her open mouth before she could reply, thrusting his tongue inside, loving the taste of the wine that lingered in her mouth.

When he ended the kiss, he smiled when he saw her face. Eyes closed, face flushed, she was so beautiful it tore at his heart to look at her. "I can't believe how much I want you."

"Oh, Ashe, I never dreamed this could happen, that you and I... But it's real, isn't it? We're here, together. Lovers."

"Lovers, in every sense of the word." Reaching down, he loosened her sash belt until her robe fell open. Seeing that she was naked beneath the green satin, he swallowed hard. "My God, Deborah!"

Her shaky fingers grasped the metal pull on his jacket zipper and opened the hooded blue sweatshirt. She laid her hand on his chest. He covered her hand with his.

"I don't really know anything about this. I don't have any experience. Teach me, Ashe. Show me what you want."

"Take off my jacket," he said.

She obeyed, sliding it off his shoulders and tossing it on the floor. "Now what?"

"Remove my jeans."

Without hesitation, she unsnapped, unzipped and tugged off his jeans. He kicked his shoes off and to one side, then spread the satin robe away from her body, allowing it to fall to her feet.

They stood, only inches separating them, naked and unashamed, passion wild within them both. He took her hands in his, lifted them for a kiss, then placed them on his chest before lifting her in his arms.

Ashe was magnificent. Big, tall and lean. He carried her back to the chaise, but set her on her feet.

"Night before last we were so hungry for each other, we didn't take the time to savor the moment. Not the first time nor the second time. Tonight, I want to learn every inch of your body, and I want you to know every inch of mine."

"Whatever you want, Ashe." She moved closer, her breasts brushing against his hair-rough chest. She gulped down a sigh as shivers of pleasure shimmied through her.

"No, honey. Whatever you want." He cupped her buttocks, bringing her completely up against him, letting her feel his arousal, telling her, even without words, how much he wanted her.

"I just want you, Ashe." She slid her hands up his chest and around his neck. "I just want you."

He kissed her until she was breathless, then he painted a trail of warm, moist kisses across her shoulder and down to one breast. All the while he caressed her hip with his other hand. She quivered, then cried out when he suckled her breast. Her knees weakened. He stayed at her breast long enough to have her panting, then knelt on bended knee and delved his tongue into her navel at the precise moment his fingers found the soft inner folds of her body. Her knees gave way and she would have fallen if she hadn't caught Ashe by the shoulders, bracing herself.

He covered her stomach in kisses, then moved back and forth from one thigh to the other, kissing, licking, nipping her tender flesh. She moaned with the pleasure, shivering as she dug her nails into his shoulders.

Lifting her, he laid her on the chaise and came down over her, one knee resting on the side of the cushion, his other foot on the floor.

"Touch me, Deborah. Feel me."

She sucked in a deep breath, then began a timid exploration of his chest and belly. Garnering her courage and enticed by his glorious body, she ran her fingers over his hardness. He groaned, but she knew the sound was one of pleasure and not pain. She circled him. He covered her hand, teaching her the movements that pleased him. But as quickly as he'd instructed her, he pulled her hand away and laid it on his hip.

"I can't take much of that, honey."

Lowering his head, he captured her nipple in his mouth, teasing it, then sucking greedily. She arched her back up off the chaise. He delved his fingers between her satiny folds, finding her most sensitive spot. She writhed beneath him as he fondled her. Within minutes she shuddered and he swallowed her cries of completion in a tongue-thrusting kiss. As the last wave of pleasure shook her, Ashe lifted her hips and entered her. One sure, swift move that joined their bodies and began the mating dance.

Slowly. Precisely. In and out. Hands roamed. Lips kissed. Bodies united in pleasure. Soon the rhythm changed, the waltz became a wild fandango. Slow. Quick. Slow. Quick. Deborah clung to Ashe as the tension in her body mounted. He thrust into her harder and faster, sweat forming on his body.

She called his name over and over again as her pleasure climbed upward, closer and closer to the apex. Ashe's movements became frantic, his need for this woman growing hotter and hotter.

She cried out in the moment of release, spiraling out of control and into oblivion. Ashe thrust once, twice more, and followed her over the precipice. His own hardy male cry blended with her feminine ones, their breaths ragged, their bodies coated with perspiration.

Ashe maneuvered Deborah so that they fit together on the chaise, their bodies stuck together with the moisture of their love-making.

"We're going to stay here all night," he told her.

"Yes. I know." She kissed him, taking the initiative, smothering him with all the passion she'd buried deep within her eleven years ago when he had walked out of her life.

But he was back and for however long Ashe McLaughlin stayed in her life, she planned to be his lover. Maybe nothing lasted forever. Maybe they didn't have a future. But for tonight, she would pretend. Tomorrow was a million miles away. Nothing mattered tonight, nothing except loving and being loved by Ashe.

* * *

Deborah opened the door to her bedroom. Ashe circled her waist with his arm, pulling her back against his chest, nuzzling her neck with his nose.

"Get in your room. It's nearly six. Mother will be up and about soon," Deborah said, but turned in his arms, kissing him.

He shoved her away, turned her around and swatted her behind. "See you downstairs for breakfast in about an hour."

Deborah stood in the open doorway, watching until Ashe disappeared down the hall and into his room. Smiling, she walked into her sitting room, humming "Goin' Out of My Head," the tune that had been playing on the cassette when she and Ashe had made love right before returning to the house.

"Good morning," Carol Vaughn said.

Deborah came fully alert, stared across the room and saw her mother perched on the edge of the window seat. "Mother!"

"Come in and close the door. I think we need to have a little talk, don't you?"

"How long have you been waiting in here?" Deborah closed the door and walked across the room, sitting down beside her mother.

"Only a few minutes." Carol took Deborah's hand. "I awoke early. I'd had a difficult time sleeping all night. The sedatives don't last very long. I walked around and just happened to stop by the windows and saw light coming from the pool house. I checked your room and found it empty, then I knocked on Ashe's door. Mr. Roarke heard me and came out to see what was going on."

"Did you tell Roarke that Ashe and I were missing?"

"I told him that y'all had obviously spent the night in the pool house," Carol said. "I rather think I embarrassed the man."

"Oh, Mother, really."

"I was awake and heard the two of you on the stairs, so I came over here to wait for you."

"I'm a big girl now. I don't need your approval to spend the night with a man."

"No, of course you don't." Carol patted Deborah's hand, then released it. "But if you and Ashe have begun an affair, then I can't help being concerned. For you and for Allen."

"Mother, I—"

"Shh. I deliberately brought Ashe back here because I knew

you'd never gotten over him, that there had been no one else.''
Glancing down at her hands, Carol twisted her diamond ring and
her gold wedding band about on her finger. ''I admit I played
God in your life, but I want you to be happy.''

''I'm glad Ashe came back into my life. We've cleared up
several misconceptions we had concerning each other.''

''He told you what your father did, didn't he?''

''Yes, he told me.''

''Deborah, your father thought he was doing the best thing for
you. I disagreed, but you know how your father was. He wouldn't
listen to me.''

''I don't blame you, Mother. I don't even blame Daddy.'' Deborah hugged Carol. ''It's all right. Really it is. We can't change
what happened. Besides, I'm the one who has kept Allen's parentage a secret. I could have gotten in touch with Ashe at any
time and we both know it.''

No, Deborah blamed no one except herself. If she had been a
little older and less dependent on her parents, she never would
have agreed to her father's plan to send her and her mother away
to Europe for the last few months of Deborah's pregnancy. A
chubby girl who had been able to disguise her pregnant state with
loose, baggy clothes, even at six months, Deborah hadn't had a
problem keeping her pregnancy a secret. And once they had returned to Sheffield with Allen, no one had dared to openly question his parentage.

''I lied to Mattie,'' Carol said. ''She asked me once, when
Allen was just a baby, if he was your child. Yours and Ashe's.''

''You never told me that she suspected Allen wasn't yours and
Daddy's.''

''I lied to her. I convinced her that her suspicions were wrong.
She never questioned me again.''

''If she'd known, she would have told Ashe.''

''She does know, Deborah.'' Carol kept her eyes downcast. ''I
told her the truth when I asked her for Ashe's telephone number
in Atlanta.''

''Mother!''

Carol's chin quivered as she looked directly at her daughter.
''She has promised not to tell Ashe, to give you time to tell him
the truth.'' Carol clutched Deborah's hand. ''You must tell Ashe.
You can't keep putting it off, not now the two of you are lovers.''

"Mother, I'm not sure telling Ashe would be the best thing to do, under the circumstances."

"What circumstances?"

"Ashe and I have made each other no promises. He hasn't committed himself to me for any longer than his business here will take. Once I'm no longer in danger, he's going back to Atlanta."

"I see."

"If I tell him about Allen, I have no idea what he might do. He could tell Allen. He could demand joint custody. Or he could make a commitment to me because of Allen and not because he loves me." Jumping up off the window seat, Deborah walked around the room. She stopped abruptly, then turned to face her mother. "I'm afraid to tell him. I'm afraid I'll lose him all over again."

"Deborah, dear child, you musn't—"

"I know. I know. I'm not fooling myself. It's just that I want whatever time we have together to go on being as wonderful as it was tonight."

"You must tell the man he has a son." Carol shook her head. "You can't lie to Ashe if you love him."

"I didn't say I loved him."

"You didn't have to. I see it in your eyes. I hear it in your voice."

"I can't tell him. Not yet."

"I go back to the doctor for a checkup and more tests soon," Carol said. "If you haven't told Ashe by then—"

"No, Mother, you musn't tell him."

"Then you tell him. We should have told him long ago. Besides, if you don't tell him before he leaves Sheffield, Mattie will tell him."

"But what if he tells Allen?"

Carol stood, walked across the room and laid her hand on Deborah's shoulder. "Ashe isn't going to do anything to hurt Allen. Don't you know him any better than that?"

"Give me some time, Mother. Please, just let me do this my way and in my own good time."

"Don't wait too long. My heart tells me that you'll be sorry if you do."

* * *

Ashe came out of the shower, dried off and stepped into a pair of clean briefs. He didn't know when he'd ever felt so good, so glad to be alive.

Deborah. Sweet, beautiful Deborah.

She was, in so many ways, the same innocent, loving girl she'd been eleven years ago; but then she was also a woman of strength and courage and incredible passion.

Whoever she was, part innocent girl, part bewitching woman, Deborah Vaughn was honest and trustworthy. She would never lie to him. Never!

He had tried to put Roarke's suspicions out of his mind, and for those magic hours he'd spent with Deborah he'd been able to do just that. But now he had to face them again.

There was no way Allen Vaughn could be his son. Deborah would have told him if she'd been pregnant. She'd have come running to him. She'd been so crazy in love with him that she would have...

She would have come to him after he'd rejected her, after he'd told her that he didn't love her the way she loved him?

Allen isn't your son, he told himself. He looks just like Deborah. He's her brother, dammit. Her brother!

Besides, Mama Mattie would have told him if she'd thought Allen was his child.

Don't do this to yourself! Don't look for similarities between you and Allen. Don't let Roarke's outrageous suspicions spoil what you and Deborah have found together this time.

Miss Carol never would have dared you to come back to Sheffield and face the past if Allen was your son.

Ashe dressed hurriedly, then rushed downstairs, eager to see Deborah again. He would not look at Allen Vaughn and search for a truth that didn't exist. He trusted Deborah. His heart told him she wouldn't lie to him. And just this once, he intended to listen to his heart.

Chapter 11

The trial had lasted eight days, everyone saying the case was pretty well cut and dried since the prosecution had a reliable eye-witness to the murder. After three and a half hours of deliberation, the jury had rendered a guilty verdict, surprising no one. Five days later, the judge had sentenced Lon Sparks to life in prison, and Deborah Vaughn had been free from threats and harassment for nearly two weeks.

Ashe had been waiting for Buck Stansell to strike, but nothing had happened, not even a wrong number telephone call. He'd thought about paying Buck a visit, but decided against it. Why take a chance on stirring a hornet's nest? He had talked to his cousin Lee Roy, who'd said little, except that *people* weren't overly concerned with an insignificant guy like Lon Sparks, that the man wasn't worth enough to cause trouble over.

Roarke had suggested it might be time to think about returning to Atlanta, but Ashe kept putting him off. How could he take a chance on leaving Deborah undefended? She'd come to mean far more to him than she should. He had allowed himself to become too involved with her, with Allen and Miss Carol. This was a job, but not like any other. These were people he cared about, a family he'd started thinking of as his.

Maybe he had reached the age when he needed to settle down, to start considering marriage and children. He wasn't sure. He and Deborah were attracted to each other, always had been, although he'd fought that attraction when they'd been younger. Maybe somewhere deep down inside him, he'd always thought he wasn't quite good enough for Deborah. Not just because her parents were wealthy and socially prominent and he'd come from white trash hoodlums, but because he'd never been innocent or pure or good, and Deborah had been all those things. Even now, at twenty-eight, she still personified everything right with the world.

And he still wasn't good enough for her.

Ashe paced the floor in the doctor's office, waiting for Deborah and Miss Carol. He'd told himself that he would hang around Sheffield until they knew the test results. It was as good an excuse as any. This way he could justify his reluctance to leave, to Deborah and her family, as well as to himself.

Sitting, he flipped through several magazines, then stood and paced the floor again. He glanced at the wall clock, checking it against his watch. Nearly an hour. Dammit, how long did it take for a doctor to explain test results?

Just when his patience came to an end, Deborah and Miss Carol emerged from the office, solemn expressions on their faces. Deborah's arm draped her mother's slender shoulders.

"We're ready to go home, now, Ashe," Deborah said.

Ashe didn't ask any questions, didn't say a word, simply nodded his head and led the ladies outside and assisted them into the car.

Miss Carol, sitting in the front seat beside Ashe, reached over and touched his arm lightly. "Can you stay awhile longer?"

"Yes, ma'am, of course I can stay." He pulled the car out of the parking lot and onto the main thoroughfare.

"Deborah and Allen will need you," Carol said.

"Mother, please don't—" Deborah said.

"Hush up." Carol swatted her hand in the air. "Ashe is like family and I want him here. Even if you think you can handle this alone, I believe you'll need a strong man at your side."

"I take it the tests results weren't good." Ashe kept his gaze fixed straight ahead.

"The cancer has returned and Dr. Mason has scheduled surgery for the first of next week." Carol opened her purse, took out a lace handkerchief and wiped her hands, then returned the hand-kerchief to her purse.

"I'm sorry, Miss Carol."

"No need for all this gloom and doom." Carol sat up straight, squaring her shoulders as if preparing herself to do battle. "I licked this thing once and I can do it again. But I'll rest easier knowing Deborah won't be alone, that you'll be at her side."

"You hired me, Miss Carol. I won't leave Sheffield as long as you need me."

"Thank you, Ashe." She patted him on the arm.

Little more was said on the short drive home. Indeed, what more could be said? Ashe wondered. Life certainly didn't play fair. Not when it heaped more trouble on one family than it could bear. But then, Deborah and Miss Carol were both strong women. They were fighters despite their genteel backgrounds.

Sirens blasted, shrill and menacing in the quite, lazy atmosphere of Sheffield's main street.

"Oh, my." Carol shivered. "I do so hate the sound of those things. Sirens always mean bad news."

"Look at that black smoke," Deborah said. "It's coming straight up Montgomery Avenue."

"My goodness, you don't suppose it's one of our neighbors' homes, do you?" Miss Carol leaned toward the windshield, her gaze riveted to the billowing smoke filling the blue sky.

The closer they came to home, the darker the smoke, the louder the sirens. A sudden sick feeling hit Ashe in the pit of his stomach. Allen was still at school. Roarke would be with him. Ashe blew out a breath.

Before they reached the Vaughn driveway, they saw one fire truck parked at the back of the house and another just turning in behind it. "It's our garage!" Deborah gripped the back of her mother's seat. "It's on fire!"

Ashe pulled the Cadillac up to the curb, stopped and jumped out. "Stay here." He ran across the front yard.

"Stay in the car, Mother. I'll come back and check on you in just a few minutes."

"But Ashe said for both of us to stay here," Carol said.

"Ashe isn't my boss."

Deborah jumped out of the car, catching up with Ashe at the back corner of the house, where he stood watching the firemen do their job. He grabbed her around the waist, pulling her to his side.

"It's just the garage," he said. "And it looks like they're getting the fire under control."

"Mazie? Where's Mazie? Is she all right?"

"She's at the grocery store. Remember? This is Wednesday morning, her midweek trip to pick up supplies."

"Oh, yes, of course."

Deborah leaned against Ashe, watching while the firefighters extinguished the blaze, leaving a charred three-car garage, a blackened Mercedes, a soot-covered BMW and swirling clouds of gray smoke spiraling heavenward.

Fire Chief Greg Wilbanks nodded, removed his hat and wiped his face with the back of his hand. "Damn curious blaze. Whoever set this baby didn't try to hide the fact that it was out-and-out arson."

"What do you mean?" Deborah asked.

"The place was doused with gasoline and torched. We found two empty gas cans at the back of the house." Greg looked at Ashe. "I've called Chief Burton. I'd say your job isn't finished, Mr. McLaughlin. Looks like somebody's out to get himself a little revenge."

"Ashe?" Deborah grabbed his arm. "Do you think that—"

"I don't think anything," he said.

"But Greg said—"

"I know what he said. There's no point jumping to conclusions. We'll take every precaution, but we're not going to panic." He grasped her by the shoulders. "Go tell Miss Carol that everything's all right. The fire's out. Tell her the truth, but play it down. There's no need to worry her any more than can be helped."

"You're right." She slipped her arms around Ashe's waist and sighed when he hugged her close. Pulling away, she tried to smile. "I'll take Mother in the front door. There's no need for her to see this until later."

"Don't read anything into this," Ashe said. "Not yet. Let me handle things. I'm not going anywhere, not until you're completely out of danger. Trust me, honey."

"I do trust you. With all my heart."

Ashe watched her walk away, a tight knot forming in the pit of his stomach. She expected a great deal from him. Was it more than he could deliver? Would he let her down again, or could he be the man Deborah wanted and needed?

Ashe approached Greg Wilbanks. "When Chief Burton arrives, tell him I'd prefer he not bother Miss Carol or Deborah. I'll talk to him. And once you've filed your report on this fire, I'd like a copy."

"As Miss Carol's representative?" Greg asked.

"Yeah, as Miss Carol's representative."

"No problem."

Going in the back door, Ashe met Carol and Deborah in the hallway.

"I'm taking Mother upstairs to rest," Deborah told him, then turned to assist her mother. "I'll fix you some tea and bring it up in just a little while."

"Tea would be nice." Halting on the landing, Carol grabbed Deborah's arm. "Let him do whatever he has to do to put an end to this."

"Mother, what are saying?"

"I'm saying that Ashe knows how to deal with those people. However he chooses to handle the situation, I don't want you trying to persuade him otherwise."

"Ashe is not a hired assassin, Mother. He's not going to kill Buck Stansell."

"You two go on," Ashe called out from the downstairs hallway. "I'll fix you both some tea and bring it up."

"Thank you," Miss Carol smiled.

"Mother!" Deborah glared at Carol. "Do you honestly think Ashe would murder someone?"

"Not murder, my dear, kill. There is a difference. And Ashe McLaughlin has been trained to kill. There is no doubt in my mind that he would kill anyone who'd harm you."

"I don't want him to have to kill to protect me, but... Perhaps Buck Stansell wasn't responsible for the fire. Besides, no one was harmed."

Downstairs, Ashe put on the water to boil, set two cups on a tray and laid two Earl Grey tea bags in each cup. Lifting the phone out of the wall cradle, he dialed Roarke's cellular phone number.

"Roarke, here."

"Keep a very close eye on Allen."

"What's wrong?"

"We've had a fire here," Ashe said. "Someone doused the garage with gasoline. They left the cans for the firemen to find."

"Looks like we'll be hanging around Sheffield for a while longer than we thought."

"Yeah. I'd say Buck Stansell is back to playing games with us. The question is just how deadly will his games become."

Deborah took care of her morning phone calls, dictated several letters and closed a deal on the old Hartman farm before her ten-thirty coffee break. She had wanted to stay home with her mother, whom she worried would fret the day away there at the house with only Mazie, the eternal pessimist, as company. But her mother had insisted she didn't need a baby-sitter, so Deborah had found an alternative plan.

She glanced in the outer office where Ashe sat with his long legs stretched out, his big feet propped up on a desk in the corner, situated where he could see directly into Deborah's office. He had begun work on his second crossword puzzle book since his arrival in Sheffield.

Deborah dialed the telephone, hoping her plan for keeping her mother occupied would work out.

"Hello."

"Mama Mattie," Deborah said. "I have a favor to ask of you."

"What is it, child?"

"Mother's at the house all alone with Mazie, and I'm afraid, after the doctor's news and the fire in the garage yesterday, she'll spend the day fretting."

"You need say no more. I've just baked an apple cinnamon coffee cake. I'll take it over and spend the rest of the day with Miss Carol."

"Thanks so much, Mama Mattie."

"It'll be my pleasure." Deborah hung up the phone and glanced back at Ashe, who looked up from his puzzle and grinned at her. She lifted her hand to her mouth in a drinking gesture. Ashe nodded agreement. They met at the coffeepot, one of three set up on a table in a small, open room directly across from the office rest room.

"Good morning." Holding a mug of hot coffee in one hand,

he cupped her hip with the other and brought her close enough for him to kiss.

She returned the kiss, then pulled away, turning to pour her coffee. "Get your hand off my hip, Mr. McLaughlin. This is an office, not a bedroom," she teased.

"I'm glad you told me," he said. "I was planning on backing you up against the wall over there and ravishing you. But since this is an office, I don't suppose ravishing the boss lady is allowed."

"Most definitely not."

"You've had a busy morning."

"I've accomplished a great deal."

They carried their coffee back into the outer office, pausing just outside Deborah's private domain.

"Ashe, have there been any threatening phone calls or a letter today?" she asked.

"No, honey, not a one."

"I'd thought that since...well since the fire yesterday, the harassment might start all over again."

He nudged her through her office door. "There may not be a connection. But..." He didn't want to alarm her.

"But what?"

"If Buck Stansell was behind yesterday's fire, I'd say phone calls and letters are a thing of the past. Simple harassment will no longer be the order of the day."

"I see. You're saying things will get nasty."

"They could."

"Do you think Allen and Mother are in danger?"

"Possibly."

"Oh, Ashe." The coffee sloshed over the edge of her mug. Quickly holding the mug outward so the liquid could run down the sides, she averted being burned.

Just as Ashe started to close the door to Deborah's office, a string of loud, piercing blasts sounded. The front office windows shattered. Glass blew across the room. The office staff screamed and dived for cover under their desks. Ashe knocked Deborah to the floor, covering her body with his as he drew his gun.

"Crawl to the left," he told her.

She obeyed silently, not questioning Ashe's order for one minute. Standing, he lifted her to her knees and sat her in the corner behind a row of metal file cabinets.

"Stay put."

She nodded. He made his way to the outer office where he found the staff in hiding. The front of the office wall consisted of a line of long windows, all of which had been destroyed by a barrage of bullets.

Annie Laurie looked up from beneath her desk, her eyes wide with fright. "Ashe? Oh, my God, what happened?"

"Everyone stay put," Ashe said.

Cracking his office door a fraction, Neil Posey peered outside. "Is everyone all right?" he asked. "Is Annie Laurie okay? Was Deborah hurt?"

"As far as I know the only damage is to the windows," Ashe said as he made his way to the bullet-riddled front door. He walked out onto the sidewalk. People were staring at him and at the Vaughn & Posey building. In the distance he heard a police siren and knew, the police station being only a few blocks away, the authorities would arrive at any moment. Returning inside, he made his way toward Deborah's office.

"It's all right," Ashe said. "Whoever did all this damage is long gone."

One by one the staff of Vaughn & Posey emerged from under their desks.

Neil opened his office door. "Annie Laurie, are you sure you're all right?"

"I'm fine, Mr. Posey. Just scared to death."

Ashe found Deborah still sitting in the corner behind the filing cabinets. She stared up at him, her eyes dry, her face pale.

"It's okay, honey." Reaching down, he lifted her to her feet. She shook uncontrollably. "Deborah?"

She clung to him, her trembling growing worse. "Was anyone hurt?"

"Everybody's fine. Nothing's hurt but the building."

"I can't let the people who work for me be at risk because of me."

Ashe stroked her back, trying to soothe her. "You can't blame yourself for this."

"Yes, I can. And I do. I'm Buck Stansell's target. If I hadn't been here at the office, then he wouldn't have sent someone *here* to shoot up the place."

"Don't start blaming yourself for something that isn't your fault." Dammit, she was shaking like a leaf. He wasn't getting through to her.

He grabbed her by the shoulders and shook her soundly. She glared at him, then nodded her head. Ashe pulled her back into his arms, and that's how the police chief found them.

"Deborah, Chief Burton is here," Annie Laurie called out from the doorway.

Deborah turned in Ashe's arms, but made no move away from him. He kept his arms tightly around her.

"They sure as hell made a mess of things," Chief Burton said. "A couple of witnesses across the street said they saw one man drive by real slow, coming to a stop right out front before he pulled out what they thought looked like some sort of automatic weapon. Of course, they can't identify the weapon. Said it happened too fast. He was driving a new Chevy."

"The car was probably stolen," Ashe said.

"Could've been. Anyway, I just wanted to ask if either of you saw anything that could help us."

"No," Ashe said. "We didn't see anything."

"Nobody in the office seemed to have seen a thing. Just heard the shooting." The police chief looked directly at Deborah. "Ms. Vaughn, you might want to think about staying at home for a few days, that is, unless you plan on closing down the business."

"No, I do not plan on closing Vaughn & Posey." She stiffened her spine. Sliding his hand up and around, Ashe caressed her back, then placed his arm around her shoulders. "However, I will consider staying at home. I don't want to put my employees' lives at risk."

"I'm taking Ms. Vaughn home, now," Ashe said. "If you need to question us further, you'll know where to find us."

"Fine," Chief Burton said. "I don't think we'll need either of you any more today."

"I need to make arrangements to have the building cleaned and repair work started immediately." Deborah allowed Ashe to lead her across the shattered glass and splintered wood covering the outer office floor.

She stopped at Annie Laurie's desk; the two women hugged

each other. Deborah turned to face her employees. "I'm sorry this had to happen. I'm so relieved no one was injured." She glanced over at Neil, whose round, normally pink face was a pale gray. "Let everyone go home for the rest of the day. I'll have someone come in and clean up. Rearrange things so work can continue tomorrow. Make use of my office. I'll be working at home. Temporarily."

"Certainly, Deborah. We'll carry on," Neil said.

Ashe hurried her outside and into her car. "Just hang on, honey. I'll take you home."

"I dread telling Mother, but I have no choice. You know someone may have already called her."

"Miss Carol will handle this okay. She's a strong woman, just like her daughter."

When they arrived at the Vaughn home, they found Mattie Trotter waiting on the front porch. The minute Deborah approached her, she opened her arms.

Going into Mattie's arms, Deborah sighed. "Oh, Mama Mattie, this has become a nightmare. I thought it was over, that the worst had been Huckleberry's poisoning."

"It'll be all right," Mattie said, glancing over Deborah's shoulder at Ashe. "Ashe isn't going to let anything happen to you."

"Someone called already, didn't they?" Deborah asked. "Mother knows."

"Miss Carol is fine. She's lying down in the library, taking a little nap." Mattie winked at Deborah as she slipped her arm around her waist and led her inside. "I put a few drops of brandy in her tea."

"Where's Mazie?" Deborah looked around in the hallway. "I can't believe she's not out here foretelling the end of the world for us all."

"I sent that silly woman to town on an errand," Mattie said. "I had to get her out of the house. She was driving me crazy and upsetting Miss Carol. She should be gone a couple of hours. And Allen won't be home from school until after three."

"Thanks." Deborah swayed, her head spinning. Mama Mattie motioned to Ashe, who lifted Deborah in his arms.

"Put me down!"

"Take her on upstairs and tend to her." Mattie pointed to the closed library door. ''I'll go sit with Miss Carol and finish reading that new Grisham book. If we need y'all, I'll let you know.''

Ashe carried Deborah up the stairs and into her sitting room, but didn't put her down. With her arms around his neck, she stared into his eyes and knew he was going to kiss her. She didn't resist, indeed she welcomed the kiss, needing it desperately. Quick. Hard. And possessive. Deborah sighed.

He carried her over to the window bench and sat down, placing her in his lap. She laid her head on his shoulder.

''Do you want a drink?'' he asked. She shook her head from side to side. ''A bath?'' Another negative shake. ''A nap?''

''All I want is for you to hold me,'' she said, clinging to him. He hugged her fiercely. ''Nobody was hurt.''

''This time. But what about the next time or the time after that? You can't guarantee me that some innocent person won't be harmed because of me.''

''Not because of you, honey! Dammit, why do you insist on blaming yourself?''

''Maybe I should go away. Far away. That way the people I love would be safe.''

''Not necessarily,'' Ashe said. ''Running away isn't the answer if Buck Stansell is out for revenge. If you leave town, he might target Miss Carol or Allen.''

''Oh, God, Ashe, Mother has enough to deal with already.'' Deborah grasped the lapels of Ashe's jacket. ''Promise me that you won't let anything happen to Allen.''

''I won't let anything happen to Allen.'' He kissed her forehead, then smoothed the loose strands of her hair away from her face. ''You love Allen a great deal, don't you?''

''He's the most important person in the world to me. I—I... He's just a little boy.''

Ashe caressed Deborah's face, cupping her cheek in his palm. ''I'll take care of you and Allen. And Miss Carol.''

Gulping in air, Deborah looked at Ashe pleadingly. She needed him, needed his tender loving care, needed his strength, his power.

He stood with her in his arms and carried her into the bedroom, laying her on her bed. He came down over her, turning her to one side as he eased his body onto the bed. Facing her, he removed her jacket, then unbuttoned her blouse. Slowly, carefully, stroking and caressing her as he uncovered more and more of her body, Ashe undressed her completely.

She was a bundle of nerves, her emotions raw. She needed soothing, needed to forget, at least for a few hours, the nightmare her life had become. He hated the feeling of helplessness, knowing he hadn't been able to prevent the drive-by shooting at her office. But he could give her the reassurance and care she needed now. And soon, very soon, he would have to confront her enemy.

Ashe made love to her with his hands and mouth, whispering endearing words of comfort and admiration. Never before had he felt so totally possessive about a woman, wanting her and her alone in a way that bordered on obsession. How had this happened? When had Deborah become the focal point of his existence?

Every touch, every word was meant for her pleasure, but with each touch, each kiss, each heated word, he became lost in the fury of a passion over which he was fast losing control.

He caressed her breasts, loving the way her tight nipples felt beneath his fingertips, loving her hot little cries. He kissed her inner thighs. She sighed, squirming when his tongue turned inward for further exploration.

She moaned and writhed, her body straining for release as Ashe pleasured her, his lips and fingers masterful in their ministrations, bringing her to the very brink, then pausing, only to return her to that moment just before satisfaction.

She cried out, begging him not to prolong the agony, clinging to him, pleading for fulfillment. His words grew more erotic, more suggestive, as he carried her to the edge. With one final stroke of his tongue, he flung her into ecstasy.

Covering her mouth in a heated kiss, he devoured her cries of pleasure. Pulling her close, he reached down and lifted the hand-crocheted afghan and covered her. He lay there holding her while she dozed off to sleep and the noonday sun began its western descent.

His heart beat like a racing stallion. Sweat coated his body. He ached with the need for release. But this time had been for Deborah, not for him. She had needed the powerful fulfillment, and what Deborah needed was far more important to him than what he needed.

When Ashe had sent Buck Stansell a warning, declaring Deborah Vaughn his personal property, it had been a ruse. Now it was a fact. If he had to destroy Buck Stansell to keep Deborah safe, he'd do it. No one was going to harm his woman.

Chapter 12

Deborah set up a temporary office in the library, moving in a computer and borrowing Annie Laurie for the first day. She would do whatever was necessary to protect her employees. That might mean staying away from Vaughn & Posey for a few weeks, but it also meant business as usual. Too many people depended upon the real estate firm for their livelihoods, including Deborah's family. She had no idea whether or not Whitney had any money left in her trust fund, but she doubted it. Not after nearly eleven years of marriage to George Jamison. That meant Whitney, too, depended upon revenue from Vaughn & Posey to keep her and her worthless husband from bankruptcy.

Ashe McLaughlin's return to Sheffield was a mixed blessing. He and Roarke guarded the family night and day. Anyone wanting to harm her or Allen or her mother would have to go through two highly trained professionals. But her personal relationship with Ashe had her confused and uncertain.

She could not deny that she was in love with him. Always had been. Always would be. But the lie about Allen stood between them as surely as Ashe's inability to make a commitment. If she knew Ashe loved her, if she knew he wanted to spend the rest of his life with her, telling Ashe the truth about Allen would not be as difficult. But he hadn't said he loved her and certainly had made her no promises beyond defending her with his life.

"Where do these go?" Ashe stood in the doorway, a stack of file folders in his arms.

"What are those?" she asked.

"They're printouts of all your current files on your present listings." Annie Laurie scurried past Ashe, dragging a swivel desk chair behind her.

Deborah smiled at Ashe; he returned her smile. She couldn't stop looking at him, couldn't stop remembering how it felt when they made love. She was as giddy and light-headed as a teenager in love for the first time. And the crazy thing was she honestly thought Ashe was acting the same way.

He looked incredible this afternoon, but then he always did. Tall, muscular and lean. Gray slacks. Navy blue jacket. Light blue shirt, worn unbuttoned and without a tie. She could see the top curls of dark hair above his open shirt.

They hadn't made love since yesterday and she ached to be with him.

Annie Laurie cleared her throat. "We could take a break. It's after one and we haven't stopped for lunch."

"Good idea." Ashe laid the file folders to the left of the computer atop the antique mahogany desk. "Why don't you two do whatever it is you need to do and I'll tell Mazie we're ready for some of her famous chili. I've been smelling the stuff for hours now."

"Check on Mother, will you?" Deborah asked. "She's been busy all morning working on that cross-stitch piece she wants to finish before she goes in the hospital."

"I'll see if she wants to join us for lunch or have something in her room," Ashe said.

Deborah looked around the library and wondered if it would ever return to normal once she went back to Vaughn & Posey's downtown office. Together she and Annie Laurie had managed to keep everything fairly neat, but office clutter had certainly changed the charming old room's atmosphere.

Deborah fell into the huge, tufted leather chair behind the desk. Her father's desk. Her grandfather's desk.

"So, Neil finally came to his senses and asked you out." Folding her arms behind her, Deborah placed her hands at the back of her head and stretched. "You'll need to leave here early enough to go home and change and—"

"It really isn't a date, Deborah. We're just having dinner and Neil is going to help me study. If I can't pass the test, I'll never become a Realtor. There is no need for me to leave early. Neil's picking me up here after work."

"Neil could have helped you study without taking you out for dinner," Deborah said. "My goodness, Annie Laurie, give the man a little encouragement. I think everyone, except Neil, knows how you feel about him."

"I can hardly throw myself at Neil when he's in love with you." Annie Laurie plopped herself down in the swivel chair she'd placed at the edge of the desk.

"Neil is not in love with me. It's just that he's had a sort of crush on me for years. I've made it perfectly clear that we can never be more than friends."

"I guess none of us can help who we love, can we? I'm in love with Neil, he's in love with you and you're in love with Ashe."

"I see you have this all figured out." In Annie Laurie's version of their love lives, they were beginning to sound like a modern day Southern version of *A Midsummer Night's Dream*. "But if actions speak louder than words, as Mama Mattie says, then I'd say you're the woman Neil cares for the most. After all, I'm not the one he checked on first yesterday after the gunman's drive-by attack."

"He couldn't have gotten to you without going through Ashe and Neil certainly would never try to confront Ashe."

"I'm telling you that if you want Neil, you're going to have to let him know. And I mean in no uncertain terms. Seduce the man."

Annie Laurie gasped. "Why Deborah Luellen Vaughn, what sort of advice is that? Are you saying that if I sleep with Neil, he'll fall madly in love with me?"

"No. I'm saying he's already in love with you, but just doesn't know it. Besides, a man Neil's age isn't going to be seduced unless he wants to be. And I'm telling you, he's ready for you."

"You and Ashe are having an affair, aren't you?" Annie Laurie kept her head bowed, but risked a quick glance in Deborah's direction. "I know it's none of my business, but you've been a good friend to me and I don't want to see you get hurt."

Deborah sighed, then smacked her lips lightly. "Yes, Ashe and I are having an affair. And I know only too well that I could wind up getting hurt again. But I've been in love with him for as long as I can remember. I've never wanted anyone else."

"I know exactly how you feel."

"Then don't wait around. Go get what you want. Neil isn't going anywhere, and take my word for it, you're exactly what Neil needs and what he wants, whether he knows it or not."

Ashe knocked on the doorpost, announcing his presence. "Chili is served in the kitchen. Coffee? Tea? Cola?"

"Tea," Deborah said.

"I'll go wash up and help Mazie get everything on the table." Annie Laurie stood. "Is Miss Carol joining us?"

"Yes, she said for me to come up and get her when we're ready to eat," Ashe said.

"I'll bring her down after I help Mazie." Annie Laurie rushed out of the library.

"What's wrong with her?" Ashe asked.

"I think my advice on her love life upset her."

"What kind of advice did you give her?"

"I told her to seduce Neil."

Ashe bellowed with laughter. "Good God, woman! I'd say you're sending two virgins into uncharted waters. How the hell will they know what to do?"

"I think they'll figure it out." When Ashe walked around the desk, Deborah slipped her arms around his neck.

"Annie Laurie and Neil? How long has this been going on? I thought the guy had a thing for you." Ashe pulled her up against him.

"He thinks he has a thing for me. But given the right encouragement, he'll realize Annie Laurie is the only woman for him." Deborah nuzzled the side of Ashe's neck with her nose. "Besides, Annie Laurie's so in love with Neil she can't see straight. A man would have to be a complete fool to reject that kind of love."

The moment she said the words, she wished them back. She tensed in Ashe's arms.

Taking her chin in one hand, he tilted her face. "It's all right, honey. I know you were talking about Neil, but the shoe certainly fit me once, too, didn't it?" He kissed her. Quick. Hard. Passionate. With his forehead resting on hers, he held her close. "I know what a fool I was eleven years ago. I didn't appreciate what I had. I was too young to know what I wanted or needed."

And now? she wanted to ask. Did he know what he wanted and needed now? "We can't change the past. Either of us."

"We aren't a couple of kids anymore, are we, Deborah? We can handle a love affair without either of us getting hurt this time."

"Yes, of course, we can." She nudged him with her hip. "I'm starving. Let's go eat."

Neil arrived at six-thirty, late and haggard, fuming about the workmen Deborah had hired to clear away the rubble from the office and fussing at the price their contractor was charging them to repair the damage.

Deborah tried to soothe his ruffled tail feathers, but he calmed very little, even after Deborah assured him their insurance would cover most of the costs.

She finally shooed Neil and Annie Laurie out of the house, suggesting the perfect restaurant for their dinner. When she and Ashe turned to close the front door, they realized Neil couldn't get his car started.

Getting out of his car, Neil walked back toward the house, leaving Annie Laurie waiting patiently in the car.

"I've been having trouble with the darn thing for weeks now, but haven't had time to take it in for a check-up."

"Leave it here." Deborah and Ashe met Neil on the porch steps. "Take my Caddy and you two go on for dinner. Keep it for the night. We'll call the garage in the morning and have them come get your car."

"I couldn't possible take your Cadillac."

"I insist. I'll go get the keys."

When she turned to go inside, Ashe grabbed her by the wrist. "I've got the extra set of keys you gave me." He pulled the keys out of his pocket and tossed them to Neil, who caught them, then almost dropped them from his shaky hand.

"I appreciate this," Neil said. "I'll drive safely."

Ashe and Deborah waved goodbye. Arm in arm, they returned

inside to spend the evening with Allen, Miss Carol and Roarke, both of them counting the minutes until bedtime when they could meet at the pool house and make love.

Although the company was pleasant, Ashe wished the time would pass more quickly. He had wanted to drag Deborah off to some secluded spot all day. As the minutes ticked away, he grew more and more restless.

Deborah only partially heard most of what was said during and after dinner, her mind was so completely consumed with Ashe. All she could think about was being alone with him, loving and being loved.

There was no other man like Ashe—not for her. She had always been fascinated by him, even when she'd been a young girl. Indeed, she wondered if his years as a Green Beret hadn't enhanced the very basic male drives that had been born a part of him.

They watched each other, their eyes speaking the words they dared not utter in the presence of others. Deborah had no idea a man could make love to a woman without touching her. Ashe McLaughlin could. And did.

She felt herself growing moist and hot, her body responding to his every glance. She checked her watch for the hundredth time, wishing her mother and Allen would go to bed early. Roarke had excused himself thirty minutes earlier to take a walk around the block as he did each night.

The phone call came three hours after dinner. Ashe took the call, saying very little, but Deborah immediately knew something was terribly wrong.

Ashe replaced the receiver, a solemn expression on his face. His gaze met Deborah's; terror seized her.

"What happened?" she asked.

"There's been an accident," he said.

"What sort of accident?" Carol Vaughn glanced at Allen, who had stopped watching television and looked straight at Ashe.

"A car accident. Neil and Annie Laurie. They've been taken to the hospital in Florence." Ashe's gut instincts told him the car wreck had been no accident. Neil had been driving Deborah's car.

"Oh, dear Lord, no!" Miss Carol clutched her hands together.

"They're both alive. That's all I know." Ashe looked at Deborah. "I think we should go to the hospital immediately."

"Yes, of course we should," she said.

"I'll let Roarke know we're leaving." He turned to Carol. "We'll go by and get Mama Mattie. Pray for them, Miss Carol. Pray for all of us."

Carol nodded, then placed her arm around Allen's shoulders when he started after Ashe and Deborah. "Did somebody do something to Deborah's car? Were they trying to hurt her?" Allen asked.

Ashe halted in the doorway. Deborah rushed over to Allen, pulling him into her arms.

"No, darling, of course not," Deborah kissed Allen's cheek. "Please don't worry about me."

"We don't know what happened," Ashe said. "I'll talk to the police and find out. But Deborah's right. Don't worry about her. I'll take care of her."

Allen hugged Deborah, then released her, waving goodbye as she and Ashe left.

No one, not even Ashe McLaughlin, could make Neil Posey leave Annie Laurie's side, and the doctors allowed him to stay when he told them he was Annie Laurie's fiancé.

When Deborah, Ashe and Mattie Trotter had first arrived at the hospital, Neil had been incoherent, his eyes glazed with tears as he sat holding Annie Laurie's hand. Neil had suffered a few cuts and bruises, but nothing serious. Annie Laurie was unconscious. A concussion, they'd been told. If she came around soon, there should be nothing to worry about; however, if she remained unconscious...

Hour after hour passed without any change in Annie Laurie. Mattie Trotter dozed in the big chair in the corner of the room. Still holding Annie Laurie's hand in his, Neil had laid his head on the side of her bed.

Easing open the door, Ashe glanced around the room, saw his grandmother and Neil sleeping and Deborah looking out the window, watching the sunrise. He set the cardboard carton containing disposable coffee cups on the meal tray, removed the lids from two cups, picked them up and walked over to Deborah.

"Thanks." Deborah took the coffee. "A few more minutes and you would have found me in the other chair over there asleep, too."

"Why the hell doesn't she wake up?" Ashe squeezed the cup he held, pressing a bit of the dark liquid over the edge and onto his hand. "Damn! Good thing this stuff isn't very hot."

"I wish we knew exactly what caused the wreck. I can't believe a careful driver like Neil would have simply lost control of the car." Deborah sipped her coffee.

"Thank God they were both wearing their seat belts. If that pole hadn't crashed through the windshield and sideswiped Annie Laurie on the side of her head, she'd be okay." Ashe drank half his cup of coffee, then set the container down on the windowsill.

"I keep wondering what caused the accident. Neil is such a careful driver. He said the brakes didn't work, that coming off the hill on Court Street, he realized he couldn't slow down, couldn't stop."

"I think he probably panicked," Ashe said. "He realized he was going to slam into the back end of the car in front of him and possibly cause a pileup, so he tried to take the car off the road."

"I have my car serviced often. There's no reason the brakes shouldn't have worked." Deborah clutched her coffee cup in both hands.

"We both know there's a good chance someone tampered with your Caddy." Ashe balled his hands into fists. All night he had fought the desire to smash heads together, to run out of the hospital and hunt down Buck Stansell. But he would wait. Wait until he knew for sure.

A tall, skinny nurse walked into the room. Covering her lips with her index finger, she signaled Deborah and Ashe to be quiet. Silently she went about her business, checking on Annie Laurie, then nodding goodbye as she left.

"Are you hungry?" Ashe asked. "We could go down for breakfast soon."

"Let's wait awhile, until Mama Mattie wakes up. She needs some rest."

A soft knock sounded at the door. Ashe walked over and opened the door a fraction. Detective Morrow, from the Florence police, stood in the hallway.

"Could I speak to you, Mr. McLaughlin? The chief said to let you know what we've found out. He's talked to Chief Burton over in Sheffield and also to Sheriff Blaylock. They both said to fill you in.''

Ashe stepped into the hallway, closing the door behind him. ''Let's have it.''

''The wreck wasn't an accident. Ms. Vaughn's Cadillac had been tampered with. There was no brake fluid. It had all leaked out. Looks like somebody intended for Ms. Vaughn to wreck her car.''

Deborah stood with the door cracked enough to overhear what the detective said. Biting down on her bottom lip, she closed her eyes and said a silent prayer. A prayer to end this madness, to keep those she loved safe.

Ashe thanked Detective Morrow. ''I'd like to see a copy of your mechanic's complete report as soon as possible.'' He shook hands with the policeman, then glanced at Deborah.

She opened the door, walked over to Ashe and tilted her chin defiantly. ''So now we know for sure.''

''Yeah, we know Buck isn't through playing games, and the games are getting more and more deadly.'' Ashe looked at her, his eyes hard, his face tense. ''I think it's time ol' Buck and I have a little talk. Face-to-face.''

''No, Ashe. Please.'' Deborah grabbed him by the arm. ''You can't go off alone and confront a man like Buck Stansell. He could have you murdered on the spot.''

''Yeah, he could, but he won't.'' Ashe put his arm around Deborah, hugging her to his side. ''You forget that I know Buck and his kind. He's had me checked out thoroughly and he isn't about to bring down any more investigations on him and his boys right now. Lon Sparks has kept his mouth shut, but there isn't any doubt who was behind Looney's murder.''

''But Ashe, you should let the police handle Buck Stansell. Talk to Charlie Blaylock. Let him talk to Buck.''

''Honey, you don't understand. There is nothing to link your car's brake failure to Buck Stansell. Sheriff Blaylock has no legal reason to question Buck.'' He kissed Deborah quickly, then gave her a gentle shove away from him. ''I don't need a legal reason. Your safety is the only reason I need. If I don't hunt Buck down after what happened with your car last night, he'll be wondering why.''

Mama Mattie rushed out the door, waving her hands and laughing. "She's awake. She's talking to Neil. Come see. Oh, thank you Lord, she's all right!"

Deborah and Ashe went inside, stopping at the foot of Annie Laurie's bed. Sitting on the side of the bed, Neil held Annie Laurie in his arms, tears streaming down his face.

"Guess what?" Annie Laurie smiled, her bruised face beaming. "Neil just told me that he and I are going to get married."

Everyone laughed. Mama Mattie fluffed Annie Laurie's pillow, then went around the room hugging everyone.

Neil glanced at Deborah and smiled. "Funny how it takes something like this to make a man realize who he loves and how much he loves her."

"I think this is wonderful," Deborah said. "As soon as Annie Laurie is out of this dreadful place, we'll start planning an engagement party."

"Well, I think first we need to let the nurses know that Annie Laurie has regained consciousness," Ashe said. "The doctors will want to examine her."

"I'll go with you." Deborah gave Annie Laurie and Neil loving hugs, then put her arm around Mama Mattie's waist. "Why don't we leave these two alone until the doctors storm in here? We could go have breakfast."

"Sounds good to me."

Mattie followed Ashe and Deborah out into the hallway. After stopping by the nurses' station to alert the staff that Annie Laurie was conscious, the three headed for the elevators. The elevator doors opened and Roarke stepped out, Carol and Allen at his side.

"Mother! Allen! What are y'all doing here?"

Ashe eyed Roarke, who nodded toward Allen, but didn't say anything.

"Allen has been frantic," Carol said. "None of us got any rest last night. He's convinced himself that someone tampered with your car, that you aren't safe."

Deborah drew Allen into her arms, hugging him with fierce motherly protectiveness. "Oh, darling, Ashe isn't going to let anybody hurt me."

Pulling out of Deborah's arms, Allen turned to Ashe. "They think I'm nothing but a baby. They won't tell me the truth. But you will, won't you, Ashe?"

Everyone moved away from the elevators and into the hallway.

Deborah held her breath. Ashe knelt on one knee and put his hand on Allen's shoulder.

"Somebody tampered with the brakes on Deborah's car. They wanted to hurt her. But she's okay. And so is Neil and Annie Laurie."

"But what if Deborah had been driving the car, what if—" Allen beat his fists against Ashe's chest. "I hate Buck Stansell. I'd like to tell him what I think of him. I'd tell him if he hurts Deborah, I'll kill him!"

Ashe drew Allen into his arms. Deborah's eyes glazed with tears, but she saw the look in her mother's eyes, the look that said *He's his father's son. End this lie. Tell Ashe the truth.*

"That's exactly what I'm going to do, go see Buck Stansell." Ashe patted Allen on the back, then stood and looked at Roarke. "You take care of things for me. I have to go talk to a man about revenge."

"No, Ashe!" Deborah reached for Ashe, but Roarke grabbed her, physically restraining her while Ashe entered the elevator and punched the Down button.

Ashe caught Lee Roy and Johnny Joe just as they were leaving. He pulled his car up in the drive, blocking their departure. Both men stayed in their vehicle when Ashe got out and walked over to them. Lee Roy stepped out of his car and faced Ashe.

"You're out bright and early, cousin." Lee Roy grinned, the look on his face as innocent as a newborn baby's.

"I've been up all night." Ashe stood several feet away, his gaze focused on Lee Roy.

"I'm surprised you'd leave your woman alone, even to pay a visit on your relatives."

"This isn't a social call."

"Yeah, I figured as much."

"I want to see Buck. I don't think sending him another message can get my point across like a personal visit."

Johnny Joe opened the passenger side door, got out and placed his elbows on top of the car. "We heard about that wreck last night. Sure was a shame. Guess Miss Deborah Vaughn was lucky she loaned her car out to somebody else."

"Annie Laurie is family." Ashe didn't move a muscle, didn't

even glance Johnny Joe's way. "Lucky for everyone involved, she's going to be all right."

"We wouldn't want to see Annie Laurie come to no harm." Lee Roy grunted. "Hell, we've always been fond of that girl, even though she's no blood kin to us, her being on your mama's side of the family and all."

"I want to see Buck," Ashe repeated. "Today."

"Well, Buck's a busy man," Lee Roy said. "It'll take time to arrange things. You understand."

"Then you get things arranged."

"Buck'll be agreeable to seeing you. He ain't got nothing but the best to say about you, you know. He respects you. And he wouldn't have allowed nothing really bad to happen to your woman."

"Bad things *are* happening. If he's seeking revenge against Deborah for testifying, then he'd better think again. Revenge works both ways."

"Hellfire, Ashe, Buck ain't no fool. He might have given orders to throw a scare into Deborah Vaughn, just for the principle of it, you know. But Lon Sparks ain't nothing but a speck of dirt on Buck's shoe. Not worth the trouble. Buck don't want to cross you."

"I need to hear Buck say that." Ashe turned, walked over to his rental car and opened the door. His gaze focused on the ground, Ashe laid one hand against the side window. "I'll be back this evening, around six. Tell Buck I won't wait any longer than that."

Johnny Joe jerked a .38 revolver out of the back of his belt, aimed it just to the left of Ashe and fired, hitting a nearby tree limb. Ashe didn't blink an eye.

"God a'mighty," Johnny Joe said. "Did you see that? He didn't move!"

"You damned fool." Lee Roy shook his head. "Sorry about that, Ashe. You know Johnny Joe ain't never had a lick of sense."

Ashe looked up and grinned. "Being foolhardy runs in the family, doesn't it? Remind Buck of that inherited trait. Tell him that when it comes to defending my own, I'm not much concerned with the consequences, just the results."

"Ain't nobody in our gang been behind what's happened to your woman since the trial ended," Lee Roy said. "I know you ain't going to believe me, but I'll warn you that you'd better start looking elsewhere. There's somebody else wanting to see Deborah Vaughn dead. It ain't none of us. You'd better start checking out some of her highfalutin friends and relatives. See who's got something to gain if she dies.''

"I'll keep that in mind." Ashe slid behind the wheel of his rented car. "I'll be back at six."

Chapter 13

Ashe parked outside the Sweet Nothings club, a huge blue metal building. From where he sat inside his car, he heard the loud, lonely wail of a guitar. So this was Evie Lovelady's place, huh? Ashe's old teenage girlfriend was now Buck Stansell's private property.

Lee Roy had told Ashe that meeting with Buck would clear up everything and show Ashe that none of *their* bunch was responsible for Deborah's most recent misfortunes. Ashe hadn't mentioned anything to Deborah about Lee Roy's insinuations that someone other than Buck Stansell might have reasons for wanting her dead. She'd been through enough in the last couple of months to last a lifetime, and now Miss Carol faced a second surgery for cancer. There was no point in worrying Deborah with something until he was absolutely sure.

Ashe got out, locked his car and entered the nightspot. Typical Southern honky-tonk. Nothing more. Nothing less. Loud music. Smoky air. Fun-loving rednecks and good old girls ready for a hot time on the town. A country band belted out the latest heart-breaking tunes.

Ashe glanced around, looking for the right person to ask about Buck Stansell. A tall, willowy brunette approached him.

"Long time no see, stranger." Evie slid her arm around Ashe's waist, dropping one hand to cup his buttock. She gave him a quick little squeeze, released him and laughed. "Tight as ever."

"You're looking good, Evie. How've you been?" Ashe grinned at his old girlfriend, one he and Lee Roy had both dated. The scent of her expensive perfume overwhelmed him. Damn, had she taken a bath in the stuff?

"I've been just fine, sugar. Got my own business now, and I hooked me the top dog in these parts." She held up her left hand, showing Ashe the three-carat diamond on her finger. "Of course, I haven't forgotten old friends and our good times together."

"Yeah, we had some good times, didn't we," Ashe said. "But we were just kids fooling around. We're grown up now and life's not fun and games anymore."

"Come on, sugar." Keeping her arm around Ashe's waist, Evie nudged him with her hip. "Let me get you a drink."

"I didn't come here to drink. I came to see Buck."

"Yeah, I know. He's waiting in back for you. I just wanted to be friendly and make you feel welcome, let you know I hadn't forgotten what good friends we used to be."

Ashe followed Evie around the edges of the enormous room, past the dance floor and down a narrow corridor. "You were friends with a lot of guys, before me and after me."

"You're right about that," she said. "I used to be a real good time girl. Now I'm a one-man woman. And Buck's that man."

"Lucky Buck."

Evie smiled. She was almost pretty, Ashe thought. Her eyes were too big, her lips too thin and her cheeks scarred by teen acne, scars she covered with heavy layers of makeup.

"He's waiting on you." Evie opened the last door on the left. "Just remember that Buck thinks of you as family. Your old man and his were tight." She crossed her index and middle fingers. "He's not going to lie to you. If your woman was marked, he'd tell you."

Ashe looked straight into Evie's eyes and knew she believed what she'd told him. Hell, maybe she was right. These men, men like his father and uncle and cousins, might be thieves, drug dealers and murderers, but they did adhere to a certain code of behavior when it came to their own people. And it was possible that they still considered Ashe one of their own.

"Take care of yourself, Evie." Ashe kissed her on the cheek.

She punched him playfully on the arm, stuck her head inside the office and waved at her husband. "Ashe is here, sugar."

Ashe entered Buck's private domain. Evie closed the door, leaving Ashe alone with the man he'd come to question. The man he'd come to warn. The man he would have to kill if all else failed.

"Come on in, Ashe." Buck Stansell pushed back his big black velvet chair and stood. Tall and husky, with a thick mustache and the beginnings of a beer belly, Buck looked every inch the successful no-class gentleman with money that he was. "You haven't got a drink. Didn't Evie offer you something?"

"She offered," Ashe said.

"Evie's still looking good, isn't she? She's held up well. You know she's thirty-five and had three kids. Two of 'em mine." Buck's loud, hardy laughter filled the room.

"Yeah, Evie looks good."

"She's having herself the time of her life running this place. Named it herself. Sweet Nothings. I try to keep her happy. We do that, don't we, Ashe, try to keep our women happy?"

"And safe." Ashe glanced around the office. Expensive bad taste. Money could buy just about everything except good breeding and an innate sense of style.

"That goes without saying." Buck walked around the huge, ornate desk and sat down on the edge. "I had to put a scare into Deborah Vaughn before Lon was convicted. Had to keep up appearances and let Lon think I was doing what I could for him."

"You never meant to harm Deborah or her family?" Ashe asked.

"To be honest with you, I did consider having her taken care of, but once you showed up, I had second thoughts. Lon Sparks is small potatoes. An idiot who made the mistake of doing his business in front of a witness. Guess I should have just gotten rid of him. It might have been easier, but I have a reputation for taking care of my own. You understand how it is?"

"You want me to believe that you're not after Deborah for revenge."

"Why should I need revenge? Lon hasn't got the guts to double-cross me. Besides, he trusts me more than he does the law. He knows I'll keep my promises, one way or the other. He'd rather do time in the pen than spend the rest of his life looking over his shoulder, wondering what day might be his last. As long as he's in prison and keeps his mouth shut, he stays alive. He knows how things work. And he understands I've done all I intend to do on his behalf.''

"Since the trial ended, the Vaughns' garage was set on fire, a gunman destroyed the front of Vaughn & Posey Realty and somebody tampered with the brakes on Deborah's Cadillac.'' Ashe stood, his legs slightly apart, his arms at his sides, his jacket hanging open. "If you want me to believe you had nothing to do with these incidents, then you're going to have to prove it to me."

"Look, old friend, I've given you some leeway because of who your daddy was, because of the man you've become, but I can be pushed only so far.''

"I haven't even begun to push you, Buck, if you have any plans to kill Deborah. There are only a few things in this world worth killing for and even fewer worth dying for. To me, Deborah Vaughn is both. Do you understand?''

"I understood just fine when Lee Roy told me that she was your woman.'' Buck rose off the edge of his desk, straightened the jacket of his three-piece gray pinstriped suit, and ran his hand across the top of his head, smoothing the strands of his slick, brown hair.

"All right, let's say I believe you. If you're telling the truth, then someone else has put out a contract on Deborah. Who?''

"I don't know anything about a contract, but...for a friend, I could find out.''

"For a friend?'' Ashe wasn't sure what to believe, but his gut instincts told him that he just might have to trust Buck Stansell. "Okay, Buck, old friend. Although the local and state authorities may be interested in your illegal dealings, my only concern is Deborah Vaughn. As long as she's safe, I have no reason to cause you any grief.''

"You give me your word and I'll give you mine.'' Buck stuck out his broad, square hand, each finger sporting an expensive ring.

"As long as Deborah and her family are safe, you have nothing to fear from me,'' Ashe said.

"You stay out of my business and, as proof of my innocence and a show of my friendship, I'll make some inquiries and find out who's behind Deborah Vaughn's recent problems.''

Ashe took Buck's hand, exchanging a powerful, macho shake, sealing a deal with the devil, a deal to keep Deborah safe. Ashe knew only too well the kind of man Buck Stansell was, the kind of man his own father had been. Among these redneck hooligans there was a certain code of honor, so Ashe was willing to give Buck the benefit of the doubt. For the time being.

He knew better than to trust Buck completely, knew he'd better watch his back. If Buck thought Ashe posed a threat to his organization, his old friend would have no qualms about killing him. A guy like Buck might even ask Lee Roy to do the job for him, and get some sort of perverse pleasure from seeing which cousin would come out alive.

No, Ashe trusted Buck Stansell only so far. Now wasn't the time to bring the man down. He'd leave that to the authorities. Unless Buck lied to him. Then he'd take care of Buck himself.

Ashe made several calls after he left the Sweet Nothings club, one to Sam Dundee to ask him to initiate an investigation of the people in Deborah's life, those who might benefit from her death. Buck Stansell could be lying about his innocence in the garage fire, the drive-by shooting, and the brakes tampering. If he was telling the truth, then someone else had a motive; someone else wanted Deborah out of the way. But who? And why?

He spoke with the Florence police again, then met with Sheriff Blaylock and Sheffield police chief Ed Burton. He couldn't fault the local authorities. They'd done their jobs the best they could. Ashe especially liked Burton. He respected the man. The two of them had spent the past few hours going over all the leads, all the possibilities.

Ashe had expected the entire Vaughn household to be in bed when he arrived, after all it was nearly eleven. Tapping in the numbers for the security alarm at the back of the house, Ashe unlocked and opened the door. Only the tiny night-light on the refrigerator's ice and water dispenser burned, creating a dim glow in the room.

Wearing a floor-length maroon red robe, Deborah stood in his path, blocking him from entering. Dear God, she looked good enough to eat, all soft and silky, lush and delicious. His first instinct was to reach out and grab her.

"I thought you'd be in bed." He took a step inside the kitchen. Deborah stood right in front of him, not moving an inch. "You didn't get any sleep last night. You should be resting, honey."

"How am I supposed to rest with you out till nearly midnight? Allen asked about you at supper and Mother's been worried."

What was this? She was fit to be tied. What was her problem? He didn't want to argue; he wanted to make love.

"Before I left, I told you I wouldn't be in until late." When he reached out to take her by the shoulders and draw her into his arms, she backed away from him, her blue eyes cold, their expression daring him to touch her.

"I had business to take care of," he said. "The business of keeping you safe, of making sure nothing happens to you or Allen or Miss Carol."

"Roarke was protecting us. Just what were you doing?"

"What the hell's wrong with you, Deborah? Why are you so angry?"

"I'm not angry." He took several steps toward her; she backed farther and farther away. "I was worried. You left here to go see Buck Stansell. You told us you'd be late, but you've been gone nearly five hours. For all I knew, you'd been killed or—"

Ashe charged across the room, drew her into his arms and held her close. "I'm fine, honey. You shouldn't have worried about me. I told you that I know how to handle Buck Stansell and his type."

Hell, she'd been worried about him. He should have called to let her know he was all right. But he wasn't used to having anyone worry about him.

Deborah clung to Ashe, running her hands up and down his arms, clutching him as she laid her head on his chest. She knew she was acting irrationally, but she couldn't help herself. With each passing minute that she had waited for Ashe, she'd grown more tense, more worried, more concerned that Buck Stansell might have killed him.

Smelling his jacket, she jerked her head up and looked at him, then pulled out of his arms. He'd been with a woman, someone who bathed in her perfume.

Deborah glared at him, her small hands tightening into fists. She'd been worried sick about him and he'd been with another woman! Damn him! She'd been a fool to trust Ashe McLaughlin, to believe she was the only woman in his life.

"You smell like a very expensive French whore!"

Ashe laughed. "Actually, I smell like a fairly cheap Alabama whore."

He had left the house hours ago, on a mission to confront Buck Stansell. She'd been half out of her mind with worry. When hours passed and he didn't return, didn't call, she had imagined all sorts of terrible things, but she certainly hadn't thought that he was with another woman.

"I've spent the last two hours crazy with worry, scared to death that something had happened to you, and you've been with some woman!"

Ashe covered his mouth to conceal his chuckle. He'd never seen Deborah this jealous, not even over Whitney. Did she honestly think that he'd been fooling around with someone else? Didn't she realize that he couldn't see anyone except her, that she was the only woman he wanted, that thoughts of her filled his every waking moment?

"Don't you dare stand there and laugh about it!"

"Your life is in danger," Ashe said. "There could be a contract out on you and what are you worried about? You're worried about whether or not I've been out messing around with another woman."

Dammit, he couldn't believe this! She honestly thought he'd touch another woman when he could have her.

"I don't care who you...you...mess around with!"

Ashe came toward her, taking slow, determined steps. He shoved Deborah against the kitchen wall, then braced his hands on each side of her head. "I'm only going to say this once, so listen very carefully. I have not been having sex with another woman. I don't want or need another woman. There has been no one else in my life since the day I came back to Sheffield."

Deborah's breasts rose and fell with her labored breathing. She stared Ashe right in the eye, her gaze hard, her lips trembling, her cheeks flushed. "Then I suppose what I smell on you is some sort of new aftershave."

Ashe leaned down, touching her lips with his. When she turned her head, he reached out and grabbed her chin in his hand, forcing her to face him. "What you smell is Evie Lovelady's perfume.

She wrapped herself around me when I arrived at the Sweet Nothings club tonight to meet with Buck.''

"Evie Lovelady?" Deborah spat the woman's name out between clenched teeth. "You and she used to be quite an item if I recall correctly."

"Evie and most of the guys I hung out with used to be an item. Now she's a happily married woman with three kids. She's Buck's wife."

"So you had to get reacquainted with Evie before your meeting with Buck Stansell." Deborah tried to pull out of Ashe's grip. He leaned forward, trapping her against the wall with his body. "Let me go. I've had enough!"

Ashe rubbed his body against Deborah's, then released his hold on her chin, only to pull her into his arms. "I had no idea I'd come home to this. A jealous woman ready to scratch out my eyes."

"I'm not jealous. I have no reason to be, do I? We haven't made a commitment to each other. We haven't promised each other anything." She couldn't bear having him this close, his hard body pressed intimately against her, his arms holding her tightly. "Just let me go, Ashe. I'm tired and I need some rest. Unless Buck Stansell confessed to trying to kill me and has promised to leave me alone, I think any discussion about your visit with him can wait till morning."

Her jealousy aroused him as much as it irritated and amused him. He had no intention of letting her go to bed angry and hurt and filled with jealous rage.

Ashe lowered his hands to her buttocks, lifting her up and against his arousal. "I've been with Ed Burton for the last couple of hours, discussing my visit with Buck and going over the best way to end this nightmare for you and your family."

"You've been with the police?" She gasped when he began inching her robe and gown upward, gathering more and more of the material in his hands.

He hadn't been in bed with Evie Lovelady. He hadn't been enjoying himself with another woman while she sat at home worrying about him. She should have trusted Ashe. She should have known he wouldn't betray her.

"Buck claims he ended his harassment of you when Lon

Sparks was convicted. He says someone else is after you.'' Ashe buried his face against her neck, nibbling, licking, kissing.

She squirmed in his arms. ''You—you don't believe him, do—do you?'' She could hardly breathe. The blood rushed to her head, her knees weakened, her body moistened.

''I'm not sure.''

He reached under the bunched material he held against her buttocks and stroked her tenderly, then ran his hand up her back, loosening the tie belt of her robe. Nuzzling her soft flesh with his nose, he parted the robe in front, uncovering the rise of her breasts exposed by the low cut nightgown. He took her tight nipple in his mouth, biting her gently through the maroon silk and ecru lace bodice. Deborah moaned with sweet pleasure.

He wanted her. Wanted her bad. He hurt with the need to take her. Here. Now. Hard and fast.

''We'll discuss this tomorrow,'' he said, his breath ragged. If he didn't take her soon, he'd die.

''Tomorrow,'' she agreed, reaching for his jacket, tugging it off his shoulders.

He covered her mouth, thrusting his tongue inside. She clung to his arms, holding onto his jacket sleeves, which she'd managed to bring down to his elbows. He shrugged out of the jacket, letting it fall to the floor. Deborah unbuttoned his shirt, quickly, ripping off the last two buttons in her haste. Ashe removed her silk robe, then pulled her gown down to her waist. He teased her aching nipples with the tips of his fingers. Closing her eyes, she threw her head back and sighed, deep in her throat.

''Deborah,'' he moaned her name. ''Honey...how I want you.''

She reached out to touch his chest, moving her hand back and forth from one pebble hard nipple to the other, curling her fingers in his hair. Lowering her head, she licked one nipple and then the other. She stroked his shoulder holster, then reached around and under his shirt to caress his back, her nails biting into his flesh as she urged him to take her.

Clutching the sides of her gown, he eased it down her hips. It fell into a dark red circle at her feet. He lifted her breasts in his hands, as if testing their weight, then put his mouth on her, suckling her while she unbuckled his belt and lowered his zipper.

Deborah clung to his shoulder, her body aching with desperate need. Her breasts felt heavy, almost painful. Her body clenched and released, dampening, throbbing, ready for the ultimate pleasure.

When Ashe touched her most sensitive spot, she cried out, then covered her mouth with her hand, realizing she should be quiet. Somewhere in the back of her desire-crazed mind, she knew they were not alone in the house, that they were insane for taking such a risk.

He took her hand and placed it around him, telling her without words what he wanted. They stroked and petted each other, then Ashe removed her sheathing hand and whipped her around to face the wall. She shivered. He lifted her hair off her neck and kissed her, then covered her shoulders and back with kisses and stinging little nips which he followed with moist tongue caresses.

When he dropped to his knees behind her, Deborah squirmed and tried to turn around. He held her in place, his hand parting her thighs, his fingers seeking and finding the secret heart of her femininity. All the while he fondled her, he lavished attention on her buttocks, kissing every inch of her sweet, womanly flesh.

Deborah became wild with her need, pleading in soft, almost incoherent words for him to end the torture and take her. When he turned her to face him, she grasped his shoulders and urged him to stand. Instead, he buried his face against her stomach, then nuzzled her intimately and spread her thighs farther apart. While his mouth brought her to the brink of fulfillment, his hands tormented her nipples.

The moment she fell apart, shattering her into a thousand pieces as if she'd been a glass doll, Ashe lifted her in his arms, carried her a few steps over to the kitchen table and set her down. Before she had a chance to catch her breath, he parted her thighs and plunged into her. He filled her completely. The aftershocks of her first release surged within her, gripping him as he invaded her hard and fast, with a fury born of a desire he could not control. The tension built again, higher and higher, and Deborah clung to him. He groaned, then shook from head to toe as he thrust into her one last time, emptying himself as unbearable pleasure claimed them both.

They kissed, again and again. He left her on the table while he picked up their scattered clothes. Her gown and robe. His jacket. Tossing the items over his arm, he lifted her and carried her out of the kitchen, down the hall and up the stairs.

He deposited her in her bed, kissed her on the tip of her nose and looked into her blue, blue eyes.

"Stay the night with me." She clung to him, her arms still draped around his neck.

"And what if Miss Carol or Allen find me in here in the morning?"

"Lock the door."

He smiled and nodded his head. "I'll go back to my room before daylight."

He tossed their clothes on the foot of the bed, pulled out of her embrace and locked the bedroom door. Returning to her side, Ashe lay down and took her into his arms. Tomorrow he would tell her about his meeting with Buck Stansell. Tomorrow they would discuss the possibility that someone else might have a reason to want her dead. But tonight they would keep the rest of the world at bay, they would forget everything and everyone except each other.

He could think of nothing but making love to her all night long, taking her again and again, hearing her wild little cries of pleasure and the way she repeated his name.

For now, this heady, wild passion would be enough. And now was all that mattered.

Chapter 14

Deborah sat in the hospital waiting room, her head resting on Ashe's shoulder, her eyes closed as she ended a prayer pleading with God to spare her mother's life and keep them all safe and well. The doctors had warned them after the first surgery that, although they had every reason to believe all the malignant tissue had been removed, there was always a chance the cancer could return. Now they faced a second cancer, a second surgery.

As if her mother's life hanging in the balance wasn't enough to worry about, Deborah now had to face the possibility that someone other than Buck Stansell was behind the recent threats on her life. Ashe had told her that he had considered waiting until after her mother's surgery before burdening her with Buck's denials and accusations. But with her life, and possibly Allen's, in danger from an unknown source, Ashe felt it necessary she be informed.

Ashe. Ashe. He was like a tower of strength, an endless source of comfort and protection. She could not imagine her life without him. She loved him more now than she ever had, and he had become such an integral part of her life, of all their lives, especially Allen's.

Allen hero-worshiped Ashe, adored him the way so many ten-year-olds adored their fathers. But neither Ashe nor Allen knew their true relationship, and Deborah's guilt at keeping the truth from them ate away at her conscience and broke her heart by slow degrees.

"Ms. Vaughn?" Missy Jenkins, a young LPN for whom Deborah had found a house a few months earlier, stood in the waiting room doorway.

"May we see Mother now?" Deborah asked.

"Yes. She'll be going in to surgery in about thirty-five minutes, if the doctor's schedule doesn't change." Missy's smile made her rather homely face brighten to a certain degree of cuteness. "She'll be getting groggy soon, so you'd better go on in."

Ashe stood, assisted Deborah to her feet and kept his arm around her waist as they walked down the hall. Deborah eased open the door to Carol's private room. Her mother looked so thin and pale lying there on pristine white sheets, an IV connected to her arm.

Carol opened her eyes and smiled. "Good morning, my dears. Come in. They've given me something and I'll be a babbling idiot soon."

Ashe stood beside Deborah, who leaned down and hugged her mother gently, kissing her forehead. "Roarke is bringing Allen by before he takes him to school. I expect they'll be here any minute."

"Such a precious child," Carol said. "So much like you, Deborah."

"Yes, Mother."

"Ashe, thank you for coming back to Sheffield, for keeping watch over us, for bringing Roarke here to help you." Carol closed her eyes, then reopened them, focusing her gaze on Deborah. "I want to talk to you while I still can. I want you to promise me that—"

"Mother, this can wait until you're feeling better." Deborah patted Carol's hand.

"Ashe, would you mind leaving us alone for a few minutes." Carol glanced over her daughter's shoulder at the big man standing guard. "Mother-daughter talk. You understand?"

Ashe squeezed Deborah's shoulder. "I'll be in the waiting room. As soon as Allen arrives, I'll bring him down here."

The moment Ashe closed the door behind him, Carol Vaughn

looked up at Deborah. "I may not live through this surgery, and if I don't—"

"Mother, please, you mustn't talk this way."

Carol held up a hand in restraint. "Hush up. We both know there's a chance that the cancer has spread this time."

"We have to be optimistic, to think only positive thoughts."

"And we shall do just that, but...I want you to promise me you'll tell Ashe the truth about Allen."

"Mother, please...please, don't ask that of me. Not now. Not this way."

Carol gripped Deborah's hand with an amazing amount of strength. "Must I beg you to do this? I begged your father, years ago, not to make us all live a lie. If I had been stronger and stood up to him, none of us would be faced with this dilemma now."

"I'm in love with Ashe. We're lovers. I keep telling myself that he won't leave me this time, that he cares enough to stay. But I'm not sure how he really feels about me, so how can I tell him that I gave birth to his child over ten years ago and have kept that child from him? What if Ashe hates me?"

"Ashe cares deeply for you. He always did." Carol motioned for Deborah to come into her arms.

Deborah cuddled close to her mother's comforting body, careful not to bear her weight on Carol's thin frame. "What if I tell Ashe the truth and he tells Allen?"

"I don't think Ashe will tell Allen. Not now." Carol stroked Deborah's hair, petting her in a loving, motherly fashion. "But you must tell Ashe. Tell him now. Don't wait. Do this for me. Consider it a last request."

"Mother!" Deborah jerked away from Carol, tears filling her eyes. "Please, don't ask this of me."

"I am asking," Carol said. "Tell Ashe that he is Allen's father. Tell him today."

"I can't!" Deborah turned away from her mother, tears trickling down her cheeks. She swatted them away with the tips of her fingers.

"You must tell him, Deborah. If you don't, Mattie will. She won't continue keeping our secret. And someday, you and Ashe must tell Allen the truth. He has a right to know."

Deborah swallowed her tears. Her mother was right. The lie had gone on long enough. It was one thing to keep the truth from

Ashe when he wasn't a part of their lives, but now that he had come to mean so much to Allen, now that she had fallen in love with him all over again, it was wrong to keep the truth from him.

"I promise I'll tell him," Deborah said.

"Today?"

"Yes. Today."

At that precise moment Ashe knocked twice, opened the door and escorted Allen into Carol's room. Ashe glanced at Miss Carol, then at Deborah's tear-stained face. His eyes questioned her silently. She shook her head, saying "Not now," and went over to stand by Allen at her mother's bedside.

Ashe wasn't a man who prayed often, and most people wouldn't call his supplications to a higher power prayers. He wasn't a religious man, wasn't a churchgoer, but he'd been in enough tight situations to know that even the unbelievers called on God for help when all else failed.

Ashe felt a bit out of place in this small hospital chapel. He could remember the last time he'd been in a house of worship. It was a funeral. Another soldier who hadn't made it back to the U.S. alive. A friend whose body had been shipped home.

He knew Deborah was having a difficult time dealing with her mother's surgery and the threats on her own life. It infuriated him that he could do so little to make things easier for her. At the moment, he felt helpless. He might be able to stand between her and danger, to protect her physically, but he hated being unable to defend her against her own fear and sadness.

Miss Carol's condition was in God's hands; all any of them could do was pray and hope for the best. But the continued threats on Deborah's life were another matter. It shouldn't take Sam long to get the information he needed—who besides Buck Stansell had reason to threaten Deborah? Who had something to gain from her death?

Neil Posey was her partner, owning less than forty percent of the business. But what would he have to gain from Deborah's death? And what about Whitney? Did she stand to inherit anything from Deborah? Deborah had told him that Allen and her mother were her beneficiaries.

Maybe Buck had been lying, covering his tracks, knowing Ashe would have no qualms about coming after him if he thought Buck was responsible for harming Deborah.

Ashe looked at her, sitting several feet away from where he stood. Her shoulders trembled. He knew she was crying. They had come into the chapel nearly fifteen minutes ago, and Deborah didn't seem ready to leave yet. Maybe she found some sort of solace here. He hoped she did. He'd do anything, bear any burden, pay any price, to ease her pain.

When she stood, her head still bowed, Ashe walked up behind her, draping his arms around her. She leaned back onto his chest, bracing her head against him, folding her arms over his where they crossed her body.

She smelled so sweet, so fresh and feminine, such a contrast to the medicinal odors that mixed with the strong cleaning solutions in the hospital corridors.

"Miss Carol is going to be all right, honey. You've got to hang on to your faith." Ashe kissed her cheek.

"You can't imagine how close Mother and I are. How much we've shared. How we've depended on each other completely since Daddy died." Closing her eyes, Deborah bit down on her lower lip. She could not put off telling Ashe the truth about Allen any longer. She had promised her mother.

"We're all going to come out of this just fine. Miss Carol is a fighter. She's not going to let the cancer win. And I'm going to make sure y'all are safe." Ashe hugged her fiercely, as if holding her securely in his arms could keep the evil away. "I'm going to find out who's behind the threats and end this nightmare you've been living. After that, you and I have some decisions to make."

Deborah's heart skipped a beat. This was the first time Ashe had even hinted at the possibility they might have a future together. Would he feel differently about her, about their future, once she told him Allen was his son?

"Ashe?"

"Hmm-hmm?"

She pulled away from him enough to turn around in his arms and face him. He placed his hands on both sides of her waist. She looked into his warm hazel eyes, seeing plainly the care and concern he felt.

"Let's go to the back of the room and sit. Please. I have something to tell you. Something to explain."

"What is it, honey?" The pleading tone of her voice unnerved him. He sensed her withdrawal from him even though they were still physically connected. The emotional fear he noted on her face scared the hell out of him. "Deborah?"

She took his hand and led him to chairs in the back of the small chapel. They sat side by side. She wanted to continue holding his hand, to keep the physical contact unbroken, but she wasn't sure she could even look at him when she told him the truth.

Her heartbeat grew louder and louder; she was surprised he couldn't hear its wild thumping. Bracing her back against the chair, she took a deep breath.

"Deborah, are you all right?" She had turned pale, her eyes darkening with what he sensed was fear.

"This isn't easy for me, so please bear with me. Let me tell you what I must without your questioning me. Not until I've said it all. All right?"

Ashe reached for her. Shuddering, she cringed, holding both hands before her in a warning not to touch her. "Deborah, what's going on? I'm totally confused."

"Please remember that I didn't know what Daddy did to you eleven years ago." She took another deep breath. "I thought you'd left town on your own, that you washed your hands of me and..."

"We've been over this already," Ashe said. "I don't see any need to rehash it."

Under different circumstances, there would be no need. If she hadn't gotten pregnant the night they'd made love eleven years ago. If she hadn't given birth to his son. If she hadn't kept Allen's identity a secret.

Dear God, did she have the courage to tell him? Could she make him understand? Ashe McLaughlin was a possessive, protective male, one who would proclaim his fatherhood to the world. If she had ever doubted the deep, primeval urges within him, she knew now, only too well, that the man she loved was a man to be reckoned with, a man whose strength was feared and respected by others.

If only she knew how he truly felt about her. If he loved her, if...

"Please, Ashe, listen to me. A couple of months after that night...our one night together...I—I..."

A tight knot of fear twisted in his gut. "You what?"

"I discovered that I was—" she died a little inside "— pregnant."

God, no! No! He did not want to hear this. He couldn't handle the truth. He didn't want to know that Deborah had lied to him. The one woman on earth he'd thought he could trust.

"What did you do when you found out you were pregnant?" he asked, a deadly numb spreading through his body.

Already his voice had grown cold. How distant would he become when he'd heard the complete truth? "I went to Mother. That's the reason she told Daddy. After you left town, Daddy said that I was better off without you, that he and Mother would take care of me and the baby."

"Your father ran me out of town, knowing you were carrying my child?" Nausea rose in Ashe's throat. Hot, boiling anger churned inside him.

"Daddy arranged for Mother to announce that she was pregnant, but due to her age, she was having problems. He told everyone that Mother needed to be under a specialist's care." Twining her fingers together, Deborah alternated rubbing her thumbs up one palm and then the other. "When I was six months pregnant, we went away, then returned to Sheffield several weeks after Allen was born."

Anger, confusion and hurt swirled inside Ashe's mind and body. The truth had been there all along, staring him in the face. Even Roarke had tried to tell him. But he'd been too blind to see, too sure Deborah wouldn't lie to him, too afraid to accept the possibility that Allen could be his son. He hadn't wanted to admit that he was partially responsible for not having been a part of the boy's life for the past ten years.

"Allen." Ashe spoke the one word.

Allen Vaughn was his son. His and Deborah's. Their one passion-filled sexual encounter eleven years ago had created a child. Why had he never considered the possibility? Despite his rather promiscuous teen years, Ashe had been fairly cautious, using a condom most of the time. But he hadn't taken any precautions that night. He'd been so out of his head, needing and wanting Deborah, that he'd been careless—careless with an innocent girl who had deserved far better treatment.

Deborah looked at Ashe then and saw the mixed emotions bombarding him. "Daddy gave me two choices. I could give my child up for adoption or I could allow him to be raised as my brother."

You could have come to me! he wanted to shout. She should have come to him and told him. He would have taken care of her and their child. "You had a third choice," Ashe said.

"No, I didn't. You left town. You never called or wrote. You didn't give a damn what happened to me. You never asked yourself whether or not you might have gotten me pregnant."

Ashe grabbed her by the shoulders, jerking her up out of her chair as he stood. "Maybe you didn't feel that you could come to me when you first discovered you were pregnant. I guess I halfway understand your reasoning. But later... Mama Mattie always knew how to get in touch with me. All you had to do was ask her for my phone number, my address. Ten years, Deborah. Ten years!"

"I didn't know how you'd feel about being a father, about our child. You didn't love me. You'd made that perfectly clear." She sucked in her cheeks in an effort not to cry, not to fall apart in his arms. Somehow she knew he was in no frame of mind to comfort her. Not now. Not when he was in so much pain himself.

He shook her once, twice, then stopped abruptly and dropped his hands from her shoulders. Glaring at her, he knotted his hands into fists. God, how he wanted to smash his fist against the wall. He wanted to shout his anger, vent his rage.

"Is that why you kept Allen a secret from me?" He ached with the bitterness building inside him. "You were trying to punish me because I'd told you I didn't love you?"

"Of course not!" Seeing the hatred and distrust in his eyes, Deborah knew her worst fears were coming true. "Allen has a good life, surrounded by people who love him."

"Allen's life is a lie," Ashe said, his eyes wild with the hot fury burning inside him. "He thinks Miss Carol is his mother. Hell, he thinks Wallace Vaughn was his father."

"I did what I thought was best." Deborah wanted to touch Ashe, to lay her hand on his chest, to plead for his understanding. But she didn't dare. "I was seventeen years old. My father gave me two choices. Telling you wasn't an option. If I'd thought it was, then I might have—"

"What about later? After your father died? I know Miss Carol wouldn't have tried to prevent you from contacting me."

"After Daddy died, bringing you back into my life was not a consideration. I had to take over my father's business. I had to support Mother and Allen. Besides, you were halfway around the world most of the time."

"Miss Carol wanted me to know, didn't she? Allen was one of the reasons she hired me to protect you."

"Mother has the foolish idea that you once actually cared about me and that if she could get you back into our lives, you wouldn't leave us this time."

Ashe lifted his clenched fists into the air, willing himself to control his rage. He glared at Deborah, at the one woman he thought he could trust. Suddenly, he grabbed her again, barely suppressing the desire to shake her. "I did not *leave* you eleven years ago. Your father ran me out of town. Do you honestly think that anything or anyone could have forced me to leave you if I'd known you were pregnant?"

"Are you saying that you'd have married me for the baby's sake?" Deborah pulled away from him, tears swelling in her eyes. "I didn't want you under those conditions then and I don't want you under those conditions now. I wanted you to love me. Me!" She slapped her hand against her chest. "I wanted you to want me, not marry me because of Allen."

"You've kept my son away from me all his life because of what you wanted? Didn't you ever think about what Allen might want or need? Or even what I wanted or needed?"

Ashe clenched his fists so tightly that his nails bit into the palms of his hands. Pain shot through his head. He couldn't think straight. He needed to escape, to get away from Deborah before he said or did something he would regret. But he couldn't leave her. He was her bodyguard.

"You mustn't tell Allen," she said. "Not now. He's not old enough to understand. That's one of the reasons—the main reason—I haven't told you the truth before now. I was afraid you'd want Allen to know you're his father. I just don't think he could handle the truth as young as he is."

"I won't do anything to hurt Allen." *My son.* Allen Vaughn was his child. He'd looked at the boy and all he'd seen was Deborah. That blond hair, those blue eyes. But Roarke had seen what Ashe had been too blind to see.

"He's a wonderful boy," Deborah said. "The joy of my life."

"Do you know me so little that you think I'd do anything to jeopardize Allen's happiness, his security? I thought you and I had something special between us years ago. I thought you were my best friend. But you didn't trust me enough to come to me and tell me you were pregnant. And now, when I thought we might have a future together, you still couldn't trust me enough to put Allen's life in my hands."

"I do trust you, Ashe. I've put all our lives in your hands. I know I should have told you weeks ago, but... I was afraid."

"How am I going to be able to face Allen and not want to pull him into my arms and tell him I'm his father? God, Deborah do you have any idea how I feel?"

Someone just outside the chapel door cleared their throat. Ashe and Deborah glanced toward the white uniformed young woman.

"Ms. Vaughn, I thought you'd want to know that your mother is out of surgery and the doctor is ready to speak to you."

"How is Mother?"

"She's in recovery. She came through the surgery just fine, but I'm afraid that's all I can tell you," the nurse said.

The next few hours seemed endless to Deborah. She alternated between the desire to scream and the desire to cry. Silent and brooding, Ashe stayed by her side. The barrier of tension between them grew stronger with each passing minute.

Now, when she needed him most, he was as remote, as far removed from her as if he were a million miles away. He would not leave her unguarded, his sense of honor would never allow him to desert her and put her life at risk. But he could not bring himself to look at her or speak to her.

Ashe was afraid of his feelings, of allowing the bitter anger free rein. More than anything, he needed to get away from Deborah, to go off by himself and think.

The doctor's news had been good. In his opinion, they had been lucky once again. They would have to wait a few days on the final test results, but the preliminary findings were positive, giving them every hope that Carol Vaughn would fully recover.

Neither Deborah nor Ashe had gone for lunch. They had paced around the waiting room, avoiding each other, not speaking, not even looking at each other. Their being together had become an agony for her and she had no doubt it had been as difficult for Ashe. She knew he wanted to get away from her, but he couldn't. He was bound by his honor to protect her.

When Miss Carol was returned to her private room, Ashe went in and said a brief hello. Not wanting to say or do anything that might upset Deborah's mother, he made a quick exit, telling Deborah he would remain outside in the hallway and that she should stay with her mother for as long as she wanted to.

"Did you tell him?" Carol Vaughn asked.

"Yes, Mother, I told him."

"And?"

"And everything is going to be all right," Deborah lied. "He understands."

Carol Vaughn smiled. "I knew he would. He'll take good care of you and Allen."

When her mother fell asleep shortly before five in the afternoon, Deborah kissed her pale cheek and walked out into the hallway.

Ashe stood, leaning against the wall, his hands in his pockets. "Is she all right?" he asked.

"She's sleeping." Deborah glanced at Ashe, but when she saw the coldness in his eyes, she looked away. "I'd like to go home now."

He escorted her downstairs to the parking lot, not touching her, not saying another word. The drive home was an exercise in torture. For Deborah. And for Ashe.

Suddenly her life seemed void of hope. Where she had felt the joy of being in love, the resurgence of dreams she'd thought long dead, now she felt only loss. Had she lost Ashe again? Or as in the past, had he never truly been hers?

Deborah glanced out the side window of Ashe's rental car, knowing that nothing she could say or do at this point would change the way he felt. When she heard him dialing his cellular phone, she glanced at him.

Quickly he returned his gaze to the road ahead. "Roarke?"

"How's Miss Carol?" Roarke asked. "Ever since Deborah called Allen with the good news, he's been wanting to talk to his mother."

"Miss Carol is doing real good. We left her sleeping." Ashe paused for a second. "I'm bringing Deborah home, but something's come up and I need to go out. Alone."

"No problem. Want to tell me what's wrong?"

"You were right about Allen."

"How'd you find out?" Roarke asked.

"Deborah told me. Today. While Miss Carol was in surgery."

"What are you going to do?"

"I don't know." Ashe clutched the steering wheel. "I can't see Allen right now. Keep him inside until I drop Deborah off. Okay?"

"Yeah, sure."

Ashe closed his cellular phone and slipped it back into his coat pocket. "Roarke will take care of you."

"Where are you going?" Deborah wished he'd look at her, but he didn't.

"I need to get away by myself for a few hours and do some serious thinking."

"Ashe, please... You may not believe this now, but...I love you."

Without replying, he drove up Montgomery Avenue, turned into the Vaughn driveway and waited for Deborah to get out. She hesitated for just a moment, hoping he would say something. He didn't. She jumped out of the car, slammed the car door and rushed up on the front porch where Roarke stood waiting. Ashe roared away, leaving Deborah alone, uncertain and miserable.

Ashe McLaughlin was good at that, she thought. Leaving. Maybe she had made a mistake, eleven years ago and more recently, too. But everything wasn't her fault. Surely when his temper cooled and he had time to think reasonably, he would see that he wasn't the only injured party in this situation.

She wasn't sure exactly what she had expected when she told him the truth, but somewhere deep inside her, she had hoped he would understand, that he would forgive her.

"Are you all right?" Roarke asked.

"I've been better," she said.

"Allen's helping Mazie set the table for dinner. He's going to want to know why Ashe isn't with you."

"I gather you suspected that Allen was Ashe's son."

"I saw the similarities. I knew your and Ashe's background. He told me about you, one night when we'd both had a little too much to drink."

"Ashe told you about me?"

"That surprises you?" Roarke opened the front door, placed his hand in the small of Deborah's back and followed her into the entrance hall.

"Why would Ashe tell you about me, about our... Ashe didn't love me. I don't understand."

"Maybe he didn't love you," Roarke said. "But he sure as hell never forgot you. He never got over the way he felt about you."

"I was in love with him then, you know. I'm even more in love with him now."

"Give him time to sort out his feelings." Roarke laid his big hand on Deborah's shoulder. "He has a son he never knew about and he's found out that a woman he'd just learned to trust again has kept a secret from him for eleven years."

Allen ran into the entrance hall, Huckleberry loping behind him. "How's Mother? When can I go see her?" Allen glanced around, then stared at the door. "Where's Ashe? Parking the car?"

Deborah took a deep breath. "Ashe had some business to take care of immediately. Mother is doing beautifully, and you can see her tomorrow after school."

"Great. May I call her tonight?"

"Right after dinner," Deborah said.

"Will Ashe be home in time to help me with my math homework?"

"I'm not sure how long his business will take." She wanted to wrap Allen in her arms and keep him safe. For the millionth time in ten years, she wished she could tell him she was his mother. Dear God, how Ashe must feel. But he had no idea the price she had paid pretending to be Allen's sister. Both of them had lost so much not having the chance to be Allen's parents. Maybe it really was all her fault. Maybe Ashe had every right to hate her. If she'd had the strength to stand up to her father or the courage to have gone to Ashe with the truth long ago, things would be different now.

Deborah checked her watch as she followed Allen into the kitchen. Would Ashe return tonight? Tomorrow? Or would he leave town and never return? Oh, he would return, all right. He might leave her again, but he would never leave his son.

Chapter 15

Ashe sat in his car, the window down, the crisp night air chilling him. He had to go home, home to Deborah. For the past several hours he had thought of nothing except what she'd told him about Allen. His son. Their son.

He'd stopped by a local lounge for a couple of drinks, then come down here by the river and parked. He hadn't wanted to be around anybody. He'd needed time alone to lick his wounds, to resolve his feelings for Deborah.

The fact that he cared deeply for her complicated his life considerably. If she hadn't come to mean so much to him, he could hate her. But he didn't hate her; and he didn't even blame her for what she'd done. How could he? Eleven years ago he'd taken her innocence and broken her heart. He'd tried to reject her gently, telling himself he was doing what was best for her. If he'd been a man instead of a thoughtless boy, he would have made sure he hadn't gotten her pregnant. That had been his fault. He'd been the one with experience, not her. And she'd loved him. He hadn't appreciated how much the love of a girl like Deborah meant. Now he did.

Why hadn't he, just once, considered the possibility that he'd gotten her pregnant and she'd kept it a secret from him? Hell, he knew the answer only too well. He couldn't have handled the guilt. He didn't blame her for not coming to him, after the way he'd treated her. Back then she hadn't known her father had run him out of town; she'd thought he'd deserted her.

He couldn't justify her keeping Allen's existence a secret after her father died, but he understood her reasoning. He had hurt her badly. She had been afraid to trust her life and Allen's to him.

Things were different now. She did trust him. And she still loved him. That was the greatest miracle of all. Somehow, he'd find a way to make up all the lost years to Allen and to Deborah.

They needed to talk, to come to an agreement on the best way to handle the situation. He wanted Allen in his life, whether or not they ever told the boy he was his father. And he didn't want to lose Deborah, not again. All these years she had stayed alive inside him, her gentle beauty, her unconditional love.

He didn't know exactly how they'd work things, but they would find a way. He'd make Deborah see that no obstacle was too great for them to overcome—together. He wasn't going to lose his son or his son's mother.

Ashe started the car, turned around and headed toward Sheffield, all the while thinking about what he wanted to say to Deborah. When he turned into the driveway, he noticed every downstairs light was on. In the distance he heard sirens. A police siren and an ambulance siren. His heart raced, his nerves rioted. What if something had happened while he'd been off licking his wounds?

He flew to the front door and through the house, calling for Deborah, then he bellowed out Roarke's name. When he entered the kitchen he ran into Allen, who trembled and cried and spoke in incoherent phrases. Huckleberry stood at Allen's side, licking the child's hand.

Ashe grabbed his son by the shoulders. "Allen, what's wrong? What's happened? Where's Deborah? Where's Roarke?"

"Deborah's gone." Allen sobbed, his big blue eyes wide with fear. "I don't know what happened. I heard Deborah scream."

"When did you hear her scream?"

"Just a little while ago. Her scream woke—woke me and—and Huckleberry."

"Where's Roarke?"

"Outside. In the—the backyard. I think he's dead!" Allen threw his arms around Ashe's waist, hugging him fiercely.

Ashe lifted his son in his arms, sat him down on top of the kitchen table and wiped the tears from his face with his fingers. "Are you all right, Allen?"

"Yes. But I can't find Deborah. Where is she? Did they get her?"

"Show me where Roarke is," Ashe said.

"I called 911. Roarke told me to call, then he passed out."

Ashe lifted Allen down from the table. Holding his son's hand, he followed the boy and his dog outside. Roarke's big body rested in a fallen heap on the patio. Huckleberry sniffed Roarke's semi-automatic, which he'd obviously dropped when he'd passed out. The gun now lay in a pool of fresh blood that had formed on the bricks.

Ashe leaned down, turning Roarke slightly. The man groaned, then opened his eyes.

"Hang in there. An ambulance is on its way," Ashe said. "Can you tell me what happened?"

"She was restless." Roarke spoke slowly, his breath ragged. "Worried about you. Thought she...heard your car parking in the back."

"Where is she?"

"He took her." Roarke tried to lift his head. "Told her not to go outside. Couldn't catch her. Couldn't stop her. She thought it was you."

Ashe inspected Roarke's body and discovered he'd been shot several times. Dear God, why didn't that ambulance hurry? If Roarke lost much more blood, he'd be dead before the medics arrived.

"Take it easy," Ashe said.

"I walked out—out the door." Roarke coughed several times. Blood trickled from the corner of his mouth. "The minute I stepped out... Shot me. Kept shooting."

"Did you get a look at him?"

"Big guy. Ugly. Sandy hair. Jeans. Leather jacket." Roarke lifted his hand, but the effort exerted too much of his strength and his hand fell to his side. "Failed. Sorry."

"I'll find her," Ashe said. "You just hang in there until—" Ashe realized Roarke had passed out again.

Four Sheffield policeman stormed the backyard, their guns drawn. Standing, Ashe placed his arm around Allen's shoulders. His son leaned against him.

"Come on, Allen. After we talk to the police and see Roarke off to the hospital, I'm taking you over to Mama Mattie's. I'll get Chief Burton to send one of his officers to stay with you until I find Deborah."

"You'll find her, won't you, Ashe? You won't let anybody hurt her, will you? You love her, just like I do."

"Yeah, son, you're right. I'll find her, and I'll never let anybody hurt her because I love her, too."

Ashe barely contained the rage inside him, and the fear. Dear God, the nauseating fear! If anything happened to Deborah, it would be his fault. If he hadn't left her, deserted her again, then she wouldn't have been in such a tormented state of mind. She never would have rushed outside without thinking, disobeying Roarke's orders. If anything happened to her or if Roarke died, Ashe would have to face the fact that he could have prevented tonight's disastrous events.

Ashe marched into the Sweet Nothings club like a storm trooper. Evie tried to grab his arm, but he threw her off and swept past the bouncer, making his way to Buck Stansell's office. If the man was responsible for Deborah's kidnapping, he'd kill him with his bare hands—after he found out where Deborah's abductor had taken her.

Ashe flung open the office door. Buck jumped up from behind his desk, like a scared rabbit dodging a hunter's bullet.

"Where is she?" Ashe demanded, as he advanced on Buck, not heeding Buck's bodyguard's warning.

Buck motioned for his bodyguard. Ashe turned on the burly man and, using several expedient thrusts with his hands and feet, brought the big man to his knees.

"Why are you here?" Buck asked.

Evie rushed into the office, bringing two bouncers with her. Ashe pulled his gun from the shoulder holster and aimed it at Buck.

"Call off your goons," Ashe said.

"Take them back inside the club," Buck ordered. "Go with them, sweetie. I can handle things in here."

"Where is Deborah?" Ashe asked again.

"If she's missing, I don't have her," Buck said. "I've been trying to tell you that I'm not behind the recent threats. I thought you were checking into other suspects."

"I'm still checking." With gun in hand, Ashe walked across the room, motioning for the bodyguard to sit. "Someone shot my partner at the Vaughns' home tonight and kidnapped Deborah. What do you know about it?"

Buck eased down in his big velvet chair behind his desk. "I didn't put a contract out on Deborah, but I know who did."

"Keep your hands where I can see them." Ashe stood in front of Buck's desk. "Tell me what you know."

"I checked into the situation for you, just like I said I would." Buck laid his hands flat atop his desk. "I found out that a prominent Sheffield citizen hired one of my former employees—Randy Perry—to kill Deborah. Randy just got out of the pen a couple of months ago and I didn't see fit to rehire him. He's a bad apple, that one."

"Who hired him?"

"A relative of Deborah Vaughn's, one who had a twofold purpose in wanting her dead."

"Who?"

"The man wanted revenge on his wife's former lover, the one he's cried in his beer about here at Sweet Nothings on more than one occasion. Seems his wife has always compared him to this guy and he's always come up lacking."

"Whitney's husband?" Ashe asked.

"Of course, getting back at you isn't his main reason. The inheritance is. Seems Jamison thinks that old Mrs. Vaughn hasn't got much longer to live, and with Deborah out of the way, his wife would be the logical one to oversee Deborah's estate and take custody of Allen."

"My God! Is Whitney involved in this scheme?"

"Don't know. Wouldn't know what I do if Randy hadn't stayed buddies with some of my boys and if he wasn't the type to brag to the ladies."

"Do you have any idea where he's taken Deborah?"

"I didn't even know he'd taken her tonight until you stormed in here. Why don't you pay a visit on Mr. Jamison?"

"That's exactly what I intend to do." Slipping his gun back into the holster, Ashe nodded to the door. "Why don't you walk me out, Buck, old friend?"

Buck chuckled. "Still don't trust me completely? I don't blame you."

Buck walked Ashe all the way outside to his car, then put his hand on Ashe's shoulder. "I'll find out what I can about where Randy's taken your woman. If I learn anything that can help you, I'll send Lee Roy to find you."

Ashe didn't say anything, only nodded, got in his car and headed back to Sheffield, straight to the Jamison house on River Bluff.

The Jamison home sat on the bluff overlooking the Tennessee River. Ashe parked his rental car behind George Jamison's Jaguar. The fury inside him had built to the "kill" stage. His common sense urged him to stay calm, telling him that he must remain in control in order to find Deborah before her kidnapper killed her.

The very thought of Deborah being harmed angered Ashe, and created a pain deep inside him. The hired assassin had been waiting for his chance to get Deborah, and Ashe had given him the perfect opportunity. If anything happened to her, he'd never forgive himself.

He rang the doorbell and waited, checking his gun. After endless minutes of keeping his finger pressed against the buzzer, Whitney Vaughn swung open the double doors and stood in the foyer smiling.

"Why, Ashe McLaughlin, whatever brings you to my house in the middle of the night?"

Ashe noticed she wore nothing but a thin, lavender nightgown, sheer and revealing. "Where's your husband?"

"Not in my bed." She draped her arm around Ashe's neck. He pulled free, walking farther into the foyer. She closed the doors and followed him.

"You want to see George?" she asked. "At this time of night?"

"Where is he?" Ashe went from room to room, turning on lights as he went. "If he's not here, tell me where he is!"

"What the devil's the matter with you, Ashe?" Whitney planted her hand on her slender hip.

"Deborah's been kidnapped," Ashe said. "And I have reason to believe that your husband put out a contract on her life."

"George?" Whitney's large brown eyes widened, giving her an owlish look. "But George would never... What reason would he have?"

"You tell me. For all I know you could be in on it with him."

"I'd never do anything to hurt Deborah. She's my cousin. I care deeply for her."

"Where's your husband?" Grabbing Whitney by the shoulders, Ashe shook her soundly.

"He—he's upstairs in his room."

"Show me." Ashe jerked Whitney around, grasping her wrist. "I don't have any time to lose."

Whitney ran up the stairs, Ashe beside her. Halting, she pointed to a closed door. "That's George's room."

Ashe crashed through the door. George Jamison had one leg in his trousers, the other on the floor. Ashe grabbed him around the neck. When George swayed, Ashe steadied him by slamming him up against the wall. Whitney stepped inside, but stayed by the open door.

"Where did Randy Perry take Deborah?" Ashe tightened his hold on George's neck.

"I—I don't know what you're—you're talking about." George pawed at Ashe's hand, trying unsuccessfully to loosen his hold around his neck.

"Don't play games with me, Jamison. You tell me what I want to know or I'll break your neck. Do you understand me?"

"For pity's sake, Whitney, call the police," George said.

"I'm not doing anything." Whitney glared at her husband. "If you hired someone to kill Deborah, you'd better tell Ashe what he wants to know."

"Please, believe me. I don't know what he's talking about."

With his right hand still pressed against George's windpipe, Ashe reached inside his jacket and retrieved his gun from the shoulder holster. He pointed his 9mm directly at George's temple.

"If you have any doubts that I'd kill you, then you don't know me at all. Deborah Vaughn is the most important thing in this world to me. I'd lay down my life for her. Do you understand what I'm saying, Jamison?''

"Don't kill me," George pleaded.

Ashe despised the weakness in this man. He pressed the 9mm against George's head. "Where has Perry taken Deborah?"

"I don't know!" When Ashe glared at him, fury in his eyes, George cried out. "I paid him $5,000 and promised him $5,000 more to do the job."

"You hired someone to kill Deborah!" Whitney screamed, tears forming in her eyes. "I knew you weren't much of a man, but I never realized what a monster you are. How could you do it? Deborah has taken care of us for years. I don't know what we would have done without her."

"But don't you see, my darling, I did it for us." George tried to turn his head so he could look at his wife, but Ashe kept him trapped against the wall, the 9mm at his temple, Ashe's big hand at his throat.

"With Deborah out of the way and Miss Carol dying soon, then who but to you would the courts award custody of Allen?" George said. "Who but you would be in control of Allen's inheritance?"

"I can't believe this." Whitney slumped against the doorpost, as if her slender weight was more than she could bear. "You're out of your mind!"

"I'd have never thought of killing Deborah. But once the threats started, I thought how lucky for us if Buck Stansell had her killed." George trembled. "Look, Ashe, killing me won't save Deborah. I hired Perry. Yes, I admit it. Once the trial ended and I realized that Buck Stansell wasn't going to continue with his threats, I decided I could hire someone to kill Deborah and everyone would think Stansell and his gang were responsible."

"You sorry son of a bitch," Ashe growled, then returned his gun to its holster. He grabbed George around the neck with both hands, lifting him off the floor.

George gasped for air, his feet dangling, his arms flying about, trying to catch hold of Ashe.

Whitney screamed. "You're killing him, Ashe!"

Not one rational, reasonable thought entered Ashe's head. He worked on instincts alone. His hands tightened around George's neck. With one swift move, he could break the man's neck. This stupid fool was responsible for whatever might happen to Deborah before Ashe could find her. He didn't deserve to live.

"Ashe, think what you're doing," Whitney cried out, beating against Ashe's back with her tight little fists. "He's not worth it. Do you hear me? George isn't worth it!"

"Put him down, cousin," Lee Roy Brennan said from where he stood in the doorway. "She's right. He's not worth it."

Without loosening his hold on George, Ashe glanced at Lee Roy. "Did Buck send you?"

"We found out where Randy might have taken Deborah."

"A reliable source?" Ashe asked.

"A friend of Evie's," Lee Roy said. "A gal Randy's sleeping with. He shared his plans with her, telling her he'd be coming into another $5,000 after the job was done."

"Where did she say he planned to take Deborah?" Ashe set George down on his feet, but kept his hands around his throat.

"Somewhere close to Deborah's house in downtown Sheffield. Some deserted warehouse."

"What deserted warehouse?"

"My guess is the old streetcar warehouse."

Ashe released George, allowing him to fall to his knees. With expert ease, Ashe snapped the purple top sheet from George's bed and ripped off two long strips. Using his foot, he pressed George over against the bed, jerked his hands behind his back and hogtied the man with the scraps of his own bed sheet.

"Whitney, don't let your husband out of your sight until the police arrive."

"Don't worry," she said. "I'll kill him myself if he even tries to move."

"Come on." Ashe motioned to Lee Roy, who followed him out into the hall and down the stairs.

Lee Roy grabbed Ashe at the front door. "When we find her, she might not be alive."

"She'll be alive! She has to be."

"Even if she is, it could be bad. Randy was in the pen for rape."

"Whatever happens, he's a dead man," Ashe said.

* * *

Ashe called the Sheffield police on his cellular phone, telling them where he was going and asking them to send some officers over to George Jamison's home. Lee Roy followed in his truck, the two cousins speeding along Jackson Highway, racing toward downtown Sheffield. Ashe prayed, begging God to keep Deborah safe, offering his own life in place of hers.

She couldn't bear his touch, rough and clammy. She'd screamed the first time he'd squeezed her breast, but he'd slapped her so hard she'd fallen to her knees in pain.

He was going to rape her before he killed her. He'd told her what to expect.

This was all her fault. Her own stupidity had cost Roarke his life and now would cost her hers. How could she have been so stupid, rushing out to meet Ashe, when in fact she'd run headlong into her kidnapper?

Did Ashe know what had happened? Was he searching for her? *Please, God, please let him find me in time.*

"I ain't never had me no society lady before." Randy Perry snickered as he ripped open Deborah's blouse, exposing her lace-covered breasts.

Deborah tried to back away from him, but he grabbed her, dragged her up against him and thrust his sour tongue into her mouth. Gagging, she fought him, hitting him repeatedly as she kicked at his legs.

He threw her to the floor and came down on top of her, crushing the breath out of her. "You like it rough, huh, society lady? Well, ol' randy Randy can give it to you rough."

He ran his hand up her leg and under her skirt, fondling her hip. When he lowered his head to kiss her again, she spat in his face. He laughed. Then he slapped her.

Deborah closed her eyes against the reality of what was happening to her. She retreated into a silent, constant prayer for Ashe to rescue her before it was too late.

Chapter 16

The old streetcar warehouse stood in darkness, the moonlight casting shadows across the window panes. Ashe could hear nothing except the loud pounding of his heart. He couldn't ever remembering being so scared, not even in battle. But then Deborah's life had not been in jeopardy, only his.

He drove down the street slowly, looking for any sign that someone had broken into the empty building. He circled the block. An older model Pontiac Grand Prix was parked directly across from the warehouse. Ashe eased his Buick up behind it, got out and checked the license plate. A Colbert County tag.

Lee Roy pulled his truck up behind Ashe, getting out and following his cousin across the street.

"It's Randy's car," Lee Roy said. "He got it off a fellow who brings stolen cars in from Mississippi."

"That means they're here." Ashe removed his gun from the holster before crossing the street. "Look, you may not want to get involved in this. I've phoned for the police. They should be here any time now."

"All I'm doing is helping my cousin rescue his woman. Right? I don't know nothing about nothing. We made a lucky guess as to who had kidnapped Deborah and about where he'd taken her."

"Yeah, right." Ashe nodded toward the building. "You check that side and I'll check this side. If you find them, don't act on your own. Randy Perry is mine."

"Got you." Lee Roy rounded the side of the warehouse.

Ashe crept along the wall, checking for an unlocked door, looking for any sign of forced entry. Then he saw it. Toward the back of the building, a dim light flickered.

Ashe found a jimmied lock, the door standing partially open. Taking every precaution not to alert Randy Perry to his presence inside the warehouse, Ashe followed the light source, keeping his body pressed close to the wall as he made his way inside, searching for any sign of Deborah.

A lone lantern rested on the floor, spreading a circle of light around it. Deborah lay at Randy Perry's feet, her blouse in shreds, her skirt bunched up around her hips, half covering the gleaming white of her lace underwear. Ashe garnered all his willpower, resisting the urge to let out a masculine cry of rage. He wanted to kill the big, bearded slob of a man who gazed down at a half-naked Deborah as he unzipped his jeans.

Ashe whirled away from the wall, aiming his gun at Deborah's kidnapper. In a split second, before Ashe could fire his 9mm, Perry fell to the floor, grabbing Deborah into his arms. Lifting her along with himself, he rose to his knees, holding Deborah in front of him, his thick arm around her neck.

"I'll break her neck like a twig," Perry warned Ashe. "And that would be a pity. She's got such a pretty little neck."

"You're a dead man, Perry!"

Randy Perry stood, jerking Deborah to her feet, using her body as a shield. Walking himself and Deborah backward, he kicked the lantern across the floor, extinguishing the flame and sending the room into darkness. The lantern rolled into a corner, crashing into the wall.

Ashe swore aloud. His breathing quickened. It would take a few minutes for his eyes to adjust to the darkness, but then it would take just as long for Perry to be able to maneuver without any light.

Sirens blared like the thunder of an attacking elephant herd. Tires screeched. Doors slammed. Chief Burton's voice rang out loud and clear, telling Randy Perry that the warehouse was surrounded.

"Don't look like I got nothing to lose by finishing this job, does it?" Perry called out, taunting Ashe.

"Be careful, Ashe." Deborah's voice sounded shaky but strong.

"Deborah!" Ashe couldn't see her now, but he could make out the direction in which Perry was moving from the sound of their voices.

"Don't hurt her," Ashe said. "If you do, I'll kill you before the police come through the door."

"He has a gun, Ashe. Don't—"

Randy Perry held Deborah in front of him as he walked backward, directly past a row of windows. Moonlight created enough illumination for Ashe to see the gun Perry held to the side of Deborah's face, his other meaty hand covering her mouth.

"Let her go." Ashe issued one final warning.

Randy Perry laughed. "No way in hell!"

Ashe aimed and fired. Deborah screamed. Randy Perry slumped, knocking Deborah down as he dropped to the floor. Blood spurted from the lone bullet wound in his head. Deborah looked over at the man's still body, then crawled away from him. Standing hurriedly, she ran toward Ashe.

He grabbed her, pulling her into his arms, encompassing her in his tight embrace. She gulped for air, her body racked with heavy, dry sobs. Ashe rubbed her back, petting her tenderly.

"It's all right, honey. You're safe now. You're safe."

The police stormed into the warehouse after hearing the gunshot. They found Randy Perry lying on the floor in a pool of his own blood and a partially undressed Deborah Vaughn clinging to Ashe McLaughlin.

"Is she all right?" Ed Burton walked over to Ashe. "Did he hurt her?"

"She'll be all right." Ashe slipped his gun into the holster, then removed his jacket and placed it around Deborah's shoulders. "I'm taking her home."

"Maybe you should take her to the hospital. If she's been raped—"

"No!" Deborah cried. "He—he didn't—didn't rape me. He would have, but Ashe—Ashe—"

Ashe lifted her into his arms, carried her past a row of gawking police officers and out onto the sidewalk. She laid her head on his chest. He kissed the top of her head.

Standing by the side of Ashe's car, Lee Roy opened the door. Ashe deposited Deborah inside, got in and looked up at his cousin.

"Thanks," Ashe said. "Pass it along. Okay?"

"Yeah. Sure thing. Glad we made it in time." Lee Roy grinned. "Guess I'll be seeing you from time to time. I figure you'll be staying around these parts to keep an eye on your woman."

Lee Roy walked over to his truck, got in and drove off. Ashe removed his jacket and draped it around Deborah's shoulders, then pulled her close to his side, started his car and headed southwest.

"Where are we going?" she asked.

"Allen is with Mama Mattie. Chief Burton has an officer keeping an eye on them."

"I can't let Allen see me like this, with my clothes—" She swallowed hard, biting the insides of her cheeks in an effort not to cry.

"He'll be asleep when we get there. I'm sure Annie Laurie can find you something of hers to put on." Ashe hugged Deborah, leaning the side of his head against the top of hers. "It's all over, honey. Go ahead and cry. Let it all out."

"I can't cry," she said. "I hurt too much to cry."

"Did you tell Ed Burton the truth? Randy Perry didn't rape you, did he?"

"No, he didn't. He slapped me around. He scared me to death. Oh, Ashe, how can you say it's over? Buck Stansell will just hire someone else to come after me."

Ashe pulled the car off Shop Pike and into the parking lot of the old converted train depot. Killing the motor, he turned to Deborah. She looked so pale, there in the moonlight, her eyes overly bright and slightly glazed with tears. But she hadn't cried, hadn't gone into hysterics. His strong, brave Deborah. Taking her face in both hands, he lowered his lips to hers and kissed her tenderly.

Still holding her face, he shook his head. "It's over, honey. Believe me. Buck Stansell didn't put out a contract on you. George Jamison did."

Deborah gasped. "George!"

Ashe slipped one arm behind her and crossed the other over

her body, bringing her into the comfort of his embrace. "Buck was telling me the truth. Lon Sparks wasn't an important enough cog in their wheel for Buck to make an example out of you. Especially when he found out he'd have to contend with me."

"But George? I can't believe he would... Ashe, are you sure? How did you find out?"

"I got a confession out of George, tonight."

"But—but why would George want to kill me? I don't understand."

"The man has a sick, devious, greedy mind. He thought Miss Carol would die, then if you were out of the way, Whitney would be given custody of Allen and the entire Vaughn estate."

Deborah gripped Ashe's arms. "What about Whitney? Does she know what he did? Oh, dear Lord, is she all right?"

That was his Deborah, kindhearted and loving to the bitter end. "Yeah, she knows. And she's all right. When she found out, she was ready to kill George herself."

"So, it really is over, isn't it?" Deborah sighed, her body relaxing in Ashe's embrace. "Oh, Ashe, I was so afraid. I didn't know if you'd find me in time."

Ashe kissed the top of her head, the side of her face, his arms tightening around her. "I had to find you, didn't you know that? I couldn't let anything happen to you. Not now when we've just found each other again. Not when I've realized exactly how much you mean to me."

The tears she'd been holding at bay rose in her throat, choking her. She swallowed hard. "I didn't want to die. And I was scared, so scared. I didn't want to leave Allen and Mother and...you."

"We have a lot to talk about," Ashe said. "But not now. You've been through hell these last few hours. We've both been through hell!"

"I want to see Allen. I want to take him home. Once we're all safe and together, then you and I can talk and work things out." She would have to share Allen with his father in the future. Would that mean trips to Atlanta for Allen, or was there a possibility that Ashe would return to Sheffield permanently? "We can work things out, can't we, Ashe?"

"Yeah, honey, we most certainly can work everything out."

Keeping one arm around Deborah, Ashe started the car and drove them straight to Mama Mattie's. The moment they pulled into the driveway, Annie Laurie rushed outside. The fading bruises on the side of her face were the only physical reminder of the accident four days ago. After a two-day hospital stay and countless tests, the doctors had sent her home with a caution to take it easy for a while.

Opening the passenger door, Annie Laurie grabbed Deborah when she stepped out of the Buick Regal.

A young police officer followed Annie Laurie. "I see you found Ms. Vaughn."

"You're all right." Annie Laurie glanced at Ashe. "You're both all right." She looked at Deborah's tattered clothing and gasped. "Oh, God, did he—"

"No," Deborah said. "Ashe found us before he really hurt me." She ran a hand down across her torn skirt. "I need something to put on before Allen sees me."

"Allen's asleep. Finally. He's lying on the couch with his head in Mama Mattie's lap. That's the reason she didn't come out here with me. She didn't want to wake him up. Poor baby has been worried sick and we thought he'd never rest."

"Thank you for keeping watch over Allen." Ashe got out of the car and shook hands with the officer. "The man who kidnapped Ms. Vaughn is dead."

"Yeah, Chief Burton just called. He said to tell you that George Jamison has been arrested and is in jail."

"Tell the chief that Ms. Vaughn and I will be glad to answer any questions tomorrow." Ashe placed his arm around Deborah's shoulders. "We'll go around to the back door. Annie Laurie, I hope you find Deborah something to wear before we wake Allen and take him home."

Deborah and Ashe walked around the house to the back porch, while Annie Laurie went in the front and met them at the kitchen door. Annie Laurie ushered Deborah into her bedroom. Ashe walked through the kitchen and the small dining area adjacent to the living room and stood in the arched opening, looking across the room at his grandmother and his son. His son!

Mattie Trotter placed her index finger over her lips, cautioning Ashe to be quiet. He nodded and smiled. Ashe noticed his grandmother's old photo album in Allen's arms.

More than anything, Ashe wanted to lift Allen in his arms and hold him. His child. His son. Ten years of the boy's life had already passed. Would they ever be able to make up the lost time? Would Allen ever accept him as a father?

When Deborah and Annie Laurie emerged from the bedroom, Deborah walked over to Ashe and handed him his jacket. He slipped it on, then put his arm around her waist. She took his hand in hers. He thought she looked beautiful in Annie Laurie's little burgundy-checked shirtwaist dress, her long hair disheveled and her face void of any makeup.

"Let's go get our son and take him home," she said.

Mama Mattie's eyes widened, her mouth gaping as she looked at Deborah and Ashe, then down at the sleeping child.

"What?" Annie Laurie said. "Allen is—"

"Allen is Deborah's child," Ashe whispered. "Deborah's and mine."

"But—but... Oh, my goodness."

With Ashe at her side, Deborah walked across the living room, knelt beside the sofa and kissed Allen on the cheek. He stirred, the photo album dropping to the floor. The boy opened his eyes, saw Deborah and jumped up into her open arms.

"You're all right!" He squealed with happiness. "I knew Ashe would find you. I knew he wouldn't let anything bad happen to you."

"And you were so right," Deborah said. "Ashe is my hero." She looked up at him with all the love in her heart showing plainly on her face.

Reaching down on the floor beside the sofa, Allen picked up the photo album. "Mama Mattie's been showing me pictures of Ashe when he was just a kid and then when he was a teenager. He was big for his age, just like I am. How about that?"

"Yeah, how about that?" Mama Mattie said, glancing at Ashe.

Deborah sat down on the sofa beside Allen. He laid the photo album in her lap. "Look at the pictures of you and Ashe together. You two must have spent a lot of time together. Mama Mattie has a ton of pictures of you two."

"They were the best of friends." Mattie's eyes glazed with tears.

"Hey, they told me they weren't an item, you know, that they didn't go together, but I think they had a thing for each other." Allen looked up at Ashe. "Come on, Ashe, fess up, you and Deborah were more than friends."

"Back then we were friends, but we should have been sweethearts," Ashe said. "You know what, pal? I've just realized, very recently, that I've always loved Deborah."

Deborah raised her eyes, looking at Ashe with disbelief. Had she heard him correctly? Had he just confessed his love? Here, in front of his grandmother and cousin. In front of their son.

"A lot has happened tonight," Ashe said. "Deborah and I haven't had a chance to talk about the future, but I was wondering if I could have your permission to ask Deborah to marry me?"

"Wow-wee!" Allen jumped up off the sofa, threw himself against Ashe and hugged him, then turned to Deborah. "Are you going to say yes? It'd be neat to have Ashe for a brother-in-law."

"Don't I have any say in this matter?" Deborah asked, not sure she liked being bulldozed by her two men.

Ashe kept his hand on Allen's shoulder when he spoke to Deborah. "Doesn't look like you get a vote. Allen and I are a two thirds majority."

"Is that right?" The look on Allen's face broke Deborah's heart. She couldn't remember a time when her son had been so happy. He adored Ashe. That was plain to see.

Ashe pulled Deborah up off the sofa and slipped his arm around her waist. Allen grinned from ear to ear.

"Once I was too big a fool to realize what I had," Ashe said. "But now I know, and I'll never let you go, Deborah. Never."

"Isn't this great!" Allen hugged Ashe and Deborah, then spun around to bring Mattie and Annie Laurie into the celebration. "Just think, when Deborah and Ashe get married, they'll sort of be like parents to me. Deborah's always been a second mother to me. Now, I'll have a dad, won't I?"

"Yes, son, you will." Ashe could barely speak, the emotions erupting inside him overwhelming in their intensity.

"I like this just fine," Allen said. "Everything is working out great. I sure am glad Mother hired Ashe to protect Deborah."

"So am I," Ashe said.

"Well, it's time we go home, don't you think?" Deborah patted Allen on the back.

"Could I stay here with Mama Mattie?" Allen asked. "We've already made plans for tomorrow. She said I didn't have to go to school. We're going to the hospital to see Mother and Roarke."

"Roarke!" Ashe and Deborah said simultaneously.

"He's going to be fine," Mattie said. "We've called the hospital several times. He came through surgery with flying colors. Looks like he'll be laid up for a spell, but he's going to live."

"Thank God." Deborah leaned against Ashe. "What happened to him was my fault."

"Can I stay with Mama Mattie?" Allen repeated his request. "She's going to make biscuits and chocolate sauce for breakfast, then we're going to bake tea cakes and take Mother and Roarke some. Please, Deborah, let me stay."

"Allen, I don't know. I—"

"Please. Besides, you and Ashe probably want to be alone anyway."

"He's right," Ashe said. "Let him stay. We can pick him up tomorrow."

Fighting her motherly reluctance, Deborah agreed. "Oh, all right." She hugged Allen. "I love you, you know."

"Yeah, I know." Allen glanced over at Ashe. "You'd better always love her and be good to her or you'll have to answer to me."

Everyone in the room laughed, Deborah thinking how much like Ashe Allen was.

"You have my word, son," Ashe vowed.

Deborah lay in Ashe's arms as dawn spread its pink glow across the eastern horizon. They'd come home, showered together and fallen into bed, making love like two wild animals. They had fallen asleep without talking. They hadn't discussed the kidnapping or the fact that Ashe had killed Randy Perry, nor had they mentioned Allen and their future."

Ashe stroked her naked hip. "What are you thinking about?"

"About how we need to talk."

"Yeah, I guess we kind of got distracted by other things." He grinned, then kissed her.

"I was too exhausted to think straight and I guess you were, too." She laid her hand on his chest, directly over his heart. "What are you going to do about Allen?"

"I'm going to marry his mother—" Ashe pulled Deborah into his arms "—and be a father to him."

"Are you going to tell him the truth?"

"Someday I think we should. In a few years, when he's a little older and can understand." Ashe nuzzled Deborah's neck with his nose. "We need some time to become a family, for the three of us to bond."

"What about your job? Are you willing to move back to Sheffield? I can't leave Mother, and Allen wouldn't want to live anywhere else. This is his home."

"I can find a job around here. Who knows, ol' Buck might offer me a position as his bodyguard."

Deborah slapped Ashe on the chest. "That isn't a joking matter."

"Let it all go, honey. It's over. Let's don't look back, let's look forward. What's done is done. We've all lived through a pretty rough time, but it *is* over."

Deborah knew she had to face the truth and had to confront Ashe with her fears. She couldn't marry him if he confirmed her doubts.

"I can't marry you." She pulled away from Ashe, but he jerked her up against him.

"What do you mean you can't marry me?"

"I told you that I didn't want you to marry me because of Allen. That was true eleven years ago and it's true now."

"I'm not marrying you because of Allen. Didn't you hear me tell you and Allen and Mama Mattie and Annie Laurie that I'd been a fool to ever let you go, that I realize I've always loved you?" Ashe tilted her chin with one hand while he held her close with the other.

"There are all kinds of love, Ashe. As much as I love you, I can't spend the rest of my life married to a man who doesn't feel the same way about me."

"You're confusing me, honey. What the hell are we talking about here? I've said I love you."

"Not the way I want to be loved."

"What does that mean?"

"It means that..." Pulling out of his arms, she got out of bed, picked up her robe off the floor and put it on.

"Deborah?" Ashe stood, totally naked, and followed her over to the windows.

"I came close to dying tonight," she said, her back to him. "I realized how very much I want to live. I've been in love with you for as long as I can remember, but you didn't feel the same way about me. You still don't."

He eased his arms around her, leaning her back against his chest, enfolding her in his embrace. "If a man ever loved a woman, I love you. Nothing and no one is more important to me."

She trembled. He soothed her, caressing her arms, kissing the side of her face.

"You've been a part of me forever," he said. "Maybe I didn't have sense enough to know I loved you eleven years ago, but you've stayed alive inside me for all these years. I've never been able to forget you. Now I know why."

She turned in his arms, her eyes filled with tears. "Why?"

"Because I'm in love with you, Deborah. Deeply, passionately, completely in love with you."

"Oh, Ashe."

Lifting her in his arms, he carried her back to bed. Laying her down, he eased off her robe, then braced himself above her. "Marry me. Let me spend the rest of my life proving to you how much I love you."

"Yes. Yes."

He buried himself within the welcoming folds of her body, telling her again and again that he loved her. She accepted him and his proclamations of love. Giving and taking, sharing in equal measure, they reached fulfillment together. Resting in the aftermath, they accepted the beautiful reality of their life, knowing in their hearts that love and happiness was truly theirs.

Epilogue

The whole family gathered around the shiny, new, black Mitsubishi 3000 GT. Mattie Trotter clicked snapshot after snapshot, while Carol Vaughn zoomed in on Allen's beaming face with her camcorder.

"We couldn't wait until after graduation tonight," Deborah said. "We thought you might want to drive it to your class party afterward."

"Wow! I hoped for something like this, but I wasn't sure. Thanks, Mom!" Tall, lanky, handsome eighteen-year-old Allen hugged Deborah. "I'll bet you picked her out for me, didn't you, Dad?"

Ashe grinned. "Yeah. Your mother wanted to get you something a little more practical."

"I helped, too," seven-year-old Martha McLaughlin said, tugging on her big brother's pants leg. "I wanted to get the red one, but Daddy said no, that you'd like the black one better."

"He was right, squirt." Allen lifted his little sister up in his arms. "I think I'll take this baby for a spin around the block. Want to go with me, Martha?"

"You bet I do."

"Don't be gone too long," Deborah said. "You'll want time

to go over your valedictory speech one more time. I know you want it to be perfect."

Allen deposited his sister in the car, jumped in and revved the motor. "Listen to her purr."

"Don't drive too fast!" Deborah cautioned.

"Hey, if I get a speeding ticket, my dad will take care of it for me," Allen said jokingly. "He's the sheriff, you know."

Ashe reached out and took two-year-old Jamie McLaughlin off his mother's hip, then turned to watch his older son spin out of the driveway in his high school graduation present.

"Don't worry, honey. They'll be all right. Allen won't take any chances with Martha in the car with him. Besides, he drives like I do."

"I know. That's what worries me."

Everyone laughed. Ashe kissed his wife, saying a silent prayer of thanks to the powers that be for his many blessings.

All the dreams of his youth had come true. He had married his beautiful society wife and she'd given him three perfect children. Having been elected sheriff of Colbert County when Charlie Blaylock retired, Ashe had acquired the respect and admiration of the community, especially after he'd helped the Feds put Buck Stansell behind bars and break up the local crime ring.

Ashe didn't know whether he deserved his wonderful life, his three great kids and a wife like Deborah, but he spent every day trying to be the best husband and father in the world. And not a day went by without him thanking God for giving him a second chance with the only woman he'd ever truly loved.

* * * * *

75¢ off

your next Silhouette series purchase.

If you enjoyed these two stories from Silhouette, visit your nearest retail outlet and take 75¢ off your next purchase!

75¢ OFF!

Your next Silhouette series purchase.

RETAILER: Harlequin Enterprises Ltd. will pay the face value of this coupon plus 8¢ if submitted by customer for this product only. Any other use constitutes fraud. Coupon is nonassignable. Void if taxed, prohibited or restricted by law. Consumer must pay any government taxes. For reimbursement submit coupons and proof of sales to: Harlequin Enterprises Ltd., P.O. Box 880478, El Paso, TX 88588-0478, U.S.A. Cash value 1/100¢.

Coupon expires April 30, 2002.
Valid at retail outlets in the U.S. only.
Limit one coupon per purchase.

107716

5 65373 00075 5   (8100) 0 10771

Silhouette®
Where love comes alive™

75¢ off

your next Silhouette series purchase.

If you enjoyed these two stories from Silhouette, visit your nearest retail outlet and take 75¢ off your next purchase!

75¢ OFF!

Your next Silhouette series purchase.

52603541

Visit Silhouette at www.eHarlequin.com
PSNCP-CANCOUPON
© 2001 Harlequin Enterprises Ltd.

Silhouette®
Where love comes alive™

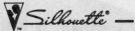

...resher Kit!

...in two proofs of purchase
from any of our four Silhouette
"Where Love Comes Alive"
special collector's editions

Special Limited Time Offer

IN U.S., mail to:
Silhouette Quiet Moments
Refresher Kit Offer
3010 Walden Ave.
P.O. Box 9020
Buffalo, NY 14269-9020

IN CANADA, mail to:
Silhouette Quiet Moments
Refresher Kit Offer
P.O. Box 608
Fort Erie, Ontario
L2A 5X3

YES! Please send my FREE Introductory Refresher Kit so
I can savor Quiet Moments without cost or obligation,
except for shipping and handling. Enclosed are two proofs
of purchase from specially marked Silhouette "Where
Love Comes Alive" special collector's editions and $3.50
shipping and handling fee.

Name (PLEASE PRINT)

Address   Apt. #

City   State/Prov.   Zip/Postal Code

FREE REFRESHER KIT OFFER TERMS

To receive your free Refresher Kit, complete the above order form. Mail it to us with two proofs of
purchase, one of which can be found in the upper right-hand corner of this page. Requests must be
received no later than March 30, 2002. Your Quiet Moments Refresher Kit costs you only $3.50 for
shipping and handling. The free Refresher Kit has a retail value of $25.00 U.S. All orders subject to
approval. Products in kit illustrated on the back cover of this book are for illustrative purposes only
and items may vary (retail value of items always as previously indicated). Terms and prices subject
to change without notice. Sales tax applicable in N.Y. **Please allow 6-8 weeks for receipt of
order. Offer good in Canada and the U.S. only.**

Offer good while quantities last. Offer limited to one per household.

598KIY DAEY   © 2001 Harlequin Enterprises Limited
                                                    PSNCP-FORM